Mignon

Mignon

CHRIS HUNT

TO JUSTINE

First published in 1987 by GMP Publishers Ltd,
P O Box 247, London N15 6RW, England.
© Chris Hunt 1987

British Library Cataloguing in Publication Data

Hunt, Chris
Mignon.
I. Title
823'.914 [F]   PR6058.U4/
ISBN 0–85449–066–3

Typeset by Best-Set Typesetter Ltd, Hong Kong, and printed
by the Guernsey Press Ltd, Guernsey, Channel Islands.

ONE

I

"...so wreck'd and welter'd by the waves...
Hapless I, God wot, poor and unknown...
Exil'd forth Europe and wide Asia both,
And have not any coverture but heaven."

O I DO make my entrance into this story and into the realm of England and upon the heaving deck of the wretched ship all most inauspicious. Scared and sullen and seasick all three. Scared with good reason because of what had gone before; sullen because it was my nature as a response to events; but the third thing was worst of all and put the final touch to the undignified, urgent and secretive manner of my departure. I was bundled out of France like a sack of apples and with infinitely less care.

"Be silent," Laurent ordered, at my querulous complaints. "We are fortunate to find such a ship."

Fortunate! It was a merchant vessel, a trader, a dealer in commerce; it bore foul sacks and dirty barrels, and the decks did ooze with slime. The captain was a man of lowest degree, half pirate, half cozener, who took our payment with a menacing leer that boded no promise of trust; and of his motley crew that climbed the rigging or slung bales and slithered barefoot down the deck hurling oaths, not one did inspire other sensation than distinct alarm.

"Mort Dieu! How can you leave me on this boat?" I whispered, appalled and full of fears.

"It is ideal," replied Laurent shamelessly. "No one will trace you on such a vessel."

"Monster, you want me to suffer," I scowled.

"Not at all. Have I not organized your departure? Have I not done everything to get you away? You owe me gratitude, not abuse. Suppose you use the experience to develop a philosophy of life. Through trial and adversity we attain spiritual grace."

"I spit upon spiritual grace."

"A remark like that convinces me that you have none," said my brother sanctimoniously.

"Ah – tis all very well for you – you ride back to Paris. You are not obliged to put yourself in the hands of cut-throats on a floating dungheap. I suppose you have not secretly paid the captain to dispatch me halfway across the sea? Nothing would surprise me."

"Don't be ridiculous, Marc," he said, with justifiable irritation. "Compose yourself to the experience."

We regarded each other coldly. Mr brother wore his priest's robes, his jewellery left at home in case of robbery, a long dark cloak obscuring the richness of his garments, his face entirely fixed into a firm and serious expression appropriate to the occasion. I was wrong to vex him; he had arranged it all; it was for my own good – but – on such a ship!

A dreadful odour rose up from the bowels of that vessel. Bilgewater; the reek of ballast gravel soaked in stale beer spilt from casks, food from the galley, and other kinds of filth and malesweat and wet rope. Black rats would run freely, and whatever cargo was below seemed to merge and mix and rise up fumily from wet wood and old holes. A sailor gave a great laugh; I winced.

"Laurent," I said, making him look at me. "Only last week I was with the King."

Laurent took my gripping hands off his arms and fixing me with a fierce stare, he said: "Any more such talk, and before all these people you so palpably despise I will close your mouth with the flat of my hand."

My lip quivered. I felt defeated. My fate loomed before me: this ship, this being hustled away, the shores of England, my unattractive cousin, ambivalence, enigma. The exchange of danger and glitter and prestige for a complete unknown, a fog of uncertainty, a wall. A little tear of self-pity plopped out of the corner of my eye.

"Ah, don't make it difficult, Marc," said Laurent, not unsympathetically. "Tis for the best."

I wiped the tear with my long sensitive forefinger.

Laurent screeched: "Take that ring off! Diable! What folly is this?"

Sullenly I took off the sapphire with the golden fleur de lys. Laurent held out his hand.

"It's mine, remember," I scowled. "I forbid you to sell it."

"I shall keep it for you. Ah, I tremble for you, Marc. I told you no signs from your past life, nothing to show an enemy who you are. And you wear a fleur de lys. You are every kind of imbecile. Have you kept anything else?"

"No," I lied with lowered eyelids.

"Well. I must leave you now. Signs of departure."

"Yes. It would be somewhat humorous if you finished by coming with me, would it not! Then you would have to learn spiritual grace through adversity also."

Laurent tightened his lips in swift irritation.

"Briefly, then, Marc, before we part... Are you feeling – not too bad, eh? Reasonable?"

"Enraptured, what else?"

"Seriously."

"Seriously I wish I had foregone breakfast."

"You do look a bit green. Unfortunately a billowy crossing is expected."

"How amusing it seems to the one not sailing."

"I wish you would abandon this attitude that I wish you ill. You really are an ungracious little cub if the truth be known."

"You are well rid of me then."

"I ignore that. Now listen. Try and be wise; show discernment. Be discreet. Oh! Is there any value in my saying these things? You have never been discreet in your life. But try now. Talk to no one. Trust no one. These are troubled times. Guise has spies everywhere. I want you safe in England, well out of the way. Haste you to Ashford with all speed. Take care. You have money, directions, and cousin Gervaise expects you. Alight at Dover, procure a horse, ride directly there, involve yourself with no one on the way."

"Just go, in effect. You are grown monotonous. I wonder you do not send me over in a sack."

"Write to me, Marc, and let me know what transpires."

We embraced. With obvious relief, my brother hurried away,

picking his way over taut straining ropes with a courtier's distaste. By then I really did not care whether he went or stayed. My stomach churned and heaved, and we were still in port. Glum dread suffused me. In contemplation of the sea voyage I had never dwelt upon the possibility of seasickness, not at all. I had been to England before, when I was nine. I remembered the journey as exceeding merry, greatly exciting. I went with my brothers, Charles, Jacques and Louis. (I have four, all older, a great trial and curse.) On that voyage I ran about, lost myself below deck, ate comfits, received beer from a sailor, became drunk, was slapped about the head by Jacques and Louis (once) and by Charles (at least six times), fell from the rigging, grazed my elbows and lost my hat. As now, our destination had been Ashford and my cousin Gervaise, and the occasion had been to betrothe me to Gervaise's sister Lettice, a big fat girl larger and older than me with ginger hair; but the sea voyage at least had been diverting. Although of course I had no intention on this voyage of running amok below deck and receiving beer from sailors, I had assumed at the age of fifteen that I would disport myself with some ordinary dignity; but I was now fearful that would be denied me.

We had ridden all night, and had taken breakfast in a squalid quayside tavern and now I was regretting it with all my heart. As soon as I had seen the ship the heavings started; no doubt my troubled sensibilities were the cause. I do believe I was in a state of secret terror, yet hardly knowing it. Suddenly I was faced with the truth, in the shape of that ship: I was leaving France, it had been a failure, my life had been threatened, I must flee. The ship rolled and shifted in its moorings. Enormous nail heads showed in her creaking timbers restraining the bulging innards beneath; dripping black ropes as thick as young trees festooned with murky weed ground against the quayside, and brown waves slurped between it and the lumbering ship. The last day of April it was, and wet, with seagulls screaming and heavy grey cloud pressing down, and here on the deck all the signs of action for the start of the voyage. Voyage – well, it ranked small in comparison with the great ones, but believe me, to a person about to succumb to most horrible mal de mer, the English coast seemed as far off as Cathay.

When we first came aboard and Laurent made arrangements I

had felt a wash of indignant shame that I should be reduced to this, obliged to voyage on a trading ship which stank, which dealt in the degrading business of trade. English, moreover, its sailors coarse and common in their manners. Laurent said it was as well, English seamen would have no idea of the nuances of French politics and would ask no questions, particularly if I kept myself apart. In order to guide me in this endeavour he had insisted I leave off all those sweet characteristics that drew attention to me – my face paint, my jewellery, my court fashions and bright colours. That year – 1587 – we sometimes wore monstrous ruffs big as dinner plates and as stiff, and trunk hose stuffed like pumpkins, like lewd swollen arses, to draw attention to that part which was so much in demand at that particular court. Whereas at court such raiment was natural and proper, even I could see the sense in moderating it to go aboard an English merchant vessel. Be sombre, Laurent advised. I was, but I still took care and was nonetheless elegant.

I wore a doublet of soft dark red leather, pinked all over with a pattern of small hearts, and fastened with little exquisite buttons, most for show, only the top section undoing to let one's head through; this over a burgundy velvet shirt with frills at the cuffs, and a stiff white frill at the neck. I had black leather gloves and soft black leather thigh boots over my burgundy stockings. Over all this a short black cloak that swirled when I walked. It was distressing to think that at any moment I might vomit over it all.

This was so likely, more so with every moment that passed and every lurch of the ship, that I did not even see Laurent's disembarkation, nor the sight of him down on the quay mounting his horse and riding away – not that I would have wished to, even if I had been well; our parting was not poignant. Of my brothers he was the kindest to me, but the others were such out and out villains that it was but a poor compliment. I daresay it suited him well enough to see me out of France. The way things had passed I was beginning to be a double-edged blessing in my position at court. I do believe that at heart he was ashamed of me. One might dress up one's fancy boys in pretty clothes and give them gifts and precedence, call them "mignons" in honeyed tones and mean it as a compliment; but everyone knew what they were for. I do think Laurent believed an ancient family like ours should not have involved itself in that.

Unsuccessfully, ultimately. Otherwise the morning would not have found me alone and dispirited, on a ship bound for England, hanging over the side and puking into the wind. I missed all sight of the receding French shores. I had no thoughts about time and distance and eternity; I just brought up my breakfast and suffered and groaned, my knuckles white on the gnarled wet wood, my long brown hair blowing into my eyes and mouth, and some sailors sniggering behind me.

Mort Dieu – I could have done without this last. It was bad enough the laughs, the comfortable superiority of people with leather guts who played dice round Cape Horn, no doubt; but apparently assuming I did not understand English, they exchanged a good few comments which I wished I had not understood.

"Neat thighs, eh?"

"And a plump little arse."

"By cock, I fancy putting *that* over a barrel!"

A member of one of the great families of France – though an obscure branch – cannot but resent being the object of crude observations by brutish disagreeable sailors, and moreover how could they tell whether my arse was plump, encased as it was in black trunk hose – half of that was the stuffing! O! to be contemplated from behind when one is throwing up makes one nervous. I would have been angry if I had not been so tormented and wracked with rising nausea. At least, however, my doublet had been spared, a relief to me. My wayward cloak, though, was blowing up like a sail and revealing all the parts that seemed to so delight the sailors. It was unfair to be so disadvantaged.

Doubled up and retching as I was then, I was astonished and, I have to admit, gratified, to think that they found me attractive enough to loiter by. I thought they would go away, having made their remarks, but they did not, and one then laid a hand on the top of my thigh.

"Oy, pretty boy," he said with a throaty guffaw.

This was too much and I half twisted round and turned my bleary eyes on him. I said through gritted teeth in a tone of anger and some dignity: "Leave me alone." But what happened was that they all repeated amongst themselves the way I said it, I mean my accent; and I stared discomfited, because I thought I said it passing well, but how they distorted it by imitation! I realised that I was going to be making my way in England with a pronounced French accent, and it was perturbing to have it emphasized by a couple of idiotic louts whom I daresay possessed strong accents of their own.

"Shall we share a cuddle then?" one enquired of me intimately.

His companion sniggered comfortably.

"We have a long trip ahead of us. It'd pass the time very well. What do you say?"

"No," I said, gulping down what seemed my entire stomach rising to my armpits.

"I heard you French were all like that," he said. It was not even that he was aiming to insult. The whole conversation on their part was done with nudges and laughs. All very well for Laurent to order me Be discreet. As soon as his back was turned I am singled out. It was not my fault.

Events obliged me to turn away and hang half upside down over the side once more. One of them patted my bottom and said:

"Courage, mon brave. It will be much worse halfway across."

But at least they went away and left me to it.

Later on, when I felt able to leave the side, I staggered limply over to where my trunk had been left, in a corner of the deck under an overhang beside some sacks, some coils of rope, and my lute. I sat on my trunk in utmost gloom, elbows on knees, chin in hands. The sea air would be wrecking my lute strings; I would be days tuning it. My trunk in itself depressed me. It had been very splendid. In order to bring it no attention we had been obliged to desecrate it. There lay my initials M.A.d.P.M. so recently set with tiny little silver studs, all gone now, and a ragged series of hollows left. Ma vie, but I had come down in the world! Marc-Alphonse du Plessis Mornay and what good was it doing me? O! Alone on a lurching bark upon perilous seas, prodded by mariners.

Sullen and resentful against my brothers I set about ignoring Laurent's instructions. I took out a small ivory mirror and rouged up my pale face a little. Ah. Even seasick I was beautiful.

I pouted at myself. My mouth tasted vile but the mirror showed me simply the lovely lips and the white teeth and my limpid blue-grey eyes. I smirked. I would be all right. My beauty would see me through. Merde, but I was pale. Eight hours sleep I needed, in a good bed. Beside a good lover, if I was lucky.

And I would be. You would not find me staying long at Gervaise's.

I fixed my small gold ear rings into my ears. Voilà, I felt more dressed. Ever since my ears had been pierced I felt stupid without ear rings, with little holes showing. Everyone has their ears pierced these days. Look at the portraits of the King.

Across the lurching deck I saw another passenger, out taking the air.

My first thought was envy. *He* was not seasick. He was strolling – strolling, Mort Dieu, as if he was on dry land. I ached with envy and upset guts. My second thought – and now I sound like a riddle. My first is in jealousy, my second in guts, my third is in seasickness four times, my last is in thighs, my whole is available for it – O what a wicked pun for somebody consumed by distress. I shock myself. The answer is Lust – is it not always!

It was plain enough to me, as I squinted through the sea-flecked wind, that the man was tall and handsome and blond. He wore a dark green cloak; all his clothes were dark. I watched him, my eyes narrowing assessively. Was it possible to tell, as everyone said? Could one Ganymede pick out another? I would have said yes. He walked so elegantly – but then, some of the women-lovers walked just as mincingly; a mincing walk was fashionable. I gazed at him again.

He had seen me; I swear he ran his eyes over me. Instinctively I extended a long blatant expanse of thigh, inviting. Immediately my stomach heaved and I doubled up with my hands clamped over my mouth. Mort Dieu, to perform like that and him watching. O! The embarrassment of it! When I could bear to lift my head I saw him disappear into a doorway.

O! He had a cabin!

Now my envy increased a thousandfold. He could go within and close the door. He could ignore the shivery wind and the jibes of mariners. He maybe had a bed in there...wine...my fancy raced, and my own bodily malaise increased by comparison. I was shivering and cold. Despondency of spirit plagued me also, brought forth by my enforced secrecy, this obligation to travel as a nobody. I believed that Laurent had been too cautious. I was not important. The Duc de Guise had better things to do with his time than to follow me to the coast; I daresay no one would even be aware that I was missing. All this was for nothing.

Yet someone had made an attempt on my life. I shuddered.

All around me the ship creaked and heaved. The sails flapped and crashed like the wings of legendary bird monsters, the ropes slithered, and the spray slapped across the slimy deck and left puddles that trickled down between the boards. It was not at all a storm, merely the choppy passage that was expected, but every inch of the way I suffered. After there was no more sickness to come, there followed a griping ache; it was torment indescribable. I abandoned myself to misery. I curled up on the sacks and turned my face away from the deck, burrowing into the sacks, my thumb in my mouth as if I was a baby, and indeed would have accepted comfort from anywhere. I felt discarded and alone and without direction, very small and insignificant, at mercy of events and weather. I began to think of all those fathoms of water below me, those churning boiling depths where dead men's bones lay polished white by the sea's insidious caress, and the naked broken ribs of long-sunk ships jutted out of the gravel and sand. How frail then seemed the bark that bore me! Its timbers creaked and strained and cracked like shot; the wind in the sails made fearful thunderings. I could imagine the splitting of wood, the bursting of nails, distorted planks that let in a tiny bubbling stream which split a path into the hold and burst it from inside. Between us and doom, I mean eternity, lay a mere thickness of oak, no more, and I began to wonder about eternity while I mumbled some Hail Mary's, a sudden panic suffusing me lest I should soon have to explain on high how it was that I had spent the last year of my life. "My brothers made me do it" – no, that would be no excuse if we believe in salvation by individual deeds and good intentions, holy living. I knew only too well the torments His Majesty suffered over the very same problem, and if the mighty cannot resolve the dilemma, how much less the small rotating planets in their sphere! Bad seasickness brings on such thoughts.

Troubled with fears and groaning with physical distress I lay hugging my knees and nuzzling my face into the sackcloth, unheedful that I might be thus observed. Had I not been so ill-disposed, I would never have lain like that – we called it the honeypot position; you are offering maximum sweetness – the knees drawn up emphasise the bum and everyone knows that trunk hose plumply padded draw attention like a gross fat invitation. The two sailors who had been molesting me before, now came to try again. A hand came from behind, groping for my crotch. I squealed like a piglet, and there was a shamefully undignified tussle. Beside myself with fury I drew my dagger and wriggled backwards into the sacks, my blade quivering like a divining rod.

"Espèce de cochons – sales bêtes – laissez-moi tranquil," I spat, insulted.

They hesitated for a brief moment, weighing up how serious my intent. Affront had made me draw my dagger; I responded swiftly and in indignation; I had no wish whatsoever to use it, and in truth I was already embarrassed, sprawled here fighting for my virtue like a virgin. The struggle had set off a whole new bout of nauseous heavings and I winced and clutched my stomach, and with a laugh the nearest sailor disarmed me.

"Little spitfire," he said, twisting my wrist with a hand like a grappling iron and embedding my weapon far out of my reach, in the woodwork above his head.

"Come now," he said. "Why fight? We have all this time to pass; let's make it a pleasant passage, hey? There's naught like a cuddle to make you forget your troubles, and I am not so ugly."

He sat down beside me on the sacks and put his arm round me and made me kiss him. Tears of mortification filled my eyes. Twas true, he was not ugly – he was rough and strong and hairy, his chin and cheeks were coarse with stubble and he tasted of ale and smelt of sweat – but he was a common sailor and I was of a great and noble family and the last person to make love to me had been the King of France. Moreover I was racked with seasickness such as no one had ever endured before in the history of the world entire and I grieved much for my sorry state.

He held me tight against him, winding his tongue into my ear and I struggled weakly. His friend sat down beside us and began to fondle my thighs. His great gnarled fingers felt for the opening of my hose, found it and groped within.

16

"O! No!" I groaned, restrained by the great arms of the other, who chuckled comfortably into my ear.

"Lay him down...put him on his back."

What could they do to me here, I thought, panic struggling with reason, here out in the open, on the deck, people about, surely nothing more than this? And I supposed I could shout for help. But would anyone respond? Even as I wondered, a sailor strolled past and saw, saying, "Give him one for me", and sneered; and one said: "They're all like that in France; they like it." It was not the last time I was treated to this blatant untruth and half London seemed to believe this scandalous rumour, as I was to learn. That was disturbing enough, but worse was the tone of raw dislike from the sailor who passed, a person who knew nothing about me and said what he said either because he was offended by a boy who was so pretty, or because he misliked the entire French nation. Either way it did not bode well for me in the days to come.

"Don't struggle, sweeting," said the sailor in a low cajoling tone. "Come play with me, come, pretty boy..."

He eased me down on to my back on the sacks, his friend still with a hot and sweaty palm all clamped within my hose and holding me down flat. I swear I would not have been so easy if I had not been weak and suffering. Shameful tears came trickling down my rouged cheeks as the sailor laid his weight full on me and held my face in his hands and kissed my lips. His fingernails were black and broken, the filthiest I had ever seen. Between my wide apart legs my prick stirred and the hand that held it tightened its triumphant grip. It was the final straw to my discomfiture when the one guffawed throatily and cried to the other: "Tis true – he does like it. Feel!"

He took his hand away; I pulled free and twisted round, and elbowing him off I hid my face in the sacks, gripping fistfuls of sacking till my knuckles were white, as if I could be saved by holding on.

I was saved, but in a manner I had not possibly imagined.

I was aware of the sailors drawing back, and a hand touched my shoulder. In flawless French a voice said:

"May I offer you the protection of my cabin, and indeed of myself?"

I squinted round at him in disbelief, the tall blond stranger whom I had observed walking on the deck. Close to, he was every morsel as pleasing as he had seemed from afar. The contrast between him and the sailors was extreme. He was handsome, clean and perfumed, dressed in dark green that flattered him immense and went well with his light blond hair. He looked about twenty-five years old. He had merry eyes with a mocking twinkle, and no doubt with some cause. I must have looked a droll sight pressed in the sacks behaving like a damsel in distress; I know I felt a fool then for having to be saved.

I sat up and tried to look as if it was sea spray that had made my face wet. I attempted to collect a few shreds of dignity.

"Thank you monsieur," I said. "That would be agreeable."

My assailants were busy slinking away. The stranger gestured politely towards the low door down into the bowels of the ship. I stood up and pulled my dagger out of the woodwork and slid it back into its sheath, then followed the stranger across to the dark little door.

Such was the way, then, that I obeyed my brother Laurent's last instructions. Be discreet, talk to no one, involve yourself with nobody on the way. I had been almost violated in full view of whomever cared to watch, come perilous close to wounding a sailor or even committing murder by accident if Fortune had so willed, and now a handsome stranger had offered me his protection, and I followed him to whatever this would lead.

II

"But what are you that ask of me these things?
Whence may you come, or whither will you go?"

THE flawless French that had invited me so opportunely to accept a rescue was yet plainly that of an Englishman speaking it, and his garb was simply that of a traveller. We went down into the dark malodorous place below deck and there he did open a door and we were within his cabin.

It was no bigger than a box, low of stature and barely wide enough to turn, but it was private, dry and warm and had a shelf against the wall to serve as a bed, with covers on it; also an old dark chest with a lanthorn; and he began by acting most solicitous to me, all being done for my welfare, which did immensely please me, as I felt I had been much oppressed till now. Assuring me that I would feel better lying on the bed, he sat me down there and did help me ease my boots off, his fingers lightly touching my inner thighs as he pulled the leather down. My knees showed and all my leg in burgundy stockings, very pleasant and shapely, and as I have oft been told a delight to the eye, for which I was most pleased just then. For if one is to have one's leg uncovered slowly how much better it is to have lovely legs as I did, and not skinny bow-legged knobbly knees as some others. He lifted my legs on to the bed and took my cloak and opened up my tight top collar buttons to relax my throat, and laid a cover over me most kindly, and began to pour me wine.

"O!" I said uneasily. "I have been monstrous sick. Should I be having wine?"

"I think you should," he said most confident. "Besides, I'm sure tis what you'd like."

"It is. I would," I eagerly agreed. "But I am not myself at present."

"Sip it slowly," he said, handing me a goblet, "and keep this nearby." And he handed me a bowl, at which my cheeks went quite wine-coloured with discomfiture although I realised it was practical. I had to smile ruefully, for what a way to make a person's acquaintance this was, expecting to be sick!

"It's hardly just," I said, "how some are struck down and others stroll about nonchalantly."

"I make the journey often," he remarked, acknowledging the reference to himself. "One grows accustomed.

He sat down on the chest, and observed me as I sipped. We spoke, by the way, in French.

"I am called Anthony Wilton," he said.

"And I . . ." I said, and stopped. What was I to say? Visions of Laurent frowning and anxious loomed about my head and instantly I dispersed them. How ridiculous it was, this secrecy! I was my own man now, I was not answerable to his protective nursemaiding. My name would mean nothing to Anthony. He would hardly be a spy from court. I decided there and then to dispense with treading this fine line of diplomacy and distrust. I was never any good at it anyway.

"My name is Marc-Alphonse du Plessis Mornay," I said, watching him for reaction.

"Many names for one small person!"

"In France it is not unusual. Marc will do. Alphonse is not pretty, is it?"

"It sounds Spanish to me."

"Oh, I think not," I shrugged. "Um, but do you think that's what I am then?"

"What? Spanish?"

"No! A small person."

He laughed loudly and set about to study me. I wriggled the blanket down a little to help him.

"Well, you are not over tall," he remarked, "but you are yet tolerable young, I would suppose..."

"Fifteen," I offered.

"...and may grow. *Slight* I would say, not small; and, if I knew you better, I would add: except around the thighs."

His eyes were very merry. I gasped with pleasure at his daring.

"O!" I remarked with a smirk, "so you think my thighs are well shaped? Most people do," I added modestly.

"It is a subject for general discussion?" he enquired quizzically.

"Oh, yes, among the people I know."

"I count myself fortunate to be part of such an honoured circle."

It was most foolish of me to be swigging back the wine, for any number of reasons, not the least because it was certainly loosening my tongue and affecting my judgement – which was limited at best. The flirtation I would have indulged in anyway; that was not the wine, that was myself. I had taken the cover right off for him now, and lay on my back, one knee bent to show off the subject under discussion.

"Yes, I did notice it before," said Anthony.

"Before?"

"Yes, upon the sacks, spread out."

"O!" I blushed a little.

"It seems that many seek a closer acquaintance with you," he observed. "I wonder you dare walk abroad."

I peered under narrowed lids. Of a certain he was laughing at me. I frowned. I was convinced he fancied me. Surely I had not been wrong.

"Filthy brutes," I muttered.

"I suppose you are more used to civilised swains..."

"Indeed I am," I blurted out. "That is what so disgusted me. I have never seen such foul finger nails. No, indeed I am not used to common people."

"Oh – royalty, no less, I suppose," he smiled easily.

"Well..." I said shrugging, leaving him to make of that what he would, implying that his guess was not so far out.

"Ah, I could tell you were quality," he said, "but come, now you are boasting."

"Indeed I am not," I protested. To my annoyance I was beginning to be cumbered once again by heavings. O! It was odious and tedious. In the presence of this smooth and pleasing gentleman whom I know I could have seduced with ease and passed the time most agreeably, here was I so troubled and distressed and possibly green-tinted too, my beauty obscured. Life was full of ironies – O cruel fortune!

"May I ask what such a precious cargo does aboard such an inferior vessel, and all alone?"

His tone was teasing and a little cynical, yet not without sympathy, I thought.

"I am travelling to visit my relations," I grimaced at the prospect.

"Without excess of joy," he observed.

"Exactly. It is a sort of cousin. We call him cousin, as one does, for simplicity. He is a branch of my family on my mother's side. You see, I have English connections."

"Do I know them?"

"I doubt it; they are not famous. Gervaise Blysshen, living at Ashford. Just one more country gentleman, as I understand. From what I remember, he is extreme uninteresting, and not at all handsome. More depressing for me, he has a sister very like himself, and her I am not looking forward to meeting. She has ginger hair!"

"Monstrous!" shuddered Anthony, twinkling.

"Seriously! I was intended to marry her."

"But –?" Anthony enquired.

"Circumstances intervened," I said loftily. I leaned up on one elbow and eyed him. "You see," I said earnestly, "even if she had been as beautiful as Venus I don't think I would have married her."

I somewhat hoped he would have responded with a like suggestive remark about himself. But he did not. Most sure, it was apparent to any but the most inattentive that the fair Anthony offered no information about himself and gave nothing away. Me, I did not notice this. I thought that we were merely conversing. In effect he was carefully finding out about me, in return for nothing.

"It seems to me then," he said, "that you must be either brave or foolhardy. Attractive as you are, you travel alone and if I may say so, vulnerable to accidents; and you go towards a situation where all may not go smoothly for you. Speaking no English –"

"I do!" I cried. "Extremely well."

He folded his arms severely. He clearly intended I should prove myself. I was equal to the challenge. I launched into a verse from one of my favourite poems.

"When other lovers, in arms across,
Rejoice their chief delight,
Drowned in tears, to mourn my loss,
I stand the bitter night
In my window, where I may see
Before the winds how the clouds flee:
Lo, what a mariner love hath made of me!"

"Oh," said Anthony impressed. "So you know that! Do you know the tune that goes with it?"

"Yes, I can play it. The Earl of Surrey is one of my favourite poets, and I also know some Thomas Wyatt."

"Talented lad," he marvelled. "And your accent is delightful."

"Yours also," I retorted, at which he had the grace to bow. English people are so patronising. They forget they too have accents when they speak French.

I allowed myself a long slow look at Anthony. Guarded as he might be, I was convinced he had rescued me for his own purposes. Assuredly I hoped so. Lean, tall and languid, one elegant thigh crossed over another, he was coolly attractive. His hair was soft and smooth and wavy on his collar. I would like, I thought, to see him without clothes. What he wore was more concealing than what I wore – he had his doublet well padded down the front, in the style they call peascod, and he had those bulky knee breeches that obscured the line of his thighs.

Turning to English to show that I could, I said bluntly:

"Why did you save me from the mariners?"

Briefly, he was disconcerted. But he immediately regained his poise.

"Would you believe it if I said it was because of a wish to help any one who suffered?"

"Yes...if I were old and ugly," I challenged.

"Lord!" he said. "You think much of yourself, do you not?"

He seemed a little vexed, but people only become so, I find, when there has been some truth in the accusation.

"Should I not?" I shrugged. "You want me to pretend I do not know that I am pretty? Most people think I am. You too, you are good looking. I am sure you know it. If you do not, I tell you it is so, you are. I was pleased when you saved me."

Anthony laughed, as if speaking was beyond him.

"It is agreeable to be saved by a handsome stranger," I explained reasonably. "I will be very happy to show my thanks in any way you like to name."

As I was stroking my thigh with studied carelessness, he could hardly have been in doubt as to what I meant.

"Surely you are not tempting me to a crime?" he said carefully.

"A crime?" I said blankly.

"Yes, you lewd wag, a crime."

"O – for the common people," I shrugged.

"Yes, for the common people," he said, "and when you land on English shores you will be a common person, *whatever* you were in France," he added, as if he had some idea.

"Why are you angry with me?" I asked meltingly. "Do you not want my thanks? Tis not a commonplace offer, that."

"I am not angry with you, except perhaps at your in-discretion. I cannot help feeling that you have no idea what England is like just at present. For instance, do you know how highly they value the French? If I say one hairsbreadth up from the Spanish, do you understand me?"

23

"Yes – but, we are nothing like the Spanish, nothing at all."

"That may be so, but I fear no one will believe you. If you must slaughter Huguenots in their thousands!"

"I?" I gasped affronted. "I have never slaughtered Huguenots – O!" I grinned sheepishly. "That! You mean what occurred upon the Eve of Saint Bartholomew. But," I cried indignantly, "they were plotting to kill the royal family. It was kill or be killed. Everyone knows that."

"Indeed they do not," said Anthony severely. "In England the nation was shocked. We could not believe what we were hearing. The streets ran with blood – indiscriminate butchery . . ."

"It has nothing to do with me," I said in exasperation. "I was one year old at the time. I was not to blame."

"Then you appropriated Calais," continued Anthony.

"I –? O, we. But Calais was French," I said reasonably. "It was ours."

"It is not seen so in England. It is regarded as a loss of English property. And even if we could forgive you stealing it, there are many other reasons why you will find it hard to convince an Englishman of your good intent. There are those Popish practices in which you indulge."

"What do you mean?"

"Don't be naif. I mean your religion. I assume you are not a Huguenot."

"Naturally not."

"Well, in England now it is against the law to hear Mass. To secretly maintain a private priest is a felony. To be that priest and to be caught would mean a most terrible and public death. Do you feel easy now about your chances of survival when you land?"

"I have no malign intent and I am assuredly not a priest. What should I fear?" But he was certainly succeeding in making me most uneasy. My brothers had told me that I would be safe in England. I was fleeing an assassin. But were there other dangers more obscure, which they had not considered? And did they care, as long as I was safely off their hands?

"And then," Anthony pursued implacably, "what about all those plots to kill the Queen?"

"What plots?" I gulped.

24

"The ones organized by the Duke of Guise. We hear so many tales – he is in league with Philip of Spain and with the Pope – they plan a Holy Crusade against England – they plan to land on the Sussex coast with hireling soldiers from all over Europe. Why, the nation lives in mortal terror! Every village yokel has his pitchfork ready, every brawny huswife her broomstick..."

He began to laugh, but I was white as a shroud at the mention of that name.

"What do you *know*?" I gasped. "You are not anything to do with *him*?" I knew that when my panic had subsided I would certainly be sick.

"Ah, that alarms you, does it?" he said, almost pleased to have proved his point, that I was indiscreet and innocent. "Suppose I was? If I had been in his employ and wished you dead, you could be dead ten times over, drinking poisoned wine and putting yourself in my power, in this dark little room..."

Truly, for a moment I thought he was serious; I thought he meant the wine was poisoned. I trembled all over and stared with eyes like dinner plates and might well have fainted had I not been lying down. My terror must have been visible, because he leaned over to me and reassured me with his arm. "Comfort you, I'm nothing to do with all that, nothing at all; you are safe enough. All I meant to do was warn you. I wanted you to understand that you are on thin enough ice without inviting a person to indulge. What if I had been a worthy upright gentleman who reported your suggestion to the captain?"

"But I knew that you were not!" I screeched. "I would not have asked you else – one can always tell. And I asked you so deviously that I would have told the captain you must have misunderstood. And then you would have been at fault for thinking it." I was shaking from my fright. "The captain!" I sneered. "Have you seen him? He would most probable ask you for a turn on me after you had finished."

"Mm, yes," said Anthony, lips twitching, "tis possible. But do you see my drift?"

"Yes. I must be more careful and discreet."

"But you were right in your judgement of my state," he added in a low vibrant tone. "It would please me to receive your thanks. I do desire to lie with you."

I groaned at Fortune's mockery. "Please, Anthony," I said

unhappily, "please turn away and do not regard me; I am not well."

He obligingly moved further off. I lay on my stomach, hunched over the bowl, my shoulders heaving, my bum shifting about in a horrible parody of something else. "Do not watch!" I squeaked slurpily in between.

"I am not watching," he called cheerfully.

"I shall kill you if you look," I moaned.

"Believe me, I dare not."

"O! How can a person suffer so and yet live?"

"You will be better when you touch dry land."

"All that lovely wine..." I groaned.

"Spare me..." he winced.

"How can you ever want me after this?"

"I have every confidence that I will, and even greater confidence in you regaining your former beauty and your pertness."

"You cannot imagine how I feel," I writhed.

Eventually we both judged that I had finished, and Anthony came and stood by me and did very sweetly put his arms about me in firm and reassuring fashion while I lay with my face to the wall sniffing and moaning and surely not at all desirable. But Anthony must have found me so nonetheless, for he ran his hands over my back and all over my trunk hose – with little satisfaction no doubt, because they were most saucily stuffed in the style of the day, and all he would be able to feel would be the padding.

"Take them off if you want," I said.

"You are in no condition..."

"It does not matter. I'll just lie here...do what you want."

"God's light – the generosity of the boy!" he marvelled. "Truly, Marc, what kind of a brute do you think I am, to behave like that, while you are so indisposed?"

"I don't think you are a brute, but I owe you thanks, and moreover it is what I would like. The voyage will finish and we will separate, and so if that's what you want, do it."

Instead he covered me up with the blanket and told me to try and sleep.

"Do you not want me?" I squawked horrified. "Am I repulsive?"

26

"Do as you are told and go to sleep. I'm thinking of something."

"Anthony! Answer what I said!"

"You are temptation, minx, and infinitely desirable and I intend to make full use of you. Now go to sleep."

Appeased, I dozed off under the blanket, thumb in mouth, lulled by the ship's mighty creakings to hazy dreams. Some of these were so alarming I woke up gasping. I was at heart a very frightened youth. I felt threatened because of the past, and the future was so vague. The present was not so admirable either. No wonder I slept fitfully. But I did sleep.

Anthony awakened me, and I turned round to face him, bleary eyed and strained, like a child prince, pawn of rival factions, woken in the night to be told to flee the place in secret.

"Listen, this is a good idea," he said. "Leave the ship with me. I am not going on to Dover. I am leaving by a small boat and you must come with me. We will alight at a cove and make our way to an inn I know. We spend the night there, and you may sleep in a tolerable bed, and next day you will travel on to face your cousin much fortified. And we will have some time together."

I absorbed this startling idea.

"But I told my brothers I would go to Dover," I said. "My route is all planned."

"Dover!" said Anthony shaking his head. "'Tis a bad place for people with secrets."

"Why?" I gasped.

"All is not well there. Those in authority at the port are under orders to spare no effort in their vigilance...continually on the look out for Jesuits and spies. The customs men are jumpy as cats. They rifle all luggage for slanderous books, they handle your clothes for secret linings, they keep you detained while they check on your past history and future plans – ugh! It's something to be avoided at all costs, and you can avoid it. You can come with me in a small boat which I have already arranged. I would advise it, Marc, believe me."

"O – I do not know –"

"Listen. Do you want to have to explain to customs officials who you are? Are you ready for that? Can you picture it? Suffering with vestigial seasickness and warding off great brutes who want to know everything about you? You could be spending tonight in prison while they decide what to do with you."

"Prison?" I quivered.

"O yes," he shrugged. "That's where they put the ones they are not sure about. Remember what I told you, that they do not trust the French – if they had any doubts about you, they would put you in gaol. If it was to turn out that you had the slightest connection with the French court, I can confidently tell you, you would be assumed a potential assassin. O, and sodomy is a burnable offence," he added for good measure.

I shall never know how true this terrible picture was because I believed him and I did not go to Dover. Weak with fear and sickness I lay there helpless and malleable.

"O! Anthony! What shall I do?"

"Come with me. You are in no condition to be alone. I will look after you."

"O – but a small boat –" I groaned.

"But for a little while. Then you will be on dry land."

"I'm so – I don't know what to do..." I trembled.

"'Tis decided. You come with me, and tonight we'll sleep together. Agreed?"

"Yes, Anthony; agreed."

A person not racked by seasickness would have wanted to enquire of Anthony why it was that *he* needed to avoid the customs men, why it was that he had arranged for a small boat to secretly take him off this ship, avoiding Dover. That never crossed my mind. Tempted by the thought of sleeping with him, desperate to be on dry land the sooner, and petrified by the images conjured up by Anthony, of monstrous brutes who'd strip me down to nothing to get at my seditious pamphlets and assassin's bodkin, I was only thankful that Anthony could offer me a better prospect. I needed no persuasion. Laurent would have had a fit.

At dusk Anthony and I left the ship and entered the small boat. Mariners rowed us ashore. More dead than alive I leaned against Anthony and we bounced like tennis balls tossed by a sportive sea, splashed by spray. Hideous images assailed me, of the great soaring sides of the ship as we rowed away, of myself bundled like a sack over shoulders and under arms, shrieking for them to be careful with my lute; and looming vistas of boiling churning black-green water and evil curving waves with wicked tips, and constant nausea and fear. O! My arrival in England was so undignified, so unheroic.

"Look," said Anthony, with his arm around me. "England."

I daresay to a native the word is an emotive one and fills the heart with joy. I blinked at those grey cliffs and dark lowering clouds without elation. Truly, anywhere would have done as long as it was solid earth – the coast of Madagascar, the Americas, northern Muskovy, anywhere at all.

But it was England, and I was here.

A shingled beach lay ahead of us.

III

"We two will talk alone – what words be these? (*Aside*)"

WHEN the boat was in the foamy shallows and it became apparent that we would have to put our feet into the water in order to reach the shore, I hesitated and hung back.

"What? You are not afeared to wet your feet?" Anthony cried.

"O! Anthony – my boots –" I whispered tremulously. "They are of the very best leather."

A sailor, who heard in disbelief, guffawed scornfully: "Throw the little popinjay right in!"

How fortunate that I had Anthony to protect me!

"I will carry you," he groaned. "Let us by all means spare your boots of very best leather."

And so with my arms round Anthony's neck and my legs dangling, I arrived on English earth dry footed. Of course, it was not earth, it was shingle, and Anthony soon put me down upon it. As my boots crunched the hard firm pebbles I did feel a lift of the heart to be on land.

"What? Will you not kiss the stones?" he teased. "Christopher Columbus did, you know, on the shores of the New World."

"O – you think I should claim this land for France?" I retorted. "It does not look so inspiring."

"H'm. There are plenty who would disagree with you, I fear. But let us not deal in contentious issues."

Anthony paid the sailors, and for a moment all was action, because atop the dark ridge there was a man with two horses waiting, so all must be going to a smooth plan. The sailors, having carried my trunk up the slope, and Anthony's small box, put back to sea, where the ship lay, speckled with lights. I let Anthony deal with all.

"So, can you get his trunk moved? You know the Blue Boar on the road north...before morning...no, I will keep my box with me...Marc, will you take your lute? Yes, one horse will be enough...O, yes, a reasonable enough crossing...I will meet you in Canterbury on the seventh..."

I rode in front of Anthony, astride a fast horse, his steadying arms each side of me, and his face brushing my cheek, ear and neck; he made no pretence of not doing it; he nibbled my ear, and I pressed myself back against him. Night came on apace. Around us there were dark trees in their small new leaves, and big bushy shapes of blossom, some bare forked branches and some enormous evergreens. It was very quiet save for the sea wind whipping up the long grass and bending low the hedgerows. Sharp raindrops flecked our faces, and sudden bitter gusts like someone throwing water. Already I was feeling much better. It was true, the moment my feet touched dry land my state improved, and I was contemplating the coming night with the greatest of pleasure.

I did not notice much about the Blue Boar inn that night. It was a wayside inn and we arrived there in the dark. I saw a tall bulky building with a swinging, creaking inn sign. I could see the leaded panes of many windows, all illumined from within by candlelight or firelight so that the smudges of light glowed amber. Above the door a blazing torch flared, gusting in the wind, and the innkeeper hurried forth, lanthorn in hand, speaking to Anthony about weather and rain and the promise of the morrow. We dismounted and went under a low archway into a yard. An ostler came for the horse and led him to the stables. Anthony made all the arrangements, and I stood by, my thoughts on food. Astonishingly I was ravenous hungry – or maybe not so astonishingly, since I was completely empty – I felt like a peapod without peas. Before long, Anthony and I had been escorted inside and up a twisty stairway to an upper room which was to be ours for the night.

When the innkeeper had gone I examined the room in great delight.

"Oo, Anthony, it is most jolly! Two chairs! A dear little table, and such a bed!" I bounced on it and winced. "Not too soft, eh, but good and wide...O – are we going to eat in our room? Can we have steak?"

"Lord, lord, how you have recovered! Steak is it? And best wine, no doubt? Do you think I am a rich man?"

"Anthony!" I screeched affronted. "You do not pay for me – what do you think I am? I have money." And somewhat recklessly (but I was indignant) I undid my purse and slung coins all over the bed to make everything quite clear.

"Put them away, you little fool. Do you want us robbed as we sleep? Very well, we go halves; I didn't realise you were sensitive about your position."

"Extremely," I said haughtily. "Just because I am bouncing on the bed it does not mean that I am without sensibility."

So Anthony arranged for the arrival of our meal and I tuned my lute. I was right, the sea air had played havoc with the delicate balance, and I was long perfecting it. I frowned and twanged, concentrating.

"You hold it oddly." Anthony commented. "What are you doing that is different?"

"I am left handed. You have to have it strung differently."

"Left handed! O – a fairy's child, eh?"

"You believe that, do you, even you?"

"In part I do. It is hard to shake off what one is told as a child, even when manhood brings a more logical way of thinking. You do have a certain elfishness, Marc. Mischievous eyes, like Puck, a certain otherworldliness. And those two moles on your face, so close to your lip." He laughed then. "Why, everyone knows that means you are under the protection of a witch."

"Dare you be alone with me?" I enquired provocatively, making sweet shapes of my lips.

"It adds a certain piquancy to feel that we are in the presence of the otherworld."

"And tomorrow is the first of May. Poor Anthony then, alone with a witch's brat tonight of all nights. You like to toy with danger?"

"If you are danger, yes," he answered.

"Anthony," I began. "You do not think they are ugly, my spots?"

"No, not at all. They are like beauty patches. I have known ladies who wore false spots to draw attention to their best features. It's like that with you. They show off your petulant lips."

I thought so too, but I wanted to be reassured.

"I know they say that about witches," I began carefully.

"Oh, in part I jested..."

"No, but it is true, is it not? People have said it to me before. They also say they jest but they look at me thoughtfully as if they wonder quand-même. It is because I am so exceptional pretty," I added earnestly. "A boy who is as pretty as a girl, yet with two so obvious marks, and others, smaller. As if something so perfect has to have a blemish in order to go in the world, with the vulgar. Sometimes even intelligent people, you know, feel uneasy."

"And how about you? How do *you* feel, to be so singled out? It is not everyone who has the mark of the otherworld upon them."

"I suppose I do feel special. Rare, tu sais."

"And just a little puffed up with conceit," he smiled.

"O no," I said perfectly seriously. "I have always believed that I was to be famous and exceptional."

"Indeed?"

"O yes. The question was, in what manner? I thought at first as a poet."

"But?" he said politely.

"When I began to read the poems of real poets – Ronsard, for example – I knew that mine were – quoi – infantile. So, not a poet. Then, I thought, a lute player. I play very well."

"I look forward to a recital."

"Yes. Gladly. But you will have heard better. I do play well, but like any cultured boy from good family. And so –" I shrugged.

"And so it was not to be as a wondrous musician. What next

then, O seeker after immortality?"

"You know the King Edward and Piers Gaveston..."

Anthony raised his eyebrows; but then the dinner came in, and we busied ourselves around the table, the innkeeper's lad arranging our food and pouring our wine, and all conversation lost in the general business of eating and placating hunger. We had green pottage, cold roast beef and also ham and veal – they had warned me that the English ate much meat – and we had a jelly set with violet comfits; and rough grained bread. Eventually when we were alone again and had finished praising the meal and grunting noises of appreciation, I wondered: "Do you think it is an unworthy ambition, to want to become famous and renowned?"

"Why, no. I believe no less a person than Her Majesty has such an ambition: to do some act that would make her fame spread abroad in her lifetime and, after, occasion memorial for ever."

"Ah, tis easy for a queen," I grumbled, munching.

"Yes, we ordinary mortals have to work harder. And you felt that your special talent lay in a close connection with a king?"

I grimaced. "I was wrong, like with the other things."

"Really?" he leaned forward. "But why?"

But I would not be drawn. It was too near.

"I shall think of a way," I grinned. "I am determined, one way or another, I shall be famous down the ages."

"Down the ages!" he cried. "Not satisfied with mere fame in the moment. Famous down the ages, no less. Have you anything planned? Anything particular?"

"No," I giggled.

"Amazing imp," he said exasperated. "Why do I attempt to take you seriously, and pander to your self love?"

"Because I am so lovely," I told him frankly.

His amused eyes met mine over the rim of his wine goblet.

"Tell me something, elf," he said thoughtfully. "If a person interested in the dark arts wished to meet you, having heard of the magic signs upon you...in the pursuit of knowledge... would that frighten you at all?"

"What do you mean? It would depend who it was, and what he wanted."

"Of course it would. Think no more about it. Talk to me

about yourself instead. Tell me about Piers Gaveston and Edward the Second."

"O, I am sure you know all that," I teased with fluttering eyelashes. "English history."

He was a little vexed. He wanted to hear gossip. He poured me more wine and I drank it.

"You were at the French court, presumably?" he said.

"O yes," I remarked grimly.

And then, very delicate, he talked about courts, and monarchs and fashions and such, nothing provocative, but directing his remarks to answers from me, which made me aware that he was gently pressing for information. It was most subtle, and warm with wine I may have been wrong. I know I began to get a wicked pleasure in teasing him by seeming to misunderstand his questions and sidestepping his remarks. As far as I could tell, it was a question of how close was I to the King and did he talk to me of policy, and what other nations were strongly represented at court. And what did they truly think of King Henry of Navarre at the French court and did the King fear the Duke of Guise, and did the Duke hope to gain the French crown, and would he kill for it? How powerful was Marguerite of Navarre – O, all the jumble of policy and intrigue that was as much a mystery in France as it was beyond the seas. Did I speak other languages besides English? Surely Spanish would come very easy to a French person, much easier than English?

"O..." I grimaced. "They made me learn English. I was almost strapped down and fed it through the ears. Because of Lettice Blysshen, you see."

He looked blank, reasonably enough.

"The big tall girl with ginger hair," I said. "The one to whom I was betrothed at the age of nine. I was made to learn English since that day, and she was made to learn French. And so here I am, not too bad in English, but no, I don't know Spanish.... Anthony, please, shall we make love now?"

I smouldered enticingly across the table. He was momentarily diverted from his attempt to milk information from me.

"And can I have hot water please?" I said.

I think Anthony would have gone without washing but I feel sure the French are more practical and I knew well enough how lovemaking left its odours. So he procured a bowl for me and I made us a good atmosphere with some sensuous singing on my now tuneful lute. "Belle qui tiens ma vie" was what I rendered and it sounded most melodious. Anthony said it was exquisite. And then he gently took the lute from me and leaned down to me and kissed me on my lips and he stood me up and began to unbutton my doublet. I helped him, all the while kissing him, save for when it was coming off over my head, of course, and then I helped him divest me of all my other clothes. Considering how tormented I had been all day, I was wondrous recovered and pleasantly replete with food and wine, and I was most happy for him to peel off my clothes and see me in my beautiful nakedness. His eyes were alight with pleasure as I stood stripped before him; he murmured little noises of delight and touched me and turned me round, and I held out my arms wide and said: "How do you want me? Ask anything you like!"

Blinking like a child at a fair, Anthony surveyed me, and then pointed to his crotch. I set about undressing him. O, our fashions, with their tiny little buttons and delicate hooks! I grumbled in French as I fiddled with the hindrances, and he said now more than ever did I look like a wicked imp. Hobberdidance, he said, or Flibbertigibbet.

"They are always pictured naked and sullen. What a shame you ever have to dress! You should be obliged to go around exactly as you are, so sweetly perfect, molesting travellers in the wood and taking off their clothes."

"I would but seduce the handsome ones," I said, "like you. I've wanted to see you naked ever since I first saw you. O! Anthony! You are so blond there! And so big!"

I gazed at his beautiful privities – O! – he was a joy to behold, I knew he would be. I set about kissing him – I darted round him, kissing and licking and teasing, till finally he took me by the head and pushed me down, down the soft skin of his belly and the curly fuzz of his crotch hair till I was kneeling on the floor and my lips were enclosing his excited prick. I took it deep in my mouth and sucked excitedly, I nuzzled him all round the groin, my arms around his arse; I felt soft blond down all over its surface. His wide apart thighs were golden-haired. I murmured glad appreciation. He was a beautiful sight, Anthony.

He leaned down and eased me to my feet.

"On the bed," he said, his eyes all glittering with lechery.

I went over to the bed and pulled the covers back. I glided inside, watching Anthony's approach. I gulped with excitement; I was very roused myself. My heart was thumping as he turned me over on to my front. I slid my prick into my hands and started moving.

"O," shivered Anthony. "Your arse — your lovely arse!"

Others also had found it a delight. I was often told it was my best feature, that is, if one likes them well rounded and smooth, and it is certainly an acceptable asset in a boy who hopes to make his way pleasing older men. Nonetheless I was much delighted with Anthony's pleasure and I wriggled in anticipation and jutted my globes enticingly as he eased my thighs apart. I sighed at the touch of his fingers on my skin. He greased me, his two fingers slurping deep, and then carefully and gradually, his long hard prick. He lay down on me, his arms around me. I was moving in the lovely rhythm, and we groaned in whispers, candlelight flickering all over the walls. His thrusts grew harder, and his gasps loud in my ear. Myself, I was very near coming and I erupted with a yell. He slammed a hand over my mouth and held me tight as he finished. In a rush of generosity I told him what he wanted to know.

"The last person to do that was the king of France."

Anthony gasped. "So it is true — you were his boy."

"Yes, I was his boy. Only he calls them his mignons."

"So I had heard. Well! Holy ground, eh?"

"Not really. You are very much better than him."

"Treason, Marc! To the dungeons with you!"

"Ah no, Anthony, do not joke. That is not droll at all."

"Pardon me. Well, I'm pleased to hear that I was better."

"And much more beautiful."

"Is it true that he is bald?"

"Anthony," I winced. "That is not in good taste."

"Tell me about him."

"I owe him I think at least to stay silent."

Anthony grumbled and eased himself out. "What a tease you are, telling some and then retreating. The things you must know!"

"No, truly I do not," I assured him. "Believe me, I was nothing politically. I was just a pretty body to play with in the evening. A kind of lute."

"H'm," said Anthony, reaching to pinch my arse. "Yes, I suppose you are rather lute shaped."

"O! I meant symbolically!" I gasped indignantly. "Cease pestering me with hints and questions. I know no more of intrigue than a lapdog – and Henri had plenty of those as well. Lapdogs, boys, no difference; he tells his secrets to his important favourites – Epernon, Joyeuse – not to his playthings. I have no information, I was an ornament, that's all."

I sensed an irritation in Anthony. He was vexed that I had realised he had been trying to wheedle gossip from me. He assumed I was too fuddled with wine, or too stupid. Maybe too he was disappointed. Maybe for him the sexuality had been unimportant and he had been hoping for information, and secrets that only I would know. He could not doubt my blunt honesty as I told him he erred to think me a source of political information. Maybe I was disappointed too. It is pleasant to lie afterwards in each other's arms, but Anthony got out of bed and turned his back on me. O, he had enjoyed his use of me, but already his mind was elsewhere, and diverting as I might have been, that was *all* I was, it seemed.

"Marc, I am expecting a visitor," he said, beginning to put on his clothes.

"You want me to help you dress?" I said, watching him.

"No. You stay in bed. Go to sleep."

"Is he coming up here, your visitor?"

"I do not think so. Possibly. I know not." Anthony sounded preoccupied. He finished dressing, and bent down to open his box. He took out writing materials, and sat himself at the table.

"Anthony," I said, up on one elbow. "You did *like* me?"

Anthony suddenly laughed, looking at me. "Of course I did – God's light – how vain you are, always demanding praise! Indeed I liked you; how could I not? The skin of your bum is like fine silk and the texture of your insides is like warm velvet. I can't believe you haven't been told that before."

I bit my lip. It did not sound very pleasant how he said it; it was a compliment but it sounded like a jibe. I felt criticised for having given him pleasure. Was he one of those who think less of you for having allowed them access?

"Listen, poppet," he said. "Tell me something. After you have dispensed with your unattractive cousin Gervaise and his even more unattractive sister Lettice, where will you go?"

"Truly I have no idea," I shrugged. "How can I know? It depends upon so many things. Maybe I will stay with them. That is what my brothers intend."

"Can you ever fancy your wanderings taking you to London, perchance?"

"O!" I said starrily. "Yes, of course I can *fancy* it. I would love to go to London."

"It is after all, the proper place to be, for a person who intends to be famous," he smiled.

"Yes, I suppose it is. I should never be famous living with cousin Lettice!"

"*Famous down the ages,*" he reminded me.

"Exactly," I replied solemnly. "Well then, tis possible I shall go to London."

"I wonder if you could deliver a message."

"You understand it is not certain I go to London. Please don't entrust me with anything urgent."

"This is not urgent. Simply a letter I am about to write. If you go to London you deliver it. If you don't go to London, throw it away."

"Very well, if you wish."

I thought it was a little odd. I wondered why he did not go to London himself; we were not so far from there. Why send me, on his vague and obscure premise? However, it made no difference to me. I could easily do what he said.

Anthony wrote a short letter and sealed it, folded over securely. He stood up and handed it to me. I took it and read what was written on the outside: Christopher Marley, at the Phoenix Tavern.

"Who is that?" I enquired.

"O," said Anthony vaguely. "He's a bit of a poet."

It was odd to be lying in a bed holding a letter to be delivered to a poet. I slipped it under the pillow.

"Listen to that," Anthony remarked. "Pissing with rain."

We could hear the rain outside, noisy and sharp like metal.

"I will wait downstairs," he muttered. I yawned. I was of a sudden extreme sleepy. Anthony handed me a goblet with a little wine left.

"Here, drink it down, and you'll sleep the better. I want you fast asleep when I come back."

He left me with the goblet in my hand and blew out the candle. He went out of the room. I did not drink; I got up and slung a blanket around me – at this inn they had a privy closet along the landing. The inn was quiet and creaky. It must have been well into the night by then. Strange time for an assignation. I would have liked a wash, but I had the impression that Anthony wanted me well out of the way asleep, and if I lit the candle he would know I was awake. I stood for a moment by the window. I peered through the dark leaded panes, out into the hissing rain. It was coming down like bodkins. Glistening trickles coursed down the glass. Huge smudgy trees shook and swayed. Not a night to be out. I shivered.

I saw a dark horseman dismount and hurry to the door, a dark figure move to meet him. I ran from the window, flung the blanket back across the sheets, and dived into bed. It is curious how you know when you are not supposed to see something. I burrowed down the bedclothes deep, the top of my head showing, no more.

It was as well I did, for very soon the door opened and Anthony returned, with a stranger. I heard his boots squelch water, and the slap of wet cloth as he took off his cloak and shook it. I made my breathing deep and slow as if I was asleep.

"The devil of a night..." said Anthony.

"But who have you in that bed?" The voice was foreign. Not French. Alarmed, moreover.

"Some little quean I met upon the voyage."

It was all I could do to remain placid. The careless contempt in Anthony's voice made my mouth open with shock. I trembled with indignation.

"Sound asleep, I hope." He sounded aggressive.

"O yes," laughed Anthony. "It would be the worse for him if he were to wake up now!"

"*Him*?" echoed the man, momentarily distracted and intrigued. "*Him*, Anthony?"

"Him, Felipe. A juicy little catamite."

A throaty snigger followed – Felipe was indulging in a little teasing, so it seemed. And then they muttered in low voices – in Spanish! They stood at the window, where I had so recently been standing, and watched the rain. I daresay all they said was

What dreadful weather, and I hope it soon improves, and other such banalities – but O, how sinister does whispered Spanish sound at dead of night! What did he mean, it would be the worse for me? Would he be obliged to slit my throat for having seen him with the Spaniard? What was Anthony involved in? What had Spain to do with England? Was it true all these rumours of plots? Or was I being over fanciful from having been at the Valois court, where rumour and plot were as commonplace as eating?

I did not dare look, or even move, but it seemed that Anthony gave Felipe some papers from his box, and there were further murmurs and finally the sounds of parting – the rustle of glove and cloak, the goodbye words, the closing of the door. Anthony turned back into the room.

Without relighting the candle, he came over to the bed, sat and took off his boots. Then he laughed to himself, and I knew he was turning his attention to me. He gave off a glow of being pleased with himself. The night had gone well then. I felt the sheet and blanket slowly drawn from my shoulders so that I was lying there uncovered. I squeezed my eyes tight together and forced my breathing to remain deep and regular. I was frightened, and I knew I had to seem asleep.

Anthony ran his hands lightly over my body, raising goose pimples on me.

"You sluttish thing," he murmured, "with your wanton ways. So the King had you, did he, paddled in that white flesh, did he, and you opening up like a lily?" His fingers played with my flesh. I could not understand how he could think this treatment would not wake me. It was only afterwards, when I realised that the wine in the goblet had been drugged, that it became clear. He thought that I had drunk it, as he had told me to, and confident in its efficacy, he gloated somewhat at my expense.

"Famous down the ages!" he sneered. "Never! Your only claim to fame will be as a fine piece of arse. I should have left you to the sailors."

He climbed off the bed and padded away out of the room, to the closet.

Trembling and gasping I sat up. I reached down for the wine to soothe my shattered state. I swigged a great mouthful. The

40

goblet dropped from my grasp and rolled away across the floor. Probably it saved my life to take that drink. I really was drugged then, though of course I did not know it. I could not have feigned a drugged sleep if Anthony had seriously chosen to test me. No doubt he did, later. So when he came back, there I lay, truly limp and helpless this time, sprawled face down on the bed, a trickle of wine at my lips.

More surprises awaited me on the morrow.

TWO

I

"And then – what then?"

I WOKE, with something of a headache, to find myself alone.
Warm sunlight lay in diamond streams across the musty
hempen sheets. The day was well advanced. I slowly
emerged, crawling up from sleep, confused, surprised, and
sorting out my thoughts.

As I paced dozily about the room it became apparent to me
that I was the victim of mischance. Anthony was gone, without
explanation, and he had called me a sluttish thing and said I
would not be famous except as a fine piece of arse. Anthony had
drugged the wine to make me sleep, and I had slept. Anthony
had met a Spaniard by arrangement and sounded menacing and
sinister, and had brought me here because of what I was and
what I might reveal to him. While I was asleep, my trunk had
come, and there it lay, but more, it had been searched. The key
had been taken from my purse and my possessions handled.
More, the most part of my money had been taken, and though
he had left me some, I was now almost penniless.

I knelt beside the trunk, still naked, warm in a patch of
sunlight. My thick head prevented the full impact of anger and
humiliation I was feeling. I winced to recall myself all limp and
bare, while he strolled about handling my luggage, and for all
I knew, myself as well. I felt indignant and abused. The day
moreover being under way, he had stolen too my time. I felt
gullible and foolish.

Nothing had been taken from my trunk, even though some of
my possessions were valuable and would have sold well. The
King's present to me, a belt with amber studs, was still there,
which I was glad about because it was very cunningly wrought.

Well, I would have to learn from my misfortune and take care whom I enticed into my bed. I grinned ruefully; I knew that I would not.

I set about bathing, taking much pleasure in washing my limbs and removing the traces of the night. I enjoyed cleansing my body, which is a pleasant sight and praised of many. Slight, as Anthony said, slim and graceful. I scented myself all over with a wash of musk rose, and dressed in that I wore before, the dark red, burgundy and black; and then I attended to my face. Cleansed it with elderflower and patted it with a marigold paste, then lightly rouged it, tracing a fine black line along my lids. My blue-grey eyes smirked back at me from the mirror, and though my sleep had been drugged it had been deep, and I looked the better for it. My ear rings twinkled. I combed my tangled brown hair into sleekness, and arranged my fringe. Now I was hungry.

I had not supposed that this early in my travels I would be obliged to fend for myself, and I must admit that it was with some trepidation that I descended the stairs to arrange breakfast. But all went well. At this inn so near the coast they were used to foreigners, and I was understood, though myself, I found it harder to understand the words of country folk than of the cultured. I had bread, cheese and wine. I was offered ale and beer, but these looked unappetising. I took my fare back to my room to eat at leisure. The bread was rough and grainy, very brown, and I feared for my teeth on the small stones I found within it. When I reached cousin Gervaise's house, I promised myself, I would eat well. I would be at Ashford by night.

Two things I remembered then, the first being the letter. I took it out from under the pillow, and turned it over.

Christopher Marley, at the Phoenix Tavern...surely I was under no obligation to deliver it now? I did not feel I was betraying any confidence to read it. Moreover, my curiosity was too strong. So I broke the seal and opened the letter, and this is what I read:

"Most dear...I send you this box of sweets – marque français – knowing you will find something therein to your taste. The flavours are many, as I have discovered. But ask it *who nibbled before*...Yours in love, Anthonie Wn."

When I read that, I flushed all over my cheeks and down my

neck, hot with embarrassment and rage. For just a moment I had wondered what he meant by "box of sweets" as if there could ever have been a box somewhere that I had overlooked; but of course the truth then struck me, that the box of sweets was *me*, and I was being *sent as a present*. To think that he had evolved such a trick at my expense – to make me deliver it myself, all innocent, offer myself so sweetly, as something to be nibbled! O! How I did resent his mocking tone, his foolish pun on my name – marque français – his unconcern for my dignity. O! He had writ it there with me watching and believing he was writing a real letter, politely agreeing to deliver it – and all the while it was a jest upon me, between two sophisticated people laughing over the head of a gullible boy. I stared at that offensive letter, till the words danced mockingly up and down in the sunlight – ask it who nibbled before – *it*, mind you, not even *him*. I was angry and indignant.

Now anyone else would have crumpled up that wicked letter or burned it on a candletip. Why did not I? Did I have some prescience? Did something hold back my hand? Strange are the workings of Fortune! I merely folded up the letter tight and hard along its creases, and thoughtfully I put it in my trunk, under a white silk shirt.

I said that I remembered two things. The other was that it was the First of May, and I had not made any celebration. So I decided to make amends at once, and left my room and went downstairs, and out into the open air.

I found the day was like a different world. The rain had fallen all night, but now the air was fresh and bright and full of sunshine. My head cleared rapidly, and I tripped off towards the woodland that lay on both sides of the track. I had only to walk a little way to leave known things behind. The track was soon lost to sight and I was entering further and further into the forest. There was no one about, and a lovely welter of birdsong piping flute-like from the sweetly green trees, and underfoot many kinds of flowers, some white, some blue, but mostly the pale yellow of primroses. Around me as I walked, my doublet brushed blossom – starry white petals and bourgeoning clumps of pink, and in the breeze the blossom fell like snow and touched my cheeks, fragrancing me with pink and white, dotting my sleeves and hair, tickling my lips. The warm sunlight speckled me with patterns of light and shade and filled my heart with gladness.

When I felt completely alone, and surrounded solely by trees and birds, I knelt down and bathed my face in the primroses. They were deliciously wet from the rain. I licked raindrops from their wrinkly leaves and buried my nose in the softly scented petals. I picked a little bunch and took it to a hawthorn tree and laid it down as an offering. I knelt down, shut my eyes tight and said the little pagan prayer, and then because I was in England now I made a swift translation – and even a rhyme, which somewhat pleased me:

"First of May, First of May
Send me my true love today."

Ardour was in my voice, the glow of prayer upon my face. Then, the secret rite and the heady scents and sun's warmth all conspiring to make me feel amorous, I looked furtively about me and undid my hose and started to excite myself. I fell forward over my knees, and plunged and lay in the primroses, rolling over and over in pleasurable abandon. I rubbed myself in primroses – there were even some in my mouth.

Then, a little shamefaced now, I laughed at myself and got to my feet. I tidied myself up, picking primroses out of my hair and my buttonholes, and I prepared to return to the known world, the ancient gods and goddesses appeased and gratified.

I was somewhat shocked then, when a girl appeared, pushing through the bushes. In truth I blushed crimson, because I feared she might have seen me being primitive, and it was bad enough to be caught with primroses in my hair. She smiled at me.

Now this girl was as pretty as I was. Beautiful even. She was slim and supple with long golden hair and large breasts and a small narrow waist and winning manner. A man might think she was a wood nymph and accept the spell she cast.

"You are celebrating May," she said winsomely.

"Yes," I admitted, pulling primroses from my person hurriedly.

"O no," she protested. "They looked lovely. I am celebrating too."

"I have to go," I mumbled.

"O! Please!" she invited persuasively. And she undid her

bodice! I stared bemused. She quite mistook my attitude. She took hold of my limp wrist and put my hand on her breast. O! I could feel her warm bare skin!

I tore my hand away, gulping. She stared at me astonished.

"What ails you?" she asked in disbelief. "I thought you were celebrating May – look, we can lie in the primroses."

Truly I could think of nothing to say. In female form she was so perfect and she had most surely never been refused before. She had offered unasked what any man would have considered himself blessed to receive. I stood there stupidly, tongue-tied and still wincing from the unpleasant touch of the bulbous shape against my hand. I wondered whether to say I was a eunuch but I could not. She misunderstood my confusion and laughed, and put herself against me, her arms round my neck.

"Come," she cooed. "Don't be coy. I'll show you what to do."

I unhooked her arms and fled. As I pushed my way through the undergrowth away from her, she called out "Why?" all uncomprehending.

I felt most vexed. She had spoilt my celebration. Women are so meddlesome. They think that all they have to do is be there and men fall over themselves to court them. I wondered if the earth goddess had a merry wit. I had knelt down and asked for my true love to appear – and look what I was given! Perhaps I should have offered more than primroses? Or perhaps the spilling of seed is an invitation to procreation? I shuddered. Luckily I had brothers enough to carry on the family name.

Back at the inn I enquired about the possibility of transport to Ashford. I would have liked a horse, but I did not want to be separated from my trunk, and so when I was told that a carrier's cart was going that way within the hour I was very pleased to accept a ride and pay out my dregs of cash for the privilege. A servant carried my trunk downstairs, and I passed the time eating. I had salt beef with mustard, also a venison pasty, and a sweet pudding made up of eggs and sugar. I was ravenous. I suppose that I was making up for yesterday. Yesterday! How far away that seemed already. I hoped the memory of Anthony would fade as fast.

The carter was a dour and silent man, who drove his heavily laden vehicle placidly down the track, idly switching the horse's rump from time to time, and thoughtfully chewing a long grass stem. I sat in the rear with the luggage, not at all uncomfortable, lying on my back, arms behind my neck, looking at the sky and the tree tops, one leg crossed over the other, my elegant boots outlined in all their beauty. I lay on sacking and straw, philosophical about my change of station. One week satin, one week straw – Life was like a rhyme with cherry stones. Maybe I could make a refrain out of my lovers – stable boy, courtier, mignon, monarch, spy – and then what ? Ah, but they were not lovers, except Gilles. Not lovers, not real lovers, not to do with love. Was anything ever? Was all not a cynical dance, a circle, shifting links in a long cold chain?

To think that but yesterday I had been tossed upon the seas that divided our two nations' shores, and now I was in England! All around me seemed pleasant, and my eyes for the first time opened to see the land itself.

I had heard two varying tales of what England would be like; and it was like neither. One was that every tree was hung with the cadavers of poor Catholics who had been caught secretly attending Mass, and that people lived in fear and dread, and hid in doorways. The other was that the people were all simpletons and brutes, caring nothing for culture and less for policy. On my journey both extremes proved false. The track we followed, though miry and rutted after the rain, passed through lush woodland whose trees were hung merely with leaves and blooms, and the waysides and ditches were yellow with cowslips and celandines, the hedges white with may, the high banks dusky blue with violets. Between the woodland we found villages and fields, where the people seemed in no wise fearful. And whoever we met had an opinion on the state of the world, for I was told by those at the inn where we stopped to eat that King Philip planned to do this and that, others arguing and saying that he did not, just as if these villagers were privy to his inmost council!

The common people of England are like this wherever you go, I find. They listen to all gossip of great personages till they feel they know them well, and talk of great ones as if they lived further on in the next village. They will tell you what the Queen thinks and why she did so and so, and whether such and such was a disappointment to her, and who she wants to marry and

47

whether she intends to have children; and others nod sagely, or contrariwise assure us it was not so, for in truth the Queen thought thus – they swear they know her favourite colours, foodstuffs, jewels, and what she said to Walter Raleigh and he to her.

Me, I said nothing but stayed beside the carter, and drank the noisome ale and ate the coarse-grained bread we shared. I listened, and I worked hard to understand their rough speech, and when we were back in the cart again I watched all that there was to see along the way.

And there was much to see, for everywhere we went they were celebrating the First of May. It was the first time in my life that I had been so close to such especial merriment. I saw laughing crowds carrying a maypole which was all twined about with leaves and flowers and ribbons; and I saw another being set up and decorated even as we passed. Mayboughs were fixed above cottage doors, and girls with armfuls of flowers were making garlands. There was music too – not very well rendered, but played with much vigour – mostly tabors and flutes; and people dancing. Further on there was a fight with cudgels and some wrestling so violent it seemed to be in earnest, but the carter said it was in play. In a meadow beneath the trees there was an archery contest underway, the targets decorated with greenery, and the contenders all dressed up in green, and one man as a female in a long dress simpering and giggling and much teased; and as I gawped the carter explained to me as if I was stupid: "That's Robin Hood and Marian – it's their day today. Don't you have that in France?"

I stared wide eyed at the dancing and longed to join in. Someone seeing me staring then beckoned and called cheerily: "Join us!" but I hesitated, and besides, the carter had to be on his way withal and did not want to stop.

"Do you not want to participate?" I asked him curiously, looking back in regret at such merry scenes, which I felt sure would later lead to lovemaking in the long grass.

"Tis for the young," he shrugged, and said no more upon it; and I felt wistful, being young, and solitary.

I thought surprisingly little about my cousin Gervaise. And so it was with almost a shock that I realised we were approaching Ashford village. You understand, time had passed.

We had delivered packages at cottages. Hours had ticked by, I was older.

And so I found myself at the manor gates, cumbersome wooden things bordered by lush trees, and down a curvy path the timbered shape of the house. The carter dumped my trunk in the grass. I pleaded with him sweetly to carry it to the door. Surprisingly he did. I sometimes do find with big muscular men they show off their strength like that – some primitive need, I think. I do not know whether they are boasting and gloating because they are strong as men should be, or whether they assume that because I am as pretty as a girl I must be treated like one and spared the carrying of luggage. And so I thanked my manly friend most cordial, and he snorted as if I was no better than I should be. In fact I am most sure I heard him mutter: "Little..." with a forceful sniff as he plodded away.

Looking about me I noticed how pleasant and controlled it was here, trees and shrubs in their proper place and extreme neat. By comparison, a huddle of wagons over behind some elm trees showed up as wild and wayward, brightly painted, even garish, and not the kind of thing I would have associated with my cousin Gervaise. I stood on the steps, travel sore and crumpled, morsels of straw sticking to my velvet, my lute strung across my back, my trunk at my feet, and thus I met my cousin.

He was in every way as drear as I remembered. He was about thirty years old. He had a white face, minutely freckled all over, save that on his cheeks some were like little ginger coins. His hair was ginger and receding. He wore it flatly smoothed across his head. His clothes were dull and plain, though rich, and his manner most pedestrian. It was clear to me that he did not like me. His little piggy eyes said so, and very soon he made his general position clear.

Now Ashford Manor was an old place, the hall, I believe, a hundred years old, and into this we went, where the remains of a meal were in progress and at the table were several gentlemen. They all figure in my story to a greater or lesser degree, but mostly Thomas Hodgkin, a merchant of some forty-five years, and Cuthbert Hodgkin his son, a Puritan. The other three, Gervaise's friends, were ciphers and of no importance.

What caught my eye was that at one end of the hall there was a

49

trestle stage just new built, and open-lidded chests whence coloured cloths did spill in great luxuriance. On the corner of the stage a youth sat playing a lute, and to one side on a chest, a young man was writing, his back to me, his curly head bowed over his work.

"We have players in," shrugged Gervaise carelessly. "A May Day performance. Nothing special."

The youth with the lute raised his eyebrows but continued to play. Adequate. Not as good as me. I itched to go and join him.

Gervaise introduced me to everyone at the table, which I managed with formal politeness and they with indolent hostility, appraisal, curiosity. Cuthbert was in full Puritan gear, the black garb, the white ruff and cuffs, the buckled shoes, and though I had seen Huguenots and was not over surprised, I could not help a flicker of unease which I knew was foolish. Was it true they intended to undermine the security of the state? Did they plot against us? Did they intend to wreck our churches and smear insults on the images? But of course in England they had already done so, had they not? They were powerful, and it was Catholics who were seen as subversive. For me Cuthbert took on the aura of a black spider; I found him sinister.

Gervaise's manner was cool towards me.

"Do help yourself if you are hungry. If anything on the table takes your fancy."

I was hungry and there was plenty to eat on the table – I saw beef, chicken, bacon, a leg of mutton and several roasted pigeons, as well as bread and beer, white wine and claret. I picked away at chicken and poured wine, and tried to persuade myself that I was but imagining my discourteous reception. I did not see why I should be received with all his friends about, so publicly; but this seemed to be a feature of Gervaise, insensibility. For instance, he was ignoring the players. To me they were the most vibrant part of the room. The makeshift stage was enticing, and the boy with the lute had floppy fair hair and needed some help with two of the chord changes. The one writing had an attractive back, and I wanted him to turn round. He was wearing a cream-coloured shirt with a slight frill at the neck. Yes, his back view was very pleasing...lean...and his leg that I could see, in black, was well shaped, with a neat firm thigh.

Gervaise paid no heed to the players; he behaved as if they were part of the wall, as rich men often do in front of servants. He must have thought he was inside a kind of bubble, which prevented his words from sounding. Everything he said to me, was heard by the players and by whomever was yet at table, and I knew this even if he did not. His attitude gave the impression to his friends that I was of no account. Certainly it seemed to be so, for one of them said, in a plain clear snigger:

"It would seem that straw flecks are worn this year at the Valois court!"

I could not help my cheeks colouring up, and I brushed at the straw bits with my hand, which made them laugh the more. I flashed a glowering glance at the man who had discomfited me, and he raised his tankard, and Gervaise did not even notice all that. But did it mean that he had told his friends about me – I mean privy things? Had he then explained what I had been to the King – had they been discussing it between themselves, and wondering what this interesting object would be like, the French king's boy? I blushed afresh, and averted my eyes from Gervaise's smirking friends. At about that point the two Hodgkins did leave the room, and Gervaise took the opportunity to begin his talk with me.

He sat me down upon a stool, near the players, and he paced about in front of me.

"I should tell you," he said, "that it has been monstrous inconvenient your coming here."

"O?" I said warily.

"Your brother Charles rides roughshod over everything in his path. What does he think I am, to be played about with like this? Hey? What has it been like for Lettice? Has any of you thought about her? When it suits you, one thing; when a new opportunity turns up, cast off the old; and when it all falls through, back to the original. This idea of dumping you here. It is most over mighty insolence."

"I understood you were in accord," I began, vexed.

"Yes. But you shall hear why. I have some ideas of my own. Charles is not the only one to use the opportunities that come his way."

"Believe me, I am not responsible for what Charles does or thinks," I scowled. "On the contrary, I am habitually a victim."

"I assume you do remember that at the age of nine you were

betrothed to Lettice? Here in this very house, in our private chapel? You accept responsibility there? As I recall, you spoke your lines well enough. All the correct procedures were carried out. Is that true?"

"Yes, but –" I gasped. "You released me from that – Charles arranged it – you agreed – all that was cancelled last year, when I –"

"When you became a royal catamite," he said firmly, and loudly too. I winced and looked round uncomfortably. For all that I hated Charles I wished he was here to browbeat Gervaise and bludgeon him back to acquiescence.

"And now it seems that the plan misfired," said Gervaise, "and you had to leave France in a hurry."

"Laurent thought it best," I muttered. "He was unquiet for my safety. You agreed I could come here."

"Yes. But it's not quite as simple as that. I will not be used as a laystall. I am a man of substance, you know, a person to be reckoned with."

"I understand your irritation," I said unhappily. "But please have some respect for my feelings too. You should have told Charles if I was not to be welcome. What am I to do? I am here now. And I have had a difficult voyage," I added quiveringly. Really, I was not strong enough to take all this dislike and rancour.

"It is not easy for a Catholic gentleman nowadays," said Gervaise, to no purpose as it seemed; but I saw that he was proffering an explanation.

"Yes?"

"I have to attend to my reputation," Gervaise lowered his voice. "I may well decide to shift my inclinations...it is the only way to rise. To continue in the faith is crippling. Debilitating fines for not atttending church, constant suspicion, sudden searches whenever there are rumours of priests in the area. I have to feather my nest. I have been busy putting my house in order. Making connections. Suitable people."

We looked at the door whence Thomas and Cuthbert Hodgkin had gone out.

"Yes," Gervaise said, "Thomas is a fine Protestant fellow, and extreme – you understand me – comfortable of circumstance. Cuthbert – well, everyone may see what an upstanding

Puritan he is, monstrous zealous. I am cultivating these gentlemen, and I would advise you to do the same."

"Me?" I squeaked. "They are nothing to do with me."

"They could be. They could be a great help."

"O – I think not," I said.

"This is the plan I have for you," said Gervaise.

I scraped a pattern in the rushes with my boot toe. It was Charles all over again. All my life I had been the victim of someone's plans. It was complicated being the youngest. I twirled my lute idly by the neck.

"Marry Lettice," said Gervaise.

All my lute strings jarred. The boy on the stage grinned.

"Marry her as originally planned," Gervaise continued. "She considers herself betrothed to you. She has fluent French, poor girl, learnt for the purpose. I am sure we can arrange it. That, and that alone, is the only reason why I agreed for you to come here at all, so that we could discuss the terms of your marriage. In spite of your vile and shameful recent history, you are yet a good match. Personable and healthy. No doubt you could produce strong children."

The boy on the stage was giggling into his hand, his whole face pink with amusement. I wriggled on my stool and plucked at the lute strings aimlessly.

"I am a Catholic," I said in great relief.

"O, you could easily change that," Gervaise shrugged. "A public recantation goes down very well indeed; all would relish it. You would be welcomed like a lost sheep."

I gulped. "Become Huguenot?" I squeaked.

"Protestant," he corrected kindly, as if that was less extreme. "O come, Marc, you do not care about the intricacies of religion! I know your family, remember. Political schemers, reprobates, disciples of Machiavel. You could easily twist your beliefs if it suited your purpose, hey? Who needs all those chanting priests, all those ave marias and stinking incense? Mass – communion – it's all the same thing in the end. It cannot be that you are devout! Indeed no, considering what the Holy Writ has to say about Sodom!" And he even laughed, most sneeringly.

I wiped my forehead.

"Why not shout it from the tops of houses?" I muttered. "I

wish you'd not refer to it. It's painful for me when other people know."

"My jest," he chuckled cheerfully. "I had not supposed you so sensitive. But then, why did you *do* it? It cannot have much troubled you. Everyone must have known in France. I suppose it is more common over there, the King being one. I suppose that all must do it."

My eyes met those of the boy with the lute. I was much discomfited. He was puce with mirth. Gervaise's friends at the table were listening also. I felt as if they were picturing it wildly, luridly, the entire Valois court, the men busy embracing in alcoves, the king strolling daintily by, picking out whom he wanted, to the music of lutes.

"Never fear," said Gervaise intimately. "Forgive and forget, eh? Put it behind you –" and everybody guffawed. "No, what I mean is, all that is finished now, and I know you'll have much merriment in learning what men and *women* do together. Believe me, tis very much better!" And he nudged me smuttily, which was horrible. "Lettice is a lovely girl. Big, buxom, healthy..."

The boy with the lute collapsed with a snort. The beautiful bending back in the creamy shirt quivered. Swine, I thought savagely, enjoying the sight of my squirming.

"About that," I mumbled, looking at my knees. "It is kind of you, Gervaise, to want me as a suitor for Lettice but in spite of what you say I do not think I am the kind who marries..."

"Nonsense. Every man has the wherewithal to satisfy males and females both. Just because you have been with men up till now, Marc, it does not mean you are not capable...Why, all of us here," he said expansively, "have played around with other men, tis only natural. We've all been naughty in that way, and it was quite delightful. But we have women too; the one does not preclude the other. Face to face with a pretty girl you would soon change your tune. And I intend you shall be given the chance, with Lettice."

I felt vexed and angry.

"Why do you want me for Lettice? I have two disadvantages you know about – my past, my religion. I am not suitable. Why do you not try one of the Hodgkins? Rich Protestants...ideal for you."

Gervaise laughed ruefully. "H'm, well. Neither would take

54

her!" And everybody laughed again, and me, I felt doubly insulted. She had already been refused by them!

"You, Marc," said Gervaise in a sugary tone. "You are my best hope. You are young and handsome and your family is one of the oldest of the French nobility. It is a *name*. Moreover I daresay you still retain some of your influence with the King, hey?" He chuckled. "A little smile here, a little caress there, and who knows? A morsel of land, a small château, a fat purse from a grateful lover? Hey? So think about it while you are a guest in my home. While I am offering you the protection of my roof!"

He nodded at me pleasantly, his inferences perfectly clear. Accept or be thrown out, but let us be agreeable and friendly. Myself I was speechless with disgust, and sat staring ahead of me, wondering what to do now.

"You will wish to see Lettice," said Gervaise.

I did not deign to reply. He strolled off down the hall, and his friends got up from the table and followed him out.

The beautiful back turned slowly round and its owner looked me in the eye.

He was lovely. He had curly brown hair; he was handsome and comely. His shirt was open at the neck. He had sheaves of paper in his hand and a quill pen between his fingers.

He smiled at me.

I did not just at that moment remember my May Day prayer for true love, made that morning amongst the primroses; but that was how I first met Nicholas.

II

"Then never say that thou art miserable,
Because it may be thou shalt be my love..."

YOU could always hide under the stage," Nicholas offered quizzically. "We'll make you a priest's hole between two helmets and a dragon's head mask, and swear we did not see you."

"Do not accept," said the fair-haired boy. "It's monstrous

dusty under there and you would spoil your fine clothes.
Besides, below stage always does for Hell or for a tomb. Or
maybe you think with Nicholas Hell would be Heaven?" he
teased provocatively.

"Maybe I do," I grinned shamelessly. "But even so I could
not accept. I must see the lady."

"I would not," he grimaced.

"I owe it to her; tis polite," I said.

"I have seen her," said the boy. "She has little chance of
converting you to loving womankind."

"Diable!" I muttered. "My chosen preferences seem to be
common gossip."

"Don't be peevish, Marc," said Nicholas laughing. "I may
call you Marc?"

"Yes; but how did you know?"

"I heard Gervaise. And – um – you have been an object of
discussion all day at the table. We were all very excited when we
heard you had arrived. We expected something between Queen
Elizabeth's Frog and the Whore of Babylon. But, *painted*, my
dear, and *dripping* with precious pearls!" And Nicholas minced
shockingly, so that I had to smile.

"His name is Nicholas Henshaw," said the blond boy, "and
mine is Amyas Ellis, since we know yours."

"O!" I cried pulling an expressive face. "To make the
friendship of someone whose name I can't pronounce!"

With much merriment they tried to teach me to say Henshaw,
till I was falling over aitches like a drunk over a logpile. But to
retrieve my dignity I showed Amyas the chord change he
needed, and we bent earnestly over our lutes, and he tried to
play a lute strung for the left hand, unsuccessfully. I must say
Amyas was delightful. Blond and plump and dimpled.

"I play ladies," he simpered.

"Me, I'm just the poor old author," Nicholas grumbled. "I
sweat my guts out unappreciated; they eat up plays like hot
dinners and then demand another one."

"Yes, Nicky's plays *are* much like hot dinners," Amyas said.
"Full of meat and sauce and spice and sudden gobbets of
undigestible matter!"

"What are we having tonight?"

"O," he laughed, "Your unsavoury relation was right –

56

nothing special! You know that wretched little Puritan? He insisted no violence, no blood, no lechery – that rules out all the best ones, so what you will see is a real delight. *The Sweet Sobs and Amorous Complaints of Shepherds and Nymphs – a Fancy.* Don't laugh. It's droll enough and there is music and dancing in it. Shepherds are always well-received."

"They die for love," said Amyas.

"Without violence?" I disbelieved.

"Offstage. They do not really die; they just think they have."

"Do not tell him the plot," said Nicholas.

"What plot?" sniggered Amyas comfortably.

"Surely not just you two, entire?"

"No, not us entire," said Nicholas grinning. "The others are about somewhere. Rehearsing in the knot garden, no doubt."

"Or knot," said Amyas, much dimpled.

"You do not play?" I asked Nicholas. "Only write?"

"*Only write*, he says!" cried Nicholas. "But what can you expect from a person who cannot sound his aitches?"

"Nicholas! I don't mean Only. I mean you are too – I mean you should be seen, not hidden away."

"Very true," he agreed. "Yes, I do play small parts – I run around changing from soldier to Persian to demon to priest and so forth. And I do direct the others," he added modestly.

"I thought you would have been the hero," I said innocently, but fluttering my lashes a little.

"Ah – wondrous though I be, we have one even more beautiful – Gabriel Pollock, known for visible reasons as Angel. He plays the hero."

"Have you ever acted, Marc?" said Amyas, "speaking of being pretty."

"Just a little," I murmured. "I know it will ruin my reputation to confess this, but for me also it was ladies."

"Oh! Truly?" they cried with interest, and not laughing at all. "You would be beautiful! Would you like to be a nymph tonight? You need not speak, just entice and flutter!"

"O! I would indeed but I dare not..." I went quite pink.

"Surely not stage fright!"

"No! I like performing. But I don't think I could bear the ridicule – they already think I am effeminate and soft, and more..."

"They are uncouth, Marc, ignore them," said Nicholas firmly.

"How can I? I have to stay here," I said gloomily.

"You do?"

"But yes – " I shrugged. "It is my journey's end."

Nicholas eyed me smiling. "You know what they say about the end of journeys!"

"No. What do they say?"

"Journeys end in lovers meeting," said Nicholas.

We looked into each other's eyes. His were grey. I tried to read the messages in them. It seemed too fortunate to be true, that he should mean something deep, about himself and me. We stared, like lovers in a play. Then Amyas spoilt the moment with a giggle.

"Journeys end in lovers meeting." he teased. "And here she comes!"

Cousin Gervaise was escorting in Lettice.

Amyas and Nicholas fled back to the stage.

I must admit my heart did sink as Lettice and Gervaise approached. Him I blatantly disliked; she I felt a little guilty about. I think our family had treated her badly – obliging her to learn French and tempting her with the prospect of me! – only to withdraw that plum and leave her fluent in French to no purpose.

But O! She was bigger than me even now, just as she had been when I was nine. She was about seventeen, and bulky. Most sure, it was in part the clothes. Ladies' fashions flattered slim girls, but they made big girls look like ships. Lettice bore down on me all sails. With great dignity I took and kissed her hand, and very conscious of Nicholas and Amyas all ears and eyes, I said firmly: "Shall we walk in the garden?"

"Sssss!" murmured Amyas disappointed, offstage.

I escorted Lettice out of the hall and sneaked a look at her. Yes, her hair was very ginger, and she had pretty little pearls twined in it. Her dress was goose-turd green silk and swayed from the wide hips below the rigid wasp-waist bodice, which effect she had produced with tight lacing.

"I want it understood," she said bluntly, "I do not overmuch want to marry you."

"Oh, good," I agreed relieved. Short lived, however.

"But if I must, I will. There seem to be advantages on both sides."

"What are they?" I said curiously.

"Well, you receive some money; I mean my dowry," she said. "Apparently your family have need of it. Did you know that?"

"It is not true" I lied. "We are very rich."

"Please yourself," she shrugged.

"Can you bear to marry without love?" I tried.

"Most people do," she remarked philosophically.

As we approached the knot garden I gasped. The most beautiful man I had ever seen was walking there in a small group of others. His hair was as gold as the sun. His lithe muscular form was clad in scarlet and tawny, and he gestured much with his arms. It was surely Gabriel Pollock, known as Angel. My eyes and mouth all opened into O's.

"O," I said nonchalantly. "Let us walk in the knot garden."

"But there are *players* in it," she objected. "Besides, the ways are so narrow we could not walk two abreast. My skirt is too wide."

I felt like Adam outside the Garden. I gawped at the Angel within. What sweet perfection!

"We should be talking about our marriage," Lettice said comfortably.

The world erupting all round me with beautiful males I could not take seriously the presence of Lettice.

I leaned across and gave her a swift kiss on the cheek.

"I can never marry you," I murmured. "I have taken a vow to be a monk."

I left her blinking in surprise and I darted off to the knot garden. I burst among the group of actors like a sunbeam.

"Nicholas sent me," I lied shamelessly. "I am to be of help. I can do anything, whatever you like."

"Who are you?"

"You know who he is, with that strange accent. That boy they've been talking about all day – the one who – you know."

"Yes, that's who I am – Marc-Alphonse du Plessis Mornay, and I have performed before the highest in the land."

"H'm, yes, so we've heard! But doing *what*?" they teased.

"I am a skilful lute player, and I am beautiful in a dress."

"Come and read Amyas's part."

Truly it was that simple. They accepted me as I was. It was easy come, easy go, though later when I was more deeply involved, the greatest commitment was expected, as I found to my cost. But that was all afar off. That first day of May, late afternoon, it was all merry and at ease, and there was I reading words of love to Angel Pollock in the knot garden of Ashford Manor, most happily, and the sun did shine.

There was Jack Unsworth, who was in charge, and they were his wagons. He was in his thirties, a big stocky muscular man, plump of stomach, black of hair and beard, broad of shoulder, strong of arm. He played kings and fathers and gaolers, and sometimes God if it was an old play. Jack's wife Madge was also with the company. She was in the wagon, sewing costumes. She was also big and plump. Her wayward wispy hair was tied up with bright braid, her face was kind and apple-cheeked and she had many chins. She looked after people and made clothes; she was very important. Their two children Martin and Geoffrey were players, they were aged twelve and ten, and they played pages, princes, messengers, ladies, and various beasts, particularly a dragon. There was Angel, who was exquisite, and played the hero, and Francis who played ladies unwillingly and clowns with more relish, and small parts with many changes, like Nicholas. Amyas played the female lead. Nicholas wrote new plays and fiddled around with old ones, and John and Ralph played instruments, and lifted heavy things and saw to the horses.

They took me over to the wagons to meet Madge, and I sat on the wagon steps holding yards of taffeta that she hemmed. Within moments she had winkled out enough of my past history to convince herself that I was a poor orphan boy who had never known a mother's love. Anything I may have done wrong was pardonable; I was led astray by those who should have known better. I needed care. I happily agreed; and I in part believed it to be true. Anyone who wanted to mother me I gave my affection to entire. I would have followed Madge around as a puppy does. Sitting holding the taffeta I was most glad and felt so comfortable. I passed pins and scissors, and stroked my cheeks with fur scraps and ribbons of velvet. For I did like women, as long as they did not try and get me into bed. I thought Madge most lovely.

Everyone pestered me to take part in the play that night. I could be a nymph or a shepherd, whichever I perferred, and when they heard my lute playing Jack said I was good enough for a solo and it would be a great help to them if I played something pastoral while the scenes were being changed. You may fancy how all this went to my head. From being all on my own, near shipwrecked, seasick, abused, betrayed, robbed and ridiculed, I was of a sudden surrounded by pleasant people praising me, people moreover with the startling flamboyance of performers, and people whom I already felt part of.

And so buoyed up and fortified was I by everyone, and particularly Nicholas, I agreed to take part in the play, and when Gervaise said he thought it was a stupid idea, I knew I had done right!

However, I was not yet bold enough to be a nymph. I was a shepherd, which meant I had a sheepskin slung across my chest, and my habitual clothes beneath. I took off the boots because they were too elegant, and Amyas tied some fur scraps around my leg below the knee, with leather threads. This did emphasise my shapely thighs, as Nicholas pointed out. I was delighted that he had noticed!

"And what did you think of Exquisite Angel?" he said teasingly. "I hear you have been making love to him in the knot garden."

"Yes; it was very agreeable. Unfortunately it was all done with a script, and some way apart."

"So it will continue. There never was a more manly male than Angel. I fear you must be female to make any advance with him!"

"How do *you* know, Nicky?" I grinned.

"By observation, Marc! What could you think I meant?"

This play, this *Sweet Sobs and Amorous Complaints*, was a May Day fancy, an excuse for twanging and dancing. It was a version of that story where the lovers meet in the forest and there is a bear and a bloodstained handkerchief, and a missing lover who is thought dead, and an almost suicide by the one remaining, who sings his playnts in a song of seven verses, at the end of which the lady returns just as he lifts the dagger to his manly breast, and everyone comes on and sings loudly and dances, and there follows a celebration with flowers and poems in praise of Hymen the goddess of marriage. We all had a marvellous good meal before, I'm pleased to relate, as I was ravenous again, and it was delightful to be munching in such a noisy merry group and thigh to thigh with Nicholas. He did not move his thigh from mine and I could feel all the warmth of his leg. He had a lovely leg, did Nicholas. But I did not really know how he felt about me because we were always in the group and getting ready for the play.

We performed by candlelight. Gervaise's old hall was a perfect place for that, transformed by the shivering light into timelessness. The early summer twilight fell, deep blue, with one bright star, Hesperus, twinkling on high, visible through the leaded panes. A few birds sang, most melodic. Within, the hall was warm. The stage was ready and the players, and Gervaise and his friends were finishing their meal, jovial with wine, and Lettice was there with her maid. I found I was most happy. It was easy being a shepherd who did not speak. My lute playing was much enjoyed. I did "L'aube vient tantôt", just with the melody. I sat on the edge of the stage, my legs much to the fore, and if Gervaise's friends had truly played around together and found it delightful, then I daresay I was desired as I sat there.

Cuthbert Hodgkin sat with folded hands and prim lips throughout. He had hair like straw and a face like a weasel, very long of nose. His father Thomas Hodgkin was portly and impressive. He had a good bearing and silver-black hair. His clothes were dark and sober but very fine. His face was square and lined, with heavy brows. He looked like a stage lord mayor. I have seen one in *The Shoemaker's Holiday* very like.

As I sat there, it seemed as though the whole world fell into place for me. Upon the stage everything was so enjoyable and lively. It was beautiful to watch Amyas and Angel speaking words of love; Amyas made a lovely maiden. The sight of Gervaise eating did nothing to spoil my pleasure in the moment, nor even the sounds of trenchers shifting and the clink of pewter tankards and the barely concealed loud whispered remarks. It was for me a sweet and bitter sort of happiness, because I was part of it and yet not part. When the play was over and all the thanks and fêting and politeness, the players went to one side to begin to pack their things away, and I stood torn, wanting to be with them, but beckoned by Gervaise.

I went to him because I still did feel an obligation.

"Come now, Marc," he said gruffly. "Enough of this nonsense now. Take off those bits and pieces and let's see if we can retrieve some dignity. You will have to grow up some day, you know."

I took off my sheepskin and sat down to undo my thongs. I ran back with them; Francis would have received them, but I ran past him to Nicholas and bundled them into his arms.

"I wish it was me," I blurted in a passionate whisper. I thought I would never see him again and so much immodesty would matter little. He stared as if he wanted to say something, but Martin and Geoffrey came between us, and Gervaise was waiting for me.

"Sit down, Marc, I want to talk to you."

I sat on the bench, and Thomas Hodgkin slid a goblet to me full of wine, which I was most ready for.

"Lettice tells me," said Gervaise, "that you did not treat her with proper seriousness. With flippancy, even. Do the years count for nothing? All the letters you and she have exchanged – is that all to be for nothing?"

"Mm," I nodded carelessly, and giggled.

Gervaise gripped my wrist so hard my goblet tilted, and a pool of red spewed out across the table. I was taken aback. I stared into his little piggy eyes and they were furious.

"You have spilt my wine," I complained insolently.

"Peevish milksop boy," he growled.

I looked at him scornfully and then down at my wrist which he still held. He pulled his hand away.

"Will you agree to discuss terms of marriage with Lettice?" he demanded aggressively.

"I will not," I answered. "I can tell you now, I would not marry her if she was beautiful, which she is not. You tell me she was rejected by him – and him – and you offer her to me. Well, I am somewhat particular. I am accustomed to quality." I added provocatively: "Remember who my last lover was."

"You are offensive, Marc," said Gervaise stiffly. "We will speak further of this." And he stood up and set off to escort Lettice to her room. I watched them go.

Thomas Hodgkin called me over to the fireplace. I was impressed. It was the first occasion that I had been treated to the favour of privacy. He draped himself on one side of the hearth, leaning his arm against the panelling, so that his fur-edged coat hung open, showing its black silk lining. I was not magnificent enough to drape myself at the corresponding edge, so I merely stood, shadowed by firelight, sipping wine.

"You are unwise," he murmured, "to offend your cousin. He has set his heart on this marriage. It is the answer for him as to what to do with Lettice."

"The idea is ridiculous; anyone can see," I shrugged.

"No, no, there are advantages..."

"Even if it were not for the other reasons, well, she is bigger than me and she has red hair." I then added: "You refused her yourself."

He maintained a dignified impassivity. It was after all none of my business. He said: "Even if you intend to refuse the offer, it would be discreet to refuse it in terms of studied politeness. Did you not learn diplomacy in Paris?"

I did blush then. It was like being reproved by one's father. Unlike Gervaise, Thomas had presence, and the attraction of a puissant and capable older man.

"I've always been indiscreet," I muttered. "I am no good with mysteries and schemes."

"Let me tell you then, it is no secret that if you do not go along with Gervaise's plans for you, you put yourself in difficulty, danger even."

"How, danger?" I frowned.

"As a Catholic you are an embarrassment to him; as a Frenchman an object of suspicion; and as a – er – person who was close to the Valois, an impossibility. You are only acceptable as – do you know the term recant? Unless you behave as he wants, I am most certain he will attempt to rid himself of you."

My stomach turned over. Not that I was scared of cousin Gervaise, but that it brought back to me the life I was escaping from – the threat, the menace, the fear of dark corners and perfumed gloves. I thought that I had left all that behind; the sinister language reminded me.

"He would not dare," I said, my heart thumping.

"I believe he would. There are many ways of procuring a person's disappearance. He doesn't want you here. You know, I have heard of a young man, a player on the virginals, who was kidnapped to spite an ambassador, and *he* was sent to the galleys. He was released...eventually...but think how he must have suffered, that sensitive young man..."

I did! I went all hot and cold. That sea! Those churning waves! Perpetual seasickness – and they whipped you, did they not? And it wrecked your hands. I shuddered.

"Such extreme measures are not needed," I laughed nervously. "I will gladly leave and rid him of the burden."

"Ah – tis not so simple," said Master Hodgkin. "The laws against vagrancy are severe. You may not go where you will. Vagabonds are whipped through the streets – persistent vagabonds are condemned to slavery – the cheek is branded, the ear is lopped. Then there are the houses of correction... I hope you do not think that life on the road is joyous and carefree?"

Suddenly he reminded me of Anthony. "The port authorities are so strict...search your luggage...throw you in gaol...do you want that?" And Anthony painted that picture in order to persuade me to go with him. Of course it may have been the truth – no doubt it was, as with this similar black picture created for me now. But what was his purpose? Did he, like Anthony, have a better plan for me? I eyed him curiously.

"If I cannot stay here," I began carefully, "and if to travel would make me a vagrant, what can I do?"

Master Hodgkin said frankly: "I would like you for my page."

I began to laugh.

"I am most serious in my intent," he frowned. "I think you would find it was the answer to your problem."

"But how is that possible?"

"I would take you to my London dwelling. You would live with me in my household. I am a man of some importance. It would be a very good step for you."

"Excuse me, you are a merchant," I said distastefully.

"Yes?"

"But – trade! Commerce! It is like a grocer."

"I see you know nothing of the mercantile world," he said evenly.

"Indeed I do not. I am nobility," I said haughtily.

"In England it is not the same as in France. In England the

merchants are respected, indeed, are the support of the crown, the prosperity of the nation. The country would not be great without commerce. Sometimes people think it is the nobility that rule the land. It is not so. Let me tell you this: some of the barons might maintain over a hundred retainers, but in the service of the iron smelters in the north there are some four thousand workers. Commerce is the nation's backbone. You need never think you are demeaning yourself to accept the offer I have made."

"But I *would* be – indeed, I would be!" I said, peculiarly insulted. "I am not interested in your facts and figures. I know nothing about your iron workers, nor do I want to. Of course I cannot be your page."

"Surely in France it is the same as here? It is no shame to go as page into a rich household."

"Ah – but the household must be noble, quoi? A family, a name. There is no honour in attending to a merchant."

"I refuse to take offence, because I am sure you do not realise that in England one is proud of mercantile success. Let me tell you, a cargo of nutmeg, from the East Indies, or a load of cloves from Moluccas or cinnamon/from Ceylon is a bounty worth any sacrifice. When Magellan set off to sail around the world he had five ships and nearly three hundred men. Three years later it was a crew of just eighteen that came home, but the cloves they brought back were treasure every bit as rare as that which spills from captured galleons down in Plymouth. To bring home spices justifies all losses, so dearly are they valued. And spices are my business," he added modestly.

"I am very happy for you," I said sarcastically. "But they are not mine. O! How can you imagine that I would – my family is one of the oldest in France – you think I would pour out your wine, hold your cup?"

"And anything else I asked, yes," he said firmly. "I begin to think that a time in my service would do you good. A little respect to your elders would well become you! What have you done to deserve a noble's privileges except to be born? It is a good offer I am making you. You would do well to accept."

I curled my lip. "I could not. Your name is ridiculous. Hodgkin. It is ugly – it means 'relation to a pig'. That alone would prevent me from accepting."

"I warn you, boy," he said in a low voice, "I am successful because I know how to get what I want. As I watched you on the stage, playing your lute and much delighting all, I conceived the idea that you should become my page. You would enhance my standing considerably. And I shall achieve my design, believe me. Sooner or later, and noble though you be."

I laughed scornfully, to disguise the uncomfortable feeling his words gave me.

"No," I said. "Find your Ganymede elsewhere."

I wished I had not said that. I could have bitten my tongue – I had almost accused him of wanting me in his bed. I had no justification for that jibe and I regretted it at once. I knew he was angry now. Maybe more determined to pursue his intent? What would he do – secretly arrange something with Gervaise? But he could not. No one could make me page for them. You could not serve at table and wait beside chairs with a cudgel at your back; it had to be done sweetly, politely, voluntarily. And they could not make me act so.

"Excuse me," I said peevishly, and left him standing by the hearth. I returned to the table and sat down. The players had dismantled the stage and they were leaving. They were being careful and quiet, on their best behaviour so as not to disturb the ones who paid them. I could not see Nicholas. He must have gone out while I was talking to Master Hodgkin. So; was it to end like this, before it was begun? No meeting of our minds, no words said between us, only brief eye glances in a crowd? Perhaps I had imagined it. Perhaps I had not kindled his affections, as I thought. And I would not go running after him. If he could not see my worth and want me, then there was nothing to be done.

But O! I was extreme disheartened.

"Is he gone?
Ay, but he'll come again; he cannot go;
He loves me too too well to serve me so"

I SHOULD have gone to bed; it was very late. Gervaise's
friends were lolling over the table, not exactly drunk, but
replete and lazy, unwilling to move while there was wine
left and the remains of the meal. The table was a shambles,
strewn with gnawed bones and pastry crumbs and spilt claret.
They were telling jokes and gossiping and already they were
settling on me as matter for merriment.

"Give us another song then, sweeting."

"Sing us one about King Henry."

"Don't be coy – be kind to us."

"How puffed up he is! And all because he's bedded royalty.
Let me tell you, my lad, one brave Englishman is a match for
any snivelling monsewer, crown and all."

I had about decided it was time I left, when Cuthbert Hodgkin
wriggled close to me and, astonishment waking me up, I saw I
was to receive a proposition from him as well as from his father.

Cuthbert, I would say, was about twenty-five, and unprepossessing and unpleasant in appearance. His Puritan black
was oppressive; his expression was odd. I recognise it now for
bigotry and possession. Assuredly I was possessed too, as will be
noticed, but mine was with beauty and fame and they are not
sinister. Cuthbert was sinister. Well! He was a Puritan, was he
not? They wrecked churches and pissed on altars, they kicked
the faces of holy statues, and melted down chalices and crosses,
and tortured priests. One is right to fear the worst of Puritans.
So it was most disconcerting to have him sidle up to me. He laid
his hand on my arm.

"You are in grave danger, Marc-Alphonse," he said.

"Why?" I said, reasonably enough. Everyone looked up with
interest.

"I am talking about your soul," Cuthbert explained.

"O," I said, relieved.

Gervaise's friends sniggered. "He's talking about your soul," one laughed, "all neatly packaged up as it is in burgundy coloured stockings and luscious lips."

Oddly enough, they were taking my part, sharing my own amusement and perplexed wariness at Cuthbert's advances. They too found Cuthbert strange. They did not share my unease at the differences in our beliefs, but they did share my scorn.

"You may laugh," said Cuthbert primly. "But you would do well to consider. Think of your life up till now. If you were called to your Maker tomorrow, how would it stand, your account? If all that I have heard is true..."

"You should not listen to gossip; you always hear scandal."

"You tell him, Marc. You are an old huswife, Cuthbert."

"With that already weighing in the balance against you," Cuthbert continued, "is it wise then to ally yourself with players? Steeped in sin as you are – sin too dreadful to name –"

"Sodomy!" someone sniggered in a loud whisper.

" – steeped in sin, you tread further in the odious mire. Let me be the one to tell you what you provoke when you go upon a stage. The spirits of darkness do attend on players and on those who write plays for the sinful stage. All the demons of Hell do lie in wait. Now, before you are too far in, O! Withdraw!"

"And make a mess on the sheets!" cried some buffoon, half choking with mirth. I was grinning myself.

"Ah, fools laugh who shall weep hereafter!" said Cuthbert.

"All I did was play a tune," I said mildly.

"No, it was more!" protested Cuthbert, "You put yourself on show. Displayed yourself. Invited us to look, flaunted those charms which you possess..."

"He desires you, Marc. Ho, master Cuthbert, so you are human kind even as we are!"

"Brutish beasts," muttered Cuthbert. "Your thoughts are all on carnal matters. My spirit is more elevated. I am beyond such. I know how to subdue the recalcitrant flesh –"

"And you would like a chance to try that out on Marc!"

"Listen to me, Marc," Cuthbert persisted. "Plays corrupt the young who know no better. They show lewd lascivious actions and vile wicked plots. Bad people go to watch. Both the matter on stage and the company that goes to watch are a source of corruption. I tell you these things because I fear you simply do not know. You must not mingle with the damned ones."

"I do not," I said glumly. "I do mingle with you."

They shouted bleary encouragement. "Good for you, Marc. We will not corrupt you — you stay with us; we'll show you what true purity is! Eh, Cuthbert?"

"I have to tell you, Marc," said Cuthbert when it became silent enough, "players are evil, but the men who write the plays are worse. They turn their back on the trusty old plays of the church, that satisfied our forefathers. They make their own. They visit Italy and learn wickedness we cannot even dream of. They live by their wits and they are wild-natured; they lurk in a deadly underworld, like a living vision of Hell. They fight duels, they riot, they indulge in all manner of vice, and they work against the peace of the realm. They are all atheists and they turn the gullible against God. They know only too well the insides of prisons and brothels and the lowest taverns — but they know no happiness, no, their sinful existence brings them only misery, gloom and regret. Fiends and monsters, debauched and despairing, they contaminate whom they touch."

"Look at Marc — his eyes are out on stalks!"

"But not with horror, eh, Marc? With excitement, I fancy. More jolly than religion, eh, lad? Like to meet one of those fiends and monsters, would you not, I'll wager?"

I blinked at my own transparency. I had listened enthralled to Cuthbert, unaware that my interest showed. I wriggled and grinned at having been found out.

"I don't know why he tells me," I shrugged. "There are no playwrights here. I suppose my soul is safe for the moment."

"We never know where our paths may lead," said Cuthbert. "It is as well for you to be prepared. A young boy, alone, a foreigner, you will be susceptible to wickedness if you are not warned. You were foolish to take part in the play tonight. You showed that the devil has access to you. Luckily I was here and saw that you were half seduced —"

They chortled happily.

"By wicked ways!" cried Cuthbert vexed. "I do not mean fleshly things. The pure are always misunderstood. Marc!" he appealed to me, quivering. "Put yourself in my hands! Let me guide you. Let me turn your feet from the path of sin and bring you to peace through submission of evil desires. Trust me! I am the one who can help you."

"There is no temptation here," I said reasonably.

"Accept my father's offer," Cuthbert urged. "Be his page. While you learn to accommodate yourself to his needs in the daytime I can instruct you in the evening. We can read Holy Writ and I can explain it to you. I can bring you to salvation. Spiritually it would be a challenge for me, and it would bring us both closer to perfection."

"Marc is eager to accept – look at his face!"

"Say yes, Marc. You will never have another offer like that one."

"Snuggling closer to perfection with Cuthbert..."

When their mirth had subsided I found I was extremely sleepy, and could not compose a worthy reply to Cuthbert's proposition.

"I must refuse," I said politely.

Cuthbert put his face very close to mine and his fervent eyes glowed with a weird predatory lust.

"I am talking of your soul!"

"I think not," I murmured. Close to, in contact with such passion so restrained, it did not seem like things spiritual. I could see the tiny sweat beads on his temple, and his trembling lip.

"I shall pray for you tonight," said Cuthbert – the ultimate threat of the godly. He stood up, preparing to go off to his bed. Myself I meant to leave also, but a heavy weariness came over me and my limbs were like wood. I put my head on my arms on the table and fell straight asleep, my cheek in pastry crumbs.

The next thing I knew I was floating up from a haze, and dimly aware of conversation. As soon as I knew they were talking about me I became alert and listened.

"So, Hodgkin wants him for his page?"

"O yes, French pages are very much sought after now. Francis Seymour has one. They are more elegant and dainty than English ones – polished, better groomed. Did you not notice how he ate? And how often he washed his fingers! I can see him waiting at Hodgkin's chair, all demure and obliging."

"And so should all the French be used. It keeps them in their place, shows them who is master. Having a French brat obeying you in public is to proclaim your belief in the rightness of things. O yes, tis well done on Hodgkin's part; and folk will be impressed."

"But what about the other? I mean, is Hodgkin that way inclined? Everyone knows what happens to pages when the candles are blown out!"

"What, you think he wants this little Ganymede for his bed? O, I doubt it. I don't think Hodgkin is...well, I've heard no rumours. Perhaps he is especially discreet!"

"Amazingly, Toby, some men do not lust after boys!"

"More fools they! He is a banquet I for one could feast at."

"Huh, probably riddled with pox. It's not for nothing they call it French pox and Morbus Gallicus."

"Ah surely not – that King Henry would not go with poxy boys. This one is clean, you can be sure of it. Even I could fancy a roll in the hay with this fair little foreigner."

"Don't grow too doting. Before the night is out, Gervaise may well ask our help to rid him of the lad. Quiet, like."

"What have you heard?"

"Only what Gervaise has hinted. If the boy won't play, then he's every kind of encumbrance to our host and his new found Puritan leanings. He doesn't want to offend the boy's family by simply throwing him out. He contemplates a judicious disappearance of some kind. I said I would lend a hand. I like old Gervaise."

"Well, I'm with you. You can both count on me – what are friends for? Is it to be tonight?"

"Enough now...he but dozes..."

I shifted meaningfully and stretched an arm.

"The maiden wakes. Maybe tis time we staggered to our beds," they decided.

I sat up and yawned. The candles were burned down and it was very dim. I stood up and we all said goodnight – just as if I had not heard and they had not been plotting.

The vast staircase creaked as I walked up to my room. A pale glow of moonlight shone behind the huge embossed window. I turned into my chamber and closed the door. I did not light a candle; a shaft of moonlight laid a wedge across the wooden floor. I opened the window and looked out into the night. I could see the moon big and round, and the dark trees and the garden. Somewhere out there the players would be asleep in their wagons. Were Nicholas and Amyas lovers, my jealous heart wondered? O! Was Nicholas thinking of me?

I thought of all the sweet and poignant separations. I was

Hero looking across the Hellespont and thinking of Leander; I was Criseyde looking back towards Troy where Troilus suffered. O! Between Nicholas and me there was a gulf as wide, the gulf of silence, of not having told our thoughts, of parting too soon, with everything fancied and nothing done. At dawn, I supposed, they would leave. And me, what would become of me?

I left the window and sat down on the bed.

Assuredly I could not stay here. It would be foolishness to wait and find out whether Gervaise did have any malignant plans for me or not. I would stand no chance against him and his friends, whatever their intent. The picture that Master Hodgkin had painted of life on the road terrified me, but that was where I would have to go. Maybe I could earn my living by playing my lute. My complete ignorance of the ways of the road alarmed me. I would be so vulnerable; I knew nothing. All my past life, with its crooked twists and turns, had in no wise prepared me for this moment. I could bow as gracefully as anyone at court; I could sing, dance and play the lute; I was of noble birth. And what good was it to me? I would have to steal a horse in order to travel. Would I be reduced to thievery then? And after that, what? Where could I go?

I sat there in a state of cold fear, frozen by indecision.

Then I began moving around, gathering up my things. I would leave; I must; and I would go tonight. It was my only course.

"Oy, Marc!"

I spun round, my hand on my heart.

At the open window Nicholas was looking in.

"I'm on the ivy," he explained, as no doubt I looked ghost struck.

"Come in," I whispered, disbelieving my eyes.

I helped him climb through the window.

"I'm parting," I said. "I'm packing my things."

"You won't be able to carry that trunk," he observed.

"No," I agreed glumly.

"You should put everything in a sheet and knot the ends. Then you can drop it out of the window and I'll catch it for you. Come on, I'll help you do it."

I never questioned a word; it seemed the ultimate in wisdom. Together we folded all my clothes and bits and pieces into a heap, and knotted them into a sheet from the bed. My belt with amber studs I noticed, and the silk shirt which rustled with the paper of Anthony's letter to Christopher Marley at the Phoenix Tavern. Our eyes met, over the bundle.

"Nicholas," I murmured, "what made you come to me?"

"Did you think I'd go without a word? I watched, and I saw you at the window. It seemed like an action with meaning."

I fiddled with the knot.

"Marc, let us waste no time," he said. "We'll both go out of the window and down the ivy, and let's go now, very quiet."

Our attention was then all given to the business of manoeuvring through the window, and dropping the bundle and passing my lute through, and climbing down the ivy out into the sweet night air.

The scents of flowers assailed me as I reached the ground – those that grew beneath the window gave off a most lovely perfume. Gilliflowers. I stood a moment, and Nicholas turned me round and kissed me on the lips. Yes! Suddenly as in a waking dream we were kissing, lips on lips, my eyelashes brushing his cheek. He was just slightly taller than me. I was dazed with perfection. Gilliflowers now I always connect with kisses.

But Nicholas was practical, and shouldered my bundle manfully and set off across the grass.

"Nicky," I gasped, running after. "I know I said I'm parting, but I have no plans. I know not where to go."

Nicholas jerked his head towards the dark shapes of the players' wagons, and towards the wide world itself.

"With *us*, of course," he said.

THREE

I

"Fortune hath favour'd thee, whate'er thou be,
In sending thee unto this courteous coast.
A' God's name, on!"

MY ARRIVAL was manifestly expected and my situation had been much discussed, for the players accepted my appearance with placid unsurprise and made me pleasantly welcome. The grey light of dawn was in the sky, and in the dewy grass amongst the trees a scene took place which I was soon to know so well – the breaking up of night time's camp and setting forth upon the road. All Jack did say to me at first was that I had been taken on largely on account of Nicholas' persuasion, and though Jack was glad of my being there, it was a gladness conditional upon my willingness to work, and if I thought a player's life romantic I would be sadly disillusioned. Vehemently as I insisted that I would willingly work at anything at all, I truly did not realise quite how hard it would be! I thought a little work, and much occasion for Nicholas and me to further our acquaintance. But that first day I had barely a moment's conversation with him, not intimate I mean. We worked as we travelled.

There was a covered wagon big as a hut, and herein lived Jack and Madge and the boys, and much gear; there was a smaller wagon very bright painted with stars and moons and lions and dragons breathing fire; and two great carts all laden down with properties and covered over with cloths; we either rode in these or walked beside. The little boys led the horses, and all the time for those who sat there was work.

Nicholas wrote out scripts and shortened long plays, and what with repairing costumes, practising tunes, tuning instruments and learning lines, the pleasures of leaning back admiring the hedgerows was one to be foregone. Most laborious of all was the learning of parts, and I was involved in this like everyone else. Jack was determined we should do *The Spanish Tragedy*, a new play, full of blood and very gory, and Nicholas transposed it from its many characters to fewer. This play was so new that it was even now being performed in London, and what we had was a quickly garnered copy, which someone had brought on his way south. Because he had not been able to get it down word for word we had a shortened cobbled version with much missing, but nonetheless it made a good play, even if it was not what the author had first writ. Jack was passionate to play old Hieronimo who prowls the stage in eloquent despair looking for revenge and the murderers of his son. Amyas was to be Bellamira the beautiful courtesan. She stabs Balthazar and herself. Truly the last page is a welter of violent stage directions: stabs him, stabs him, stabs herself, shows his dead son, runs to hang himself, bites out his tongue, stabs the duke and himself. Jack had the idea that I should play Isabella, for with all these being Spaniards and Portuguese, one could yet speak with an accent if it was loud and clear. Isabella was not a big part – the mother of the slain son – however, she does go mad and stab herself, so it is very jolly. Unfortunately for me her first line is "O monstrous homicides!" I believe I permanently distorted my mouth and dislocated my jaws coming to grips with that. So I spent that day being helpful and useful, and all the time pronouncing and learning. And this, as we travelled to Canterbury.

I barely did observe the route for the learning of my part, but I could not help but see that lovely trees did pass and hedgerows thick with blossom, with the song of the birds on every branch most melodious.

Amyas was a trial to me. Under guise of helping he sat by me in the cart and made us weak with laughter showing me how I sounded. "Rent them up" I thought I said, but no, it was "Rent them erp"; and my aitches dropped the more I concentrated – "Make haste, Hieronimo, to hold excused" was a great stermbling blerck to me! Nicholas said I had great strength of character to be able to talk at all after Amyas' teasings, and to make me feel better he spoke some halting French. Truly I was touched. That Nicholas should know some French was to me astonishing and charming, and only went to prove that he knew at heart we were destined to meet one day.

"No," he said modestly, "but though you see me travelling the road with these buffoons, these layabouts, I am in fact an Oxford man and very civilised."

An Oxford man! I did not realise what he meant, until when later circumstances placed me in the company of Cambridge men and it became more clear. Reasonably enough, when Cuthbert Hodgkin painted me that dark image of the playwright I never thought of Nicholas. Desperate, subversive, malcontent and melancholy, he seemed to be none of these. And yet when I grew to know him better, I understood that he might well have been so if circumstances had been different and he had not become playwright to a group of travelling players. When I told him all that Cuthbert had described, he said:

"If playwrights are gloomy and embittered and live amongst thieves and cut-throats in the poorer parts of the town it is not their fault which brings them to these desperate means. Who properly values a man who writes plays? Who pays him well? Tis poverty, not wickedness, that obliges him to keep bad company. An author can do nothing unless he finds himself a rich patron to support him. I have nothing but sympathy for the men that Cuthbert maligns."

Francis said if I was to be one of them and if I was to use oaths – for living a player's life would certainly cause me to do so – there must be no pardieux and diables, and he set to teach me English oaths.

"A pox damn you!" I uttered carefully, and: "A plague upon it! Godamercy! By cock and pie!"

"But never 'in sooth'," Francis told me frowning. "In sooth is for the lily livered, the milksop, the green girl."

So, since oaths were being shared I passed on the favourite oath of the king: "By the twenty-four balls of the apostles!" which everybody liked, and used henceforth in many a conversation.

Francis was of burly stocky build and short of stature. He had an enormous mouth, it quite filled the lower half of his face and when he smiled it seemed to reach his ears. In female attire he was somewhat grotesque and therefore had to play nurses or beggar women or aged maidservants, though he was extreme hilarious in comic parts and played Noah's Wife as brilliant as could be. He was of nature affable and placid.

John and Ralph were brothers, stringy black-haired boys of hardworking, willing dispositions and both most skilful with the horses, yet also good musicians. Their father was a blacksmith up in Gloucestershire and when players had visited their town they had become smitten and had run away to join them.

Amyas was pleased with me for being the only person who had not heard his two jokes – How many pieces of string does it take to reach the moon? One, if it be long enough. Who was it killed one fourth of all the people in the world? Cain, when he killed Abel. Amyas did not talk about his past, but only smirked. His father was a country parson. Amyas had been a choirboy. There were rumours of a deeply religious background, and of a disgraceful incident in Winchester cathedral.

Martin and Geoffrey with much merriment undertook to teach me English foul words, the others agreeing that in the company we kept these would be words I'd need. Geoffrey was most pretty, and would soon play ladies.

Angel, well, he was one of those who have to prove their manliness by a certain boorishness. It was a shame, I thought, that someone so exquisite should be so ill-bred. He sat beside me and read the part of Hieronimo to my Isabella, as we wept over our slain son. ("Sweet lovely rose, ill pluck'd before thy time.") He said to me:

"I hope you are not thinking of attempting anything with me."

I was, of course. How could I not? He was angelic.

"Assuredly not," I replied affronted.

"'Tis well," he said pompously. "I want it clearly understood. The word is about that you like men, in the way that Nicholas does." (My heart leapt.) "So don't try any of your craft with me."

"Excuse me," I said with icy politeness. "I have this foolish weakness, I like my lovers to be polite."

I do not think he even supposed that I was criticising him.

"Some people assume," he continued, "that to be a player means to be an ingle, that the two are one and the same. It is most troublesome particularly when you are fair of face and form as I am. I've had offers from nobility, you know; I mean *men*. But I'm a full blooded male and know where Nature intended our interests to lie. I tell you this now to save confusion."

Many ugly men assume this, that if you are a lover of boys they are not safe in your presence. Unfortunately Angel had some justification, and I was annoyed to be put in my place, like a child slapped for touching the comfits. His ungraciousness of character, however, was some comfort, in that even had I enjoyed his body, no harmony of mind would have been possible.

We stopped at a wayside tavern for a meal in the middle of the day. Little more it was than a tumbledown thatched cottage, one of a scattering around a small village green.

As I munched delicately at the coarse brown bread I realised I must accustom myself to a change in my manner of eating. It seemed to me that much from the field was in this bread, and I was not entirely wrong since it was often made from tares, peas and acorns; but it always did alarm me when my teeth ground upon a stone big enough to hold between the fingers, and I half expected to encounter horse shoe nails and scraps of plough-man's boot leather. Beer I savoured for the first time, and somewhat to my surprise I found it was agreeable. My companions encouraged me to persevere, and with much back-slapping poured me more and praised me and set about teaching me some drinking songs and how to slam the tankard on the table. I sighed – Diable! I would never be like the English, I knew it, so monstrous cheerful over food, so undiscerning in what they ate, so noisy and so rude. *Everybody* belched, and cared not who heard it.

But beer did certainly induce well being.

We sat on a bench outside the inn, with our feet in the daisies, and discussed immortality.

"The only way," said Nicholas earnestly, "to cheat death is to write a poem."

"No," said Amyas. "There are three: write a poem, plant a tree, and father a child."

"O well," shrugged Nicholas comfortably. "What I first said is true then."

I beamed happily that he seemed to have no desire for the other two.

"Planting a tree is pleasant," Amyas decided.

"Ah, but who can tell it was you that did it?" said Nicky. "One more holly, one more elder, what difference does it make in a great forest?"

"It may not show," I said, "but at least you have done it. The tree would not have been there without your existence."

"Tis but a poor second to the joy of seeing your name in the printed word."

"Are you eager for fame, Nicky?"

"Of course. Who is not? My problem is a small one — my poems are never good enough."

"They are not *bad*," Amyas conceded.

"They are; they are insipid. I know what I want to say, but it comes out all milk and water."

"Yet worse than yours are published," Amyas said, "if some rich lord does choose. All you need is a patron. That way, any dross effort sees the light of day."

"O, thank you for your praise!" cried Nicholas.

"I did not mean that yours were dross — well, not *all* of them," Amyas giggled, ducking from Nicky's blow. "But if you will not sue and grovel, as other poets do, then you must suffer obscurity, must you not?"

"I find it hard to write the plaintive stuff that's necessary to get myself such a patron — O most wonderful Sir this and that from whose fat arse the sun doth shine and gladden this poor earth, accept these paltry lines that have no meaning without you sneeze upon them in your goodness."

"Then you must write a play," I said.

"O yes. So easy," Nicky grumbled.

"Poems are best for immortality," Amyas explained to me. "Poems — with a patron — do circulate in print. Nobility do read them, and more, if some bright musician do set it to a tune and folks do sing it — well, your fame is made. Songs will last. If you do write a song, your name will live, and you will be eternal."

"Then, Nicky, it must be a song."

"Well. I persevere."

"I'll set it to music for you," I offered modestly.

"O Marc — you greedy for immortality too?"

"Most sure! At first I thought a famous poet — but my poems are like blades of grass in a meadow. Then a lutanist — but the same — all bright boys play the lute. Then I thought — excuse my lapse into vulgarity – a famous concubine –"

"Yes, immortality, not immorality," agreed Amyas.

"Exactly – the one I achieved but not the other," I admitted. "And so here I am. How will I achieve my fame? Will it be by putting music to Nicholas's words? Will it be when I take the London stage by storm? Will people say as they leave the play: who *was* that Isabella? How exquisitely did she go mad! With what finesse did she plunge the dagger into her chest! How passionately she declaimed the immortal phrase: *Rent them up!*"

"You will be famous for your beauty," Nicky said seriously. "People will say: I remember this boy player in *The Spanish Tragedy*. He had beautiful eyes and a perfect smile. I shall never forget him."

I basked glowingly. But Amyas said: "I shall never forget him, but I shall certainly forget his name. Peascod Murray? Parsnip Mermaid? What was it now?"

He was right, and we attended to it in all seriousness. On our playbills then I went down as Mark Morny. Not that it made much difference to the course of history. But that afternoon all things were possible. The sun was shining from a blue sky, and we were drinking. Sweet rose-coloured petals of blossom blew down from the trees into our hair. I touched one to loosen it.

"Don't move it," said Nicholas. "It suits you."

It suited him too. How pretty hair does look flecked with blossom!

"Of course," he said, "it is my ambition to write a play, but I still believe that for immortality a poem is best. I mean, to be *famous down the ages*. You see, a poem *is*, like a little monument wrought in words. A play is messy, as live things tend to be; in its life it's handled and used, and hacked about and sold and re-sold. Other companies lay hold on it and reshape it. Eventually no one knows who wrote it, and the author gets no glory and no money, and dies forgotten, swearing at his bad luck. But a poem is clean and courtly. I wish it had been me, and not Thomas Wyatt who wrote: 'They flee from me that sometime did me seek.' Now that, that is a poem!"

We sat, reverent among the daisies.

"I wish I had written every poem in the whole world," said Amyas modestly. He reduced all to foolishness.

II

"Why talk we not together hand in hand,
And tell our griefs in more familiar terms?"

As we moved toward Canterbury then, I sat at the back of one wagon, boots dangling, and Jack who drove the main wagon sat at the reins following behind, and heard me shout my part. I had to make myself heard above the horses' snortings and the bridles jingling, declaiming Isabella's lines loudly and feelingly. Jack said I would do. It meant that I had joined the company. Our name was Sir John Fordham's Players.

Late afternoon we came to Canterbury, and found a fair outside the walls.

We made our settlement somewhat on its edge, and ran around to see the entertainment. There was everything merry there – stalls for buying and selling, sweets and drink, country dancing and morris men and a maypole still beribboned from the preceding day, and tents and fortune tellers and pedlars and dwarfs. I found it strange to be amongst ordinary folk. I had never done this before, to wander at will through a crowd of common people – huswives buying eggs, sellers of herbs and flowers and earthen pots, horse dealers leading marvellous inferior animals to sell, which I could see at a glance were broken down old nags; countrymen herding sheep and pigs, and unkempt children clamouring for comfits, and a great noise all about, of English voices in accents almost impossible to understand. Certainly many there were townsfolk, but there were as many who were not – strange men of the roads, stinking and dirty, with daggers at their belt and dangerous eyes; and foul beggars who tapped your legs with their crutches if you tried to walk past, and whined and cursed and tugged at their clothes to show you wounds and scars they promised you were got in holy wars.

"Come *past*," said Nicholas laughing in exasperation. "You must not give to all and nor must you believe each tale of woe."

"Shall I take him instead to see the Bearded Woman?" suggested Amyas.

But too many others were waiting outside her tent to see this marvel, so we saw instead the Biggest Fish Caught in Any River, in a different tent, and some performing fleas in another. Then we decided to visit the astrologer and have our characters divined. Nicholas insisted he did not believe in the truth as told by the stars. We had a noisy argument all round the tent.

"How can it be the same for him?" he demanded, indicating me with a casual thumb. "He was born in France. He would see different stars. If he is Gemini in France he would probably be Taurus or Cancer here, the heavens being further on."

"Don't be silly, Nicky. All the signs have the same name, in France and probably all over the globe."

"O? Are you telling me the savages of the Americas are all Geminis and Librans and such also, the same as we?"

"We don't know," said Amyas reasonably. "I daresay Columbus did not think to ask them."

"Even the astrologers themselves can't decide upon the best way to cast horoscopes," said Nicholas. "Do we take the moment of conception or the time of birth? And if all is ordained from the first, why do not all those born on the same day die on the same day, and have such varied fortunes in between?"

"One supposes it is a similarity of character which the stars cause," I said. "Once born, then it is Fortune, Chance, geography which shape the life."

"But twins, who are born on the same day, are often of entirely different character. Jacob and Esau for example."

We considered this extraordinary pair.

"In spite of what you say, many eminent and intelligent persons believe in astrology. We have many astrologers in Paris..."

"It is the same here," said Amyas sagely. "I am an intelligent person and I believe in it."

We sniggered.

"I can't accept it," Nicholas insisted, "because we have free will, which raises us from beasts. With free will we make our own fates and cause our own destinies. If all is ordained by the stars then why should we ever strive or work, or even bother to live? We might as well lie down in a ditch."

"My brother the cardinal says that astrology is devilish."

"Marc! Have you really got a brother who's a cardinal?"

"No; it is a jest. You know the Duke of Guise?"

"Intimately!" they cried. "I saw him but last week."

"Well, he had a brother who was a cardinal. They were the most powerful men in France. That is, you understand, not the present Duke of Guise but the previous one. Although he too . . ."

"Dear Marc," Amyas sighed. "There is absolutely nothing we would like better than a swift history of France."

"Well, my brother is a very minor priest. So we call him my brother the cardinal – to show that we are equal and superior to the Guises."

"And he says astrology is devilish."

"Yes. He says you find out what God does not think you are ready to hear. Which implies a lack of faith."

"This is of course true," began Nicholas.

"Well, Laurent proved it for himself when he went to an astrologer."

"Your holy brother?"

"Yes; he is an imperfect priest," I grinned.

"What did he learn? Bad things?"

"For France, yes; but it need not concern you."

"Seriously, Marc? War and such?"

"O – astrologers are never explicit. He saw blood. He saw the death of a great man. He didn't say particularly war. But blood and slaughter. But in France, not here."

"Marc, I should keep it to yourself henceforth," Nicky advised. "People are suspicious about predictions concerning blood. They might think you knew something . . ."

"But I do not," I shrugged.

"Do we still want our characters analysed?" said Nicholas, "now that I have proved conclusively that it is all logically impossible and incredible?"

"Yes!" we said clamouring.

"Gullible babes! And tell me another thing – why are astrologers always to be found in the tumbledown parts of town, the darkest streets in the vilest quarters, the most sinister tent in the fair ground? Look at this one here, with all his signs and symbols on the cloth. He wants you to believe he is in close commune with the heavens, with his zigzag lightning and his shooting stars. He wants you to be afraid, and enter his domain all quivering with dread, as the simple are! And to pay money

84

for being sent anxiously away!"

But our astrologer could take no more, and having certainly been listening, he emerged from his tent to put us right. He was a scholar, he said, not a charlatan or magician, and astrology was a science. We knew that the humours in our bodies were affected by the planets, did we not? We knew that the water in our bodies responded to the pull of the moon? By studying the changing face of the heavens and applying mathematical calculations, the skilled practitioner could help a man understand the shaping of his own life and lead him to avoid pitfalls and mistakes. Why, no less a person than the Queen herself believed in horoscopes; she had hers cast every day.

Chastened, we went in and learned our characters. Of what I remember, Amyas, who was Leo, had "an itching desire to rule and sway where he comes; prudent and stately, affable, humane, loving magnificence, no sordid thought entering his heart, proud, sometimes foolish, endued with no gravity in words or soberness in actions, a spendthrift, a mere vapour!"

Nicholas, who was Taurus, was "not given to quarrel or wrangling, not vicious; pleasant, mirthful and clean, musical, delighting in baths and honest merry meetings or masques and stage plays, cheerful, jealous, of no faith, a lewd womanizer, spending his time in alehouses amongst scandalous loose people, irreligious and lazy."

Of Gemini, of which I took most note, it was said: "Intelligent, eloquent, a searcher into mysteries, learning almost anything without a teacher, desirous of travel and seeing foreign parts, a man of unwearied fancy, curious in the search of occult knowledge, able by his own genius to produce wonders, a great liar, boaster and prattler, busybody, given to wicked arts, easy of belief, a trifler, a frothy fellow of no judgement, easily perverted, constant in idle words and bragging, and given to ungodly knowledge."

We could not afford to have our futures told, so we came away, with much to mull over and argue about. We did tease Amyas for being a mere vapour, and Nicholas for not being given to wrangling; and many times later on did Nicholas have cause to upbraid me for the things whereof I was accused. They said I frightened them, with my penchant for wickedness; and Nicholas said it was true that he spent his time with scandalous loose people – we two. We congratulated him on having landed in the right profession and sniggered much at the idea of him pursuing women. We were very merry as we went into the town.

I thought Canterbury a most fair city. It had a mighty wall about it with battlements, like a castle. Passing through the West Gate we saw above us two fine turrets and narrow slit windows. There were more than twenty watch towers upon the walls and, I was told, dungeons within! We walked along Mercery Lane towards the Christ Church gate of the cathedral, and this gate I found most magnificent, with windows and arches and shields carved upon it.

As we passed under the gate, prompted by what the astrologer had said we earnestly discussed whether we considered ourselves phlegmatic or melancholy, choleric or sanguine; and if it were but reason that enabled us to maintain the balance then how did we fare, how well possessed of reason were we all?

"I not at all," said Amyas loftily. "Tis passion that rules me."

"That would make you a beast," I observed.

Amyas barked at me foolishly and cried: "O go on apace and I will *dog* your footsteps!"

"We refuse to be *cowed*," sniggered Nicholas. "And we will *ram* your barking down your throat."

"Then will I be *horse*," chortled Amyas.

"Who cares for words anyway? Words cost nothing; they are *sheep*."

"O!" I cried, delighting myself and them. "Enough – I can *bear* no more."

"He *is* a beast," concluded Nicholas comfortably. "He has excess of earthy humours."

"But even if I was all air and fire," said Amyas, "I would be no better. For though these are noble qualities they counterbalance reason even as earthy humours do. They make the body fall out of harmony."

"All air and fire," laughed Nicholas. "That combination is one you will never need to trouble yourself over."

Amyas disgraced us all by grunting like a pig to show he was a beast, and grunting did he enter in the cathedral.

Here we found a little difference between us. For Nicholas and Amyas did laugh about the old time relics, but I thought it was

86

sad. There used to be in that place a tooth and bone of St. Benedict, a finger of St. Stephen and some of the stones that killed him; the pillow of holy king Edmund, the bones of St. Lawrence and a morsel of his gridiron; a twig from the staff of Moses, and a splinter from the crown of thorns. All these went, just over twenty years ago, and the priests' gorgeous vestments were cut up to make dresses for the canons' wives, and cups and chalices and holy rings were sold. Nicholas and Amyas saw this as a triumph for common sense and practicality, and did snigger much about the gridiron and the pillow. I did not think any of it amusing, and whether I believed in the genuineness of relics or no, if they comforted worshippers I thought they had a value. Indeed I sulked, and I would not even concede it was a pretty church. I said we had better ones in France, and stacked full of relics – teeth and bones and toenails and hair and skin. I fixed them with a frowning stare and dared them to laugh. Amyas laughed, behind a pillar. Nicholas did not, because he was always sensible of my feelings. He took Amyas outside and well clear of the walls he shook him, and reminded him he was a Mere Vapour. Amyas kept on sniggering and said Gemini was Easy of Belief. I did sulk more, and did say when they cast away relics they cast away much more and never did replace it, things invisible, like reverence and spirituality; and Amyas said: O, was his religion not spiritual then?

"I think the time has come," said Nicholas firmly, "to go and have a drink and see the inn where we shall spend the night."

"O – will we sleep at an inn?" I demanded, lust for Nicholas taking precedence over religion, for I did wonder if I would ever get him privily to myself.

"In a town we usually sleep at an inn; in the country in the wagons. Either way it's very communal," said Nicholas, I'd swear reading my thoughts.

Considering all this, I trailed along through the little streets. Earlier on, at the fair, I did sell a pair of gloves of mine, finely embroidered, and gave money to Jack and kept some for spending, so I was not always begging off the others. We had a good meal in the inn, which was very full, and we found that Angel had found himself a friend. Nicky nudged me and said that it was usual.

"He always finds a girl, wherever we go. He says they can't

resist him, and pester him for his love, but I think he seeks them out and makes them sit with him in company to prove he is not feminine."

Angel waved to us cheerily, his arm around the girl. Not being one to notice girls much, I did however observe that she was dark haired and good looking, and knocking her drink back like any man. She would cost Angel somewhat if he was paying. She must be marvellous bold, sitting there looking so comfortable amongst all the smoke and joviality. Angel several times did lean across and kiss her on the cheek.

"O Nicky!" I said suddenly, all envious of the privileges of ordinary men and women.

"You and I will sleep in the wagon," murmured Nicholas, "to guard the property. I'll arrange it."

My heart turned over. I flashed him a look of vivid excitement. Beneath the table our knees touched and tingles of warmth ran up my thigh.

I spent my first night with Nicholas in a wagon outside the walls of Canterbury, a little distant from the fair.

The night was dark but starry and all over the meadow small fires glowed beside the tents, and little snatches of music sounded as fair-folk strummed before sleeping, notes of melody tossed up on the breeze, isolated, like handfuls of tawdry beads slung into the air. Sometimes a dog barked, its owner growled a reprimand; sometimes an argument burst forth and as suddenly was silent. The other players dispersed to wagons or inns, and Nicholas and I were together at last.

It was an unusual bed; the wagon, high-sided, deep of gut, its shafts embedded in the grass. Across it, a great cloth was pulled taut, covered with sacking in case of rain. Below, stage properties were neatly folded, fur on top making a cosy nest. We wriggled in, and the dark warm mustiness enclosed us. We took our clothes off lying down, bumping limbs, exciting ourselves with touch. The pallor of our skin faintly showed; we hurried to be naked. We rolled into each other's arms. O! That was a very good moment. We pressed together eagerly, our lips touching in a thoughtful kiss that grew hot and greedy as we tasted. Our hands stroked and squeezed, our mouths never leaving off kissing; we were like beggars at a banquet. We entwined our limbs, panting, each making the other hard and long, sometimes in turns, and sometimes together in an equal rhythm, till the excitement grew so strong and we were gasping and we brought each other to release.

"God's teeth, the fur!" muttered Nicky. "Jack'll kill us – what a mess we've made!"

"We'll say rain came through the sacks," I beamed, contented and uncaring.

"Rain was never this sticky...Well! You have a magic touch."

"You also."

We kissed more, in mutual satisfaction, till our hearts had ceased to thud like galloping hooves and we were less breathless. Nicholas took me in his arms and held me close. Without greed or lust or dominance he held me and stroked my hair, till suddenly, uneasily, I pulled away, threatened.

"What, Marc?"

"I don't know, Nicky. I felt suddenly – anxious."

"There is no need."

"I'm not accustomed, I feel –"

"We were only loving, that's all."

"O," I sneered, "O, l'amour, tu sais, quoi!"

"What's this – an unbecoming cynicism on the subject of love, unusual in one so young?"

"If you *knew*..." I muttered, rolling on to my stomach, half turned away. "In my experience, love makes you weak and vulnerable, and other people take it and turn it into something to sell. I've no time for love."

"Oh," groaned Nicholas. "My misfortune! I fall in love with someone torn with troubles. Lucky for you I'm tolerant and understanding, and a little older. You're marvellous young to be so world-weary."

"My experience has been large. And bad."

"Marc, is it really true you were the lover of the King of France?"

"It seems bizarre *here*, does it not? So different...No, of course I was not a lover. You don't understand how it is there. It is not to do with love. Nobody knows what that means. Love is a thing that you can weigh with jewels and gifts of land as a balance. So let us not talk about love. Don't spoil the thing that happened with us. Love spoils."

"Suppose you tell me what happened?"

"No, I could not," I said bluntly.

"I wish you would. I want to understand you. I care about you."

"Tis hard to explain," I floundered. "I cannot suddenly begin to trust people. I'm scared to."

"Merciful heaven! What do you think I'm going to do to you?"

"I had to learn to be defensive."

"Yes. I had thought to point out to you that you have no need to wear your dagger with us. Myself, I think the dagger is a diabolical weapon – tis so small and dainty you forget its deadliness. People who wear daggers end up using them, you know."

How awful true his remark was to prove! But at the time I just smiled ruefully. "I know not why I wear it. I cannot imagine using it. I faint at the sight of blood."

"Why not leave it off tomorrow? Sell it, and buy lute strings and songbooks."

"I've been afraid for so long, you see, it has been a way of life. Even being here with you and the others I feel as if I'm still running, that if I stop and think, I shall be afraid all over again. I feel I am in hiding."

"Who from, Marc? Who would pursue you *here*?"

"Exactly! – in all commonsense, nobody at all! Particularly now that I'm clear of the court and have abandoned my pretensions to advancing my family's position. You see, in Paris *everyone* was scared – or if not scared, then plotting! It was so sinister. People died mysteriously. Someone tried to kill me. But what frightens me most is that we had no idea who or why, and it was so habitual that nobody bothered – you had to expect assassination if you lived at court. It was only a week ago that that was my way of life. You cannot suddenly say to me: O, all's well now, open up, trust people, cast away your weapon..."

Nicholas most wisely did not try. He eased me back into his arms, and held me close and stroked me. It was so pleasant I had a little weep on his shoulder.

"I wish you would tell me," Nicholas said. "I feel responsible, to you, for you. It was my idea you came with the group. I don't want you to feel it was in panic, to do with running. You can be so good for us, with all your talents; and we can be good for you. I want you to be happy. And for myself...I loved your body just now because I could not stop myself. I've been hard for you all day just watching you move about. But I want to know all of you. Your thoughts...whatever is really you. In truth," he added apologetically, "I love you."

Ungraciously I muttered: "Love was the cause of all my trouble."

"Tis no use you threatening me with sulks," he said easily. "You are loveable and I do love you, and you will have to grow used to it."

"I am not loveable; you're wrong. If I told you what I was like, you'd soon dislike me. How I let people use me...my horrible liaison with the King. I've nothing to be proud of in my past. You should not love me; I am vile."

"How you do fight it!" he said, holding me close. "Go to sleep," he told me. "Go on, I know you're tired. I shall look after you."

I snuggled up against him and slept.

He woke me in the early dawn with sweet kisses. I put my arms round his neck sleepily, like an infant waking. He touched my nose teasingly.

"You suck your thumb," he said, "when you are asleep."

"I know."

"You are endearing."

"I am infantile!"

"So sophisticated with your ear rings and your flirtatious ways. And such a little boy."

"Not in what I *know*," I said darkly.

"O yes, I know, you've seen it all and done it all."

"Maybe I will tell you, Nicky, maybe you ought to know."

"I fully intend you shall. But meanwhile, I woke you so you could get dressed. The others will guess we made love, but I don't think we need be found lying here like Mars and Venus, eh?"

We stayed outside the walls of Canterbury for about a month, sleeping in the wagons, and performing our repertoire for the citizens. I learned our plays and my days were very full with that and practising songs and handling the properties. The players owned a host of lovely clothes, many of them handed down from noblemen – orange doublets finely trimmed, trunk hose in scarlet striped with silver, whole boxes of buttons, a pearl coloured doublet, ruffs and rufflets, many detachable sleeves in green taffeta and white and horseflesh, mulberry and rose; and hats, tall ones with three feathers, flat caps sewn all over with small buttons, another in peach coloured beaver; and wigs made of real head hair or silk, and some of gold and silver wire. The dresses were even more wondrous, with yards of coloured cloth in taffeta and velvets, with chemises and smocks, petticoats and bodices with laces, and many ruffs and caps and stockings and gloves. We had strange things too, as horses' heads, shields and weapons, and the amazing dragon which spat fireworks; and false flowers and false grass, phials of pigs' blood (ox blood was too thick) and bellows that puffed out smoke. I spent much time with Amyas translating songs for us to sing in duet. Sometimes this was serious and sometimes it was foolish, for he often told me wrong words to sing, to make the others laugh.

"It is some weakness of character in him," Nicholas assured me, laughing as much as anyone. "He must have us in stitches or he is not happy. At least you do not fare as badly as that poor Italian..."

At the memory everyone guffawed afresh and I pestered to be told.

Amyas had met an Italian juggler at a fair and drunk with him and set him up to be the victim of a trick. Amyas had three pennies in his hand and said he would give them away if only he were asked.

"Hold out your hand," he said, "and say to me Give me the first, and I will do so."

"Give—a me da first," said the obedient Italian, and Amyas handed him a penny.

"And now: Give me the second."

"Give—a me da second," Amyas recounted, in a voice much as Englishmen supposed Italians to speak.

"And now: Give me the third."

"Give—a me da turd," said he, and half splitting his seams

with mirth Amyas handed him one – a dog's, he said, into the palm of his hand, which he had nearby all ready, and everybody roared and laughed afresh, and I did slightly, and winced somewhat also.

"Come now," Jack ordered cheerily. "Sitting and gossiping is wasting time. All you young sprigs take some time to wrestle and play – the happy man is the active man, and leaping and dancing keeps the vital spirits lively and banishes melancholy. Up with you – the planets move, the stars move, and so shall you!"

"Sometimes," Francis murmured, "Jack thinks he is still upon the boards."

In between wrestling and running I learnt then the many tricks and skills needed for our plays. There was a little book of instruction, with pictures of stage movements and stances and I memorised and practised them. There were for instance Modesty, Fear, Reverence, Indignation, Suspicion, Deep Thought, Aggression, Impatience. All these and more were conveyed by gestures which had to be much larger than was ordinary, to be seen from afar and to better convey the meaning.

"Marc, whatever your background," said Jack, "you walk and move most pleasingly. Look at him, Amyas, you might learn from him. I have heard it said the French pay more attention to the graces – too much so, they sometimes say, for it makes them seem effeminate and artificial. But for the play-house, Marc, this is a virtue. You will do well in London. They will love you."

"O! Are we to go to London?" I cried, shining eyed.

"We are. But not till Autumn. We will perform in villages and houses in the summer months and reach London when the Summer ends. Meanwhile, perfect your art. You are graceful, but you have much to learn. You do not," he looked at me curiously. "give of yourself. You are all outside. Bring out the inner man, the heart."

I looked downcast. I could not do that. Inside, I was all fear. I was still fleeing.

III

"...for I am full of fear."

A ND SO we took to the road.
We trundled our way about the southern parts of
England, playing in villages and small towns, in country
barns and in the houses of the gentry. It was not a comfortable
life. The tracks were dry and rutted and sometimes overgrown,
and after bad weather they were mulchy with mud. I sometimes
wept to find myself drenched in rain heaving at a cart shaft when
a wheel was stuck, I, who had known satin sheets. Sometimes at
night there seemed nothing more uninviting than a rough-hewn
wagon with a sodden cloth athwart it, weighed down by a pool
of water, and at such times we would be far from village succour
and obliged to sleep all tightly pressed, so that it might be John
or Ralph I lay against and not a loving time with Nicholas.

Unsavoury persons frequented the roads also. Although
mostly our fellow travellers were homely folk – pilgrims,
farmers, carters and such – there were the other kind. I saw men
with strange disfigurements, the result of punishment for
crimes, and once a gang attacked our camp and we had to fight
them off with swords and staves. Players through their trade
become skilled with weapons and we were successful. Another
time two thieves were discovered filching from one of our
coffers, thinking there was money in it when there were only
costumes, but even these they would have taken, so desperate
was their poverty. We shared a meal with them and parted
kindly.

But there were sunny days when all went well, and we would
wake to birdsong and the sweet scent of sunlight on wet leaves
and I would notice how well our food tasted in the open air. And
though it sometimes happened that men in authority did not
wish us to play at certain times or at such a place we were mostly
received everywhere with welcome and delight, and that was
very pleasurable.

I thought then much about the ways of Fortune. I who had
lived all my life in another country was now in England, every
day hearing the English tongue about me, and sometimes that

tongue so countrified that even Nicholas and Amyas were hard put to understand it clearly. I thought in French and translated my thoughts, but now and again I thought in English and that pleased me, and I would feel modest pride, until some bizarre mistake embarrassed me again. And I wondered unhappily about the situation I was in, here now, with players, sleeping in a wagon. In part it seemed a childish game, a dream, as if I would awake and find myself back in Paris and in winter, and I shuddered at the thought. But was this to be my life instead, I wondered? Was it possible for a scion of noble house to live this way, with riffe-raffe on the road? Simply because I loved playing and singing and dressing up in gaudy gear – was that enough? Or was this pleasant life merely a flight, the fear still in me, and not an answer at all? One day, I knew, I would have to stop running and look over my shoulder and see if anything was there pursuing, or whether all my demons were within and summoned up by me, my fright, my dread. Fortune had brought me here – I was tossed to and fro by her careless hand, a leaf borne on the wind. And even as I thought so I remembered my philosophy:

"Fortune does us neither good nor harm; she only holds out to us the seed and the matter of good or harm, which our soul, more powerful than she, turns and applies as she pleases, being sole cause and mistress of her happy or unhappy condition."

And so if Fortune had brought me here I could not blame her for what then followed. I could make of it what I would. O! But I was so weak and small in the great world.

"Have you heard about the one who lost a silver spoon?" said Amyas, pressing his face close to mine.

I had not, and I smiled happily to be diverted from my thoughts. The others howled at hearing this old tale brought out once again and tried to stop him, but he would not be stopped.

"There was one who lost a silver spoon," he shouted. "And did go to an astrologer to ask him who had stolen it. I see it clearly, said the astrologer looking very wise and serious. It is someone who has long legs and wears a black coat and a pair of red stockings. He has a beaky nose and he must be a foreigner, for he speaks no English."

"Yes? And did he find such a one?"

"Yes!" screamed Amyas. "It was a Cornish chough!"

As I looked completely blank, his joke had fallen quite flat. Cornish chough was a word I did not know, and the others thought this was funnier than the joke itself, and praised me for my ignorance, though Amyas beat me about the shoulders very fierce.

Along the dusty country tracks Amyas and I pooled our knowledge of musical instruments. We both played the lute, and I played the recorder; but he could play the sackbut and trumpet – most fearful loud. Also he had an interesting one I had not seen before, a small portable organ in a leather case like a large book. I sat and taught myself to play it. As my horoscope said: learning almost anything, without a teacher. We shared our repertoire of songs. It was most curious to see how many songs were the same in the two languages. "J'ai vu pleurer ma dame" Amyas knew as "I saw my lady weep", and I began to learn it in English, which was hard enough with him nearby.

"*Weep*, Marc, not whip! What can you be meaning: I saw my lady whip? It calls to mind all manner of lewd practices!"

"Amyas, I thought you were a *pure* boy. Your horoscope said no sordid thought ever crossed your mind. What can you possibly know of ladies who whip?"

Amyas giggled and so did I, and I fear he made up a crude version of the song, too vile to write down.

Jesting with Amyas all morning was curiously conducive to lechery. Amyas was so pretty. It was no surprise that he played ladies and was so good at it. He had a sweet oval face and beautiful ears – I could not resist touching his neck just below the ear, that little hollow, and when I did he nuzzled me like a kitten. He was wearing pale blue. His hair was soft, like growing barley, and its colour was the pale gold of corn. We sat on the back of the cart, legs dangling, strumming our lutes. It was so warm we took our boots off and opened our shirts. His chest was smooth. He always responded to advances – both of men and women. Amyas would offer himself to all the world if he liked the look of them. Many men desired him, as I was to find in London; but women too, particularly older ones, found him irresistible. Perhaps he did not tell his jokes between the sheets.

We made camp early, to do repairs to the wagon and to wash the clothes. Amyas and I sat in the grass and he showed me his make-up. It was in a carved wooden box with a velvet lining. We sat, sharing lip salve and eye shadow, and powdered our cheeks.

"What do you use?" enquired Amyas. "In England the fashion for ladies is to be pink and white and golden, and they secretly bleach their hair in the sun. I, of course, do not need to," he simpered. "But I have used apple pressings and hogs' grease to make it shine, and one year I crisped it with hot irons and made curls. But it did not suit me."

"I comb rose water into mine. For a pale face I tried white fucus and poppy oil. It is better than ceruse because that makes the skin dry up and gives you aches in the stomach; and red fucus is worse. Someone I know was awful scarred from that."

"I have a lip salve I like; I'll give you the receipt – it's one that tastes good too. Do you use burnt cork for the eyes? And I have belladonna which I plop into the eye with a feather, just a droplet. Eyes go *enormous* then. Look into mine!"

I could not, without laughing.

"And what perfume do you wear?" he asked.

"It is made from rose oil and rosewater, sugar, musk and ambergris."

"Ah, that's too costly for me..."

"You may share it."

"Thank you! And I have some violet water left; you may share that. And may I ask you, Marc, have you ever tried removing those moles near your lip? They are not flattering, you know. I have so many receipts for removing spots. You may not believe this, but when I was younger I did suffer much from spots. My present clear complexion I believe is due to birch tree sap and Tristram's Water."

"What is that?"

He grinned. "A magic potion I swear, for it does all. As well as clearing blemishes it cures toothache and bad-smelling breath, and it is said to keep you young. It takes weeks to make!"

"Even so," I said, "I have been told the marks on my face are pleasing, in spite of what you say, and I shall leave them where they are. I know someone who made a mixture to remove such blemishes..."

"And...?"

"He removed them. But he removed his skin withal."

We shuddered, and then smiled, sharing mirrors.

"Have you two been perfuming yourselves?" groaned Francis.

"Only a little dab in one place and another," protested Amyas, and then he giggled; but the damage had been done.

"A little *dab* in one *place*?" cried Francis delightedly. "I don't believe what I'm *herring*!"

"We *flounder* in amazement," added Angel. "But Jack will soon bring you to *eel*."

"There is no need to *carp* on so," Amyas pouted.

"We will, by *Cod*," said Angel.

"No blaspheming," called Madge firmly.

"But what about these painted popinjays? Amyas was bad enough before, but with Marc to encourage him..."

"Give them something useful to do," Francis said, hammering a nail into the wagonside and patently being useful.

To everybody's delight except ours Madge slung us a whole load of clothes to wash. Vigorously we protested.

"Nicky needs me to help copy out scripts," I tried.

"No I don't. Do as you're told, like a good boy."

"Tis not fair —" Amyas pouted.

"If you make yourself so pretty you should expect maids' work," sniggered Angel.

We flounced off, wiggling our hips and making petulant gestures, and gathered up all the dirty washing, grumbling to each other as we went.

We were beside a brook. The wagons were further up, on drier ground in a flat meadow surrounded by lush trees. It was all most idyllic. Down beside the water we were in a beautiful glittering world. Trees and bushes came right down to the brook's edge, trailing low boughs into the clear water. Lovely low willows hung like curtains, and on the sloping banks were buttercups, and delicate white cowparsley like bundles of lace. Upon all this wealth shone the gold of the sun, making the water glister and dance. Darting insects hummed close to the surface.

"We shall be bitten," Amyas grumbled. "Marc — why do you look so star struck?"

"O!" I breathed. "I am truly in the countryside."

"You truly are," laughed Amyas. "You will be bit by flying

gnats, and stung by nettles and snakes, prickled by brambles, and you may drown. Ugh! The countryside! Poets may call it Arcadia – but who wants to live in a world of Corydons and Phyllises? They are all clownish clods, they do not know the latest songs, they smell of cows, they *look* like cows, they *talk* like cows – give me London any time. When I see all the spiked and mangled heads of traitors on London Bridge then I know I am back in the civilised world at last!"

I laughed, a receptive audience.

"Ah, but Amyas – I've been in the town so long – I spent all the early part of this year in dark narrow streets and close rooms. Soon you feel like clothes stored in a chest, all fusty and oversmelling of dried lavender. Now suddenly from darkness and rain I am emerged, I am in sunlight."

"You are sweet, Marc," said Amyas, kissing my cheek. My heart quickened; my prick twitched.

"You and Nicholas make love at night, don't you?" he enquired.

"Yes," I said.

"Do you love him?" he asked curiously.

"I love nobody," I shrugged.

"Me neither," dimpled Amyas. "'Tis so much easier."

We giggled. It was somehow understood that we two were shameless and without consciences. We sat down in the buttercups and took off our stockings. We watched each other as our legs appeared.

"You are quite hairy, aren't you!" he observed.

"Your thighs are so plump and – I think – soft."

"Feel," he offered, spreading his legs wide.

First I felt with my hands, but then I had to put my lips there, kissing all his inner thighs till he was almost squeaking, like an excited mouse. He began to tug at his trunk-hose and I sat back as he took them off and made his body naked from the waist down. O! but he was charming. I lowered my head and holding each plump thigh I opened my mouth and put my lips around his prick, now very big and hard and glistening at the tip. He stroked my hair while I was sucking. My bare knees pressed the buttercups down, my tongue weaving liquid patterns on his prick. I made him excited, he was writhing on his back, his legs splayed out abandonedly. I gulped his juices down, my cheeks bulging. He sat up, pink and blinking.

"Ooh Marc," he cried. "Thank you."

There were still the clothes to be washed. We paddled into the water up to our thighs, and Amyas looked so pleasant it made me want more, and I went back to the bank and quickly took off all my clothes, and when he saw me he took off his shirt and doublet, and we went back in naked, and first of all just bathed and sat, and glided about gasping, for it was not as warm as it looked. Then in a rushed sort of way we began to wash the clothes, but it was tedious, so we played a while and touched each other, and Amyas looked over his shoulder at me, lewdly inviting. I gasped, excited. The sight of his fat bottom, half in, half out of the water, the faint golden down of his hairs all wet and gleaming, it was too much. He slid over to the bank, so that willow leaves tickled his skin and lay on him like long green ribbons. His bum was just out of the water, big and round and white, and now and then splashed by an impudent little ripple. I rubbed myself against him, my face in his neck, the sun warm on my back. He bent forward, holding on to clumps of purple flowers. I separated his cheeks, and entered him slowly, push by push. The brook water plashed against my balls as I fucked. My jiggling thighs made ripples. I was too roused to take a long time. Then, weak, I pulled out, and he wriggled up from the greenery with petals in his hair. We washed ourselves in the water and, cold now, attempted to finish washing the clothes.

Martin and Geoffrey suddenly came dashing down, shouting: "They're bathing! They've taken off all their clothes! Can *we*?" And next thing we knew everyone had joined us because it looked so lovely in the water. Amyas and I, shivering, got out and dried ourselves and dressed, and watched the others.

I was very interested to observe Angel, who as I suspected was beautiful all over. O! What a waste that he liked women! He was well proportioned with a manly chest and muscular arms and lean thighs, and his body hair was gold. I almost wished I was a woman, that I could know his lovemaking. Watching Nicholas, I felt pride. That beautiful man loved me – and O yes, he was beautiful. On his chest he had curly brown hair and a great lovely mass at the crotch. His thighs were well shaped, and his cock large even unaroused.

"There is no need," murmured Amyas confidentially, "to

mention to Nicholas what we did."

"Naturally," I agreed.

Madge had made us all a steamy vegetable broth, with bread and ale, and we ate it around the fire whereon it was cooked, most companionable and pleasant, and all clean from bathing. Amyas and I played and sang, and everyone praised us and said that all the men in London would be in love with us. And although they teased us for our mincing ways they were very proud of us. Companies know when they are lucky, and they are lucky if they have two pretty lads who can be convincing when they are dressed as girls.

Privily Nicholas said to me, a little severely: "Well, Marc-Alphonse, and who are you sleeping with tonight, me or Amyas?"

"You, please, Nicky," I said, fluttering my eyelashes.

And so it befell, that at night time, we prepared as before to sleep in our covered cart.

An odd thing happened. we discovered a faery ring just nearby, a little under the trees, with low white blossom hanging over it. We stood, neither of us stepping into the ring. In the half light all things seemed possible. There was the rutted road, curving away towards a village, but all around, there was the shivering wood, so pleasant in the sunlight, so mysterious in the dark. Without saying anything, it was understood between us that we both believed in the otherworld. I know not what I mean when I say that – the possibility of magic, I think, the actuality of a strange twilight kingdom of shadows and elves; that a shape could disassociate itself from a tree, that a trailing branch could be a long green sleeve, that a princely arm could beckon, and a door in a hillside open. Charms, spells, invocations.

"If a faery prince called, would you go?" I asked.

"Yes," said Nicholas.

"To what, I wonder?"

"To escape from what is wrong with the world that we know, to lose the human condition, with its sorrows and responsibilities."

"A faery prince would steal away your soul; they are merciless, you know; no half measures and no turning back."

"O, you know all about it, eh, Marc-Alphonse?"

"Naturally," I said mysteriously. "I am a faery prince."

Nicky half laughed, but he looked at me almost seriously. "I do believe you are," he said.

"Look, here are the marks of the otherworld on my face," I told him, touching my impressive moles. "I drop into your life. I tell you I come from France, but how do you know? Maybe I come from secret places – I am a wayward star that does not know its orbit; I speed across the sky without a proper sphere. O you should beware of me, Nicky. I am sent to bewitch you."

"Indeed you have," said Nicky. "I have never fell in love so sudden as with you."

Francis noisily coming back through the undergrowth from having a piss called in a human voice: "What are you two doing? Go to bed, why don't you?"

We called goodnight and standing by our wagon we took off our clothes. It was very silent then. We heard the myriads of leaves rustle, and the liquid rippling of the brook. One of the other wagons creaked, and Amyas giggled, from within.

I took Nicky's hand, and led him back to the faery ring. A sliver of moonlight cast a sheen upon the hedges white with roses.

"Dare you follow me?" I said, and went into the ring.

I knew how I must have looked; performing comes naturally to me. All naked and beckoning, I was lucky no underworld creature rose up there and then and carried me off; I was all invitation. My offer – and Nicky's acceptance – were both extremely bold. If I was magic he would be in my power, and if I was not, we were both tempting true magic. I held out my hand and he took it, and crossed over into my magic circle. Shivering a little we embraced, and stood entwined, in a long sweet kiss.

"Shake petals on us," I insisted. Nicky made a bough sway, and as if in the wind a snowshower of white fell on us, settling on our hair and lightly touching our skin.

"I made a ceremony on the first of May," I said, "in a wood with primroses. I asked to meet my true love, and I met you. Now it seems we are indeed bound. A charm will hold us together. It might be called the possibility of magic."

"Love, maybe," said Nicholas.

But I just laughed. Love I did not want. Love made you weak, love threatened.

"Don't spoil it, Nicky," I said pulling him out of the circle. "Love is too serious and it puts a person into chains."

"O yes," snapped Nicholas. "Tis much easier, is it not, to fool about with Amyas and I wish you joy of each other. He won't threaten you with finer feeling."

"Don't be angry," I pouted. "Tis you I prefer, you know it. It is for you I came away to live this life, to sleep in wagons and to live as the vulgar – it was to be with you."

"And must I be grateful?" cried Nicholas. "You think you demean yourself, do you, associating with me and my friends?"

"But of course I do – how could I not? I am of noble family and I have lived at the court..."

"You will never let us forget that, will you? Don't you understand how lucky you are to have landed with us? Without us you could be alone and fending for yourself. You would not survive a mile on the roads by yourself. Where would you go, speaking as you do, and with some of your puffed up ideas? You have seen the kind of villains and vagabonds that travel the roads – you would have been robbed by now, even killed for your finery – or maybe taken as some rich man's bedboy – anything could have happened. But we took you in – gave you a livelihood –"

He stopped. I think he was regretting he had said so much. But I did not help him. I put a cloak about myself and withdrew into my thoughts.

"I was angry; I didn't mean it," said Nicholas.

"You meant it. It's good to know what we truly think of one another."

"O, well, if you prefer to sulk..."

And so what began as a happy occasion was all sour and marred, and the bad flavour was still with me on the morrow when we performed in the house of a young Catholic gentleman.

IV

"I know not what you mean by treason, I."

I T WAS the first time that our troup had played in a nobleman's house, and so it was the first time that I, while seeming to be with the players, was amongst folk of higher station, and feeling as I did at that moment, my instincts were to ally myself with the gentry.

The house was very beautiful. It lay in a little valley thick with trees. In its fields we set up our encampment, and for a moment I stared, shocked by the contrast. Our camp – my home – was poor and shabby. Our washed clothes hung to dry upon hawthorn bushes, smudges of tawdry peach taffeta and torn cloth, cast-off cloaks and discarded hats shoved upon branches to lose the musty smells in the clear air. Madge beside the pottage pot could have been a peasant mother, and what was Jack with his slop breeches and his woollen hose but a common man, as a blacksmith was, or a butcher? What was I doing here, with people who teased me and did not value my proper worth, inferior in station to me and yet treating me without any deference?

The house, of biscuit-coloured stone, lay mellow and elegant, the sunlight warming its ancient walls, doves cooing upon its roof, house martens darting below its eaves, a shield carved above its imposing door; the whole betokening peace, stability, and ancient wealth. A ditch about it showed it had been fortified of old, and a lake beyond was lush with water lilies. If I had stayed in France – if I had pressed for my share of my inheritance – could I own something like that in good time? Did I want that? But did I want to be allied with raggle taggle player folk? Surely not.

To make matters worse that afternoon, the folk at the house unwittingly fostered my growing discontent by recognising quality in me and making much of me, and when it was clear that I was French and Catholic and bearing the name I did, they treated me as an equal, even though I was with poor players.

I was suddenly struck by the difference between real noble-men in stylish clothes, and false noblemen – the players, in old cast-off finery discarded by the gentry and displaying by extravagant gesture sham nobility which they did not possess. I was reminded of a situation I was once familiar with, in which one gave orders to servants and drank out of silver, and then went upstairs to sleep in postered beds with testers and hangings. I suddenly ached to be pampered. I responded shamelessly to the interest in me showed by Sir Philip and his lady. They were cultured as well as noble. There was a young man visiting, and his tutor, one Master Pendry, both of whom spoke French to me, and knew Paris and Rheims.

We performed in a cool stone-floored great hall with a minstrel's gallery at one end, a raftered roof of fine old timber, and shields embossed carved into the walls. I sensed a further similarity between myself and this family – an ancient name, a present straitness of circumstance. One understands these things, the very air speaks of it. I remembered Gervaise talking of the heavy fines imposed on Catholics; there was a startling poverty here behind the superb frontage, the fine silver, and the fiercely polished wood.

Sir Philip and his wife Lady Margaret were a young couple, not much older than I was. He was dreamy-eyed, with black hair, slight of build and very elegant in dark blue satin. She his wife wore her long hair loose in tiny abundant curls about her shoulders. She was marvellous fair, like a painting from times past, very small in height, and with a clear sweet voice and an angelic face. They made many solicitous enquiries about me, and after the play they congratulated me upon my performance and my lute playing, and enquired how did I come to be with players and did I plan to return to France; and they asked other questions, about my religion, questions which I could not see the point of, for religion had never been a matter of close concern to me, and I was embarrassed at being asked my thoughts on matters of conscience.

I could see both Nicholas and Jack eyeing me with visible disquiet and frowning at me like the picture in the stage direction of "He frowns", and I ignored such pointed hints which I put down to jealousy.

"Marc..." Nicholas even interrupted. "We should be leaving now."

I hesitated; his interruption seemed impolite, and I felt embarrassed, for I was sure it seemed so to my hosts.

"Stay a little if you wish," said Sir Philip. "We may talk

further."

"Yes," I said. "I would like that." I thought at that time that these kind people might know of some solution to the problem of my future, some alternative to a life on the road, something more conformable with the dignity of my position. And besides, I liked them. And so in the cool of the evening the players left the house to return to the wagons to sleep and wait for me, and I stayed at the house.

Behind the house was a garden, which was entered from a terrace. One passed between two conical posts carved all over with fruits and flowers, and descended steps into a fine broad walk between cultivated rose bushes planted in triangular beds and having a fountain in the centre splashing water. At the end of the garden was a covered walk, a passageway of low arched trees, so tightly planted that it was like a corridor of green shade, and wherever the arches came, little glimpses of the garden showed. It was most cool within, most private.

"It has happily befallen that you came here today, Marc," said my host now that we were quite alone. "If you would like to, you may hear Mass tonight. I am sure you have not been able since you set foot in England?"

"It is true, I have not."

"Would you like to?" asked Sir Philip, his eyes all brightly gleaming.

"But yes," I shrugged. "How?"

"Master Pendry is not entirely young Sir Francis' tutor," he said to me softly. "He is a priest. A travelling priest. One sent from Rheims."

I made no reaction, but I remembered then a meeting with one such priest, in Paris with my brothers. Lionel Fulbrook was his name and in my mind I saw again his dark contorted features, heard the passionate intensity of his voice as he boasted of his plan to work in Southwark, in disguise as a serving man in a cookshop, selling pies. I had then found him grotesque, but now I felt uneasy, as one does when stirring up dark waters.

"Ah yes,' I said, as one who understands all, but who evidently did not.

"You know what he risks...It is wonderful that there are men so brave and dedicated, bringing comfort to the faithful. Tonight you shall hear Mass if you so wish it."

"Thank you." I was aware that he was doing me an honour,

106

and favouring me with his confidence. I could then hardly refuse. We were nobility; we had things in common.

Swiftly then he turned to other matters, as, how did I like Canterbury, and English food, and had I been to London, and I must visit the playhouses there for I would see good meaty matter, so he had heard. When we returned indoors we sat again in the great hall and I was asked to sing and play again, which I gladly did. Listening to me there was Sir Philip and Lady Margaret, Sir Francis and that same tutor which now I knew was a priest, and two from the village also come for the purpose of receiving the sacrament. All seemed very pleasant, and between my songs bright conversation and loud laughing, and the tinkle of Venetian glass.

Suddenly there was a knocking at the door, a loud knocking which made echo throughout the hall. It made me start, but that was nothing to how the others behaved. Lady Margaret shrieked, and all of them jumped to their feet, either crossing themselves or putting hands on heart as those do who portray terror. And terror this most palpably was, true terror like a wave washing over us all, all caught in its surge.

A servant stepped forward, hardly able to frame his words for fear.

"Shall I answer the door, my lord?"

"You must," said Sir Philip, his face quite white, and as for the priest he had sat down again, and I watched his efforts to control himself, all shown in his face, as if one were working strings behind his cheeks.

The servant unbolted, and instantly in came a burly red-faced figure, seeming to be some kind of farmer, bursting straight to the purpose of his visit.

"Ah, Sir Philip, I've disturbed you at your table – do excuse me – I was passing by – though the hour is late – I came to tell you that the matter of the fallen trees is all resolved, and he will pay the cost of the timber as we hoped – I knew you would be pleased to hear all settled –" and the rest of his tale being lost in the general cries of delight and appreciation which surrounded him. I knew the fervency of these had something to do with the matter of the fallen trees, but far more to do with the relief of tension and the gratitude that this beer-faced neighbour was himself and no one whose unexpected presence at the door was threat. They gave him drinks and sent him away with thanks.

After he had gone they sank back to their places, laughing, crying, sighing, praying – and now it seemed it was only me who was afraid. I found that I was shivering, and my fingers on my lute stem slippery with sweat.

I stood up.

"You must excuse me," I said stuttering. "I dare not stay."

"But Marc, all is well now. It was nobody. All is as before."

"For you perhaps. But I am too afeared. I don't know why. I think because *you* were and I thought that I had done with fear and put it behind me in Paris. But it is not so, and it was here tonight."

"But Marc..." A secondary fear now touched Sir Philip's face. I understood it.

"I will say nothing," I assured them, looking at their anxious faces. "I give you my word. Not even to the players, who are my friends." I winced, to remember how I had implied to Nicholas that these friends had been of small account. Suddenly they seemed most dear.

"Very well," said Sir Philip. "We understand. We do accept your word. I regret your choice, but each must do what his conscience dictates."

"Conscience," I laughed weakly. "I am in too deep waters here. I am but a poor player and I should return to my own kind."

Sir Philip escorted me to the door and let me out. I ran away, across the ancient moat and up into the field where the wagons lay against the high dark hedge. O! How warm and welcoming they seemed! The embers of the fire, the soft sound of Amyas' lute, the bickering of Martin and Geoffrey, the whinneying of the grazing horses, all sounds which suddenly I valued most immense.

Nicholas ran forward to meet me and slung his arm about my shoulders. He knew at once I was upset. Jack did not and he was angry.

"Sirrah," he said. "I did not like the way you played this day. And less the way you played this night."

"I did not like it myself," I tremulously agreed.

"Are you too good for us?" he continued loudly. "Are we beneath your feet? How you did look fond upon that lord! And how you did turn your back on us!"

"I am ashamed..."

"You did not even speak your lines well in the play. There was no passion. First strutting like a Peacock of the Ind. Then, stiff and rigid as a post. A *post* would have made a better Isabella. A *post* in a farthingale with ribbons on its top would have made a better Isabella than you."

"Leave him, Jack, he knows it," Madge said, drawing him back. "Marc, there's pottage left; come eat."

"Was I too rough?" said Jack amazed. "If I was I am heartily sorry. He should know by now I only chastise those that I hold dear."

My sixteenth birthday was celebrated in a very enjoyable way, for Nicky and I took ourselves away from the others for an afternoon and lay in a hayfield. The hay had been gathered and what was left was the white and sun-dried grass, and when we saw it we could not help but fling ourselves upon it. It was soft to lie on, and we gathered bunches of it in our arms to smell. We ate strawberries from the hedgerow, and pulled rose petals to put in each other's hair. We lay close together, our clothes flecked with petals and grasses.

"Nicky," I began. "Is England a safe place?"

"For certain it is."

"Yes, but for all?"

"What can you mean? Against attack? We are surrounded by sea, and our seamen and ships are the envy of the world."

"But, within?"

"Within? Look at us, lying in each other's arms and no one to bother us."

"What would happen to me if I secretly attended Mass?"

"O Marc," wailed Nicholas sitting up. "Don't talk of religion. I know you're not devout. Why start things –?"

"My brothers told me I'd be safe in England. In Paris I was not safe. You've seen the mark along my ribs where one tried to kill me. But I thought *here* . . . And my first impressions, tu sais, the first of May, the maypoles – it was as if I were in a Pastoral."

"Yes, May is lovely . . ."

"But is it an illusion? Below the surface is it just like Paris? If you are a Catholic?"

"Promise me, Marc," said Nicholas, "that you will not involve yourself with secretly hearing Mass. It is not worth it, and it will only cause trouble, to all of us."

He looked at my dubious face.

"Marc, you know the conspiracy that led to the execution of the Queen of Scotland..."

"No. What conspiracy?"

"Wicked men intended to kill Queen Elizabeth. They were just discovered in time. It would have been a calamity. She lives in constant danger from the hand of an assassin. And so she cannot take chances. Tis not that she hates Catholics, not at all — no, she loves all her subjects equally. So laws have to be made. It's perfectly easy to comply. Go to church, think what you like in your heart, but don't play with fire, don't toy with danger for the excitement of it. Promise me, no secret Mass."

"I promise," I assured him. "I have no wish to be a martyr!"

"Believe me, Marc, England is a place of peace and well being."

And the others would have it no different. The Queen is a marvel, they told me, a goddess. Gloriana! Cynthia! The moon! She loves us dearly and has kept us safe these many years. She loves both poor and rich; she will take the hand of any common man when she makes her royal progresses through villages and lanes. I saw her once in Cheapside...I saw her at Greenwich...I touched her horse...I saw the jewels on her glove...she wants us to pray how we will...she wants her people happy...it is her dearest wish...no other monarch ever cared so for her people!

And I could see that they truly believed this. They spoke of the Queen all glowingly, with shining eyes and affectionate smiles, all of them, from noisy cheerful Jack to exquisite Angel ("I would *die* for her! I would die just for the chance to kiss her hand!") and they politely reminded me about the state of other realms. "Does your King Henry come down into the streets and show himself to his people and talk to one and all? Does old King Philip?" Neither, I had to agree, was famed for such familiarities. And they plied me with ale and fêted me and drank my health. Nicholas gave me a pomander to wear at the waist; Amyas gave me a bowl of the biggest strawberries he could find, to eat all myself and I am ashamed to say I did. All the others gave me new lute strings and comfits, and a grand celebration in a village barn, with cider and ale at trestle tables and singing and dancing with people from the village, till the moon rose and the owls hooted in the meadows beyond.

And I laughed weakly as I sorted out my thoughts. Yes, I was in a safe place, my brothers were right. As long as you believed that the Queen was the goddess of the moon, and you kept away from secret priests, England was all celebration, all merriness and music. And I thought about Lionel Fulbrook the seminary priest I had met in Paris, who knew Rheims cathedral and the mystic incense, who had come over secretly to spread the Faith, and was now selling pies in Southwark as a cover for his plots, and I wondered how it went with him, and how he fared.

English people seem monstrous pleased for any excuse to have festivities. At one village we were invited to join in their celebrations over having just heard that Sir Francis Drake had burned some ships in Cadiz harbour. There was dancing in the village street, and images of King Philip were stuck up and pelted and later burned, and I had to keep quiet all evening because there was such savage delight in the burnings that any foreigner might have been seized and flung upon the pyres.

The festival of Midsummer, however, was entirely pleasurable. There was drinking and feasting in the village ale house, and music and dancing on the green, and bawdy songs and a tug of war and an archery contest, and at night Midsummer bonfires. We performed some of the ballads of Robin Hood, which now I knew, and I enjoyed it all so much and was so shining-eyed that Francis asked me in all seriousness:

"But don't you have Midsummer in France?"

It was simply that I was remembering how on the First of May I had watched the celebrations as an onlooker and had felt apart; and now I was within. The feeling made me very happy; and better was to come.

Nicholas, who loved faery and all these old customs took me off to a glade in the woods, and there we wandered hand in hand, alone beside a bank of honeysuckle, where white and pink briar roses grew and purple foxgloves as high as overselves. Here in the green gloom he kissed me and I responded so fervently that we lay down to enjoy each other the better.

We lay for a long time there, watching the evening star Hesperus rise in a little patch of sky beyond the foxgloves. Birds carolled in the trees above our heads, and a marvellous strange thing — we heard an eerie sound, like the notes of music

111

a faery fiddler might make, or as if a tree were singing. It must have been two boughs that rubbed together in the wind – but on Midsummer night?

"I love you," Nicky told me. "Sometimes when we're busy or travelling or with the others I cannot tell it you as often as I would like. But I do tell it now – a Midsummer gift. I give you this glade, these roses, the perfume of this honeysuckle, everything that grows here – they are all for you, all created entire for your pleasure. Elves did it a thousand moons ago, knowing you would be here today."

I smiled comfortably, nestled in his arms.

"You don't believe me, do you?" said Nicky smiling also.

"O I do!" I promised. "And I am remembering something. I made a solitary celebration on the First of May, and now it is Midsummer and I am no longer alone. I feel grateful to – somebody, someone of the forest who answers that kind of prayer. We should give thanks. You know what I mean," I murmured suggestively.

We set about undressing, secretly, whispering, looking about us, because we could hear the sounds of other lovers laughing and chasing and the rustling of bushes, and the music of a flute – mysterious but companionable. All naked we embraced kneeling, our arms around each other, our bodies touching, skin to skin. I kissed my way down his body till my lips closed on his cock, and I could not help thinking that this was a more satisfying celebration than when I had been alone amongst the primroses. And if, as they say, this is the real way of worshipping a maypole, I must agree it is more pleasing than the dance.

Then Nicholas returned the favour to me, and I lay upon my back amongst our strewn clothes and tossed and writhed in pleasure, and I watched the foxgloves sway, black shapes against the turquoise sky, and the scent of honeysuckle hung upon the air. That night we did not go back to the wagons, but slept in the forest. In the morning we were cramped and damp, but magic was about us – perchance the elves had touched us while we slept.

I knew then I was ready to tell Nicholas my story.

FOUR

I

"This is no seat for one that's comfortless –
For though my birth be great, my fortune's mean..."

IMAGINE, I said, a tower that's old and strong and without beauty, built for defence, a place to leave behind. Tall pointed turrets very high and narrow, a courtyard down below, a crenellated wall with stables. In winter icy blasts through windows and no warmth in those thick and massy walls. The only walls the sun warmed were the stables.

I do not tell this how I told it to Nicholas, which was haltingly with conversation interposed; I tell it how I remember it; some things I kept from him. But lying in his arms I did find that episodes became clearer as I told, and made me understand it all the better myself.

For now it came to me quite clearly why it was my brother Charles hated me so much. And even then it was not exactly hate, for in spite of all, there was a kind of odious bond between us, some obscure loyalty that curiously we all shared. He was thirteen when I was born, and I see now that he had adored our mother. She had been very beautiful, and to him I think almost holy. Small wonder then I was a poor exchange. I started life with a great awareness of guilt, dreadful irresolvable guilt, and I was made to feel it was no less than murder, which I suppose it was. So I would always have to expiate my crime and be punished by those who judged me guilty. When shortly after her death and the same thing, my birth, our father died of natural causes, it meant I was brought up by my brothers. Charles hurried into manhood, and the others followed him: Laurent, Jacques and Louis.

You would think, being of an ancient name and living in a

castle, that we would be rich. On the contrary, we were poor. Of course, one does not compare oneself with peasants. I mean by comparison with other noble families. In the recent power struggles there were close to the king three great families, Guise, Bourbon and Montmorency, and the nobles clustered about them for advancement. Unfortunately the Guise who were most successful, were our enemies, and therefore political changes left out family impoverished. What it meant was our velvet wore thin, we ate off old silver plate, we gave our servants no rewards, and schemes for getting money were common talk. Eventually Laurent accepted the church as a way of advancement, leaving us four to scrabble over what could be got from the property. In any kind of mathematics that meant that I received nothing.

For the first years of my life I was left to run wild, like a weed, which was what I was considered to be. I played in the dirt and ate where I could, and fond servants gave me their own food and time for my poor mother's sake. So Gilles was to me always close. Gilles was a stable boy, his parents peasants on our estate. I slept in his bed regularly, long before we made love, because though it was a pallet of straw near the horses it was warm and friendly; my own was cold and drear and far away in a turret. Icicles regularly formed part of the window shape in winter.

I kept out of my brothers' way as far as possible, because there was endless opportunity for ill treatment when we crossed paths. You know those quintains, those posts that twist round, with two arms and a weight you punch which swirls round and hits you on the head if you are not swift enough? They put me in a bag all folded up and used me for the weight; I would have been about five or six. When they let me out I was covered in bruises and aching all over. Charles carried me on his shoulders, proudly almost, as if I had suffered all that willingly, and laced me with wine till I was drunk. Another time they sat me in a pail and lowered me down a well. They gathered at the top to hear me scream, and scream I certainly did. They said if I climbed the rope they'd stone me, and I believed them; and so I sat in the bucket, my legs over the side, down there in the curious darkness with the circle of light far above, and bottle green weeds trailing from the black stone all round me, and earth-iced water below.

Laurent came home on a visit, and I heard the arguments rage up and down the stone stairways.

"You must educate him – he must have tutors – I did not recognise him in the yard – I thought he was a servant's brat – Mort Dieu, he is a little savage."

"That's right, he is. He always has been. He has always played in the muck and kept company with cooks and vassals."

"He must be educated; he will be worth nothing."

"Pay out good money on that little scab?"

"I'll find someone." It was always Laurent who saved me in the end.

Charles must have realised that to educate me provided a whole new area for punishment and suppression, so he gave in and allowed Laurent to organize my civilisation. I was brought in and scrubbed and tidied up, and taught to read and write and pray. I can remember being dragged into the chapel by my ear, the hot sunlight slammed away, the cold perfumed interior as I was slung to my knees.

"A thousand Hail Mary's, and he's to stay on his knees; see to it!"

I resisted learning with all my being, and escaped so often that finally I had the indignity of being tied to the chair and each day began that way. I learnt all my lessons tied, arms on the chair arms, legs wide apart to fit the chair's legs, my feet not touching the floor; and there I learned, and there each day Charles visited me and sat opposite, languid and pouring wine, till he was satisfied I could recite all I had learnt. The whole of my education was entirely due to fear of pissing in the chair in front of Charles; I could not leave till I had learnt, and so I learnt.

Before it might be thought that I regularly wore a coat of many colours and was nearly sold to the Egyptians, I must explain that sympathy to the poor ill-treated child is out of place, and in truth I was a malevolent little boy. I kicked everything in sight – my brothers' legs, tables, dogs – and threw things – trenchers, food, goblets; they could not use glass if I were present. Worse, I killed things. I threw stones at birds, trapping sparrows for the pleasure of slaughtering them; I smashed eggs, I drowned kittens without remorse; I wrung the necks of chickens. I was so full of venom. The kittens of course no one minded, but the chickens got me a bad beating. What was worse about it was that Jacques tied me to a post in the yard where everyone could see, the chicken corpses piled around my feet, so that the servants knew it was me who had done it. More than my smarting back I minded the disgrace; everyone now knew I was not a poor sweet boy, but brutish and vindictive like my brothers, and after that I received less kindliness from the servants than before. Gilles came and cut me free. I pleaded with him not to: I knew they would beat him for releasing me. They did. We were then about eight years old.

Down beyond the village in the forest there was a witch; her name was Jehanne. She lived alone in a vile hovel and worked evil; it was common knowledge. Her home was half underground, scooped out from the earth. Worms writhed in her walls; and above, the rain dripped from the leaves and boughs that made her roof.

"You want him dead?" she offered me. "You want your brother dead?"

Her hair was thick and fair like thatch and hung down to her waist. Her face was fat and overblown and brown like rotten fruit. She had heavy breasts as soft as pillows and she pressed me to them till I was half stifled. In her mouth there was one tooth only but her lips were painted berry red as if she thought herself a lady.

"Pretty boy," she cooed to me, and touched the moles upon my face. "Witch's boy. *My* boy..."

And truly she did fascinate me and I visited her again and again. With my finger I stirred the brews she made – the cold remains of toads, hogs' grease, moles' blood, and the floating eyeballs ripped from forest creatures. I learnt spells – a cure for lameness using ash twigs and a shrew mouse buried alive; a sleeping apple made of hemlock juice and henbane seeds and poppies – and other things, as how to cause a person prickling in the limbs and sudden pain. And she held me close, this witch, and handled me, and sometimes said for this or that to work I must be naked, and I would be so, pulling the wild herbs for her, great bunches of them, with the rain drops coursing down my skin. Then in the foxy earth we lay, and she pressed sweet tasting ointments to her dugs for me to suck as if I were a baby, and her body was a tangled mix of foul and fair; and while I sucked she held my privities, which I confess I found agreeable and, as I guess, so did she.

She gave me a dark grey toadstone, taken, she promised, from the head of an ancient toad in the throes of death.

"Keep it by you," she said. "If ever someone means you ill or if the wine you drink is poisoned, the stone will sweat. You will feel it clay-cold in your hand."

This seemed a useful thing to own, and many a meal time at the castle I sat smugly clutching it, comfortable in the knowledge that I would know if my brothers intended to poison me. But they never did.

I saw the wax images she made, with twisted nails stuck in the heart and vitals; there was not just Charles and Jacques, there were people from the village, with a morsel of torn cloth to identify them, or a curl of hair.

One day men from the village came to the witch's hut with stones in their hands, and I was there. They dragged her screaming from the hovel and they would have taken me, but someone said:

"Leave him, you fool, do you not know he's from the castle?"

So I was thrown back and left to shiver in the earth, while they pulled it apart about me, tearing bough from bough and making a great bonfire from all within. I ran away as soon as I dared; I ran to the safety of the castle.

"I hear they stoned the witch," said Louis in the evening, munching bread. "Stoned her dead."

"What – not Jehanne?" said Charles, putting down his wine.

"That gap-toothed hag who mixes questionable potions for the credulous."

"Indeed..." said Charles, and smiled and shook his head. "So...is she dead? She had other skills than witchcraft, Louis." Half to himself he added: "In truth, she taught me all I know..."

With Gilles one day I visited his grandmother in the village. As we returned home in the dusk, on foot, we passed the doorway of a rough hut where an old woman sat. She saw us, and she turned and spoke to one within, and then she spat at me.

"Witch's brat!" she croaked, and the figure behind her came right out and picked up a stone and flung it. It landed in a deep rutted puddle close by, and spattered all my clothes with mud.

I never went back into the village on foot then, only on horseback, with servants.

At nine I became the focus of a new scheme, the potential bridegroom of Lettice Blysshen.

"How would you like a wife, pig?" Charles asked me cheerfully one day.

"Don't be stupid," I replied.

"Unmannerly rude brat, you'll have to change your ways. A wife you shall have, whether you will or no. And we must educate you, and make you courteous!"

He chortled happily, for the humour of the challenge appealed to him.

"You'd like to see England and voyage on a ship – all little boys want to travel! And we'd like to be well rid of you, so all shall be best pleased."

Before our journey to England I had to convince Charles I could pass in civilised company, and he rapidly tutored me in good behaviour. His method was very simple, a smattering of information gleaned from Castiglione's treatise on courtliness, and a stout cane. I learnt politeness at the expense of welted legs, and I went along with the idea out of curiosity and a natural excitement at the idea of seeing England and voyaging on a ship. Gervaise had money, we had a noble name, we were all Catholics, and so the plan progressed. My views on Lettice are known.

After the betrothal my education became more serious, and the crux of it was the learning of English. I was no longer tied to the chair because amazingly I began to see the value of education for its own sake, and I seriously applied myself. I learnt English, Latin, history, poetry, geometry and astronomy. I particularly remember a vast drawing I made of the twenty-two rings that surround the earth. Using compasses you begin with Terra, then progress to Aqua, Aer, Ignis, and on to Luna, Mercuri, Venus, Sol, Mars, Iupiter, Saturnus, Caelum Stellatum, Angeli, Archangeli, Virtutes, Principatus Potestates, Throni, Dominationes, Cherubin, Seraphin; and then a big impressive face with "Deus" writ beside, and sunbeams protruding. I became almost as cultured as Charles, and certainly more so than Louis who only read Rabelais.

At this age I was given my first lute, and a musician came and taught me. Lettice sent English songbooks and I knew some Thomas Wyatt and the Earl of Surrey and also "Greensleeves".

The elements within me were little better mingled than before, though I had stopped killing chickens. I was sulky and secretive, difficult and provocative. I could be relied on to behave badly. Once an ambassador visited us with a courtly entourage, and at dinner I pretended I was an idiot and deformed. I tied a cushion under my shirt between my shoulder blades, and I stuffed apple halves in my cheeks, and I let my lips dribble, and I stroked the ambassador's fur, and I lay down in the rushes and pretended I was having a fit – I had seen a boy in the village do this – and all stared at me. Charles carried me out carefully. Once well clear of the hall he dragged me to my room and locked me in. We fought all the way. I bit his leg till it bled through his stocking. Later that night all three came and tied me to the bed and leathered me and left me there two days and nights. Before I was untied I had to swear to Charles that I would be good. Weeping, shamed and aching, I pretended penitence and was released.

As soon as the welts on my body eased I took Charles' best horse and rode him stupidly, and it being winter we slid on ice and I did more damage than I intended. I had meant to ride him hard and indeed I did, for he stumbled in a ditch and broke a leg. I was scared to go home. I lay in that same ditch, blue and shivering, tormented by the horse's agony, for he lay close by. I knew I would be beaten stupid. Eventually a mad hope that something could be done to save the horse made me limp home. I was hurt from being thrown, but I would heal and the horse would not. I daresay they would have preferred it the other way about. Charles was obliged to kill the horse. He returned in wrath and sorrow to where I shivered huddled by the hearth, guarded by Louis and terrified to near insensibility. Charles might well have flayed me alive, but Louis and Jacques said I was not to be beaten as I was still black and blue from the last, and also there were people visiting, and ladies added their requests that I should be treated leniently. So I was not beaten, but Charles said he could not stand the sight of me, and so I was chained in the stable and there left in the straw. They told Gilles to bring me food.

They had no idea that this was a sweet delight to me, that Gilles was my dear friend. They saw him as a menial. This present incident occurred when I was about eleven or twelve, Gilles also. It pleased me to think of him as my twin, for being Gemini I needed an embodiment of my other half. Gilles was the reason why against all odds I remember my childhood as agreeable. We fished together in summer brooks and lay in meadows sucking grass stems, and climbed trees and fought, and shared our thoughts and fancies. We slept together often, like two puppies cuddled together. To become sexual then was the most natural thing in the world. I suppose it is the same for boys who go with girls, the budding intimacy, the curiosity. I never felt the slightest interest in girls at all, I never cared what was under their skirts or wanted to see them naked; I knew what breasts were like. But I was curious with Gilles, to see him naked. Was he beautiful all over, was his cock like mine, could he make it hard? Gilles made me secure; like Nicholas he had the natural assurance of people who comfort. He had curly brown hair and brown eyes, he was very sunburned and he spoke with a country accent. He was muscular and strong. I watched him heaving hay on a pitchfork; the muscles rippled from arms to shoulders and down his back. It was Gilles who held my cock and gave me pleasure. We did it in the hayloft, with the sun on us. It was my first real taste of love's ecstasy.

"I love you!" I said. "With all my heart."

And so being chained in the stable was no punishment to me, sleeping and eating with Gilles and experiencing each other's bodies, innocently at first, but gaining in experience.

When I was allowed back into the castle, soon after that, Charles made me go as page into a different household. I did not object to this, except for leaving Gilles, because I thought it would be better. In most ways it was. It was the castle of a nobleman who unlike us was truly wealthy, and I went there to be "polished". I suppose polished is quite a good word for what happened to me. The nobleman was called Pierre de Villeneuve and he was a refined and cultured man. I had lovely clothes to wear there. He liked me in white stockings and plumply padded trunk hose, and a pale pink satin doublet and a stiff starched ruff that prickled my neck and made me hold my head high. It was here that I first learnt I was pretty.

"I'll give thee sugar-almonds, sweet conserves,
A silver girdle, and a golden purse...
And stick these spangled feathers in thy hat."

I WAS about twelve or thirteen, and still part innocent. I did not notice that there were not many ladies at the castle and the men were very painted and powdered, not at first. I simply thought how elegant they were. At last, I thought, I have found my true sphere, I feel comfortable here. I blossomed. And they were very agreeable to me. They let me play my lute as long as I wanted, and eat comfits and play games, and here I learnt to dance. My duties as page were very light; it was quite hard to see them as duties – I simply had to be there and be obliging, which was easy. I handed round wine and violet comfits, and gentlemen praised me and pinched my cheeks and patted my padded arse and tickled my knees. Most evenings I sat on someone's lap. They called me Ganymede and said I was pretty. They encouraged me to walk with mincing steps because it was so charming, and they gave me some pretty shoes with high heels that pattered on the stone, with little blue bows at the toes. They gave me gloves and stockings and a cap with a feather – more new clothes than I had ever had in my life. I was most happy. O, they said, and smiled, and could I show my appreciation with a little kiss? So I would kiss their cheeks as I sat on their laps, and sometimes one would move so my lips touched his, and so sometimes I would kiss them on the mouth. And one would call me across to fill his glass, and I would mince over to him daintily, and bend and pour his wine, and his hand would be upon my well stuffed trunk hose as I poured, and I would always smile because they liked their page to be obliging.

One night Pierre came into my bedroom when I was in bed, and lit a candle and sat down beside me, and under guise of asking me if I was well content, he began to stroke me. He did this for a long time and it was very pleasant. And he admired my bottom and handled it most lovingly, and asked if I liked what he was doing, and I said yes. And then he grew more daring, with Did I like that, and that? And now he would put his cock where his fingers had been and I would be sure to like that too. I did. It was my first time. He said I was a sweet, sweet boy.

I knew he would be back for more.

He had two special friends whom he sometimes brought into the room when he came to see me at night, and sometimes all three would do what he did that first night. It was all done very tastefully and gently, and speaking to me most agreeably and always praising me – I had the whitest thighs, the smoothest roundest rump, the dearest little prick, the lushest little bush of maidenhair, the most delicious balls; I was a gem. They taught me all the intricacies of sucking cocks, directing my lips and encouraging me with compliments. And they liked me to wear only my white stockings, with blue garters and the high heeled shoes, and they liked to see me walk about like that, or to sit on their laps while they played with me.

All this began to seem most natural, the more so because at these intimate times they would talk in pleasant voices about cultural things, and talking to me too, as if I was quite properly dressed, till sometimes I almost forgot my near nudity. Everyone wrote poems and read them out loud, and we wrote songs and set poems to music, and Pierre even discussed philosophy with me and the current state of France, and talked to me about life at court and the character of our king, Henri III.

The castle of Pierre was not like the gaunt and crumbling stronghold in which I had grown up. Its walls of apricot-coloured stone seemed in the changing lights of the passing season sometimes amber, sometimes pink, its ornate crenellations the home of darting swallows, its circular towers topped with pointed mouse-coloured turrets.

Within the castle walls lay the garden where I sat so often with Pierre, as the sun warmed all the flowers to life. We sat within a railed trellis upon which peacocks perched. The turf at our feet was set all over with a flowery mead of daisies, violets, muguet des bois and buttercups, and the bench whereon we sat was turfed also, so that instead of woven cushions one sat on a cushion of little tiny flowers. There were red carnations growing in an ornamental pot, and both white roses and those striped red and white ones called rosa mundi tied against the trellis – the ancient roses that you see on paintings from a bygone age marvellous flat, as if sliced across, or packed with myriads of petals; the newer ones round and whorled, and soft as velvet.

A white hound lay nearby, a crimson collar about his neck. Bees droned in a tub of lavender.

There was a song written long ago set at this time of year and I learned it then; men had been singing it for hundreds of years.

> Li noviaus tens et Mais et violete
> et rosignols me semont de chanter,
> et mes fins cuers me fait d'une amourete
> si douz present que ne l'os refuser.
> or me laist Dieus en tel honor monter,
> que cele ou j'ai mon cuer et mon penser,
> tiegne une foiz entre mes braz nuete,
> ainz que voise outre mer...

It spoke of love, of May, of nightingales and violets, and a prayer to God for the achievement of love's desires

Amongst music and daisies, Pierre spoke to me of the King. "I was at court in the old days," he told me, "some ten years ago when Henri first came to the throne. They had obliged him to become King of Poland, you know – his heart was never in it, and as soon as he knew that he was needed in France he made all haste to get away. He had to escape from Poland like a figure of romance, through secret postern gates and hidden paths, hiding in peasant huts. They were sorry to lose him, the Poles, they had never seen anything like him! Such an ornament, so painted, so exquisite...Of course, no need to relate that back in France everyone was quite relieved to see the demise of King Charles – even his own mother couldn't wait for him to hurry up and die, so that her favourite son Henri could mount the throne. Maybe she hoped it would distract him from some of the other mounting he was doing – but let us not be vulgar! The nobles had high hopes of him – well, anything would have been better than King Charles – but poor Henri managed to upset them all. He would be privy and to make certain his privacy was respected – he ate his meals with a little velvet rail about his table to be sure that no one spoke to him. It was a very pretty little rail and I'm sure contributed to good digestion, but those noblemen were accustomed to bursting in whenever they chose and telling all their grievances. And there was so much more they did not like – the darkened room where he would closet himself with free-thinkers to discuss theology and philosophy but who knows what else? I believe that was when the rumours of sorcery first began to circulate. People are so credulous, young Marc – why, the things that were supposed to have gone on in that dark room of his! Satanic masses – abduction of poor peasant boys for nefarious purposes – the calling up of demons – once the rumours start, no smoke without fire, people say! His wild extravagant carnivals through the streets of Paris did not help his cause – the rich at play, while the poor looked on, their noses, so to speak, pressed against the opulent windows of the Louvre. And Henri somehow managed not to put matters right. He did not show himself in the streets dispensing largesse to the masses...a monarch must be seen to do his kingly tasks. But they are a strange family, all of them. None was exactly a God–given gift to the nation..."

I knew that their mother Queen Catherine de Medici had always been held in suspicion. Naturally her Italian background did not endear her to anybody. Everybody has always known that Italy was the country of unspecified vices, poisons, and princes who put into practice the cynical philosophy of Machiavel. When Catherine first came to France she brought with her a knowledge of secret potions, the sort that could be mixed in food or wine to cause a natural–looking death to those she wished removed; she had read the works of Machiavel and knew all the tricks to make herself powerful and successful. She had always been the silent power behind whichever of her sons was on the throne.

"She had this astrologer," Pierre continued, "a swarthy Jew from Provence called Nostradamus. He prophesied that her sons would be Kings of France – it was an open secret. Now how could he know that? And yet it came to be. There was first, poor François II, who married the lovely little Queen of Scotland, and died so painfully. Then there followed his brother Charles IX – and what a disturbed and unpredictable character that was! They said his mother ruled him, that he was a dog and she held the leash. He was tall with stooping shoulders, victim of his humours, one moment fierce and violent, the next passive and gentle. He was curiously attracted to the thought of pain -he whipped both servants and animals – I remember the squeals of his hounds...It was he who ordered what occurred on Saint Bartholomew's Eve...

"It is twelve years ago. King Charles is on the throne. After years of Catholics and Huguenots warring together, a peace is planned, with the marriage of the Huguenot Henri of Navarre to Marguerite sister of the King. Thousands of Huguenots come to Paris for the wedding. The Peace of St. Germain is to end our civil war. But there are those who do not want peace, and one of those is the Pope himself. Plot and counterplot behind the scenes, rumour and suspicion on all sides. The mother of the King of Navarre comes to Paris in the June. Queen Catherine recommends that she should buy perfumed gloves from her own Florentine glovemaker. Shortly afterwards the lady dies. What does one make of that? You know, Marc, do you not, that the perfume of a glove may conceal a deadly scent whose odours may bring death?"

He paused to sniff a rose. "They say this rose once grew in Persia, the treasured possession of a sultan. I like to think as well as roses he appreciated the sweetness of a fresh young boy..."

From contemplation of the ancient east, Pierre returned to what had happened in Paris.

"Regard the personalities of the marriage itself – the beautiful black-haired Marguerite – she has no wish to marry Henri of Navarre – he is one of the sturdy masculine breed, coarse and crude – he does not wash or change his linen, and he has a string of mistresses of whom he makes no secret. Marguerite's first amour, they say, was none other than her own brother, our King Henri with whom she has so much in common – beauty, culture, a fastidious nature, unconventional ways – but now her love has turned to hate. Her one true love is now the Duc de Guise whom Henri hates. Why should he not? The Duke is tall and fair and handsome, and the people of Paris worship him. Wherever he goes they call Vive Guise! They call him King of Paris. King Charles hates his brother Henri – all their lives they are plotting one against the other, jealousies and rages no doubt started in the nursery, twisted passions, envies, slights real or imagined. The youngest brother, the Duc d'Alençon, is the worst of all – named Hercules at birth he is growing up to be most unHerculean – small, monstrous ugly, pockmarked of skin, of nose enormous. Henri calls him The Maggot.

"And now the streets of Paris are alive with provocative Huguenot gentlemen, ah, such an insult! The marriage is celebrated – at the threshold of Notre Dame, not within, for Henri of Navarre is a Huguenot. He does not look worthy of her; he looks vulgar. It is the Duc de Guise the people cheer.

And then what happens? Someone tries to kill the Admiral Coligny as he walks through the Rue des Poulies – a shot is fired from a house in Saint-Germain L'Auxerrois – whose house? a servant of the Duc de Guise. The assassination fails, but the Huguenots clamour for justice. And is it that they plot then to be revenged, to kill the entire royal family, and place Henri of Navarre upon the throne? My boy, it is to be hoped they did. For if not, then what followed is the outrage which the Protestant world holds it to be. So let us hope the Huguenot leaders plotted, and needed to be destroyed.

"All the bells rang out – a signal to the initiated. The massacre lasted three days and nights. Originally I believe it was at the instigation of Queen Catherine, to make sure that this time the Admiral died, for he had begun to have influence over her son Charles and she feared to lose her power. The Admiral did most certainly die, most violently, and his body was flung into a courtyard, where the Duc de Guise kicked in its face. All the obscene indignities were then perpetrated upon the wretched corpse. There was indiscriminate slaughter – private feuds settled under cover of religious fervour. People hid in their houses and dared not go out. *I* hid – and I was a Catholic! For days afterwards there was blood in the streets, bodies to be found in alleyways, mangled corpses in the Seine. You did not dare look about you for fear of what you might see...

"I have read Protestant pamphlets on the subject. They say that King Charles was tormented by hideous nightmares as a result, and that when he died – young, two years later – he saw the ghosts of the slaughtered victims haunting the passageways of the Louvre. Don't you believe it. He thought he had done right, and the entire Catholic world supported him. King Philip of Spain sent congratulations, and in Rome they lit bonfires and rang all the bells.

"Even in France, you know, they thought that God approved, because a miracle occurred in the Cemetery of the Holy Innocent. A hawthorn tree at the foot of an image of Our Lady, which for four years had shown no signs of life, burst into bloom. The people flocked to look at it, and celebrated with music and prayers – the sick claimed to be healed and pilgrims came to honour it. It seemed to me that Paris was a very unhealthy place and for the moment it suited me marvellous well circumspectly to withdraw and tend my roses here."

Studiously we sniffed roses. Paris seemed far away and these events to me mere history.

"Your family is no friend to the Duc de Guise, I hear," said Pierre. "I should watch your step. He is almost certain to be the next king of France."

I had never smelt roses with such a perfume; it was as if it were something that one drank, and I drank it in.

"O yes," said Pierre, "Guise has his eye on the throne, doubt it not. He is the Catholic hope, the people's choice, and somewhat indirectly of royal blood. Let him bide his time. Henri's own character will finally cause his own undoing."

Pierre told me that Henri was an enigmatic king, full of contrasts. He was noble but degenerate, clever but indecisive. They said he secretly scourged himself in the convent of Capuchins, only to emerge and indulge in all the excesses which had caused his guilt.

"He was a lovely-looking man back then – dark like an Italian, very neat and slim and elegant. He has the most beautiful hands in France. O, and the clothes he wore, the jewels! He was even late for his coronation, so determined was he to be perfect as he made his entrance, changing his costume, rearranging his jewels to best effect. Of course, from the first there were his mignons. He had always had boy lovers; indeed he took several of them with him to Poland when he became king there. And now in Paris they were very much in evidence. You will have heard that they were pretty fellows, painted, perfumed, decadent. But they were more than that – they were brilliant swordsmen who lived at fever-pitch, recklessly, fearlessly. They were superb! Ah, the festivities we had then, the glittering evening balls. The court was all debauchery, all carnival. They said it was The Court of Silk and Blood, and Henri was the Prince of Sodom . . . You know what that means, do you not?"

"Well, I suppose . . ."

"It means that what I have been doing with you, the King does also. And in those days he cared not who knew it, and was lavish with his favours to the lovely youths who surrounded him. Some were quite humbly born – impudent rapscallions. Others were of noble blood, exquisite beings – it is a joy to remember them. Conventional people hated them. The King's enemies spread stories, they circulated books, scandalous ac-counts of daily life at the Louvre, saying that the entire palace

127

was given over to the pursuit of beautification, that whole rooms were used for the frizzing of hair, the powering of faces, the arts of love, and that all manner of lasciviousness was practised in beds with sheets of red satin...Ah, how the staid, the dull, the sanctimonious are threatened by the glittering, the exotic, that which is different ...And all of Henri's family detested those beautiful creatures. They were jealous of them, of their influence over Henri, even though many of these boys truly loved him, would have died for him – and did. His sister Marguerite, infamous creature, and that vile woman his mother had the Sieur de Guast murdered, stabbed to death in his bed. Henri was devastated – he gave his lover a splendid funeral and ordered all the court to attend. In St. Germain l'Auxerrois he raised a great monument over the young man's tomb. But still the enemies were hungry for blood, and the Duc de Guise put his services forward. A man of his, d'Entragues, insulted the Comte de Quélus, the loveliest of all the lovers, and the young man responded with a challenge. They fought a duel and Quélus was killed – he died in Henri's arms. In the brawling, Louis de Maugiron was killed also. Henri never truly recovered from Quélus' death. He had a jewelled reliquary made, and in it placed a lock of Quélus' golden hair. The court was put into mourning and another elaborate funeral followed, another impressive tomb. Soon afterwards, a Guise-backed band of ruffians killed the Comte de Saint Mégrim, as he left the Louvre late one night. He was slaughtered near the Rue Saint Honoré and left to die. Another ceremony, another tomb...

"The frivolous days were over, and for a while the king involved himself in penitence. He wore a hair shirt, he wore simpler clothes, he indulged in flagellation. People did not understand his sincerity – some thought it was a new fashion, and the foolish aped it, hoping it would lead them to pleasures. Again the air at court felt most unhealthy. Again I withdrew from court. Roses need much tending. I was afraid, you see. I too had known the King's embraces and I feared some indiscriminate continuation of the tragedies. They said the King lost all fleshly desire after Quélus' death, but I know it was not so. He still had boys – but – carefully, more circumspect. He has two particular favourites now, the Duc de Joyeuse and the Duc d'Epernon; but of course, he still has an eye for a pretty lad. You never lose that! But now he is more wary...now there is a very extensive bodyguard...

"But people do not forget, and the rumours are sometimes stronger than truth. Henri is a good man, with good intentions, misunderstood. Yet the gullible populace will cheer for Guise because he *looks* well and has the common touch – or Henri of Navarre because they think he's manly – Nom de Dieu! He is far more licentious than the king, but since he does it with women and with bravado, the misguided mob adore it – what a hero, they say, what a lover!

"The King, I fear for him. Paris hates him; and there are those others waiting to step into his shoes..."

I heard all this as if it were a tale of no connection with myself. I shivered for the mignons, I sympathised with Henri, I feared the Duc de Guise and Henri of Navarre. I wondered uneasily how our family would suffer from political changes. If Guise took over we would be ruined. But Henri of Navarre was a Huguenot; if he came to power would he impoverish Catholics? How threatening the world seemed when you thought about it. Better to forget it and lose yourself in love and music.

"Ah, Love!" cried Pierre extravagantly, as we sat with his friends in the garden. "As a young man one believes it is the justification of life, the only good thing in this wicked world. For longer than I care to remember, I carried a miniature of the Queen of Scotland about my person, close to my heart. I spent many fruitless but absorbing hours planning her rescue, leading a faithful band across those misty northern hillsides, crouching in the undergrowth, watching for a signal, and then one day achieving the desired fulfilment, to stand face to face with my darling, to kneel at her feet, to receive her grateful thanks as I led her to freedom..."

"From what I have heard, you would have done better to have offered your services to her pretty husband – he who was found with his manservant murdered in his garden, their nightshirts well rolled up around their waists!"

"No, no, my motives were of the purest, I insist. It was a passion such as a trouvère of old might have sung about, of most courtly sentiment. Ah, the adventures I imagined us to share, in disguise, sleeping in peasant hovels, travelling on horseback or in a dear little boat, until eventually she achieved the English throne and came to her rightful inheritance. I know that it was pure love I felt, for I had no desire for any reward for my care of her, simply the act of so doing. But I am older now..."

"And now you would take a reward – albeit modest!"

"How you misjudge me! I did not mean that at all. I meant that now I know love is not all. Hélas! The Queen of Scotland is still a prisoner and I have long since abandoned my romantic dreams; no, love is not the answer. Ah, you may smile, yes, all of you. Love does have a place, but in correct proportion. It is philosophy that enables the thinking man to survive."

And he introduced me to the essays of Montaigne.

"How can one not approve of the fellow," Pierre said, "when he writes so beautifully of his friendship for another man? 'In the friendship I speak of, our souls blend and melt so entirely, that there is no more sign of the seam which joins them. If I am pressed to say why I loved him, I feel that I can only express myself by answering Because it was he, because it was I.' "

Pierre pointed out to me that while others were at war over the finer aspects of religion, Montaigne was writing: "I do not share that common error of judging another by myself. I can readily appreciate in him qualities differing from my own. Although I am tied down to one line of conduct I do not as others do, oblige the world to follow it, and I believe in and conceive a thousand contrary ways of life."

I knew that though Pierre loved fine clothes and perfume and had a merry manner that made all perceive him as of a shallow nature, he did think much about the human condition and each person's relation to the great scheme of things. For particularly he liked: "We carry our fetters along with us...our soul cannot escape from herself...Let us so conquer ourselves as to be able to live really alone and then we live contentedly...Truly the sensible man has lost nothing if he has himself...we should have wife, children, worldly goods and above all health, if we can, but not be so strongly attached to them that our happiness depends on them. We must reserve a little back-shop, all our own, entirely free, wherein to establish our true liberty and principal retreat and solitude...the greatest thing in the world is to know how to belong to ourselves."

I lived in Pierre's cultured castle for some seven months and I owe him much. From him I learnt sensual pleasure and that I was desirable. He also touched my mind and improved my musical talents and shared with me poetry and dancing and pleasant talk. He gave me countless presents and a love of pretty clothes. It was a pleasure to be a page in his household.

Suddenly Jacques and Louis came and took me away. It was a surprise to me, though of course I knew my stay there was only temporary. But I was full glad to be going home, because I was missing Gilles, and had great longing to try out my new love skills with him. Once we had left Pierre de Villeneuve's château, my brothers were quite open about why I had been removed. They happened to know that Pierre would be in disgrace; somebody who coveted his land had worked for his downfall. It was political. They did not want our family name to be involved at all, and I was well out of it. I felt sorry for Pierre but relieved to have been rescued. I was grateful my brothers extricated me. Whether it was to save me or the family name it mattered not, and I had rather be with them than with Pierre in disgrace.

After dinner that first evening back, Charles called me over to him. "Where do you think you're off to, Marc-Alphonse? Come here, you little runt, and talk to me."

I sat on the edge of the table by his chair. He had called me that objectionable name all my life, but tonight it sounded different, like a term of grudging admiration or maybe acceptance. The difference was that now I knew I was pretty.

Charles eyed me thoughtfully, half amused, half wondering-ly. "Well. *You've* changed. De Villeneuve has done a good job on you. You even *eat* nicely now. What's happened to the little barbarian we nurtured?"

"I am glad you approve," I murmured, a little sarcastically.

"And what's this?" he teased, pinching my leg. "Silk stockings! White silk stockings!"

"They are more interested in fashion than we seem to be," I said pointedly.

"I see. You like to look pretty then, my little blossom?"

"Why not? I deserve to."

"Indeed, I think you do," he said. "You know, runt, I always considered you a surpassingly ugly infant. You were thin and scruffy and you had those noxious moles on your face just by your lip. I found you repulsive."

I put my hands over them instinctively and blushed. I found them ugly too. I would never forget that some uncouth peasant had once called "witch brat" at me.

"Pierre said —" I mumbled, "they were like beauty spots. He said intelligent people would see them as an enhancement. He

131

said only the ignorant would say a witch had put them there."

"Mort Dieu!" cried Charles. "Who said that to you? Has someone mentioned witches in connection with –? But this is monstrous."

"A long time ago," I said, uneasy. "I was called witch's brat."

"You should have told me. I'd have burnt his lips off."

"Truly, Charles..." I protested, alarmed.

"No, tis a slur on our mother, a monstrous insult."

"O!" I realised. Nothing to do with me at all.

"Well, Pierre is right," Charles decided. "Tis unfortunate that you have blemishes on your face, but they do add something not unattractive. You've become quite good looking. Pierre's taken off your rough edges. You bear yourself well now. People will observe you. How old are you now?"

"Nearly fourteen."

"I must think about your future. I suppose you let your English fall by the way these past few months?"

"Um..."

"Well, you'll have to make up for it; not disgrace us when you meet up with your bride, eh? Tell me something now, runt..."

"What?"

Charles assumed a foolish crafty leer, and poked my knee. "Did old Pierre ever come to your room?"

"No," I said, colouring up like a summer rose.

"No?" he teased. "Really no?"

"Certain," I snapped, wriggling off the table. Charles caught my wrist and held me.

"Tis said that Pierre has some rather odd habits?" he said significantly, I should add, by the way, that Charles was now twenty-six, with a wife and two brats and a third expected.

"If you had heard that," I said carefully, still gripped, "perhaps you should ask yourself whether in all honour you should have sent me there as a page?"

I do believe a little flash of momentary disconcertment lit his narrow eyes.

"I never listen to rumours," he said.

"Apparently," I said, "odd habits are in fashion in high places."

"Oh–ho!" said Charles. "We grow a pace, don't we? Well, hear my words and mark them well. Wherever they be, in whatever sphere, high or low, sodomy is a filthy vice. Anyone who practises it is a loathsome beast. All sodomites are."

"Yes, Charles."

"Go down to the village, Marc," he told me. "Find yourself a wench tonight." He peered at me quizzically. "I hope you are not still a virgin!"

I pulled free from his grip and his laughter, and turned my back on him.

It was about a year later when they caught me and Gilles in the hay, and set events in motion that finally led to my coming to England so hurried and alarmed and seasick.

III

"I would have a jewel for mine ear,
And a fine brooch to put in my hat,
And then I'll hug with you an hundred times."

IT HAD not been a bad year at all. I spent it studying and riding and lute playing and travelling. Charles thought I was civilised enough to go in company now; we visited and rode; I met people; we stayed with other families and there were banquets and dancing and watching masques and taking part; I learnt swordplay which I enjoyed as movement but hated in actuality. Tis true I faint at blood. Once some youth was badly wounded and several ladies swooned, and also me. Charles knew not where to put himself for shame.

I was desired of ladies in dark corridors, but I told them I was betrothed, pretending I was deep in love and faithful. As to youths, I did not dare indulge my preference in case my partner told, and caused a scandal. So I saved myself for Gilles, who I arranged to come with us and look after my horse, and under cover of concern for the animal, I spent much time in stables. Our friendship was loving and warm. We shared fantasies that we could go away to a perfect place where there were not lords and servants, and boys could love each other and not have to be secret. As to that monstrous blot on my horizon, my marriage, I put it from my mind. I wrote curt letters to Lettice and I had to keep up my English lessons, but it was never a reality to me. Now that I was older I was not mistreated, and I reached the age of fifteen happily.

And then they discovered us. The capture was so cunning and well timed I believe they had suspected for some time and waited for their moment. I turned and looked back over my shoulder as a creak on the ladder alarmed me, and found myself facing Jacques' dark visage. Gilles was naked, lying on his back, his arms around me. That was bad enough, but there is a certain brave honesty in nakedness – I was wearing a pink satin shirt, open, and white silk stockings with pink garters; all other parts of me were quite bare. Foolishly I clapped a hand over my visible bottom.

"Down," Jacques ordered, jerking his thumb behind him.

"Please let us dress," I gulped.

"Get the little buggers down," called – O! Charles was there.

"You dress," I told Gilles, and I went down with Jacques as I was.

Diable! I had never been so embarrassed in my life as I stood in the circle of my brothers, and some servants further off. Ordinary daylight it was, and the stable doors wide open, and I was spared nothing, from the sniggers as I climbed down the ladder, to the rage now I was amongst them. They were furious, in that curious way that people can be over that kind of misconduct – it rouses them like nothing else, except religion.

"What is he *wearing*?"

"Just look at him – have you ever seen anything like it?"

"Vile filthy brat – you have been fucking that stable boy, eh? I'll whip the hides off you both."

I twisted about imploringly. "I made him do it," I wailed. "It is all my fault – he had no choice – do not hurt Gilles –"

"Liar, you've been at it for months – I *thought* you showed an unnatural interest in horseflesh – and all the time you've been swiving in the hay like animals – Get him up against that post!" Charles ordered brusquely. "Rip the shirt from him."

"No, no!" I squealed, writhing about in the grip of Louis and

134

Jacques, who tore the satin off me and slung my wriggling body face first against the post, and tied me by the wrists, hands high, as when they used to leather me as a child. I started whimpering and snivelling, monstrous alarmed at the idea of having my beautiful white body marked, twisting around, all unconcerned for the moment about what I must look like. From the corner of my eye I saw that Charles had taken down a horsewhip, and I screamed and pleaded and promised every kind of repentance and good behaviour. I thought my appeals had touched him, because nothing happened, and dimly I heard Louis' voice saying: "Wait a moment – *look* at him!"

Then there was an odd little silence, and then whispers and quiet talking. I moaned from the suspense. And then they came and put their plan to me.

I knew our family was in dubious fortune, did I not? I knew I was an extra mouth to feed, I knew I cost money to keep? Here was a way – a most unusual and daring way for us to rise – How would I like to go to court and seduce the King!

The persuasion followed thick and fast. I knew the King was a lover of boys? Look at me – they'd never realised till now what a tasty little thing I was, wriggling about like a harlot in my silk stockings – I was a perfect peach! But they would never have suggested it to me had I not shown I liked it and I was that way inclined besides – just like the King! Twas so delightfully convenient! Henri would be much more exciting than a stable boy! Did I not know his court was full of pretty boys, his mignons, and once they reached the royal bed they could ask for anything – gifts, land, castles...Why, with sufficient guile I could be as Diane de Poitiers was to Henri II, a famous and established mistress with influence surpassing the queen. Charles said he had *wondered* when I came back from Pierre's – he had often suspected I had learnt some bedroom tricks there. And so that was why I never chased women, eh?

"I am betrothed to Lettice –" I gasped faintly. "I am promised..."

"We will arrange – fear not – leave that to us –"

"I am not courtly," I moaned. "I don't know how to behave..."

"You shall be trained..."

"Ah no," I quivered. "'Tis horrible."

"How can it be, if it pleases you to do it with men? The King is not repulsive. He is not even old. What is he, thirty-six, something like that? You must! It's the way out of our difficulties."

"Charles, I *know* about the mignons – Pierre told me. They *die*...Everyone hates them...the Queen Catherine...the Duc de Guise...the King's sister Marguerite...these people organize murders, horrible murders...I would be too a feared.."

"No, no, that was mere rumour...and some while ago, assuredly. I daresay those young men were in part to blame in that they somewhat flaunted themselves and strove to offend. But you would not act thus. Besides, I think Marguerite stays not at court these days; I thought she was in Navarre with her husband. All that was long ago, was speculation, tis nothing to do with you. In truth, Marc, this is a wonderful chance – we would be foolish not to try our luck..."

"No!" I screamed. "I won't! I won't!"

"You will!"

"I won't. And you dare not horsewhip me now to force me because I shall be marked, and my value spoilt!" I crowed.

I was still praising myself on that brilliant deduction when Charles said calmly: "You will. Gilles shall be put in the dungeon. What transpires there will depend on how amenable you are."

I stared, stunned, my mouth hanging open. Servants had bound Gilles' hands and were leading him away; I saw them go through the door, Gilles hunched and bowed, and hustled by his guards. I began to weep.

That was when I learned that love makes you vulnerable, and people use it against you to achieve their ends. I sobbed against the post. Its splintery wood prickled my body. I pressed my hot wet cheek against it, defeated.

"He will," said Charles. "He will do as we say. He'll go and be a mignon. Will you not, Marc?"

"Yes," I said. "And I detest you."

"There is much work yet to be done," Jacques said. "But I wager we'll have him installed in Paris by Christmas."

O! But at the Court of Silk and Blood!

Throughout that Autumn I was trained for my new role. My feelings about it were split, as you might expect from Gemini. I was both alarmed and excited. Most sure, I was heartily relieved to be rid at one blow of Lettice and the dismal future she had represented. Suddenly I was very much the centre of attention, and I did not object to that. I and my body were suddenly very valuable commodities, so much so that to some extent I could make terms. At least I bartered for Gilles' release from the dungeon – not to freedom, they did not trust me enough for that, and rightly so – but to a small room in a tower. I knew he would be unhappy, and he would feel enclosed and stifled, but at least he would not die from cold and dirt and be gnawed by rats. He would be well treated as long as I was compliant. So I set myself to do all they wished, and some of it I tolerably enjoyed.

A man – le Sieur de Breussy, a highly civilised courtier – came and instructed me. He taught me court behaviour. One of the oddest lessons was how to bow in a peculiarly lewd way, according to the King's wishes – very, very low, with your head right down near the floor, the while making a sweeping obeisance with your hand. What this does for the behind can be imagined. I had to learn the tune "Belle qui tiens ma vie" on the lute, because the King had writ it, and everyone was singing it to gain favour. I had my ears pierced so I could wear the pretty ear rings he liked to give as presents. I had some new clothes – a cream doublet embroidered all over with curly green leaves, and pale green trunk hose very short to show off every inch of leg; and many pairs of white and cream stockings, and shoes with bows and heels. I had a wondrous hat decked with small pearls, and the stiffest ruff you could possibly imagine, and wider than I was used to; also matching rufflets at my wrists. Then I was given my dagger and instructed how to use it, but not how to cope with my sentiments on such an occasion. Sometimes I enjoyed my preparation so much I half forgot what it was actually *for* and that Gilles was locked up alone; and then I'd feel dread for the one, and fear and guilt for the other. As I grew more courtly and supposed I was giving satisfaction, I asked Charles to let Gilles go. He would not and I flew at him in a rage, and he held me off at arms' length saying: "Do you think me an imbecile? You would not go through this without the hostage."

Would I not? I could not say. I knew only that what I was embarking on did seem as reasonable a course as any, and suited

137

to my tastes, and if Gilles had been set free I cannot think I would have chosen to go back to the idea of Lettice, or to follow any other. My determination must have been passing great, because I did not baulk at what I had to do next.

The Sieur de Breussy was not an ugly man, but he was not the sort I fancied. He was pallid, effeminate and affected, and his voice was high and silvery. Yet when he set about to make sure I could manage lovemaking, I did not give any resistance. I was glad to have had Pierre and Gilles first, one for courtliness and one for true love, for if that man had been my first I would have found it all a cold dispassionate business. My mind strayed to other matters as I allowed him all liberties and watched him panting over me. I felt some scorn for him – but who knows, maybe he did for me? He was paid to break me in.

All was reported back to Charles, who viewed me with some wonder. Charles for all his other vices had never been a sodomite, and could not decide whether I was a martyr or perverse; certainly he did not understand me. But he appreciated my dutiful sacrifice for the family name, and when it was all over and I was a mincing painted little ingle in apple-green satin, he said I was a good boy, and I could take the key to Gilles myself and let him out.

Then I went pale under my powder. Take myself to Gilles like this? Show him what I had let them turn me into? The shame I felt was not for me but for Gilles – to think that our family had the power to deprive him of his liberty for three months, without justification, and now could set him free and were answerable to no one for what we had done. In another story, perhaps, I would have set Gilles free and sneaked away with him and joined a band of outlaws and travelled, had adventures and made love; but not in this. My guilt and shame were so great I never saw him again. They let him go, but I did not seek him out; I could not have met his eyes.

And so we went to Paris, and as Jacques said, I was installed by Christmas.

Paris was enormous. It was eight times as large as London. Never had I seen a city so big. From afar it was all spires and ramparts; within its city wall it was a mass of streets and squares, narrow winding alleys, and huge impressive buildings; some inspiring like the great cathedral of Notre Dame and the Sainte Chapelle, some sinister like the Bastille with its dark towers and its cannon. Around the church of St. Severin there were colleges and convents, a place of passage-like ways and little cramped courts where Pierre Abélard had preached to students sitting upon bales of hay. And there was the hill of St. Geneviève, where there were dens of thieves and every kind of disreputable character. Beggars were everywhere, sleeping on the cobble-stones, pestering at knee level as one rode past. And all was built around the river, gliding its silver way beneath the bridges, beside the waterfront; and there at the water's edge the noble palace of the Lourve, where lived the King.

Since I was only there in Winter, my memories are all of that time. Streets of snow and slush and rain, snow puddles splashed by hooves, shuttered windows, diamond-paned, the arrow tracks of birds' feet in the snow on the wide window ledges, the snowflakes seen at windows framed by pointed arches. Within, the tapestries, the bright-painted panelled wainscotting, ela-borately designed; and everywhere the blue and gold of the fleur de lys, the symbol given to Clovis by an angel. Fires burning in small rooms, dark cold corridors between these warm places, the bare edges of the glinting halberds of the doorway guards. And more, it never seemed silent. Even when it might have been, when silence was expected, there was always music, always a distant lute somewhere, hidden, melodic but eerie, as if a ghost played it.

I lived in Jacques' lodgings, in the Rue de l'Arbre Sec, and we lurked at court as visitors, coming away at night. The main gate of the Louvre on the Rue d' Autriche was opened by the guards early in the morning, and from then onwards the corridors, the antechambers, the galleries and staircases were thronged with courtiers all eager to press their causes. Some spent days and days waiting to be seen. I caught sight of the King long before I was presented, a dark-looking man in sober clothes with a small linen collar, his eyes hooded, his face languid and serious. When he dined in his antechamber, musicians played for him, and I noticed that all his food and wine was tasted by another first, and a large bodyguard surrounded him.

Some evenings we attended balls. My first impressions were of intense darkness in the shadows, intense brilliance in the light.

139

So much jewellery, so much glittering! I had thought that there might be but few women in attendance, but this was naif; there were many women there, and what fashions! The wheel far-thingale was then the style, as if the lady protruded from the hub, with spokes all round, floating in a circle. They had peascod waists and sleeves slashed open to show other colours beneath; and ruffs like fans. All the men wore ear rings and high heels, and in the light of many candles and flambeaux they sparkled from the myriads of small jewels sewn into their brocade. They wore long padded doublets with heavily puffed out sleeves, and some wore Venetian breeches; and the more daring wore short culottes and pale stockings, so that anybody might admire a well shaped leg as they danced branles, courantes and gaillardes. I saw raiment of crimson satin patterned with gold, green, azure; black velvet, peacock blue velvet, tawny velvet; white leather slashed over crimson lining. On the prettily tiled floor small dogs frolicked – indeed, it was hard to dance without treading on them; along the walls there were arched niches wherein statues stood in graceful postures; and the King sat under a crimson canopy on a dais with a red carpet, and a coat of arms above.

He did indeed have lovely young men about him – all bright and rich and very painted, glowing in mulberry taffeta and copper gold and blue velvet. But there were lovely women also, and nothing I saw seemed particularly outrageous or publicly shocking, as some Protestant pamphleteers would have us believe. Moreover, there was also a queen, Louise, and I had the impression that she and Henri were devoted to each other, and most assuredly gave a show of their being so.

Jacques took the earliest opportunity to strew me in the path of the King.

"My brother, Marc-Alphonse du Plessis Mornay..." and I made that incredible bow.

It was over in a moment, and as far as I could tell I had made no impression at all, for nothing happened. I noticed in that brief moment that the King wore black and white silk and a small black velvet cap, and he was bearded and wore long pearl ear pendants. His perfume was musk and violet powder. His hands were glittering with rings. But I seemed to have made no reciprocal impression and assumed I had been seen as one more face in the dazzling crowd about him. I remember I felt some relief, thinking that my brothers would sense it had all come to naught and take me home again. Certainly not. We are here and we shall stay, I was told; these things take time. And so I was encouraged to take part in any festivity I was offered, and I made friends with one Matthieu who had already caught the attention of the King, and we took part in a masque at the celebration of the Purification, and I played Andromeda.

I could not fail to be noticed in such a part, dressed as I was in a white silk robe and chained to a rock, which was wheeled on and off when needed. At this court people seemed to take especial pleasure in dressing in the clothes of the other sex. I have seen men with beards accoutred as women and much relishing it; and some of the ladies looked marvellous attractive in doublet and hose. In this masque some ladies wore short Grecian tunics and sandals, and carried swords; and boys were dressed as nymphs and sirens. Behind me on my rock, a servant with bellows crouched to blow the folds of my dress about as if it were the wind; and sweet music played, and there was Neptune and a monster, and melodies sung by the nymphs, and new poems read about the majesty of France; and finally Perseus saved me. He was a bearded muscular nobleman who had many affairs with married ladies, and seemed untouched by the nearness of youthful male beauty, and assuredly showed no proper tenderness as he tore away the chains and carried me to safety. However, others had been moved by my plight and my sweet voice as I sang a doleful playnt, and I was sent for by the King.

O! You would think, would you not, that to be so summoned would merit pages of description, rivulets of emotion, many superlatives – it was not so. I was far too nervous to appreciate the honour done to me; and barely able to take in the wonderful richness of the tapestries that lined the walls, the presence of the many guards past whom I was escorted, the paintings and the ornaments – they were as in a mist. The King was in a small warm room upon a couch, and lapdogs about him – seven at least, which he tried to order into a basket, but they would not go, and servants had to lift them away.

The King wore a dark blue velvet robe and a velvet cap. He was not quite bald, but he did not have much hair, and he was vain. He had a clever pointed face and a small beard and moustache, and melancholy knowing eyes. Drear to report, he had a very poor skin, visibly so. I was sorry he was not more beautiful, though his natural elegance was so striking that it more than compensated. He was glossy and scented, musk and violet emanated from him, and a feline grace, together with unmistakeable intelligence. From the first I admired him immensely. I admired him because he was not secret. Take the Queen of England (if you want to) – she is secret. If she has lovers she hides it; she tells the world she's virgin, but what about Robert Dudley, what about Thomas Seymour, and O, so many others? She is all counterfeit. Take the King of Spain, a spider spinning secret silent threads from a fortress in the mountains. Who knows what he is really like? But Henri cannot hide it; he loves boys, he loves the decadent, the bizarre; he cannot help his ways, he must show the world. Let the world make of him what it will. Chance has made him king – I do not think he welcomed it and I do not think he is overmuch interested in politics. Why cannot the people love him, he wonders, as they do the Duc de Guise and the King of Navarre? What is it that makes the populace love a monarch, and historians to nurture a good legend to live on after his demise? People seem not to love Henri overmuch – no, not even his lapdogs do. He wants to be peaceful – people keep fighting. Why is the world so difficult? But here in this room it is not difficult. We can shut out the world. There will just be young boys' flesh, firm smooth skin, yielding limbs – and tomorrow presents, for you to remember a king desired you. That was the atmosphere of that room.

His long pale hands were very cool on my skin.

"Remind me of your name," he said.

"Marc, mon roi."

He gave a cynical laugh. "How subtle are Heaven's ploys to keep the conscience squirming. I ought to send you away. I *will* send you away – I am not so dominated by the lust of the flesh that I could not put it aside if I chose. No need to look so bewildered. The last boy I sent for was called Matthieu; I tend to see the Almighty's hand in these coincidences, the Almighty Eye, like the one that followed Cain, twinkling through the arras! We shall not be prevented, eh, Marc? No divine signs, no mysterious patterns. I shall simply hold you in my arms, but I shall swear a private oath and say Heaven save me then from Luc and Jean!"

Naturally I could think of nothing to reply; but it was not expected of me, nor was it wished.

"I suppose you have thoughts in your head, Marc?"

"Yes, your Majesty."

"Carefully built up over the years, lovingly nurtured by tutors...philosophy, history, manners, political views..?"

"Well, to some extent..."

"I want to hear none of them! If there is anything I do not want to hear about it is thoughts. Thoughts would be superfluous in a boy like you. A boy who looks as charming as you need never bother with thinking. And if that body of yours can manage to banish some of the thoughts I am obliged to entertain, then you shall receive presents in the morning."

"Mon roi, I had no thought of anything but pleasing you, and I certainly expect no reward for what is also pleasing to me..."

"Enough, Marc," he said, kissing me. "Indignation is inappropriate. Just give pleasure. Then let the good Lord send all twelve apostles! Yes! Let him send them all at once, and as soon as he pleases!"

It was my first taste of satin sheets and I found them enchanting. But I could never forget it was a king I lay with, I could not forget where I was; everything conspired to keep it to the forefront of my thoughts. For all that I had been schooled in lovemaking, I felt that I must have seemed inexperienced and gauche, with nothing but the natural attraction of youth to recommend me. He said I was a lovely child. A servant escorted me back to the main gate when it opened in the morning.

Later a messenger came to my lodgings, and I received pearl and silver ear rings, wrapped in black velvet.

"This is no life for men at arms to live,
Where dalliance doth consume a soldier's strength,
And wanton motions of alluring eyes
Effeminate our minds."

THAT arch-enemy, the Duc de Guise, I saw quite often
from afar. Tall and manly, with fair hair curled above each
ear, a pointed beard and moustache, and a prominent scar
upon his face, he was handsome and distinctive, and one could
not miss him. I watched him with macabre fascination. I noticed
that his hair was turning grey, that he looked sometimes tired.
His famous scar so distorted his good looks that sometimes
when he smiled, he could be seen to be also weeping, for the scar
made his eye run on one side of his face. How sinister he
seemed, our enemy! But I never spoke to him nor he to me, and
now, well clear of it all, I cannot help but realise how much fear
stems from rumour. Pierre had told me that it had certainly been
Guise's man d'Entragues who killed the beautiful Quélus, and
to the King's face Guise had said that anyone who killed
d'Entragues in revenge would find himself spit upon the point of
Guise's sword. And so it was true the Duc despised all mignons,
and with the antipathy between his house and ours it made my
position a vulnerable one. Such sophisticated entertainments as
we indulged in to enliven winter glooms must have seemed
provocative and offensive to one who already despised frivolity
and effeminacy, and I believe that foreign ambassadors who also
felt threatened by the different sent scandalized and hostile
reports back to their masters.

But rumour and fear spread rarely without some justification.
One week in February I was seized with stomach pains so
griping I could not leave my bed, and when I met with Matthieu
again, where he lodged in the Rue Béthisy, I learnt that a like
case had befallen him, and a lad named Raoul who had been a
favourite of the king some months ago. Weak and shaken from
our recent illnesses and the obvious conclusions at which we had
arrived, we stood at a window watching the white sky beyond
the gabled rooftops and the thin spirals of smoke from winter
fires.

"It would have been the blancmange," Matthieu decided. "Do you remember, portions were handed to us – it was not on the table already – and there was excess of almonds, to disguise the taste."

In a gloomily matter of fact way we both assumed poison, and neither of us wasted time suggesting other.

"Last year some bunches of grapes were laced with a poison from Italy," said Matthieu. "I have never touched grapes since. A boy who ate them died. We suspected," he lowered his voice, "the King's mother, the Italian woman."

"A witch once gave me a toadstone. If someone wishes to poison me it will sweat and turn cold in my palm."

"And has it done so?"

"I can never tell. Since I have been at court my palms sweat constantly from fear and my hand that holds the stone is always cold. And so the stone has no effect."

"There is nothing one can do against an unknown assailant. Remember what happened to the Queen of Navarre – never accept a present of a perfumed glove nor any gift which smells unnaturally sweet. And meanwhile take every delight in such moments as are fair, and cheer yourself with the hope that you will surely have a lovely funeral!"

We smiled wanly, and outside a fine sleet rattled against the window. Far below, walked people hunched against the cold, who shivered only because it was Winter.

I was amassing presents from my visits to the royal couch – a belt with amber studs, the one I have with me in England, a second pair of ear rings, each with a small pendant pearl; a fleur de lys ring, and some embroidered gloves; and once in view of all the King did ruffle my hair!

My brother Charles sent for me, to his place in the Rue St. Honoré, where he was with his wife and children. Out of politeness' sake I knelt down with the brats and played with them beside the hearth. When Charles' wife came in, she gave me a look one might give to a worm, and hissed: "Filthy little beast!" at me, and snatched her infants from me as if I would by breathing turn them into catamites – O! Perhaps she thought I wished to swiftly bugger them while I had a moment to myself!

Charles patted her in the doorway: "Calm yourself, my love!" he said, and came into the room alone.

Then he poured me wine and spoke me very fair, and said how all knew I was regularly with the king; and then I had to smile, because he wanted to ask me how it was going, was all progressing well? And yet he floundered over his words, because it did embarrass Charles to talk about men making love together, and he went all delicate. Truthfully he felt the same as his wife – it would come naturally to him to spit abuse at me for foul practices, and he had to pretend a worldliness and nonchalance he did not feel. His problem was he wanted some land and he needed me to ask. It was a portion of a duchy, and many nobles wanted it, and all those who had the friendship of anyone close to the King were busy applying themselves, cajoling, begging, bribing.

"The time is ripe," he told me fawningly. "A word in his ear tonight, eh? For the family?"

Suddenly I realised what power was. Truly it had never much struck me before. I watched him flattering me; I was detached.

"Charles," I said casually. "Kiss my hand."

He thought that I was jesting, and he frowned.

"No, truly," I insisted. "And kneeling. Otherwise I don't ask for your bit of land. You are begging now, and must act submissive."

I extended my hand cynically, with its royal ring there to remind him what I was; and he knelt down. What he thought and suffered as he seethed there on his knees I can only fancy; but he kissed my hand as I commanded. Maybe he thought I was gratified – that my position at court had gone to my head and inspired me to demand this tribute. But no, it was nothing of that kind. I did think to pay him back for all that he had done to me, and for what he had helped to turn me into. But I found I felt nothing. I did not care if he kneeled or rose. I wonder if that were the saddest – I did not want revenge; there was not even passion. I just said coldly: "And tell your wife to treat me better. For what she said to me today I could have her punished, and you too."

This was not true – I would never have asked mean things of the King, and he certainly would not have pampered any whim of mine for the asking – but Charles was not to know that. Next time I came to Charles' house his wife curtseyed to me and did look a little pale. I favoured her with a haughty glance. Yes, I suppose I did enjoy their dread, a little.

Towards the end of February we heard the dreadful news of the execution of the Queen of Scotland. The entire nation went into mourning, and the court was stunned, scarce believing it could be true. On the twelfth day of March the cathedral of Notre Dame was draped in black and we attended a requiem mass there for her soul. Guise was there also; he was related to her. Thirty years before, Queen Mary had been married in that very cathedral as a beautiful young girl. And now she was dead, and in such a way!

"O vanity of human greatness," said the preacher, "shall we never be convinced of your deceitfulness..."

People clamoured in the streets and cried she was a martyr, a saint. I thought of poor Pierre who had cherished dreams of saving her. Many men had been devoted to her, for her beauty, her helplessness. She had thrown herself upon the mercy of the Queen of England, only to be treated so! What a cruel unfeeling woman Elizabeth must be, what a monster! The very air quivered with outrage and fevered agitation; and I who had never been particularly deep in my religious fervour was introduced to a crusading priest. His name was Lionel Fulbrook.

I was dining at Charles' lodgings in the Rue St. Honoré, not far from the English embassy.

"My youngest brother, Marc," said Charles, and I noticed now the difference in his tone. To this stranger, brought here by Laurent, Charles seemed quite proud of me, and indeed I did look rich and fine. I had never owned so many suits of clothes, for it was well known that the courtiers changed their outfits every day so that no one could accuse them of poverty or monotony, and it amused me how my brothers sweated to make sure I was the same. I even heard Charles' wife complaining to him that he put me first before his family, and his reply: "Be silent, Isabelle, Marc is our nest egg!"; and I had sniggered; I have been called many things – but *that*!

"I leave tomorrow," said Charles' visitor. "More than ever now – since the execution – I am inflamed with a sense of urgency. I am unsure what the political effects will be – whether the authorities will relax now that the figurehead of potential rebellion is gone, or whether their vigilance will increase, to batter home their vile assault."

"The figurehead may be gone," said Charles. "But not the

147

potential for rebellion. All the world knows that King Philip has his eyes on England. All he needs to be sure of is that if he were to land, the English Catholics would rise up in support. If one comes as a deliverer, one needs those that are crying for release."

"Well, that is why I am needed, and others like me," said Lionel. "Some Catholics are fainthearted, others are true, but unable to contact those of like mind. It is for me to keep their faith alive, to bring them hope."

In my ignorance I found Lionel a somewhat ridiculous figure. A heavy English accent distorted his speech and he had a way of talking that contorted his face and made him ugly. He was of unprepossessing appearance moreover, ordinary, forgettable of feature; and to hear him talk of bringing hope and being inflamed made me want to snigger behind my hand.

"You were trained by the Jesuits, I assume?" Jacques enquired.

"And what of that?"

"You are an Englishman. Do you see your mission as religious or political?"

"Religious," answered Lionel shiftily.

Charles scoffed. "How can you make the distinction? If you take proscribed religion to folk to whom it is forbidden by law, then that is political. What are the penalties for Catholics in England these days? Monstrous fines – prison? And you think you are dealing with the good of their souls? Moreover, you, an Englishman, are by implication working against your Queen. How can you reconcile that?"

"Charles, you are insulting," Laurent interposed. "Lionel faces indescribable danger – if caught, a vile and unspeakable death..."

"Of course, forgive me," said Charles graciously. "I admire your dedication."

He did not sound as if he did.

Lionel explained: "I believe in liberty of conscience. Everyone must be free to believe what he wishes to believe."

"No, there I cannot agree with you," said Laurent, "and nor would the citizens of Paris – what, would you have the world overrun with Huguenots?"

"Logically, yes," said Lionel earnestly. "If you allow liberty of conscience to one, it must be to all."

"Ah, you are English; it's different in England," said Laurent.

"You have not had years of religious wars."

"I am speaking in ideal terms," said Lionel. "Ideals are always hard to reconcile with the particular."

I sat and watched Lionel's mouth move as he chomped his food.

"You don't look like a priest," I remarked. "Even Laurent my brother has a more spiritual air."

I sensed Charles holding himself back from slapping me, as he had been so used to do before I became important.

"Excuse Marc," he said hurriedly. "He still has things to learn as regards good manners."

But Lionel laughed. "I don't look spiritual, do I? And that will be the secret of my success. Even you, Marc, must know that on a mission like mine one goes in disguise."

I sniggered. "I could lend you a lady's dress and an exquisite wig."

Charles silenced me with a look.

"I have a contact in Southwark," Lionel answered, equally enough. "The south bank of the River Thames, Marc, a somewhat disreputable place. He runs a cookshop. I am to be his assistant. Tis true, mine is the kind of face that looks at home in a tavern of the meaner degree. I shall blend in with my surroundings very well. Do you see, I shall deliver pies!"

Charles shuddered. "And how does that accord with the elevation of the Mass? The two seem far apart."

"You would be surprised to hear the tales of the adventures of travelling priests, I think," said Lionel wrily. "The strange hiding places, the deceptions...Some country houses in England have special secret hidey-holes built in – between floorboards, behind panels that open with the pressing of a carved knob, staircases in the wall that begin from the seat of a big old chair...Divers more unfortunate priests have on occasion hid in haylofts and horse troughs, or in disguise as pedlars. So, as to delivering pies I embark upon it cheerfully. If it achieves my ends it will be no hardship."

"Tell me," said Charles thoughtfully. "I believe you when you say that you are for liberty of conscience, and I believe your intentions are well meaning, to keep the faith alive and to cheer and refresh the faithful...But there are other men, less scrupulous, who make the journey to England – intelligencers in the pay of King Philip. Their intentions are wholly malicious, in that since the Holy Father gave his blessing to anyone who undertook to work against the Queen of England, they may claim divine approval for whatever they do. If such a man came to you and asked you – in the name of the religion you both share – to deliver messages – seditious documents, weapons even, concealed in your famous pies, what would you do?"

"In all honesty, I know not what I should do," said Lionel, his face blank and empty.

"Because then, you see, your mission would be political. You would be a traitor."

"My mission is religious," Lionel persisted.

"You may find it is not possible to be the one without the other."

"It must be possible," said Lionel. "The only truth is freedom of thought."

"For spies also? Are they to be free to think, and cause what havoc they will?"

"I believe they are."

"A spy who worked for the Pope would be doing God's will," muttered Laurent, "whatever his mission."

It was understood what he meant, and we shifted uncomfortably.

Charles shook Lionel's hand.

"I wish you well," he said, "with your pies. I also wish you well in the intellectual juggling you will have to do as you try to work out your conclusions."

"You are a brave, brave man," cried Laurent emotionally, clasping him in an embrace. "A brave, brave man..."

Inconsequentially I tried to imagine Laurent as a travelling priest. I knew he was a coward, or should I say a peacemaker, and I could not picture him in England, secretive and cunning, facing the threat of a vile and unspeakable death. I giggled foolishly. None of this had any connection with me.

One day I was alarmed to find in a heavily crowded gallery at the palace that I was within a little distance of Queen Catherine de Medici. She was surrounded by ladies in waiting of exceptional beauty, and a throng of courtiers pressed about them. Even so, for a moment I had a clear glimpse of her and, I swear, she of me. She was dressed in black, and she was monstrous fat. She did not look at all regal, but very bulky in build, though her clothes of course were marvellous rich. Her face was yellowy pale, her eyes large and bulbous, her lips heavily painted and her neck extreme thick. I stared in dreadful fascination, as Perseus might have done at the Medusa. Through my mind tumbled in chaotic sequence the terrible tales I had heard about her, a fiery whirlwind of stabbings, poisonings, revenge and plots, slashed across with four thousand screams, those who had perished by her command that fearsome August night. My lips parted, bone dry, and I swallowed. She moved her head and spoke to an attendant. He looked at me. My face paled beneath its powder. It was almost as if she had said: Who is that? Who is that young man? and as if there had been answer, and the information absorbed by her, secreted away for some time in the future when she might need to make use of it. The moment passed; the dazzling courtiers between us hid her from view.

For myself I was all of a shiver, my palms clammy-cold, my heart thudding like an unlatched door in a thunderstorm. That night I asked Charles if I could be taken home.

"Home?" he frowned. "To Jacques' place?"

"No, home away from Paris. I'm so frightened... you cannot know..."

"O!" said Charles irritably. "What have you to fear, now that you have lain with the king?"

"Everything! And for precisely that reason!"

"Calm yourself. Your fears are fancies."

"What about the poisoned blancmange? What about that?"

"What indeed? The cook had dirty hands – a dog pissed on the almonds in the kitchen – anything could have contrived to give you stomach ache!"

"Pains so fierce I could not walk!"

"You have always exaggerated your pain, even as a repulsive little boy."

"But Matthieu also, and Raoul?"

"You are all of that nature, and you know it. By all that's holy, if the summit of your fears is a poisoner so inept that all three of you recover within the week, you will live to molest us for many years to come!"

Naturally I was in no wise reassured by Charles' easy dismissal of my terrors. And these were further fuelled by an incident that happened shortly after. I was walking back to Jacques' lodgings when two men came out from a doorway and seized hold of me, and each in turn did spit into my face and call me sodomite and slut. It happened very quickly and they ran off and I knew not who they were; but I was very shaken at having their hands on me, and revolted by their spitting, which did trickle into my ruff.

"You were fortunate," Matthieu said gravely. "Spit will wash off; it could have been a weapon. Someone told me he had heard that the Duc de Guise intended killing us all one by one."

"Us all? Who exactly?" We each moved closer to the hearth and put our shivering bejewelled hands to its blaze.

"Every boy who might have pleased the King. They say he cares what foreign ambassadors are saying about the court. Other countries think we are all depraved, licentious and effeminate. They believe everything they hear, the wilder the rumour the more greedily they lap it up."

"My brother Laurent says that ours is a degenerate age. He says the religious wars have gone on for so long that we have lost all moral values. The finer aspects of taste have dwindled to vulgarity. All is affectation and vanity and lavish display."

"He would say that; is he not a priest? Priests always say that sort of thing."

"He says some of the fashions at court are so garish and gaudy that we look like Italian travelling players."

"What does he know of Italian travelling players?"

"Laurent has never been the most holy of priests. He knows about many things that ought not to concern priests. O! Will the Duc de Guise ever become king, do you think?"

"All Catholics hope so."

"I don't! What would he do to us? It does not bear thinking of!"

"Our case would be as Gaveston's. You know, the handsome favourite of King Edward of England. The jealous nobles murdered him. We had better pray that the succession goes to the King of Navarre."

"A Huguenot – he would make us repent, and walk through the streets in our shirts, with people slinging mud! Fortunately," I cheered myself by remembering, "the King is not old. He will live for many years."

We fell silent. We knew that some wanted him dead, and that he was constantly guarded for fear of an assassin's blow. It was true that wicked rumours were spread about him – that he practised necromancy, that he debauched young boys, and squandered money upon banquets while the poor starved outside his walls. It only needed a resourceful and dedicated fanatic to slip through the guards, believing he was his country's saviour...

"Marc," said Matthieu, touching my hand. "Let's go to bed..."

Matthieu was not a lover like Gilles had been, but we very often did make love. It was a necessary antidote to our most lively fears. Mostly it was in the afternoons that we lay upon his little bed with its four ornately carved wooden posts, its tapestried coverlet. The sheets were cold and strange in the chill of the daytime, and the sounds of the street, and passing of horses and trundling carts came up to us only as muffled noises softened by snow, distanced by the heavily fastened window. Above, the white plasterwork ceiling was curiously whitened still further by the effects outside of light upon snow. Sometimes when Matthieu's lips were about my loins I would look upward at this ceiling with its wrought vine leaves, grapes and dancing figures, its lyre players and twining garlands, and it would remind me of the court. I would imagine those white grapes painted with glossy poison, the vine leaves lightly laced with venomous powder. The dancing figures served but to remind me how vulnerable we all were to those who wished us ill. They could mix poison into your face powder, your lip salve. You expired in agony. The flesh burned away; everyone knew it. Then, startled from my dismal litany by Matthieu's kisses, I could forget, and lose myself in love; but only to lie shuddering after, as the ceiling whirled back into place and the leaves and figures once more took up their inevitable dance.

I had thought that the king's especial favourites, the Duc d'Épernon and the Duc de Joyeuse, might show some resentment and dislike of those who were the king's passing fancies; but no, so secure were they in their position high in his favour that they could treat us with tolerance and affection, albeit with some condescension therein. They even had mignons of their own.

153

I was standing in a crowded gallery amongst a throng of others when the elegant Joyeuse paused beside me in passing to commend me on my lute playing; and even gave me some advice upon which colour of doublet would best flatter my skin. I was basking in the warmth of such interest long after, and I became engaged in conversation with a gentleman who stood beside me almost before I realised it. With the buzz of talk around us and the milling of those gathered about, I did not give him my full attention, until it suddenly dawned on me that his words were laced with dubious meanings. I looked at him.

Cleverly he had begun our conversation as if he were someone to whom I had already been introduced, and I had assumed that in replying. Now I realised that I had no idea who he was. His face was of that sort that looks familiar, but then again not distinctive, and you cannot quite place where you met, but you are sure that you did meet. He was about thirty in age, bearded, neither handsome nor ugly, a face in a crowd, a passer-by.

"The King needs those about him that love him and wish him well," he was saying, idly watching Joyeuse. "Yes, these are troubled times. The faithful and devoted are to be sought and cherished. True friendship is a very precious thing."

I agreed with him politely. There was nothing to disagree with there.

"So many loyal courtiers...the King is very fortunate," my companion continued. "I am sure that you would count yourself in that happy number."

"I have that honour." I felt wary then. Whatever did he mean? He must have known who I was. Most assuredly I was considered loyal.

He confirmed this. "Everyone knows," he said, "that *you* are loyal to the King."

"Indeed I am, monsieur!" I said, insulted that anyone might ever doubt it.

"And young..." he purred, unmoved by my hostile tone, "and eager to demonstrate that loyalty, if ever one were to call for proof."

"I think you should explain what you mean, monsieur. No one has ever suggested that I am anything but devoted to the King."

"Calm yourself!" he laughed lightly, moving back a little as one or two turned to stare. "I am pleased to find you so proud. I would be interested to know your opinion..."

"On what, monsieur?" I said stiffly.

"On whether it is possible for a King to be completely safe, ever."

"His Majesty seems to me to be always perfectly well guarded."

"I do not doubt the efficiency or the bravery of his guards. But I ask myself, how is it possible for a king ever to feel safe, as long as he has...enemies?"

While I was perfectly aware that such random remarks about the state of the nation must be leading, however windingly, to some particular purpose, I could not conceive what it could have to do with me. I waited for him to continue. He turned us a little to one side.

"I am speaking of one particular enemy," he said quietly. "One whom your family has no cause to love." He eyed me closely, satisfying himself from the look on my face that I knew well enough whom he meant.

"Yes," he continued. "And many others feel the same. There would be strong support for one brave enough to...move him from this place."

I had some difficulty suppressing a highly mistimed snigger. The Duc de Guise was immensely tall. A foolish picture came into my mind of someone attempting to bundle him out of the room, and he immovable. But the seriousness of this gentle-man's business prevented him from supposing mirth anywhere.

"I know it to be true," he said, "that of all the King's enemies, this is the one he truly dreads. You know it, do you not, as we all know it – this man intends to be king, make no mistake. He is the most dangerous man in the kingdom. Those that love the King will know where their duty lies. I put it to you – one man could rise to fame this way, and earn the King's undying gratitude."

"Monsieur," I said, pointing out a fact so obvious that I hardly thought it needed stating, "I am not that man."

His face remained expressionless; the movement of courtiers and my own desire to leave his company separated us. I hoped I had misunderstood his meaning, but I knew I had not. I felt a sort of hysteria rising inside me – I dared not go within yards of

155

the Duc de Guise, let alone attempt to rid the world of him. I felt most bewildered that anyone at any level could have so misread my character as to think I could do so. I remembered that Pierre had told me that the Comte de Quélus and Louis de Maugiron were so brave that they responded instantly to the challenge of a foe. Did they think all mignons were the same? Was it assumed that if you went to the king's bed, however infrequently, you were prepared to risk your life for him? Should I be feeling ashamed for having refused? O! More than ever I longed to be far away from the court, far away from these people who left me so disturbed and confused, this troubled situation where I tripped this delicate balance between luxury and fear.

One evening soon after that, Matthieu and I were walking from the palace to Charles' lodgings in the Rue St. Honoré. These old narrow streets were a squalid mazy shambles and nobody seemed surprised at what happened to me. In the Rue du Coq, a dark figure came between us, and all so sudden that before I had any idea of his intention he had slid a dagger under my arm against my ribs. I felt pain and blood; I knew I was cut. Terror overcame me and fear made me swoon. Matthieu ran in panic and hid in a doorway. He saw the assailant look back and see me in a crumpled heap upon the stone, no doubt assuming I was slain, and then run off. Matthieu ran back to me and I revived. He lifted me and walked me to Charles', where I was lain in a chair, and my doublet and shirt removed. Wine was poured down my throat to restore me, and they gathered round me to assess my damage.

I was not badly hurt, only the skin scraped along my ribs and on my inner arm. I did bleed but they staunched it, me looking in the other direction very fixedly and shaking like a leaf in Autumn. I was left with a bandaged graze which healed neatly in time and bequeathed a scar.

"But who was he?" Charles cried once more.

"We don't know," Matthieu and I assured him foolishly.

"Whoever planned it, the assassin is always some none-descript," shrugged Louis. "Some hired vagabond, some disillusioned soldier."

"But did he not cry 'Take that, from the Duc de Guise?' Or anything?" Charles cried irritably.

156

"No, he was not so thoughtful," sniggered Matthieu nervously.

"You shall both stay here tonight."

We gladly took up his offer of a bed. My legs were like jelly, and I could not have walked a step.

"I did wonder," I suggested timidly to Charles. "It might have been something to do with a man who hinted that I might like to murder the Duc de Guise..."

"You?" hooted Charles in mirth and disbelief. "Murder? Anybody?"

I smiled wanly.

"And I refused. I wondered if I was now considered suspect, or something."

"'Tis possible. Who was he?"

"I've no idea."

"I do not fancy we shall ever know your assailant. There could be so many reasons... your role at court excites envy and disgust in people whose outward shows give away nothing. We should simply be glad that you are spared. There is yet much you can do for us with the King."

It was after that that Laurent came and took charge.

"This has gone far enough," he declared. "We cannot put Marc in danger. It has become too serious now. He must leave court before he is killed. Success at court is not worth the sacrifice of his life. And besides, *is* it success? A couple of scraps of land of doubtful value..."

How they did argue! Charles and Louis thought I should stay but have a bodyguard. It was a waste of all their work if I left Paris. But Laurent called them unnatural monsters, like the brothers of Joseph. Then he told us about his visit to an astrologer.

How sinister it sounded, as we sat there by the hearth, all lit by the glowing flames, the wind and rain pounding outside in the streets.

"It was a sordid little den on the other side of the river," Laurent said. "But not disreputable, no, some of the most famous in the land have visited that place..."

"You say that to appease your conscience," Charles laughed. "I know the place you mean. He has a backroom behind a curtain, and there goes on much that could be described as disreputable. I've seen his magic squares and amulets, his Grands Grimoires for the summoning up of spirits..."

"I know nothing of that," said Laurent quickly. "I went there with the best of intentions and solemn wish to understand something of the future fate of France."

"What did you discover?" Louis asked.

"Nothing good." Laurent shook his head. "His message was: Blood."

Charles groaned. "So what is new?"

"No Charles, it was not simply the habitual prophecies of doom. I believed him. Conflict all around, he said, to the north and south, and conflict on the sea. And within France, blood. A famous man would die."

"Who?" I demanded eagerly.

"He could not say."

Predictably Charles snorted.

"But it would be like a meteor's fall," Laurent continued firmly. "All will be confusion. And it will centre upon Paris."

"O!" I wailed.

"You should have kept it from Marc," Louis remarked. "He will be no use to us a gibbering idiot, and look at him already."

"I think tis right that he should know," Laurent said. "A man whose business it is to foretell the future has seen Paris in a state of conflict, and all this no further off than the next year. It must be obvious that the Valois court is not the place to be. I for one shall profit from his warnings, and I suggest you do the same. As for Marc, he must be got clear of this place."

Over my head they discussed me, as if I were so much merchandise. I shivered and scowled and listened to them planning my future. I was heartily frightened, there was no doubt about that. The stinging pain along my ribs reminded me that someone had made an attempt upon my life, and that I knew not who, made it so much more terrifying. I would have agreed to any plan that took me away from Paris. My fear was clearly apparent, and I daresay it was this as much as anything that convinced Charles that I had better go. If I had lost my nerve I had no use to him as a source of profit. I watched the flames that leapt high in the hearth spawning monstrous shadows on the walls. Rain hissed against the window. The dark streets outside were to me peopled with assassins. We were in the capital of European culture, the city of learning and sophistication. But what was it to me except a place in which to be afraid?

"We had better reconsider the marriage notion," said Charles. "And send him to England."

FIVE

I

"If words might move me, I were overcome..."

SEPTEMBER, and I was a travelling player and I was on my way to London!

In telling my story to Nicholas, in snatches here and there, as we travelled the southern part of England, I sensed that I was in some measure learning to free myself of my fears. The memory of those dark streets, the close perfumed rooms, the feverish gaiety that stretched taut over a surface that hid unfathomable depths of dread and deception – these were already almost dispersed by a summer spent in good company, sleeping under the stars.

When I told Nicholas about my meeting with Anthony, and the inn where I had seen him meet with Felipe whom I had to assume a Spanish spy, Nicholas shuddered. "You are not fit to travel alone! You are lucky to be here at all! How can you be so stupid? You could have been murdered for what you saw! I cannot believe anyone could be so foolhardy."

"O – please don't find fault with me," I winced. "I've told you Nicky, I am indiscreet and stupid; I've told you I am like that. I warned you I was a bad bargain."

"No," he said, shaking me. "You are lovely. I was angry with you because I care about you – and I'm sorry for you. You're so marvellous innocent, for all your experience."

"But after what I have told you," I began tremulously. "Do you not judge me? Do you not agree that I am wicked?"

"No, of course not. How can I judge you? I was brought up in a comfortable house with doting parents and two sweet sisters. You want to go to university, Nicky, you shall go – you want to go to London and write plays, well, we think that you are crazed, but if tis what you want, go with our blessing, and there is always a home for you if your venture fails. How can I judge? My childhood was all milk and lavender."

"But I, Nicky, I hardly dare well know myself, for fear of what I may find. I think it was ambition was my downfall," I maintained earnestly. "My wish to become Famous Down the Ages. I think I supposed that at court there would be opportunities...the King would elevate me...poets would sing of me...I would be a kind of Gaveston...I think I had hopes to change the world – you know – to dabble in politics, to tell the King what to do – to be indispensable, the secret power in the land." I frowned. "Nicky, are you laughing?"

"Who? Me? Indeed no!" he chortled. "O, Marc," he added, sighing but amused, "I suppose that to be indispensable to *me* would be a poor comparison for you, after the King of France!"

"No-o," I said cautiously. "No, tis pleasant to be indispensable to anyone. But I fear I have some compelling power in me – my wish to become famous – that may make me do bad things, as I have done. I fear I am going to be difficult for you, Nicky."

"I cannot but agree with you," he said ruefully. "Tis good that I am tolerant and care about you. Fortune directed you well when she sent you to me. An unscrupulous man would be a very bad thing for you. Lucky I'm like my horoscope says: mirthful and clean, not vicious, delighting in honest merry meetings and hot baths! You shall fare well with me, I know it."

I think I believed him.

Along leafy green lanes, past apple orchards heavy with fruit, I perfected the way I spoke and learnt my parts. We would soon be in London and would spend the Winter there, and I must be ready for a more critical audience. The country people good humouredly applauded anything, said Jack, as a change from working in the fields and with little to compare our plays against. Again and again we performed old plays and unsophisticated tales – things the people liked and could join in – O! I was many times a shepherdess and often did I weep for my love slain by a bear!

Between towns we would camp at night in a woodland clearing, a circle of carts and wagons with a little fire, and far

161

from finding it a raggedy eyesore as once I had done, I was growing to see it as the place where I lived. What were turrets – what were castle walls – fine monuments, rich dwellings? True security, true wealth lay in the heart of friends! This philosophy was less sweet in rainy weather when we were soaked to the skin and could not properly dry ourselves. Then did the wagons seem most unlovely, and our tempers often frayed like cloth edge.

Angel Pollock was far worse than Nicky or I as regards his amours – particularly as he had a weakness for married ladies, as, it seemed, did they for him. I was astonished women are so gullible. Wherever we went, his golden beauty attracted gazes. After performances, the foolish wenches hung about in hope that he would speak to them, and clamoured for some remembrance of him. Even foul things, as kerchiefs he had sweated into. I would not so have demeaned myself to ask for such.

And he was liberal with his favours; he would always go if one desired him. Sometimes we saw nothing of him for the night entire and he would creep back at dawn. On the days that followed, he played heroes that were half doubled up with back ache, and Jack swore at him beside the wagons. "By the twenty-four balls of the apostles!" he declared – for all had a liking for that one. "One more performance like that and I'll tan your hide off you, Gabriel. God's gift to women you may be, but I'm older and bigger than you and I will treat you like a naughty apprentice if I must." (He never did though, to my great disappointment. It was a favourite dream of mine that Gabriel would goad Jack too far one day and be obliged to take a beating . . .to struggle and resist a little, maybe, but to submit, and we all watching!) "Wield that sword as you should, and not as if it were a hedgerow switch and you were pulling hazel nuts!"

"O I am racked with pains!" Angel moaned. "I cannot understand it."

"I know a remedy for your particular trouble," Jack threatened him.

"Sick as I am, I will try to play my part," said Angel nobly.

"It is Playing and Parts that have caused your weakness."

"I swear it, Jack, I was abed all night."

"That is exactly what I supposed!" cried Jack in some exasperation. "And when we get to London you are to mend your ways. The girls are not so simple there, and their brothers will pay cut-throats to do their dirty work."

"Oooh!" we groaned and winced and clutched ourselves and staggered, as if we were all Angel when the London cut-throats had finished with him.

But it was true the country girls were simple.

One time Angel sent me to deliver a package to a wench who lived in a cottage down a narrow lane. It was a lonely place, with high wild hedges black with elderberries, dark with gloomy shady trees. I knocked upon the door, and there within was the maiden. She was not at all pretty as I was expecting, and I tapped the package meaningfully and said:

"I am sent by Angel."

She looked at me blankly, and I spoke again.

"I am sent by Angel. Angel, Gabriel." And she screamed and screamed, and I left her the package and fled, for fear someone would think I had gone there to molest her. It proved to be the wrong house, and Nicholas and Amyas were much amused to think that I had been supposed a divine messenger and the poor wench supposing my appearance holy. Angel was vexed and did not think it droll at all, for the package was for another who berated him after; and Jack said that sort of thing got players a bad name.

Another time Angel came running to the camp as if devils were after him. Gusts of thistle seed from the parted bushes flurried as he stumbled through.

"Hide me!" he panted, and we hid him inside the dragon, which lay flat upon the ground; and on his heels came two great country oafs all fists and muscles, crying, "Where is that whoreson player with the butter-coloured hair?" We protested we had no player like that but Amyas, who appeared and showed his hair and was duly brushed aside.

"No, no, not that fat boy-girl, no, he that kissed our sister..." And they stamped about and lifted coloured cloths and shook the wagons, and finally turned to the great and glossy painted dragon's head and the humps of its green body – only to pause with a yowl of terror, freezing as if turned to stone. For we had a Severed Head which Madge had made most skilfully with glass eyes and real hair and blood at the neck and gristle that hung down, and this head, disturbed by their actions, came rolling slowly forward towards their feet. Like village rustics in a play these two pursuers turned and fled, screeching and flailing their arms about – it was such a merry sight. And when Angel crawled out he was so hot from lying inside the dragon that he looked parboiled, his face as red as poppies.

But it was thanks to Angel that we returned to Canterbury, and that had an unexpected twist for me. On the wayside beside a tawny field of garnered sheaves they argued.

"Ah," Jack grumbled, swatting midges with a bracken stem. "It was not my plan to go back there. Why should we retrace our steps? They have seen our plays. We will be old stuff."

"Not a bit of it," Angel maintained. "That was back in May. Now that summer is nearly over, there will be different folk there – other travellers, pilgrims, anybody – and those that liked us will be pleased to see us back."

"And now the real reason, Gabriel?"

His exquisite features admitted a certain sheepishness – but how it suited him!

"I did tell a lady I would return."

"But Gabriel, you have told so many ladies that you would return one might make a pathway with them end to end."

"Jack!" cried Madge. "And what coarse talk is that?"

"All I meant was, it is a long way to go for one lady."

"She is special!"

Everybody groaned.

"She is!" cried Angel. "And I promised her –"

"If she is special," remarked Madge, "she will know that men's promises are nothing worth, and will not expect you."

"She does expect me. I made her acquaintance when we were there before, and between us there was something beautiful..."

"It was I!" cried Amyas spreading out his arms.

"It was not," grumbled Angel. "It was true love. That love which is swift and brief and sudden, and must be caught when it is seen, or feather-like it will blow away."

"That is not true love!" we all interrupted. "True love is –" and for an hour thereafter I swear we were all explaining what true love was.

"Ah," said Jack with a gesture of defeat. "By all the lice that

164

line a nobleman's doublet! We will go back to Canterbury."

"You are a miracle," Angel assured him with hugs and kisses I was green with envy to see wasted on Jack. "I will work like a Trojan. I will do whatever you say. I will sell my soul for you."

"Come, come," muttered Jack with uneasy laughter. "What kind of talk is that? We will have no selling of souls here. Who is this wench, then, that has caused you such a stir?"

"Her name is Joan," said Angel. "Joan Moore."

"Joan? An ordinary name for such a marvel!"

"And yet he must have Moore of her!" we chorused happily.

"Is she married? Your conquests usually are."

"Yes; to a shoemaker called John."

"How old is she?"

"But seventeen!"

I was to meet this paragon. The first night of our return to Canterbury found Nicholas and me sitting in a dark and stuffy tavern, and Angel in smirking delight, having found the lady and her as warm to him as ever. We were happy for him, and for ourselves also, merry with ale and each other's company.

Angel came across to us bearing tankards of golden mead, and sat down, complacent and manly, shaking back his glowing yellow hair.

"Is she not a peach!" he said. "A married lady too! She twists her husband around her little finger. And she likes players. She says they brighten life."

"'Tis true; they do," we agreed pleasantly.

"Are you not tired of each other's company? Why don't you let me find you a girl? I daresay Joan has friends."

"We're just like Joan herself — we like to be with players," Nicky smiled, and slung an arm around my shoulder.

"And where is she now? How could she bear to leave your company?" I wondered, leaning close to Nicky.

"She went to fetch something," Angel explained, looking back towards the door.

We sniggered.

"No," he protested. "Nothing naughty. She's gone to fetch some poems. You know whose sister she is, do you not?"

We shook our heads vigorously, eager to be surprised.

"Christopher Marlowe's!"

In truth I did not immediately connect the name with the one on my letter. I looked at Nicky, who raised his eyebrows impressed.

"Truly? You mean to say he is human after all, and came to manhood the way common to ordinary mortals?"

"Well, yes, I was somewhat surprised myself," admitted Angel. "To think that he has sisters – several, it would seem, and a mother yet alive and terrible masterful!"

Nicholas chortled happily. "All becomes clear."

"Who is he?" I said, just as I had to Anthony. A bit of a poet, Anthony had replied. Nicholas said:

"An odious puffed-up creature."

Naturally by then I had guessed it was the same as to whom my letter was addressed.

"Is he a poet?" I asked.

"Is he a poet!" cried Angel mockingly. "God's gift to poesy, if he is to be believed. O moreover, Nicholas, apparently he has had something of a success. I fear you'll have to fight the demon Envy."

"Envy *him*?" muttered Nicholas, so transparently doing so that even I could see it, who knew little of the subtleties therein. "Never!"

"What success?" I asked.

"Some play produced that's all the rage in London. I forget the name – some oriental warrior's tale, with much of blood and guts and high-blown speeches."

"Do you know him then?" I asked.

"Most surely not," said Nicholas firmly.

"Hardly at all," admitted Angel. "They use the Phoenix and the Unicorn; we use the Cross Keys."

"I have no wish to meet his sister," said Nicholas, "I think I'll go and have a piss."

He left quite pointedly as the lovely Joan returned. I think he thought I'd follow him, but I did not. Extreme curiosity kept me in my seat, my ale mug empty. From the beginning, Kit Marlowe was a source of discord between us. I partly felt disloyal by remaining; I partly felt a jaunty unconcern. Gemini is like that – split equally.

"Well now," said the luscious Joan, quite blatantly looking me up and down, "and who is this sweet jewel?"

I fluttered my eyelashes charmingly.

Piqued, Angel snapped: "Don't bother with him, my dear, you'll get no joy. That's a little Ganymede, that is."

I swear her interest quickened rather than subsided.

"Is he in your company, Angel? Are you, sweetheart? Going off to London with Angel?"

"Yes," I simpered.

"Move up," she said, and sat down by me. For a woman she seemed quite sensual, which surprised me, as I was not used to thinking of women in such terms. She had a wide grin and thick eyelashes; her hair was black and wayward, and she had a sort of mannish frankness. I make her sound odd; she was not; it was just that for a woman she seemed forward without being coquettish, as if she expected to be treated openly and plainly, and not pampered and wooed, as if she dispensed with feminine tricks and was simply a person. It was most pleasing, like being splashed with fresh water.

"Is it true, that you like men and do not care who knows it?" she enquired.

I blushed somewhat "The first part is true."

"O yes," she shrugged, looking round at the company. "These manly men have to have their feelings protected, do they not? We must not upset them by suggesting that there are other ways of looking at the world."

"Tis a shame," I agreed, "we have to be discreet."

"Are you discreet then?"

"No," I admitted.

"I daresay you've been much desired?" she said.

"Somewhat," I murmured, fluttering again.

"Godamercy," Angel sniffed. "Don't encourage him. He's full of self importance already. Thinks all who see him are beguiled by his charms."

"And many are," I shrugged reasonably.

"What are you — French? Italian?"

"French," I said, astonished at such confusion.

"Accents all sound the same to me," she said cheerfully. "Well now, I have these poems here." She slapped down on the ale-stained table a sheaf of papers that within a couple of decades were to become most priceless. "Tis some of my brother's early stuff, done when he was first up at Cambridge, and he wants it, and Angel said he would deliver it. Like I told Angel, it's only cluttering up the place at home; our mother's bound to throw them out some spring-cleaning time; she's no idea what he wants kept and what he does not care about, and I know you will be seeing him."

"Will we?" I asked Angel, frowning. "I thought Nicholas..."

"Nicholas won't be seeing him, no, but I shall. Particularly now he's had this play produced. A person needs contacts."

"Listen, dearie," said the amiable Joan to me. "You persuade Angel to let you go with him. *You* deliver some of it. I tell you, you will not be sorry."

Her expression was so laden with meaning I had to drop my gaze. Her eyes were very merry. I guessed well enough what she meant.

"You won't have any trouble finding him," she laughed, "not now he's famous!"

Well she and Angel went off then, and me, I was left alone at a tavern table with a sheaf of papers. Naturally I started reading.

All were written in a clear bold hand in very black ink; each began with a quotation in Latin which I could read. It so happened I started with this one:

> Envy, why carp'st thou my time is spent so ill,
> And termst my works fruits of an idle quill?...
> Thy scope is mortal, mine eternal fame,
> That all the world may ever chant my name...
> Therefore when flint and iron wear away,
> Verse is immortal and shall ne'er decay...
> Let base conceited wits admire vile things,
> Fair Phoebus lead me to the Muses' springs.
> About my head be quivering myrtle wound
> And in sad lovers' heads let me be found.
> The living not the dead can envy bite,
> For after death all men receive their right.
> Then though death rakes my bones in funeral fire,
> I'll live, and as he pulls me down, mount higher.

The arrogance reached me straightaway. Suddenly I recalled our conversation so long ago outside the country tavern with our feet in the daisies, when Nicky, Amyas and I had talked about fame and poetry, and the urge to be eternal and cheat death by becoming immortal through our words. I realised our hunger was quite small compared to this.

From the very first, Kit Marlowe came between us.

Not, of course, that he chose to; no, it was simply that I thought about him so much. I was the one to blame.

As Nicholas prepared the cart ready for our bed, I sat upon a stone beside a lantern and read the poems by its light. Nicholas knew it and he was grumpy.

"Nicholas – tell me – does Christopher Marlowe like boys or women?" I asked, frowning and earnest.

"How should I know?" snapped Nicholas testily.

"Have you heard *nothing*?"

"No, I have not."

"Who does he sit with in taverns?"

"His unpleasant cronies."

"Men?"

"Yes, men! Your horoscope is right to say you are a busybody."

"It's just that all his poems are about girls – they're all about someone called Corinna. "Then came Corinna in a long loose gown; her white neck...her breasts...her tears...Ad puellam ...my mistress..."

"Corinna isn't necessarily anybody, Marc. It's a symbolic name for a shepherdess, you know that? Like Corydon and Phyllida. Her name was probably Suzy!"

"No, for it is Latin."

"Show me," Nicholas took a couple and turned them over. "Well, look, Marc, they're translations, that's why. Ovid wrote them. Obviously he liked women. Shit!"

"What, Nicky?" I blinked. "We don't mind about Ovid, do we?"

"Take the scurvy things back. I said shit because as translations they're uncommon good."

"How can you tell?"

"Because they read like natural English."

"They are all about love," I said, "and quite forthright."

Nicholas snorted. "I can just picture how he spent his time at Cambridge."

"Can you? You mean reading Ovid?" I said innocently.

"Yes, in a pool of his own lust."

"Mm, some indeed are tolerable crude – about harlots and love bites on the neck, and –"

"Marc," said Nicholas, "if you don't put those poems away I

shall take each one and slowly and lingeringly burn it in the lantern flame."

I gasped, awed.

"O, Nicky, you would not!"

Nicky sighed exasperatedly. "No, I would not. Much as I mislike the fellow I would not destroy a word. Not for noble reasons, such as the world should benefit from good poesy and Latin translations rank as scholarship. No, simply because I know the sweat involved. Also, I cannot choose but smile to see that he is human and must rhyme 'arms' and 'charms' and 'mountains' and 'fountains' like the rest of us!"

"Nicky, why do you not like him?"

Nicholas came and stood by me and slowly eased me to my feet. He held my arms and looked into my face. "Listen to me, Marc," he said. "There are some things that lovers do to provoke lust. Talking about Kit Marlowe is not one of them. Now climb into that cart and turn your mind to other things, like pleasing me."

"Forgive me," I said chastened, and fluttered shamelessly so close to him. "Let us to bed."

I put Kit Marlowe from my mind, which was easy enough as I settled into Nicholas' arms. Secure in his love for me, if my thoughts strayed at all it was towards London, the goal of our journey.

In Dartford, in a market, I sold my dagger.

II

"Tell us who inhabits this fair town,
What kind of people, and who governs them."

AND so! I was in London!
I am tempted to continue: London is nothing like Paris. But how differently I reached those two cities, how divers my experiences in both! I saw Paris from brittle bravado born of fear and glittering greed; and also it was Winter, when

dark nights seem very black, and candlelight shows all faces in shadow. I saw London in sun and daylight, with the summer dust still on it, and the sights and sounds of Summer lingering on into Autumn; and my impressions were of bronze light and gilded mists, cider apples, pomanders and sweat, muskets and shouting, crowds and carts, and every kind of stink. As a city, well, I was ripe for falling in love with a place, and London was it.

Most striking as a characteristic – particularly so since I talk of bells! – was the skyline of spires and towers always ringing and chiming. For one penny you could climb to the top of St. Paul's tower and see all London spread below you. I did this with Amyas one sunny afternoon and we could see everything, the whole world, it seemed. To the north, London Wall and Alders Gate; to the east, broad Cheapside with all its shops and stalls, and all the tightly packed streets between there and Gracechurch Street, by London Bridge with the smoke of many chimneys; and to the south even as far as the river Thames at Blackfriars' Wharf, and the filthy Fleet River which did stink immense; and to the west, the noblemen's mansions on the Strand, whose long gardens backed down to the river, just beyond Ludgate.

"London is so small!" I marvelled. "You can see the fields and hills beyond."

"Small?" squeaked Amyas affronted.

"Yes, truly; you should see Paris."

"I have no wish to go anywhere near that foreign place," said Amyas haughtily. "I know not why I brought you here to insult me so."

"I do not insult; it is the truth. St. Paul's is not as pretty as Notre Dame and moreover it has no steeple."

"Why should it? Who needs a steeple? What a vainglorious idea, a steeple. I spit on steeples."

. "Are you a bird flying by, so to spit?"

Amyas giggled. "The steeple was struck by lightning a long time ago and no one has rebuilt it."

"I do not criticise London when I say that it is small. I find it very beautiful. All pointed roofs –"

"Gables."

"Gables, yes, and churches. And so many trees and gardens.

And the wall that encircles all."

"It has seven gates, also portcullises and turrets."

"I am impressed."

"All poxy foreigners are so." We fought for a while, and nearly became famous down the ages for falling from St. Paul's tower.

Our headquarters was the Cross Keys Inn off Gracechurch Street, a great big rambling place it was, several storeys high. You entered through an archway a wide rectangular courtyard, cobbled, where barrels were stored. Balconies ran round on all four sides. The innkeeper Master Meeres – red-faced and sandy haired with bushy eyebrows, and amazing strong – was not the unscrupulous kind as some are. He was good to us, providing places for our wagons and doing all he could to help us, for here we performed our plays. A stage was made of trestles upon barrels, and the nobler patrons sat on the balcony galleries, the ordinary folk gathering in the innyard, paying one penny. The profit came from the noblemen. It was a good thing for innkeepers to have plays performed in their yards, and we were a resident company there, a competent group, but not famous enough to perform in theatres. We met up with London players who joined us, and this meant we could perform larger plays, and Nicholas was constantly busy writing and editing and copying out parts. We performed several plays a week. In between learning our parts we had to perfect duels and dances and falling without hurting ourselves, as well as all the sewing and decorating and knitting chain mail. So many hours did I spend repairing the dragon's costume that I never wanted to see green linen again.

One of the first things we learnt on reaching London was that our patron Sir John Fordham had died, and so we were without a licence. This was a matter of some calamity because we were breaking the law; but Master Meeres said he would keep it a secret if it were not too long before we found another.

Meanwhile we did study and learn, indeed I worked harder than ever in my life before. But because I very much wanted to see London, Amyas helped me sneak out, and was only too glad to show me the sights. We saw the Theatre and the Curtain, two playhouses in the green fields beyond London Wall, and the archery grounds and artillery range where, because a Spanish invasion was constantly expected, citizens were obliged to train and practise with muskets and pikes. We had a look at the outside of the Tower of London, and we saw the tumbledown shacks of Wapping and Limehouse, and further off, Whitechapel Common surrounded by poor hovels and ragged streets. We gawped up at the Tower with frissons of awful fascination, and Amyas told me the names of the ones who had been murdered in the Bloody Tower.

"And the mortar is made with beasts' blood!"

"May we go within?"

"We might, but you have to pay those that show you round, and we shall either seem churlish or impoverished if we do not. Tis pity, because as well as dungeons there are caged beasts to see, and strange things from Roman times. They found casks of wine which the Romans had left and now tis all thickened up, and you may spoon it like a jelly."

"Why did they leave it? It seems a shame it was not drunk and enjoyed."

"It is a shame for *anybody* not to be drunk and enjoyed!"

Another time we ploughed our way down Cheapside, past the stalls of vegetables and shops, and there, bruised from the rubbing of hefty shoulders, my fine boot toes trodden on by clodpole feet, I paused and looked about me. It seemed that to walk among the masses one needed a different style than to walk among the great. There was not politeness and good manners and standing back to let people pass. If you hesitated for a moment, you were in fair danger of being trampled over by a country cart weighed down with hay, or thumped between the shoulder blades by someone's basket swinging aloft. Above my head the timbered buildings leaned, with brightly painted coloured signs creaking in the wind — lions, crowns, roses, mermaids. I was beside a stall that sold pears and apples and eggs, and all around me English voices clamoured — huswives shopping, servants pushing, carters yelling for a passage, and rough boys in flat woollen caps — apprentices — who shoved where there was no need, with no finesse at all, not even common manners.

Everything is different now, I thought. This way of life has to become my way of life.

I took a breath, and with a rueful laugh to think I had been taught to bow so low my face near touched the floor, I shouldered my way through the crowd.

"Look where you're going!" yelled a pedlar with a pack; and I thought: yes, I must do that, and not look where I have been.

I caught up with Amyas: he was buying suckets – orange pips dipped in syrup many times till they were fat with sugar – and as we sucked I stared beyond his head and down a side street, where of a sudden I saw an inn sign displayed. I froze with shock. The Phoenix Inn! There it was, the brilliant golden bird, its wings outstretched, and flames about its feet. I stood there staring. I could see the bulging wall, the timbered overhang, the dark-paned latticed windows.

"O!" I said. "The Phoenix Tavern!"

"Well, yes," agreed Amyas reasonably. "And so?"

I felt foolish then. It was a tavern, no more. But I had yet in my possession that offensive letter, safe tucked in my silk shirt, addressed to Christopher Marley. I had told no one, yet not a day went by without I thought of it, as if it burnt a hole in my shirt by its existence. The shock of coming upon that tavern, all unexpected, had made my heart bump and paled my cheeks. I had no explanation for Amyas.

"Well," I mumbled. "It is not far from the Cross Keys, is it?"

"No. But the Bell is nearer."

Suddenly a rush of choleric humour took me, and I sulked for no reason I could name. I did not want to leave that golden sign, but I had no reason to stay, and we were starting off back to the Cross Keys.

"And," I said vindictively, "the streets of London stink. I never knew the like before!"

Mildly Amyas remarked: "They stink far worse in Summer!"

London was a place of processions. Many times when I was out in the streets I would pause to stare at some diversion. There were funerals and weddings and the condemned on their way to Tyburn and men dragged to the pillory, with crowds accompanying that disgrace to yell and cheer; but some processions were elegant and stately. I saw courtiers pass on horseback, with liveried guards and pages, and one afternoon a slow and measured march of aldermen and merchants. They wore fur-trimmed robes and glittering gold chains about their necks. One carried a crystal mace, and upon velvet cushions there were Bibles borne, and golden cups displayed.

But suddenly I gasped. I recognised Thomas Hodgkin amongst them, as darkly impressive as I remembered him when, beside Gervaise Blysshen's hearth, he had assured me that he always achieved his desires. So! He was back in London! Hurriedly I faded into the crowd. Quickly I put a distance between myself and him. I did not think he had seen me. Surely he had forgotten me by now? He would not still cherish that old intention to make me his page. I would be safe – he would not visit the Cross Keys and discover me. Our paths would never cross if I was careful, and I would be.

But I was uneasy at heart. The procession had been to show the populace a display of wealth and power, two qualities which could both reassure and terrify.

On the first Sunday, and every Sunday after, Nicholas made me go to church and I did sulk.

"Yes," he said seriously. "You must. They always suspect players of sedition and misconduct, without us giving fuel to their fires. And you, Marc, have been foolish enough since you set foot on English soil, without adding to it by not attending church."

"But you know I do not believe in your services. They are all Huguenot here. I cannot attend. It is against my conscience," I added importantly, as if I had given it much thought.

"If you do not come, you will not only have a fine to pay but you are most like to land in prison, on the grounds of subverting Amyas and me who are good little Protestants."

"I don't see why –" I grumbled.

"You know how it is over here. We daily expect an invasion from Spain – they send us Jesuits over with every tide, to work on us and persuade us away from our beliefs."

"Are your beliefs so weak that this is a danger?"

"You know full well the whole matter is not so much religion as policy."

"Papists believe that it's right and proper to plot to overthrow the Queen," Amyas joined in, explaining it to me as if I were slow witted. "We, being tolerant, understand that you, Marc, are exceptional, but not all Papists are as reasonable and pleasant as you."

175

"You have to come to church," said Nicky firmly. "A matter of expediency. Nothing to do with religion; simply to prevent the authorities poking and nosing and finding out our company has no licence."

Because it was so plain that Nicky and Amyas – indeed, most of the company – were not devout and zealous but went to church for an easy life, I went along with them. If they had been staunch Protestants and noisy in their hatred of Catholicism I might not have gone, but I had already a loyalty to the company and did not want to bring trouble. I did not feel comfortable attending. I know it is the same God, but O how dreary it is without the golden paintings and the gilded statues and the sweet scent of incense! I found it bleak and bare and unspiritual, and my heart did not much lift, and the preacher was uninspiring. My brothers would have killed me if they knew that I had gone. But still, I thought, with a little guilty thrill, they never will. I'm free of them. And yet I did not *feel* free, not yet. My head and shoulders were clear, but my legs were still entangled.

I never grew to approve of what the Protestants had done to their old religion. The land where the theatres were was the site of an old priory – it seemed to me somewhat sacreligious to think that on that holy ground where monks had prayed, there was now noise and laughter and the merry wantonness of playgoing. Inside the churches, on the whitewashed walls, you now and then could see the faint shape of a face, some saint or apostle, now gone for ever, some scene of Hell or Heaven from the days when these were the picture books of the poor. And in the niches, emptiness, where once there stood a lovely statue or a holy chalice. One could perhaps forgive it if such spoiling had been done for honest care, but the Catholic church had been so rich. The Protestants gobbled up the land and grabbed the church's wealth. So how much was religion, how much greed?

On London Bridge there was a holy chapel dedicated to St. Thomas. Nicky mentioned it because it was well known, and we looked in – it was a grocer's warehouse. I found it sad to think of all the silence and the praying, and the candles making holy light in a small arched window over the water; a place of commerce now, where huswives go for flour.

And then I was diverted by the present – for London Bridge is very fine! It has twenty arches, and beneath the tide runs fast and swirling, and if you watch for long, you may see a boat capsize! We all did hope! Some will not dare go underneath it, but change boats the other side of it. Others have daredevil races through. Amyas said there were five prisons on the south bank, and every house there was a brothel. He said the watermen were very devils and always swore oaths, and some had compacts with brothel owners to abduct pretty boys and force them into servitude. He would not ever go to Bankside on his own.

"O," I said. "So many watermen would fight over one so gorgeous, that in the struggle you could easily escape!"

"Even so," said Amyas haughtily, "I shall not risk it."

"O – *shall* we go?" I breathed. "The two of us?"

"Zounds, no!" squeaked Amyas. "Truly, Marc, a part of you is very wayward, to go courting trouble for its own sake. What was it your horoscope said – easily perverted and given to ungodly knowledge? *You* would not be safe on Bankside either! It's true, you know, they really do have stews with painted boys that lurk in doorways, much like female harlots!"

"Well," I shrugged easily, "then you and I will never starve, and if we fail as players there is always that."

"Marc! Do not be foul!" said Amyas primly.

"I but jested...I think," I grinned.

Into my mind had come that picture envisaged by Cuthbert Hodgkin, of the sinful playwrights who diced and swore and brawled, and then fell into melancholy and despair. If anywhere, I thought, they would be on the streets of Bankside. I tried to feel a shudder of revulsion. But none came, and I knew that half of me was curiously attracted. I fear my horoscope spoke true.

Nor was that the last time I was reminded of that unsavoury Puritan whom I had encountered at my cousin's house, for often as we walked abroad we saw others of his sect about the streets. They looked sombre and unprepossessing as he – I swear I never saw a handsome Puritan, never one with merry flashing eyes and a laughing devil-may-care insouciance. But then I suppose that was somewhat unlikely, their business being to ensure that the devil did care, as he saw them spoiling the amusements of his flock...We saw a street brawl once, two Puritans caught hacking the head off a wooden statue, and a crowd about them, some enraged about the desecration, and some bawling abuse about Popish practices, and the Puritans loud in proclaiming the true voice of God, to which of course they thought they had direct access. All were still disputing when the Watch arrived, and they too then joined in and had their say, and we left them, the matter all unresolved.

Nicky and I slept at the inn in a garret under the eaves. It was so small it was hardly even a garret; it was simply a space where the roof sloped, and we could not stand upright, but did always lie – which suited us very well. We reached the garret from an outside entrance up a long and rickety wooden ladder with twenty-nine rungs. It was terrifying to mount. Even holding on with both hands it made the head feel very strange, and if by chance you looked through the slatted rungs and saw the street beneath, the world began to whirl and you wondered how mariners ever managed upon the rigging of ships. Then at the top there was an alarming moment as you reached up to open the door. It swung to and fro and like to catch you on the side of the head. You had to throw yourself in, and the door swung shut behind, creaking and thudding. But once within the little garret room all was well and safe. Far removed from the world we had our own world up on high, on a level with the birds of the air. Indeed we shared some of the privileges of the angels, for we could see the unfolding of human life below us; and sometimes affect the elements, for if we were too lazy to use the jakes we would piss into the air, and far below, the puzzled townsfolk would swear there was rain in the wind. We had a tiny window, and the sunlight covered us with golden dusty shafts where we watched the motes dance, and we had a covered straw pallet to lie upon. This little garret was a store room for apples. All the time we were there, apples were there also, rosy red, green and marvellous sweet smelling.
    Afternoons we lay on our fronts copying out parts, sharing the ink, and talking. I did most of the copying – it was this kind of thing:

>   *Music . . . he enters left . . .*
>   Lorenzo: My lord . . . *he kneels.*
>   Duke: Is't even so when under guise of friend
>   The false perfidious knave doth mock me thus

> But he shall see I am not to be vexed
> And thus (*stabs him*) do I requite his treachery.
> *Lorenzo dies. Enter a servant.*

It was quite hard work for me, being in English and my actual writing a little different from the English way, but I did persevere so that Nicky could write his Great Poem. This was a partly secret thing, and was the way Nicky intended to become famous down the ages. Long poems about lovers were very fashionable then. With your patron's name on the front, your poem might then circle about and eventually be printed and on sale in St. Paul's churchyard, where the books were sold. Nicky had not yet acquired a patron, but the poem was progressing. It was called "Lancelot and Guinevere" and it seemed to me very good and very courtly. It was all forest and faery, with something of the old ballads about it. Elves were in it, and white roses, and characters embodying virtues and vices, as in the "Roman of the Rose"; there was Love Ideal and Lust, and Loyalty and Bad Faith; all did appear within that forest, to bear out the states of mind of the characters. Nicholas was toiling with this poem, and marvellous preoccupied, because he still had to write blood and guts for us to act.

Well, I respected Nicky's work, and I very much valued his care of me, but a young boy cannot live on promises of later. As we lay side by side writing, I would stroke his back, down the lovely hollow of his spine.

"I love your shoulders, Nicky, they feel so strong, and your beautiful neck – do you know you have little tiny curls on the back of your neck, and – here – behind your ear – do you like what I am doing? – mm, your ear tastes nice – Nicky, mm, love me, Nicky –"

I contrived to glide under his arm, so that instead of his Great Work there was me, all winsome and eager, twining my arms around his neck, pulling him down on to me. He sighed and laughed, aroused, exasperated.

"Marc – how can I work? Listen to me, daisy, I've so much to do – O, when you do that – O you know I can't resist you."

And we would roll away from the manuscripts and pull off our hose, and run our hands all over each other, pressing close till the sweat poured between us, holding handfuls of warm flesh

179

and kissing skin, panting words of passion and endearment. I could not work beside Nicky without needing to seduce him, but then I was not writing a Great Work at speed. Sometimes I would ache to touch him, but when I saw his concentrating brows and the quill travelling across the page in full flow, I had to hold back; it would not be just. I respected his wish to be famous down the ages, and he must finish his poem.

And sometimes he told me so himself. "Listen, darling, I know you're bored and fidgety but I cannot stop just now. Tonight – you shall have all my attention tonight – all night – anything you want. But while it's light I have to work. Why not go find Amyas and see what amusements you can get up to? Go on, daisy, go find some sport."

You might say, then, that Nicky had only himself to blame when I persuaded Amyas to come with me to see Christopher Marlowe's *Tamburlaine*.

III

> "O, how these irksome labours now delight,
> And overjoy my thoughts with their escape!
> Who would not undergo all kind of toil,
> To be well stor'd with such a winter's tale?"

HOW COULD we not be aware of this potboiling drama? It was the talk of the town. Everyone said: Have you been? Have you seen it? I mean the people in the inn yard, the sparetime actors and the stage hands, for everyone was stage-struck and went to plays. And in the streets and in Paul's church-yard the playbills were up: "Tamburlaine the Great, who from a Scythian shepherd by his rare and wonderful conquests became a most puissant and mighty monarque, and for his tyranny and terror in war, was termed The Scourge of God – acted by the right honourable the Lord Admiral his Servants."

People who had seen it did show off by calling out lines they remembered, some jokingly, and some because they loved the sound the words made – as, when parting, humorously: "Go frowning forth, but come thou smiling home!"; and the famous one:

> "Is it not passing brave to be a king,
> And ride in triumph through Persepolis?"

And everybody spoke about how a king was put in a cage and taunted and was made to be a footstool, until he could take no more, and did brain himself against the cage. I was so excited at the thought of seeing it that I could hardly keep still, and all the way to the theatre I was bouncing and jumping and running, and Amyas puffing to keep pace.

We walked there with the afternoon crowds upon a blue-skied sunny day, jostling and jostled, over London Bridge, where the houses jutted out into the streets and carts could scarcely pass. But I was used to pushing now, and no longer landed squashed in doorways gasping at unmannerly behaviour. Only here and there upon the bridge could you see the water itself, and we did lean there whenever we could, and we heard that bellow of the watermen's that made us giggle.

"Oars! Oars!" they cry, and because it sounds like something else it was always pleasurably wicked to imagine them saying they have harlots for sale.

Down at the water's edge in places there is real sand, like the strand of a shore, which astonishes me when I think we are in the heart of a city, amongst civilisation.

The theatre to which we were going, the Rose, was new built, positioned close by the Bear Garden and the Bull Baiting. Some of the crowds were going to those entertainments, but I swore I would swoon if ever I saw a bear gorged by mastiffs till the blood ran down its sides.

"That is because you are a foreigner," replied Amyas sagely. "Englishmen don't swoon at the sight of blood. In truth we love it."

"You truly loved it, seeing the poor bear so slaughtered?"

"I have never been within," admitted Amyas. "But full-blooded Englishmen enjoy it, and therefore so would I. However, because you are a faint-hearted foreigner I will not take you to the bear baiting. But I do hope," he added with shining eyes, "that there will be blood enough within the playhouse walls today!"

And so did I. Pig's blood I could tolerate.

As we approached the theatre I felt much excitement. Passing the fine church of St. Saviour, we entered a maze of mean streets built over land riddled with ditches and marsh, little bridges taking us over the waters, and there on the south side of old Maiden Lane, west of Dead Man's Place was the playhouse. You could see the thatch of its roof edge up beyond the houses, its banner blowing in the breeze.

To my surprise, there was a small group of men in dark clothes gathered about the entrance. They seemed to be accosting the approaching playgoers, speaking to them urgently. As we drew nearer I heard what they were saying.

"We urge you, sirs, do not go in. In the name of the Lord we urge you. The Devil resides in that place, reaching out his hands for you!"

Amyas whooped with glee. "Puritans!" he cried eagerly, hustling me forward. "This is good sport – let's hear them." And he put himself on purpose where a Puritan could speak to him.

"Youth!" one declaimed. "With all your life before you – do not enter this accursed place."

"Why not?" enquired Amyas, in blue-eyed innocence. "What shall I see in there?"

"Sights which shall affright the godly and cause them to tremble. Slaughter, murder, war. And the Lord's handiwork defaced, for boys dress as women and use female ways, in a manner that Our Lord did never intend."

"O, horrible!" gasped Amyas. "Marc, do you hear? Is not that monstrous?" I grinned. The man then turned to me, tugging at my arm. His eyes were earnest; he truly believed the things he said.

"It is not simply the dreadful sights upon the stage which are unfit for a young boy's eyes," he told me, in a lower tone meant only for me. "But sometimes amongst the crowds there are low women – do you know what I mean? And they will tempt you to evil ways."

"But how do you know what takes place within, sir?" asked Amyas. "Have you seen the play? Have you entered in that den of the ungodly?"

"It is true that I have entered this place," replied the Puritan sadly. "It was my duty, as God's watchdog. Bitterly regretting it, I suffered in order to bring the message to others, that they may avoid the horrors I was forced to endure."

"But were you not tainted then? Did the Devil's hands reach out for you?"

"Fortified by the Holy Spirit I remained untouched by the evil therein. But others may be weaker than I am. And it is to those others that I bring my urgent warnings. To such as you, young boys in the flower of your youth. The door of this playhouse is like the split in the road, one way leading to the thorny path of righteousness, the other to the soft and slippery path of wickedness..."

"And we choose that one!" Amyas interrupted cheerfully. "So come away, Marc, and leave this fellow to his briars!"

We left the Puritans to minister to others with as little success. Amyas nudged me. "I half expected your friend Cuthbert Hodgkin to be amongst that motley crew," he said. "He lives in London, does he not?"

"O!" I groaned. "What a fearsome prospect, the idea of meeting Cuthbert once again! Do not talk of such. Did we not come here to enjoy ourselves?"

"We did indeed. And if you hear me giggling you will know the Devil's hands have found me and are tickling me about the privities..."

I smiled wanly. Were there any of life's pleasures, I wondered, thinking about the Puritans, that could be truly relished without some other person telling you that they were in some way harmful, wrong? Why was it that pleasure was considered such a dangerous thing?

But I forgot all such considerations then in contemplation of what lay ahead.

We entered, paying one penny, and pushed to the front against the stage which jutted right out into the audience, so we could see well from three sides. We tried to espy the hidden trap doors where devils might rise or graves be dug. We gawped about us at the galleries for the rich, with seats and a roof. We peered toward the inner stage with its curtain and balcony and watched the musicians assemble and guessed where there would be thunderbolts and cannon. We longed to play on such a stage.

We met – whether we would or no – many rough apprentices who elbowed us and trod on our feet. ("Kick them," Amyas advised amiably.) But when the play started we were all friends, to watch the unfolding of the story – indeed they lent us rotten eggs to throw if we so wished, but someone pushed us and the eggs broke against the doublet of a man in front of us, but amazingly he did not realise till after; and the play then took up all our attention.

The King of Persia was effeminate and played very humorous; he did mince and sulk and pout. When Tamburlaine came on the crowd did cheer, though all he did at first was lead on captive Zenocrate, a lady. He had a lovely speech for wooing her, so lovely that he seemed to be a man of tender sensibility, yet after, he explained: "Women must be flattered," and so it seemed it was all in cynicism, not in praise. When he persuaded the Persians to desert their king he had a noble line:

> "I hold the Fates bound fast in iron chains,
> And with my hand turn Fortune's wheel about."

And all the time I wondered *Did* he love boys, *did* he? There was Zenocrate the noble queen, no boy, and yet from time to time I could not help but think there showed some hints – the effeminate Persian king, and the description of Tamburlaine by Menaphon:

> "About them hangs a knot of amber hair
> Wrapped in curls, as fierce Achilles' was,
> On which the breath of heaven delights to play
> Making it dance with wanton majesty..."

That did not sound like Edward Alleyn, the actor who played the part; that did sound like somebody known or desired, some perfection.

This was a play that glittered. Of course, the sun did shine and the metal did gleam, but so did the words, and kept a person on his toes, all spellbound:

> "And with our sun-bright armour as we march,
> We'll chase the stars from Heaven..."

It was all jewels and flames, and many deaths on stage. And I did wonder once again:

> "Those Christian captives which you keep as slaves,
> Burdening their bodies with your heavy chains,
> And feeding them with thin and slender fare,

> That naked row about the Terrene sea,
> And, when they chance to breathe and rest a space,
> Are punish'd with bastones so grievously
> That they lie panting on the galley's side –"

for I thought: this is someone who sees in his mind the naked galley slaves; and so did I, and my prick did twitch, and not for the last time during that play. The lines were so *wicked*:

> "I will not tell thee how I'll handle thee,
> But every common soldier of my camp
> Shall smile to see thy miserable state!"

and:

> "Let these be warnings for you then, my slave,
> Or else I swear to have you whipt stark naked!"

And O it was even as everyone had said, for Bajazeth did go within a cage and be made to be a footstool, and Tamburlaine did *tread* on him, and they teased him with food; they said: "Feed, you slave, thou mayst think thyself happy to be fed from my trencher!" And then four Virgins were slaughtered-screaming! And the poor king did knock his own brains out! And we all craned our necks and stood tiptoe to see how it was done – O, very well! Blood upon the stage and little bits of brain – real brain, from a pig or a sheep, that floated in a little sticky pile. We cheered!

But I do speak as if it were all blood and gut, but no – from violence and cruelty we suddenly were assailed with poesy such as silenced all the yells and cheers. How we did love:

> "What is beauty, said my sufferings then?
> If all the pens that ever poets held
> Had fed the feeling of their masters' thoughts
> And every sweetness that inspired their hearts..."

(and divers other if's)

> "Yet should there hover in their restless heads
> One thought, one grace, one wonder, at the least,
> Which into words no virtue can digest."

I came away quite silent, not knowing where I was, my head all full of gold and flame and blood and the echo of the words. It was not enough to say we had nothing like it in France. Twas plain enough that they had seen nothing like it in London either. I felt like a beach over which a tide had rolled, churning up all my sand and pebbles. I wondered whether other people found it as seductive as I did, or whether it was just my peculiar nature, to feel an odd little shiver at the thought of panting naked slaves and forced submissions. And I was confused that so much poesy had been dedicated to Zenocrate, a lady, as Corinna in the poems. What if he liked girls, and had a mistress? And yet...

There was this one line in one of the poems that we had brought from Canterbury which had stayed in my mind: "Love is a naked boy." It was a poem about Cupid and his mischief, but how that phrase stayed with me! It jumped off the page at me – the picture of a naked boy lying on a bed ready, not Cupid at all. It sounded as if he spoke from truth, as if that was love for him the poet, he who had written this disturbing play.

"Amyas, have you ever *met* him?"

We were entering Gracechurch Street now, on our way home. Amyas minced and fluttered prettily.

"Met him? Well, not exactly. I mean not with a formal introduction. But I have seen him, most sure, often, and once quite intimate!" he smirked.

I gasped with jealousy. "How? Intimate?"

Amyas giggled. "I could tell you anything and you'd have to believe me!"

"I cannot fancy that he would have anything to do with you," I said huffily. "Someone so famous, and someone so *not* famous."

"He was not famous last year," said Amyas, "so there! He was but a mere student like Nicholas, floating about and reading his poems to people; he was only a poet. London is full of them," he added scathingly.

"About this intimacy," I prodded.

"O, I'll be honest," Amyas offered generously. "It was in Paul's churchyard. He was always there. It was especial crowded. I was in his way. He took hold of my ear and moved me out of the way, and that is all. I think ears count as intimate, do not you? It did hurt much."

"Is that all?" I said, disappointed and relieved.

"That's quite enough," said Amyas severely.

"Does he like *boys*?" I demanded.

"I do not know; and it would not surprise me. I have never

seen him with anything female, and he is very wayward. If it's different he's bound to do it, or so I have heard. He never propositioned me. But then, he did not see me well, in fairness to myself."

"If he had propositioned you, would you have gone?"

"Probably not," said Amyas hesitantly.

"Why not? What does he look like?"

"O fear not, he's handsome enough! No, it's just...I wouldn't feel *safe*. I prefer lovers who think that I am wondrous, and who, as they say, eat out of my hand. Preferably placid and rich. Well, he is not either of those, and I would have no power. You hear some odd stories..."

"What stories?"

"O ... probably untrue," shrugged Amyas, and said no more.

When I climbed up all the rungs to my garret room I found Nicholas tidying up his papers and I sat down and told him where we'd been. He was so interested he didn't sulk at all; indeed I had to tell him all my impressions and what the play was like and all, as if I were being examined by a meticulous tutor. His professional curiosity was far greater than his niggling dislike, and we did talk at length about it. I hoped he would explain his hostility.

"Why do you not like him, Nicky?" I wheedled.

"He is marvellous weird," said Nicholas unhelpfully.

"I suppose he wears a cloak with magic symbols on it?" I said sarcastically.

"Maybe," shrugged Nicholas. "And probably invisible ones at that. You know his name is sometimes spelt Merlin! I have heard it said he does not influence people for good. You know he is an atheist. He has some strange ideas, and he tends to convert other people to them. As you saw today, he has a fine line in rhetoric. I don't think he's a good influence, that's all. He leads people into trouble. And he is somewhat free with his fists... Tis odd that you should have gone to see his play today. Angel took those poems while you were gone, you know, the translations. He decided it might be a good move to ingratiate himself."

"O!" I cried outraged. "But *I* —"

"You?" said Nicky quizzically. "Yes?"

"*I* looked after them," I muttered. "*I* kept them safe. He should have asked me first."

I suppose I had planned secretly that it should be me who returned the poems and received the praise. It would have been the ideal excuse to arrive at the Phoenix Tavern, all sweet and innocent and doing good. And now Angel had done it and I was monstrous vexed.

Nicky slung an arm round my shoulder. "Let's go down and eat," he said.

The kitchen at the Cross Keys was a most agreeable place. There was always a fire burning in the hearth, with Phoebe the innkeeper's daughter at the cooking pot, and her youngest brother to turn the spit. The room smelt of breadmaking from the glowing oven built into the corner of the wall. There was a clean-scrubbed heavy table and some stools, a stack of logs beside the fire, and tubs of vegetables and sometimes fish, and hams that hung on hooks below the rafters; and all the pots and pans and pewter plates upon the shelves, and herbs bunched up to dry, and then about the fire the chimney crane and grease trough where they caught the fat for making candles. An immense striped cat was always there, supposedly to kill the mice but all he did was play with them and let them go, in spite of which he was much petted. At some times of the day the kitchen was a mass of movement with serving men and wenches darting to and fro; at others a peaceful place, as now.

Halfway through our meal, we caught sight of Angel's blond head as he passed a window, and he was trying – and failing – to look inconspicuous and slink by unnoticed. But we were so inquisitive as to what had happened we would not let him, and we rushed out to grab him and bring him in. He was much distressed, moreover he had a monstrous black eye, the cause of the distress.

"What about my livelihood? My beauty?" he demanded. "What will I look like tomorrow, and I am Corydon! If Madge can't fix me up with some remedy I shall be ruined. Worse – ugly!"

"You never could be," Nicholas assured him. "You are beautiful even now – truly you are."

"But how?" I gasped, fascinated by the purple.

"You think players are excitable? You should try poets. It never occurred to me that he would take it like that. I told him he should have thumped his sister; it was not my fault."

"What? Was he annoyed you played around with Joan?" asked Nicholas. "He was angry about you and his sister?"

"Not a morsel! He was angry about his poems!"

"What about them?"

"He said she should never have given them to us. He seemed to think we were not to be trusted with something so priceless. As if I care about his scurvy poems! He had the idea we'd snap them up and say that they were ours. I hadn't even read the whoreson things. As if I'd want to put my name to his poems – I am a player!"

Nicholas looked thoughtful. "But what he says is true. I would not have blacked your eye but I can understand the feeling. All that way, all those miles from Canterbury in a players' cart, in the keeping of players and poets. If we'd been anything less than the wonders we are, we could have had them printed up by now, and received payment. Come now Angel, you cannot have been surprised – he always hits first and speaks after."

"Thank the Lord *you* are civilised at least, Nicholas," grumbled Angel. "You manage to turn out plays at a fast rate without crippling everyone in sight. And now I must soak my face in medicaments."

Nicholas sighed. "Yes," he said. "I'm good and rational and pleasant – and unsuccessful. I suppose one has the choice – the violence and passion and glory – or to be a pleasant person whom people like."

I had not the words to encourage Nicholas. I accepted his love of me but I did not return it; I loved to sleep with him and enjoy his body, but I had not the wisdom to cheer him, and as always he did it for himself, and therein lay his strength.

It was not Madge who fixed up a potion for Angel's bruise but Phoebe Meeres, the daughter of the innkeeper.

"O let me!" she begged, and sat Angel down to minister to him, in a chair beside the great hearth.

I watched Phoebe with Angel, a little twang of jealously gnawing at my guts. She was a thin-faced, snub-nosed thing with a little stem of a neck, and a mass of corn-coloured hair which she wore beneath a little cap, curls and tendrils poking through. She was comely of build, small, and slim of waist. She wore a neat ruff atop a plain dark gown and an apron. She was always busy in the kitchen, turning her hand from gutting fish and disembowelling chicken to creating pomanders and scent bags; all her talents seemed so useful. I envied her because her care of him would lead Angel to grow fond of her, and he would take her to bed if she would have him, and her doting glances said she would. And I envied him because he had spoken with Christopher Marley in his room, and because Phoebe would be besotted just as all the others; and I envied the start of their growing affection. I blamed Kit Marlowe for my discontent. Love is a naked boy, I kept thinking, awed and quivering; love is a naked boy. And all the while depressed and tormented, since it was in no way aught to do with me.

SIX

I

"All which hemm'd me about, crying 'This is he!'"

S TOP! For this is Satan's workshop!"
      I was marvellous amazed. I ceased my singing, my voice
trailing away, my lute strings twanging tunelessly, and all
upon the stage beside me turned likewise to stare at the
interruption of our play.

"Sing on!" Jack hissed. "Tis but a poxy Puritan."

The man had come in amongst the crowd like an ordinary
playgoer, but now, having gained the attention of us all, he
pushed aside those about him, and with an assurance I admired,
and a loud bellowing voice, he cried:

"O, cease these profane fables, these lascivious words – these
are not fit matters for Christian men to talk of. It is the first step
down a path whose end is villainy and degradation. You penny
knaves," he turned to the audience. "O, shun these harlotry
players, they will turn your souls from righteousness and lead
you to the murky mire of sin..."

Our loyal followers at first thinking that the interruption had
been part of the performance, now turned in anger upon the
Puritan and yelled him down. With shouts of "Out with him,
throw him out" they heaved him bodily from the innyard, and
he still railing, still protesting. I watched it all. With my slippered
feet upon the cloth-covered trestle, a potted tree beside me, and
my lute upon my lap, I hardly felt an artisan in Satan's
workshop. Yet how bold he had been, our Puritan, to spout like
that, to offer himself to ridicule and violence. In his misguided
way, what zeal he showed, what careless indifference to his fate!
He was our first!

After him, we gradually grew used to little upheavals of that

191

nature and were ready for them. Sometimes we silenced them with a loud blast in their ear from a crumhorn or we would sound thunder at them, rattling a cannon ball in a drum – there were many ways to make them leave.

Once we had one at the door. For an hour or so before the play began he stopped passers-by and walked up and down with a banner reading "SIN WITHIN". To those who passed he shouted: "Do not enter! Within that place are drones, wasps, caterpillars, mites and maggots , crocodiles, wolves, vipers –" To the rapidly growing throng who loved nothing better than to see a menagerie, he yelled: "I mean the players! O yes! Go within if you would learn how to be faithless, how to deceive your husbands and wives, how to murder, poison, play the harlot, ravish, lie, and learn the words of filthy songs of love!"

Jack let him rant. He said they did more good than any notice we put up. Indeed some of our audience thought the Puritan was one of us in Puritan guise to draw men and women in!

Representatives of the city fathers dropped in also, in more dignified fashion, to remind us not to advertise our plays by the blowing of a trumpet. They talked earnestly with Jack.

I could not help but marvel that anyone could believe that pastorals were so subversive. We did a marvellous one called *Sir Calidore*, writ by Nicholas. Angel played this knight who on a quest did stray into a forest and there met Pastorella (Amyas) and divers other nymphs, one of which was me. The others were all good and bad shepherds, and the boys A Bear of Fearsome Aspect. We had branches in pots on the boards and some very fine false roses, taffeta, twined in the leaves. This was a beautiful play to perform on a sunny day. There was good music in it; there was sung by the company "As I my little flock on Ister bank", and a complete song by me. I did come to the front of the stage and sing with my lute "O sweet woods, the delight of solitariness", which is about the innocence and perfection of country life.

Many famous writers turned their talents to compose a pastoral. It was said of pastorals that although they savoured of wantonness and love and toying, and now and then broke the rules of poetry and became plainly scurrilous, yet even the worst of them were delightful, because they showed the harmless love of shepherds diversely moralized, distinguishing between the craft of the city and the innocence of the sheep cote.

Myself I liked pastorals, and so did Nicky. They were set in Arcadia, in a Golden Age, and all parts had such pretty names, as Phyllida, Corydon, Amaryllis, Rosalind, Cynthia, Carmela, Doron and Pastorella. And some did come particularly to watch a pastoral because it was a touch old-fashioned, and they preferred it to the blood and gore, because it was elegant and beautiful. And we did end with dancing, both with country rounds and galliards, and a stately pavane.

Nicholas said: "It is too good a chance to miss. I shall write a play where you and I may kiss on stage – I have the plot already. Of course, it will be very chaste – but think of the delight..."

Nicky longed to turn his talents to the kind of play he would have truly liked to write. "Where two boys meet and fall in love...but it can never be. Even in plays about men and women, how few are happy! We have to endure deaths and deviousness, wicked brothers, jealous lovers, power-crazed dukes – all this makes good drama, I know. But how sweet to write a play of love – a happy play, where they did question their thoughts and explore the nature of their love, and finally persuade the jealous lovers and the unkind dukes that all could be well in love! But who would come to watch such a play? They must have poison and despair. And as for love between boys! I would be imprisoned for sedition! Do you know, Marc, if once you write a seditious play, they come and search your rooms, regularly, just when they please, and keep an eye on you henceforth."

"What counts as sedition, Nicky?"

"Plots against a king which lead to his abdication and not to his victory...anything religious – I mean, anything whereby religion is questioned and explored...immoral love...Toy with dangerous topics if you will, but all your characters must suffer divine retribution. Any overreacher must be brought down. He may strut somewhat, but he must be seen to perish. I daresay I would be permitted a tale of two boys who loved each other if they both were eaten by a bear!" Nicky said, half smiling, half in gloom.

"Well," I told him, "Two boys will love each other off the stage, and their story will be no less lovely for being secret."

Nicky was not cheered. "I think we mean not the same thing, Marc, when we say Love," he said despondently.

I shrugged. "I give you all I know how."

"I know," said Nicholas, hugging me. "I'm sorry. Tis folly to demand so much."

"I cannot love," I sighed. "I told you. I tried it once. There's no place for love in the real world. It is a commodity for bargaining and I do not want it. I shall never forgive myself for what we did to Gilles – and what they did to me. I don't mean teaching me whore's tricks. I mean taking the love which was for me an innocent thing, and using it against me. I don't want love; it's too upsetting. And I cannot give it."

"It matters not," Nicholas assured me, and most certain lying. "I love, and that will have to do."

"It would be different," I sulked, "if we lived within a pastoral. But we do not."

"They show us a certain ideal."

"A false one."

"It need not be. All ideals are based upon the possible."

"No – the world is too bitter and cynical," I told him. "Ideals are only there to be perverted for bad purposes."

"Then pure love becomes all the more necessary. It is the only weapon."

I hugged Nicholas in return. "Keep believing it," I said. "I don't believe it, but it gladdens me to know that *you* do."

In those early days, you see, I did not truly value Nicky's worth.

With Amyas I had wonderful times playing with clothes. As we were the leading ladies we could have first choice and decorate ourselves as we would. There was white taffeta and mulberry taffeta and russet satin, and a surfeit of silk, and even cloth of gold for kings and gods. And we did kneel in all this richness, arraying ourselves most proudly. But I had always a fondness for green – the colour of lovers – and when I was a shepherdess (I was Amaryllis) I wore a green kirtle embroidered all over with long thin green leaves. The kirtle opened to reveal a gown of cream silk. Amyas wore blue. He played the heroine Pastorella, who did marry Calidore. He was a better lady than me, for he was plumper. In his low cut bodice he could manipulate his chest to look as if he had breasts! Truly! His flesh did jiggle and he could separate it till he had a cleavage!

"O Amyas!" I did murmur, kissing it. "You almost make me want to love women!"

"Love women then," he simpered. "I am one; love me."

"But Amyas, I am a woman too!" I giggled, in my green gown.

"It does not matter; I take all comers." And we did kiss, all decked in our dresses, and I did lick the lovely white flesh of Amyas' amazing tits. That shameless boy did love it, and did moan and sigh in my arms, indeed so exciting me that I was beside myself and he did have to pull me off by the hair.

"Hey! No love bites! What a beast you are; why, you are almost like a boy, Amaryllis, not a maid at all!"

"Forgive me, Pastorella," I murmured, flushed and grinning. "O Amyas, I do desire you in your dress!"

It was hard not to be intimate with Amyas. We dressed for the play together, and helped each other into our clothes. Women – what strange gear did they wear! We had to put on a farthingale. This was done by either sewing hoops into a petticoat or by tying around your hips a bolster, which was called a Bum-Roll. Thus accoutred, we would don the gown and kirtle, and our skirts would sway most delightfully. But tying a bum-roll on to Amyas – who wore nothing under his gown – was like to reduce me to a tremble; I did end up on my knees, cocooned in his petticoat, kissing that fat pink provocative arse, and emerging red faced and gasping. Taking pity on me, Amyas would escort me to some private place – a dark landing, or behind the barrels – and lift up my skirts for me and swiftly bring me off. We rarely needed to redden our cheeks artificially, for time and time again we did trip on stage all pink and flushed from our activities. But country maids are said to be rosy – from warm fresh air and cider and pure living!

This is the kind of things our company sang as shepherds:

> "Careless worldings, outrage quelleth
> All the pride and pomp of city:
> But true peace with shepherds dwelleth,
> Shepherds who delight in pity
> Whether grace of heaven betideth
> On our humble minds such pleasure
> Perfect peace with swains abideth
> Love and faith is shepherds' treasure"

Amyas and I were truly most popular, especially Amyas, who had what he called his Followers. Naturally, they knew he was a boy, but that increased their pleasure. They took no risks by flirting with him – no angry brothers or fathers jealous of their girl's honour, no irate matron pursuing them with a pestle. There were apprentices who turned up regularly, and there were noblemen who ogled us both, and called out saucy things, and pulled our skirts up a little way, crying: O, an ankle, a sweet white ankle! We were not displeased and disported ourselves like maidens, bashful but severe, smacking their naughty fingers with a stick of flowers. Amyas did in truth make several assignations for the nights which followed, and several fresh faced apprentices did blow him kisses and send him sonnets – monstrous bad – to "fair Pastorella" for whom they expired of love, as should a doting swain. Me, I kept myself pure and slightly apart, because I slept with Nicholas.

Because Amyas had told me that Kit Marlowe had oft been seen last year at St. Paul's churchyard where the bookstalls were, I pestered Amyas to go there with me, in the hope of seeing what he looked like. Amyas knew that was my reason for going, and did not find it surprising that I should want to see him – though I mentioned nothing of this to Nicholas. At least six times we went there, loitering around and waiting, but we never saw him there. It was so crowded always that we could have missed anybody. It was noisy and exciting, and you did feel that everyone here was a poet or a cut-throat; and there were playbills to read and strange advertisements pinned upon trees and walls, and some soliciting; indeed, every time we went there, older gentlemen did enquire if we would walk with them. We always refused politely. We were not of course in our farthingales, I hasten to add, but mere pretty boys, though I daresay we looked aimless, which we joked about, saying well, one of us is, and therefore between us we were both "aimless" and "marked" (in the sense of being noticed, it being a pun). There were books, poems and pamphlets on sale, and satirical broadsides and religious tracts; and there were fights and robberies and chasing, and street musicians, and students arguing; so time was never wasted here if you wanted to feel at the centre of the world. It was our custom to go there in the morning, because we performed plays in the afternoon. And we were yet without a patron, and Jack was most concerned.

Amyas rooted amongst the books, searching for something diverting; and I merely loitered, looking at passers-by and wondering if any were the man I sought. I fixed some of our playbills upon a tree and others on a wall, and I read some of the notices – servants needing a position, articles for sale, objects lost and found. Then one in particular caught my eye.

"Citizens! The Established Church speaks not for the Kingdom of God but for the Kingdom of England. The Prayer Book that you use is culled together from husks and scourings from the Popish dunghill. We will have no bishops, no ceremony, no pomp and idle display. Citizens, look into your souls and see what lies there. Do you need priests to tell you what to believe? Do you need the outward shows, the genuflexion?" There was much more but I did not read it all. I wondered whether it was treason or mere ravings. It was signed Nathaniel Gods-Will. Nathaniel Gods-Will! I pictured a tall and sober Puritan, cloaked and muffled, a monstrous crow, sneaking by night, his pamphlets hidden in a secret lining. Unobserved by all, except for churchyard owls and the spirits of the dead, he fixes up his broadsheet, smiles in dark delight, and slinks away. I smiled too. It marvellous amused me to think that the godly tract lay next to my playbill: "Citizens! At the Cross Keys Inn, Gracechurch Street, on Tuesday, a performance of SIR CALIDORE, with the Loves and Trials of poor shepherds, and a Bear of Fearsome Aspect."

Truly in Paul's churchyard one found strange bedfellows!

I leaned thoughtfully against a tree, watching the yellow leaves swirl and fall about me and the darting flights of swallows. Amyas turned a moment and looked at me.

"Marc, read a book or something. Standing there so dreamily you look like an invitation."

"Perhaps I would be – to the right man."

"O? And how would you know him?"

"I don't know. What do you think?"

"Make him show the lining of his cloak."

"Why so?"

"Many a poor man passes for a rich man here by wearing a fine cloak. But he holds his elbows close and keeps his lining hid. By his lining shall you know the nobleman! Choose he who

197

has satin within!"

"I would think," I smirked, "that only his breeches would be sat in!"

Amyas groaned and turned back to the bookstalls. I found that I had caught the eye of a stranger observing me with an assessive gaze. I blushed. If it had been a nobleman I would have simpered and smiled.

But the man who was looking at me was in no wise noble, and wore nothing satin. He was a beggar. He was standing by a wall and watching me. His hair was shaggy and unkempt, he wore a ragged cloak about him patched in bright colours – orange, purple, scarlet – and his feet were bare. The hand extended from his cloak was like a claw. Beside him on the ground lay his earthenware pot. Beggars I did not dread; but this one was diseased. I stared helplessly before I could tear my eyes away. I saw grey sores upon his arm, scabby mounds with sunken glistening cores. The same were upon his cheek. I should have pitied him and prayed; but I was revolted and afraid. Why did he stare at me? I put my hand to my heart and turned hurriedly away.

"Amyas –" I tapped him on the shoulder.

The beggar shifted from his place; I thought he would move towards us.

"Amyas – let us part."

"Part?" blanched Amyas. "O! I see – you want to leave. Well, as you wish."

I hustled him away, without looking back. Once clear and in the street again I felt a fool for having run away.

"I saw a beggar," I said blithely. "A real vile rascal, and all scarred and pitted."

"There are many such," shrugged Amyas.

"Who is Nathaniel Gods-Will?" I enquired.

"He that writes Puritan pamphlets? I don't think anybody knows. I have certainly never seen him."

"I picture him as a tall stern figure dressed in black, coming by night to fix his broadsheet upon the tree."

"Why would he do that?"

"Because I am sure it counts as treason that which he writes. He would not want anyone to see him."

"Treason? Tediousness, more like. It is all to do with souls and praying. I call him Nathaniel Pig-Swill!"

Doubled up in foolish mirth Amyas chortled to himself.

"Well, mayhap we'll not go there again," I said. "We are destined not to find my poet."

But Destiny was smiling on me – or maybe she was laughing – because that very day as we walked homeward I achieved my wish.

We had to pass a drunken brawl. It was two men fighting on a street corner, and a small crowd gathered. Of course we stopped to stare. They had come out of the tavern drunk, it seemed, and up and down the street had been fisting and scuffling, and of those idly by, some were shouting them on, and some were nervous, looking about in case the Watch were called and they all be arrested.

"Best go," Amyas murmured, catching my arm. And then his light touch turned to an excited pinch.

"That's him!" he squeaked.

"Who? Which?" I gasped, looking at the brawlers.

"No, no, not him," said Amyas shaking his head. "That one is Robert Greene."

"Robert Greene?"

"The writer," Amyas explained, "of novels. The other I don't know. No, I did not mean either of the brawlers. I meant he – him watching, him against the wall."

I looked. It was a moment full of movement: for I was half turned on my heel to hurry away, and he at once leaned forward, involved in the fight; and so I first saw him like that, his arm outstretched, a dagger in his hand.

"Oy! Robert!" he said, and Robert, who was disadvantaged in the fight, stuck out an arm to take the proffered weapon. Howls from Robert's opponent and his supporters, and a second dagger produced; then cries of: "The Watch! Run for it!" – and all in the blink of an eye he was gone, dashed down a sidestreet, and the two who fought were stumbling up and all dispersing, and Amyas and myself also, who had taken off down some side alley, as one does at times like these.

"Huh," grunted Amyas as we panted breathless home. "I might have known if we could not find him at Paul's churchyard we could find him in a fight. Unfair moreover. If Robert had been swifter, there would have been murder done from that dagger."

"At least he would have won," I pointed out.

"Ah – you French have no sense of fair play," he accused.

I thumped Amyas and he thumped me. But ours was not serious, and we were monstrous hungry. As I wolfed my bread and cheese and ale sitting upon a barrel in the innyard, I had plenty of time to mull over what I had seen. He had dark brown hair, lush and long on his collar. He was beautiful of features, dark browed, dark eyed, and lean, and I had heard him speak! Yes! He who had written:

> As looks the sun through Nilus' flowing stream,
> Or when the morning holds him in her arms,
> So looks my lordly love, fair Tamburlaine

had spoken! He had said: Oy, Robert!

Well, I was bedazzled! So! He was beautiful! And I did desire him immense. I even echoed to myself the immortal words Oy Robert! again and again in my head, to see if I could recapture the tone, the sound. But no, not really – only someone catching his friend's attention to throw him a dagger. And those who stood gathered in groups about me were talking noisily of other things, and I had to prepare myself for the afternoon's performance, just as if it were any other day, and not the day on which I first saw Kit Marlowe.

As it turned out, the day still had excitements for me.

After the performance Jack did call me over to his wagon, which was always in the corner of the innyard, and there upon the slatted wooden steps he put a proposition to me. I was still in my green kirtle, for we were very careless about our clothes and did sit about in odd gear. I sat upon the steps, my skirts billowing up, and my toes curled on the wood. I was comfortable in the soft sunshine and the play had gone well. But Jack looked troubled, as well he might. His plump face was frowning and concerned; he even looked uneasy. Finally he sat down by me, and the steps did creak like an old floorboard.

"Young Marc," he said, "I am in a quandary. I know what I should do and I do not do it. My problem is that our little company is the most important thing to me in the world. And this makes me put it first, before anything, and that is my only excuse for burdening you with a bad situation."

When he eventually broke through the preamble, this was

what he had to say. "The fact of the matter is, a gentleman has asked you to supper! It is Sir Edward Knollys and he was at the play. It seems he is much taken with you – and why not, indeed! We all are! – and he came privily to me and asked if I would send you to his house. I know I should have refused out of hand – but one cannot with noblemen – you know who he is; he is the Earl of Oxford's friend – one may not offend – and we particularly, who at this time have no patron. It sneaked across my mind that you could ask him to be our man – if he liked you over supper he would agree, and that would be a great relief – but – as you must be aware, sometimes when one is asked to supper one sometimes is given *more*...And this distresses me for what it makes me seem...and the situation I put you into...What are we to do?"

"What is he like?" I asked reasonably. "Young? Old?"

"O, he is young, never fear; he's no old dotard. Marc! Give me credit for some sensibility; I would not send you to some old ram."

"Handsome?"

"O, goodly enough, yes most personable. He is the Earl of Oxford's friend, remember, and your earls may have their pick."

"Then really Jack, there is no problem," I shrugged smiling. "An attractive young nobleman has asked me to supper, and by accepting, I may do the company an important service – it is an easy choice, and I do accept."

"O Marc, bless you! But," he added painfully, "you do understand what he may want..."

"Yes," I said and I knew he did feel bad about it, so I added: "You have not asked about my past history, but all the stories are true. Fear not, Jack, I can handle supper." There was an odd little poignant pause, wherein he looked at me with such sad sympathy and tenderness that I was somewhat uncomfortable. I was no poor victim and did not need concern. "I need not wear my kirtle?" I enquired with a smile.

"No indeed!" Jack looked quite alarmed, and then laughed too, and we did leave it thus and said no more about it.

I put my shoes back on and tripped across the innyard through the tangled straw, deciding what to wear for my engagement.

II

"Theban Niobe
Who for her sons' death wept out life and breath
And, dry with grief, was turned into a stone,
Had not such passions in her head as I."

MY EXPERIENCE with Sir Edward Knollys was marvellous
strange, indeed mystic. What we did between the
sheets was almost nothing, and certainly counted as
nothing with me. But the mental part was different, and one of
the most important things that happened to me.

This free-thinking gentleman lived in one of the elegant
houses on the Strand, whose doors opened on the wide street
but whose backs led to long green gardens that reached the river,
with steps to private landing stages. I had never been there
before, but I was not at all apprehensive, for in truth, being of
noble blood myself this was my element, and I was quite at ease
in rich surroundings. I knew this would surprise him. He was
expecting a pert young player, but I wore my mulberry silk
doublet and cream stockings and my fine white leather hat and
swirling cloak, and I arrived as a young nobleman.

It had been a sunny afternoon but the evening was fallen out
lightly misty, with a stale damp smell upon the air. I passed a
garden wall where heavy overblown rose heads hung down,
with the webs of many small pale spiders stretched upon them,
looking strong as thread; and church bells rang from a nearby
tower. It was not yet dark– few doorways showed a lanthorn lit
– and there were yet many passers-by. I saw a baker carrying a
tray whereon were piled most intricate loaves in shapes of corn
sheaves, thatch and harvest mice. I remembered then that
seminary priest who plotted to bear messages in pies, reflecting
how the innocent and homely may seem sinister to the beholder
in a sombre humour. The sky was a curious golden brown
and suddenly against it a great mass of rooks flew up with
powerful wings and cries. The twilight thickened as I walked,
the smudge of chimney smoke now adding to the growing
gloom, and the nearer I came towards the river that stale and
bitter smell increased and chilled the air.

A tall manservant met me at the door, and escorted me through the forecourt and across a paved courtyard, to an ancient doorway at the base of a stalwart tower. We ascended a stairway and so upstairs to a room on the third floor, a low wainscotted chamber, and here I met my host.

He was a pleasant young man, Sir Edward, with hazel eyes and fine silky fair hair. He was of medium height, graceful of bearing. His slender hands were heavily bejewelled and he wore pendant droplets of pearls in his ears. His doublet was of peach coloured satin. From his manner to me it was happily apparent that our delight in each other was mutual, and on our meeting he favoured me with a kiss on my cheek, his lips lingering a little and leaving me with a most pleasant sensation and anticipation of what was to come.

The room was elegant and full of treasures – a fine virginals with many music books lying about nearby, a chess board set with precious stones, and ornaments and comfit boxes made of gold and silver, and shelves of rich bound books. Brocaded curtains were now drawn against the encroaching night, and the firelight and the flames of candelabras glinted amber in the goblets of Venetian glass, where now the servant poured us wine.

"I thought you fair in your green gown," Sir Edward said. "But not till now did I understand just how fair...tell me more about yourself."

Yes! He was delighted with my presence just as I had hoped. I felt we were a most attractive couple as we sat down to eat, and I made no secret of my enjoyment of the situation. Sir Edward dismissed his sumptuous rooms with an apology.

"...the musty smell. It is always damp here, even in Midsummer...the vapours from the river..."

"Can we see the river from here?"

"No, this is the north side. But there is a tolerable garden, and you may see the river from there."

I had not tasted such fine wine since I had left France, and the bread, the beef, the different portions of fowl, the custards and the sweetened orchard fruits were as well as I had known at court; and afterwards we ate candied lemon and oranges. While we ate we spoke of serious things – as religion and the obligations of wealth – and comfortably relishing my surroundings I was happy for him to do most of the talking, while I listened leaving my mind open, aware and amenable to new ideas.

He commented that now as never before, the horizons of the world and of our minds were opening up, and astonishing changes lay within our reach. In the dark past, the enclosed ages now gone by, the people stayed in their villages and believed what they were told by the parish priest, and many of these were not the learned men they should have been, and so some monstrous odd notions had been bandied about. Things were different now. We were on the threshold of a Golden Age, flooded with new ideas. Next year – 1588 – was to be a Year of Wonder. It had to be – there would be an eclipse of the sun in February, and in March and August two total eclipses of the moon. Did that pressage the fall of a great nation? If so, was it England or Spain? Or did it pertain to wider issues – a revolution in mankind's way of looking at the world? Did it mean that truths hid from our fathers were to become revealed to us? Were discoveries to be made available to us, challenges that were beyond our power to imagine? What would that mean for us – disaster or joy? How would we deal with that new liberty of thought – could we go forward in a new freedom, or would we go down in an abyss of lost faith and confusion?

In this age of ours, so vibrant, so optimistic, so questioning, so probing, discovery was all – anything was possible. Anything could be dared, could be thought. What marvels lay beyond the seas, suddenly made known to us through courage and daring! And above – what if the world was not at the centre of the universe! Suppose the universe had no centre! Could there be people on the moon – other worlds, peopled with creatures unlike ourselves? Suppose the universe went on for ever, into a vast unknown? What if its centre was the sun itself? And where did Mankind stand in relation to such startling conceptions? What of the ancient framework, with its angels and archangels, its principals and powers, its solid security, with everything upon earth for Man's good alone? Where was Heaven? Where was Hell? And where, in all this new confusion, was God Himself?

I know I found this marvellous exciting. It went to my head like the Muscadel, monstrous potent. It was like lifting the lid off a bubbling cauldron and letting in light. It meant that anything was possible. It meant that we could think what we liked. It was not exactly atheistic, but it felt dangerous. It made me wonder where did the stimulating become the seditious, at what point? Once we started to question all our beliefs, whither did we go? It was like walking off a cliff.

I sat there, in the panelled gloom, and idly turned a great globe that stood by my elbow, flicking the New World past me at a glance, spinning the vast empty spaces of the south and the mysterious cold lands of the north, as if I were Jupiter and held mankind in my palm. An exquisite nutmeg-coloured cat sat on the floor immobile, staring at a candle flame. I watched the cat, with its huge soulful eyes and rapt expression, and the candle flame it watched, and the moment set in time, like a pearl in glass. And then Sir Edward's long bejewelled fingers touched my cheek, and he led me to the bedroom.

I was in no way a kept boy brought here for his pleasure; he was not paying for me and I had no obligation to entertain him. He had respect for who I was by birth, and he was not so much older than me besides – I would say about twenty-five – and we undressed as equals, sitting on the bed quite naturally and still talking, though by now it had descended to mere travellers' tales and geography.

"Dolphins," said my companion, removing his doublet, "that come up out of the sea when flutes are played."

"Lions," I said, stretching my bare legs, "so gentle that they come like kittens to a woman's touch."

"A dragon," said Sir Edward, his silken shirt slipping from his slender torso. "Ten fathoms long!"

"Ten fathoms!" I marvelled savouringly, licking my lips, watching all he did.

"Ten fathoms," he agreed unblinkingly, "with golden skin and of a charming disposition, raising its head to look about it if a stranger should approach, then breathing fire if it should like what it does see."

"And serpents," I said moving closer. "Forty yards long, and very smooth to touch..."

"Forty!" he laughed, naked now. "No, Pliny never said as much."

"Forty," I assured him ardently. "And hard and firm and marvellous warm."

205

Convinced, he turned the covers back, and we entwined and glided then within.

It was a beautiful bed, excessively carved all over; indeed, as I lay on my back and looked upward I could see the underside of the four-postered tester fine carved also, and against the headboard two slim candles gave us light. We kissed passionately and then pressed together in content at each other's beauty. I began to cover his chest with kisses, which excited him, and so I put my head down lower and I took his cock in my mouth and sucked. He lay back and abandoned himself up to pleasure. I worked hands and lips and sucked him to coming, and he groaned and said I was exquisite. He had not touched my heart but I knew beauty when I saw it and I was pleased to give him joy. When he had recovered he placed me where he was, with my head on the pillow, and then did the same for me. I was touched and surprised. I had not expected it. Naturally, I did not resist! I lay back and enjoyed it, and he did it very well. I held the bedposts, lying all spreadeagled, crying out as it became more beautiful. With a great long sigh I let it come – it almost hurt. It left me shaking. He came up and held me in his arms. I could not explain why I was affected. It was too mental. It was to do with free-thinking, and with all things being possible. I felt that I had rid myself of a heavy weight, of bad ideas that had been dragging me down. In a way, it could only have happened to me from a stranger. Nicholas could not have done it; he was too kind, too close. It had to be someone who did not know what he had done – the unknown jailor who turns the key and whom you never see again. I clung to him with an intensity quite irrelevant to mere fucking; he was somewhat surprised, I think. He patted me. He said we should sleep now.

And so I slept in white scented sheets against the bare shoulder of the Earl of Oxford's friend. Would he tell the Earl of Oxford? "I took home this young player from the Cross Keys...an affectionate little thing..." Probably not. Would I tell Nicholas? Yes, I must. It was too important not to share. The sudden unexpected freedom I had experienced must surely bode well for our relationship. Might it even mean that I could allow myself to open to love's vulnerability? I felt so contented at that prospect that I fell asleep happy, and slept well.

My mood of elation and excitement lasted. My pleasant host

must leave in the morning, but he told me to bathe if I wanted, and to part when I was ready. Tremulously I asked about him becoming our patron.

"We are a very good company, though small, and as well as the pastoral you saw, we do *Saint George*, and *The Spanish Tragedy* – I play Isabella, and I go mad very noisily – and Jack Unsworth our leader is most hardworking and serious, and would be so grateful..."

I knew he would say yes. It had been very good between us. And then I put in a plea of mine own.

"And also, we have a poet and resident playwright, one Nicholas Henshaw, who has writ a most beautiful poem, about Lancelot and Guinevere. He has no lord to address his poem to, and truly it would be only to your praise to let your name be on his title page..."

Yes! He agreed! I was elated! I had done this for Nicky. Nothing for myself – O – was it love?

I did bathe. Twas most pleasing to bathe in ease and privacy, in a large tub, with herbs to strew in the water, and here I lay languidly, far beyond the call of mere cleanliness. I washed my hair also, and then I dressed, and strolled into the garden, to let the sun dry my wet locks.

I can barely describe the happiness of that moment. It was one of those rare times when all good things come together, and make perfection.

I was in a garden that sloped down to the River Thames. Although it was now Autumn, there were many rose bushes yet in bloom, deep red ones that bespoke love, and pale pink ones for affection and tenderness, and white for purity. I smelt them all, going from rose to rose, like a meticulous bee. The sun did shine from a huge sky of pale blue, and as I approached the water I saw the sun did glitter on the surface, and a fine looking boat was approaching, which also glittered, either on weapons or jewellery, it was too far off to see. I went right to the end of the garden, and sat on the first wooden step that led down into the water. At my feet the water plashed idly – and even the pale scum looked amber, such was my mood. The sun was warm on my hair.

I thought of my companion of the night, who had been so courtly and polite. Come and see me if you need me, he had said, implying that our evening had been agreeable but there was no involvement. He had given me a ring, an onyx, and I had it on my finger where I toyed with it thoughtfully. He would never know the sweet new freedom he had bestowed upon me. As I sat there in his garden, looking across the river to the south bank and the houses and trees there, I thought now that I was free of my brothers and my past. I owed nobody anything; it was all done and paid for. I should not go back to France. I had done with being used and frightened. Courts and intrigues were not for me. Daggers and deceit, and wealth from policy – that was all over. In their place I had no idea what. All I could think was freedom. The possibility to think anything, to be anything, if only merely a part of this Golden Age, and the Annus Mirabilis that was coming next year. I felt so alive, so hopeful, so excited, so peaceful. I felt golden. I felt a living part of now. Truly, twas like being born. I felt I could start afresh now and find out who I was. My mind had come out of its Winter, imposed on it by my childhood and my past months, and I would bloom!

True to all moments of magic there was a strange and gorgeous climax. The glittering boat I noticed was now level with me, surrounded by many smaller boats that churned the water to a vibrant motion. It was the royal barge! And the Queen was in it! I nearly fell in the Thames with excitement. All those sour things I'd ever said about her were quite forgot as I jumped up and waved like an idiot – both arms! I could see the glitter on her dress, and her great white ruff and her golden hair, the sun glinting upon jewels therein. I saw the flash of weapons and helmets of the men-at-arms, and some other ladies and gentlemen around, and the scarlet and gold canopy. No, I am not inventing it – she did wave, truly; she did look toward the bank, and there I was, and she did wave!

Well! After that, I thought, all will be anti-climax. I wandered about the garden in a daze, marvelling that life could be so perfect. Guiltily I picked a rose. I picked a pink one. It was for Nicky, and you see I was yet cautious, for I did not pick a red. I suppose I was hesitant, love being new to me. I needed reassurance first – as in the "Roman of the Rose", you believe in love within the garden, but you are not so sure outside its walls. But nonetheless I felt free and hopeful, and I blew a farewell kiss to the river. I daresay I would never see it from a house in the Strand again.

I left Sir Edward Knollys' lodgings and ran – even bounded! – back to the Cross Keys on a cloud of delight, in plenty of time for the afternoon performance of *Sir Calidore*. I sought out Jack who was munching his way through a vast beef pasty, and with many hugs I told him that all had gone well and that now we had a patron. Jack's deep-felt relief moved him to tears, for our company was all to him. His arm about my shoulders, he led me to Madge who was kneeling in a heap of taffeta behind a wagon, sorting clothes.

"This wondrous lad, this blessed traveller, this hero," he explained, with many a manly sniff as emotion overcame him, "has proved to be our salvation..." And when I wriggled free in modesty and slipped away he was still telling all – "Ralph! John! Come hither! We have news!..."

I then bumped into Francis, who caught me firmly by both arms.

"You have done well, my little hero," he agreed. "But Nicholas is not best pleased."

"Nicky?" I said surprised. "But why –?"

Nicholas entered the inn yard with a sheaf of papers in his hands. He saw me at once, but turned his head and went towards the stage. I ran to him.

"I am returned!"

"I know it," he said tartly. "Your praises have been sung so loud that all of Gracechurch Street must know of your return."

"Are you not glad to see me?"

"I have been far too busy to have noticed you were even gone. So why should I feel aught for your return?"

"Nicky, this is not like you," I protested laughing. "I have such good news and I must share –"

"I know your good news – I heard Jack tell it like the chorus tells the groundlings! You have found us a patron. Along with everyone else I must thank you. Is that what you want, thanks?"

"No! Not from you!" I protested. "And that is not the news I had in mind. I meant something different, something important between you and I."

"I have no time for it; I have to put these in the wagon."

Nicky climbed the wagon steps with his papers, shoving aside

209

somewhat rudely Geoffrey, who was sitting at the top and who cried: "Nicky! Is it not marvellous what Marc has done!"

Behind us all was preparation for the play – the trestles set firm, the potted trees in place, much yelling, Francis testing out the crumhorn, and I had to find my lute.

"Come all!" Jack bellowed. "Leave what you do. All to the stage!"

"Nicky," I called urgently. "I will explain..."

My happiness a little tempered by his cool reaction I nonetheless much relished the performance, for I was still on air, and the story of our pastoral and the music played therein was such that sensations of happiness could only be enhanced. I wore the pink rose at my waist and sung my solo exceptional well. Yet I could see that Nicholas looked sullen. O, I thought, when I explain all will be well...he does not understand. And all else were so pleased with me and gave me many gladsome glances, and afterwards Jack said that we would have a feast and celebration soon as he could arrange it. With clearing things away and such, it was not till much later that I had a chance to speak to Nicholas, who pointedly ignored me until then.

We climbed up to our garret, in that kind of noisy silence of two people who have much to say, the moment being ripe.

And Nicholas began it. No sooner was our door fast shut behind us than he started. He was monstrous vexed.

"I suppose that you are feeling mightily pleased with yourself? What a little saviour! Sacrificed yourself for the common good, so now we have a patron. I suppose you are expecting gratitude now!"

"No – I did not sacrifice –" I began astonished.

"I guessed as much. No, you enjoyed it! And why not? You relish that sort of action, as I well know. And, it would seem, with anyone."

I thought this was unjust. Though I had in the past been less than virtuous, I had been true to Nicholas, Amyas being but a passing pleasure as we both knew. But I did not wish to quarrel.

"Are you not glad we have a patron now?" I asked.

"But at what cost?" he cried. "For surely you did sleep with him?"

"I did, yes, but it was merely..."

"Exactly," he said coldly. "It means so little to you – you will

210

go with anyone. I know about Amyas sure enough. But now what? Where does it end, your eagerness to oblige? Any man who needs a favour? Anyone we are obligated to? Innkeepers who will not accommodate us? Wheelwrights if we need to replace a wagon wheel in a hurry? Fetch Marc – he is so sweet natured and will go with all who ask and gladly!"

"O Nicky," I laughed weakly. "This is foolish talk. It is not thus. Last night was just the once, and it was special, but not what you suppose. Sir Edward is a courteous man, polite, and he was most kind, but it was not like how we are together, you and I, it was almost nothing..."

"But does anything touch you at all? You go with him – you say that it was nothing – what about how you felt – and what I might feel? I start to believe that there are no passions in you, that you feel nothing ever..."

"That is not true," I said, tears coming to my eyes.

"Even tears," he scowled. "I have seen how easily you weep. When you play Isabella you cry real tears every time."

I put my hands over my face and turned away. Real tears came hot and damp between my fingers.

Nicholas sighed. "You could have asked me, Marc," he said more moderately. "We might have talked about whether there were other ways of acquiring a patron, without you going to his bed."

"O," I spat. "You are plain jealous. Why not say so?"

"When you love someone..." Nicholas began, now monstrous well controlled.

"So that is what you mean by love?" I sneered. "Asking permission, saying where we shall be, never doing aught without the other knowing? And then abusing till the other weeps – *this* is what I have been lacking?"

"I do accept that you do love me not," said Nicholas bitterly. "But I knew not even where you had gone last night till I asked. Even Martin and Geoffrey knew. What do you think last night was like, for me?"

I had not considered that, and now I felt chastened. But only briefly. My deflation was too great, the contrast between my previous happiness and these recriminations. I sat, hunched and wary, and wiped my eyes.

"You say you love me," I burst out. "But you are too quick

to blame me. You would not hear what I had to tell."

"But I am angry!" cried Nicky. "Maybe you do not know me well at all. I know that I seem tolerant – and I am so – and I will say nothing, though I feel the more. Then of a sudden I can take no more and I will rage. And I have to say I cannot but wonder at your lack of scruples, your lightness...I accept Amyas, though I sometimes think you are too careless where you do it...but in this last matter you seem to have had no regard for me at all, and all throughout the play you grinned and smirked and seemed so monstrous unconcerned..."

"There you are wrong," I said defiantly. "For I thought much of you. I asked Sir Edward to accept your poem, and he will. You can now publish."

Nicky stared and said nothing.

"Are you not pleased?" I demanded. "God's Teeth!" I said with relish and some difficulty. "It is what you want. I did it for you. Are you not at all grateful?" – with a kind of grunt too French to translate.

"A plague upon you, yes!" he shouted at me. "And if I had a scrap of honour I would throw it back at you. But the truth is that I want my poem published more than I mislike your little escapade. And so that makes me every kind of hypocrite."

Indeed he was upset enough to leave me. His voice shook with reproach, and I suppose disgust, with both of us. He climbed out of the garret, leaving me sitting half open mouthed, too enraged and hurt to call him back.

I sniffed a bit, and wiped my wet cheeks with my finger. I caught sight of the pink rose lying by the bed, and I picked it up and put it on the floor and ground my heel on it, squashing it flat. So. I had come to Nicky with a little bloom of love all hopeful, to tell him of the miraculous changes in my head and let him share all the elation I was feeling, and all I had received were anger and reproach. Damage had been done. I did not feel inclined to sit and wait here until his anger subsided and he regretted his hard words. I did not feel I should be blamed so much. If he really loved me he would not be so angry. Love forgives, I thought. So if he does not love me, I owe him nothing. If he thinks I sleep with anyone, he need not be surprised if I do.

Like a devil possessing me, an urgency was upon me to reach

into my pile of clothes down to the silk shirt where I kept that letter. It was almost as if I had been merely waiting for an excuse. I had wanted to pick it up before , for reasons nothing to do with Nicky, but loyalty to him had stayed my hand. And a certain timidity and apprehension, and of course, pride. But I had not these now. I felt very abused, sullen and defiant. The sort of mood where you do foolish things.

I hated that letter writ by Anthony. It was humiliating to me, and made me look cheap and amusing. But ever since I first read it, Christopher Marley at the Phoenix Tavern had been a part of my thoughts, a sort of itch. I would have liked to have used returning the poems as an excuse to get into his presence. But they were gone now, so that was no use. And now I had seen him I knew he was beautiful; and everyone did speak of him for his fame and glory. He would be famous down the ages. And I had in my possession the means to get straight to him, if only I dare take it.

I moved over to the clothes and delved about, still sniffing a little from my tears.

I found the letter.

SEVEN

I

"For in his looks I see eternity,
And he'll make me immortal with a kiss"

I CANNOT pretend that it was solely in pique that I went
marching off down West Cheap that particular evening. If
it had been, I would have gone as I was, face flushed, eyes
red rimmed and carelessly clad. Instead, once I had decided what
I would do, I took a deal of trouble to make myself lovely. As
much as ever when I was expecting to be sent for by the king of
France, I gave myself up to self-beautification. Fortunately, I
noticed, I was still tolerable clean from my exquisite bath that
morning, and a few well-positioned dabs of musk rose perfumed me pleasantly. I wore a cream silk shirt, my apple green
doublet and bottle green velvet cap, dark green trunk hose very
short like we wore in Paris, and cream coloured stockings. My
silk shirt had a high gathered collar that frilled, also at the wrists,
and so I wore no ruff or rufflets; and I wore a pair of pale
coloured leather shoes, most dainty, with small cork heels. I
combed my fresh washed hair very smooth and shiny, and my
fringe low on my brows, and I painted my eyelids light brown
and salved my lips, wiping away all traces of my bout of
weeping, and powdering over the place. O! Would he like me?

Naturally enough, I told no one where I was going, and
indeed I sneaked out like a thief, for I had no wish to meet
Nicholas, or anyone who might ask or comment on my
prettiness. And thus I did what I had longed to do – I walked to
the Phoenix Tavern and boldly went inside. My knees were
extreme weak of a sudden, and so I found a place and sat, and a
serving wench brought me wine – jovial ale did not suit my
humour. Then I looked about me.

It was large and somewhat dark, dense with a fug of smoke. There were many of those high backed settles that made ingle nooks, and so all over the parlour men could be private and go into huddles whence only smoke and hats showed above the seat backs, and great gales of gusty laughter rose up along with the smoke. Everybody seemed to know each other, and there was much back-slapping and calling out of names, and people dragging heavy stools across the floor, to sit at the sides of tables. At the next place to me a man was reading out loud a sonnet he had writ, to a friend who was passing comments, their heads bent low over the manuscript.

When I had a second drink of wine, I asked the girl privily if she did know whether Master Marlowe was in here, and she said she would ask.

She enquired of the innkeeper, and I saw him point with his arm outstretched and his finger crooked down, which seemed to show that yes he was, and over there in a far corner and in a group deep within the high backed settles. My heart both rose and sank – at the same time, it seemed to me! I was elated he was here, but most apprehensive at how I would achieve his presence – between us it was as a copse of nettles and briars, with legs and feet and bodies and tables and smoke and brawny shoulders and bellowing laughter. Still, I would not go back now and, wine-emboldened, I began to stagger through. Not unobserved, I may say! My thighs were much pinched, and with cries of "Where are you going, darling?" and "Here's a pretty youth – or is it a maiden in disguise?" and other such, I was both helped and hindered on my way. Pink-cheeked I persevered and recognised Robert Greene standing drinking, and no worse for his street fight. He was tall and red-haired, lightly bearded, and he was something of a beacon for me, as I supposed Master Marlowe would be nearby. But so many men were about, so tightly packed, I ended stuck within a yard or so, and up against the back of the settle, being asked, "What do you want, lad?" by so many interested parties that there was no way I could keep my business private.

"I have a letter for Master Marlowe," I said a little desperately to Robert Greene. He was amused. He observed my hot and flustered look, and he could see hands straying over my cream thighs, and my wriggling. He held out his hand for the letter, thinking to do me a favour by relieving me of my errand. I held the letter to my chest as if it was most precious, and shook my head.

"Ho!" he laughed. "Confidential, eh?" He leaned down into the group the other side of the settle back. He said: "Kit – a sort of Mercury is here and brings a letter."

A most arrogant hand did rise up. I say that because without even turning his head or looking at me, Master Marlowe reached up behind his shoulder for the letter, flicking finger and thumb in that impatient way to imply I should put the letter in his hand. I did not. I waited, half leaning across a man who was patting my stuffed trunk hose in an intimate manner. I studied the hand, which was long and slim and inkstained, and the shirt cuff, which was frayed, and the long dark hair of his head, which was lush and wavy and to a length below his collar. He was not even interrupting his conversation – he said: "What, in Italy?" in a kind of laughing sneer, and his friend opposite said: "He told me so himself"; and then seeing I was still standing there, said: "Kit – your letter", and laughed and caught my eyes, and twinkled most explicitly. He was Thomas Watson, gentlemen and poet, who was much admired for his Latin verses. Either he or arm-ache persuaded Kit to turn his head and deign to look at me, and there we were, but inches apart. His eyes were brown. I thought him very beautiful. I smouldered meaningfully. His expressive black eyebrows rose.

"The quality of messengers improves," he remarked, to the world in general, but also to me. I fluttered.

"'Tis a rumour then, this letter?" he enquired ironically.

I went a little pinker and put the letter in his hand. He turned back to the table, and I blushed full scarlet as I waited for his response. Robert and Thomas and indeed the others were very merry about the letter, not reading it, but joking about the contents.

"A commission to write a play on the subject of the daily life of nuns, from one that enjoyed *Tamburlaine*!"

"A plea from Nathaniel Gods-Will that hence forth he and Kit should collaborate in all plays and pamphlets!"

"A love letter from a lady discovered to be with child and thinking he was Robert, and Robert he."

"A warrant..."

216

"From such a pretty boy? No – an assignation in Southwark!" Kit turned round to me quite baffled.

"Have you read this?" he said bluntly.

"No," I said, lowering my eyes.

"Lying wag, then who broke the seal?"

"Maybe rats ate it," I shrugged.

"Rrrrrats!" they all mimicked delightedly. "Ate eet!"

I wriggled.

"You met up with Anthony Wilton?" Kit said. "How?"

"At an inn," I confessed, aware that this conjured up images of dark bedrooms and lust-scented sheets.

"And am I to assume that there is no box, other than what I see?" he enquired laconically.

"Yes" I said, thereby admitting that I knew the contents and that I accepted my role as implied by them; in effect, I thought, putting myself in his hands.

He gave me an odd look – quizzical, penetrating, amused, but I have to admit some contempt was in there too. Eventually he waved me away, rubbing his neck, which was somewhat disadvantaged from being turned round. "Go sit over there," he ordered, "and wait."

I was obedient like a dog, partly vexed with myself for allowing him to order me, and partly grateful that he had. Everyone had heard him direct me and saw me go meekly off and sit, and I endured good-humoured sniggers and jokes I could not hear behind people's hands. I sat on a stool, with a sulky pout, and my toes tracing patterns on the floor. I fiddled with my fingers. Someone handed me wine, but it was not from Kit, it was from Thomas Watson, who was the most considerate and courtly. He was pleasant to me from the first – well, it takes a cultivated person to know one. He was passing elegant, was Thomas, older than Kit and much travelled – he had been to Italy and France and met the Earl of Walsingham in Paris. He knew Italian fashions, and dedicated his poems to the Earl of Oxford. He always treated me considerately, which was more than Kit ever did. I drank the wine quickly, to dull my embarrassment, and I *was* embarrassed. It occurred to me that if everyone knew that Kit liked boys then it would be comfortably assumed that I was something he was saving for later – like a pudding, or a bunch of cherries! Here I sat perched on my stool, in cream stockings and lip salve and ear rings and a pretty shirt – they might even think I was a boy harlot who had been paid for! I need not have worried so much, of course, because people soon grew used to my sitting there and took scarce notice of me; as for my being a harlot, I later realised that Kit could not have afforded one of my quality, and everyone knew it.

Well, there I sat, and sometimes I caught his eye between the heads of the crowd, and he gave me no response but turned back to his conversation and his ale and dice. You would think he had not sat me there. But O what power he showed, that I stayed waiting. No wonder he was arrogant. Someone said of him he "nor aught admired but his wondrous self". I think it might be true. I sat and looked at him covertly. He was then twenty-three. He had a smudge of moustache above his lip, and a dark trace of beard along his jaw; it was a young proud face, with a little line from nose to lip, which I could never tell came from sneering or smiling, both of which he did exquisitely. I did not know whether to be pleased because he had told me to wait, or insulted because he ignored me. I began to wriggle with impatience and I cast a glance at Thomas, sensing he was the one to sympathise with my position. It would serve them right if I took my leave. But I did not.

Hours it seemed I was on that stool. I darted Kit a venomous scowl, which he certainly saw, indeed, to my indignation, his lips twitched with amusement. At this point Thomas stood up and strolled over to me, and to my astonishment began a conversation with me in almost impeccable French. It was entirely of the social and polite kind – "Is it true that you are French?...From where?...Have you been over here long? Do you like London? Have you been to see *Tamburlaine?* What do you think of it? All brawl and bombast, eh, is it not?" He nudged me smiling, as one who did not really believe that.

"I thought it was most excellent," I murmured apologetically.

"Ah, you French, you take things so seriously...one forgets."

"Some things are serious," I said earnestly. "And in that instance, also beautiful."

"O well," laughed Thomas, "with those attitudes you are bound to be a success."

I felt a flash of annoyance, the implication being that I was

218

prepared to ingratiate myself, and also that his friends were taking bets on my chances.

"What I say is true," I protested.

"Indeed it is," Thomas soothed. "But he will need no convincing of this truth."

"Did he show you what was in the letter?" I asked rather painfully.

"O no," said Thomas easily, and at first I was relieved, and then I supposed that Thomas being polite would tell me what would spare my feelings. We looked across and saw Kit and Robert standing up, and Robert called for the reckoning.

"I am sorry you have had so long a wait," said Thomas pleasantly.

"It does not matter," I said, with equal courtesy.

I thought Kit would do something, say something, to make my position clearer, but he did not. He clambered his way out, with Robert towards the door, people calling out goodnight as he went. I seethed with rage, stumbling out after him. I felt I was being treated like his dog, and worse, I was behaving like it – twas too much. I also felt hot and discomfited from several drinks of wine. We all emerged into the street. Thomas turned towards Paternoster Row, and Kit, still with the objectionable Robert, turned in the other direction and I trailed after. He and Robert were sporting quite foolishly and parading themselves till I felt almost embarrassed. They were thumping people's windows in passing, and shoving each other about and singing and making silly jokes that depended on a Latin tag. I could even believe it must have been quite somebody else who had writ "What is beauty? said my sufferings then", and I felt quite demeaned by being in the same company. Finally I put myself beside him and even grabbed his arm.

"Tell me what I am to do!" I screeched.

Robert collapsed in mirth and covered up his ears dramatically. "But not in front of me Kit, please," he cried, "I am too innocent, too trusting, it may be too much for me to hear the terrible intimate details when you tell him what to do..."

Kit detached me with great dignity.

"Well, you are coming back with me, are you not?" he said reasonably.

"Am I? Nobody has said so," I seethed.

"Well," he grinned, "I say so." However, he was quite drunk, and for a first smile I did not rate it very highly. Robert, whom I never liked, was still sniggering at his own humour. "O do tell him what to do...I have oft wondered what it is you do, and all these good people in their houses probably wonder too, and if you could oblige by doing it here in the street, we would all have our curiosity satisfied...Should he bend over, Kit? Is that not how you start? I wish that you would tell him what to do, he says he does not know...Give him some intimation, look at him, poor lad, he only wants to please you...

"Enough, Robert," Kit growled.

"O come, we don't have to be modest with him – what is he, one of Anthony's little catamites? He's probably bedded all the sodomites in London – how about it, boy, have you? You need not be coy with us, we know the world." He teetered around tipsily in my direction.

"I said *enough*, Robert," said Kit irritably, and suddenly turning, gave Robert such a thump he knocked him sideways and right off his feet. I gasped. Most sure, it was not that he was defending my honour by such a thump – no, it was for the pleasure of hitting Robert, a thing I have oft longed to do but dare not, Robert being big and tall. Robert lay and writhed so dramatically I could not tell how hurt he was, but when he began to cry: "O! Murder! I am slain!" and then: "Hell, death, Tamburlaine, hell! Make ready my coach, my chair, my jewels – I come, I come, I come!" – Zabina's mad scene before she dashes out her brains – I supposed him not hurt beyond redemption; and as for Kit he stood and laughed and laughed, and to my delight we left Robert there attempting to regain his feet, and wherever else he went that night, he did not come with us.

"Do you not live in Bankside, then?" I enquired tentatively.

"No," Kit said, reasonably enough since we were walking up Coleman Street towards Moor Gate. Even tipsy he walked very swift, like someone in a great hurry; and I was half running as I kept level.

It was night now, chill and dark, save for the smudges of light from upstairs windows, and the glow of lanthorns that hung above the doorways. Beyond the roofs amongst the wispy clouds the moon showed silver pale. The streets were quiet, except for other echoes of drunken revellers far off. I felt a thrill, for where I was and who I was with, though why I scarce know, as his attitude to me promised nothing at all.

We turned into a very narrow street with closely overhanging upper storeys; we entered a door, and he going first we climbed two flights of twisty stairs in darkness and arrived in a room. This room smelt most strong of tobacco smoke. He moved about and lit a couple of candles. The light showed me a narrow bed against the wall, strewn with papers, and a table stacked with books. He gathered up the papers that were on the bed and put them on the table; and then he flung himself upon the bed, and leaning back against the wall and eyeing me, he said: "Well. Suppose you get your clothes off, then."

I do not know if I were expecting finesse, but I was I think hoping for a more subtle beginning. I stared glitteringly, and he stared back. Then I tossed my head like a plucky little fellow and began to undo my doublet. He watched me with such a studied insolence that I felt like a plain strumpet, and though I told myself: "Well, what did you imagine, true love?", yet a silent misery was rising in me to be so debased – and I mean both of us. How could he write like that and be like this? I felt confused and vexed.

He took the letter out of his doublet and slowly started to read it out loud, stopping for observations which made me squirm.

"Marque français?"

"That's a sort of pun, because my name is Marc."

"Ah...most pleased to make your acquaintance, Marc... 'The flavours are many'...well, fortunate for me, eh?... 'as I have discovered' ...so Anthony tried you out and found you tasty...a night of passion at the inn, one supposes." He ran his eyes over me coldly.

" 'Ask it who nibbled before'," I wailed. "So ask. It was the King of France. There! You are receiving best quality cast-offs, you see."

That I was now considerably upset probably escaped him, in his frank astonishment at my revelation.

"The King of France! I don't believe it."

"Tis true...I was a mignon," I confessed modestly.

"Indeed?" He blinked. He thought about it. "Christ!" he remarked. "You believe in variety, do you not? And you

221

thought you'd try a poet next?"

"Yes, why not?" I cried, close to tears. "Or are we going to spend all night talking about it?"

He began to unbutton his doublet. His hair fell over his face as he leaned forward. I turned away and wiped my eyes. I hated Anthony. I was to achieve my desire, thanks to him – but, thanks to him, most horribly. I watched the candle burn. By its light I read half absentmindedly the words:

> Stay, Sigismund, forget'st thou I am he
> That with the cannon shook Vienna walls
> And made it dance upon the continent

and I looked at him and of a sudden darted to him and helped him with his clothes. I kneeled at his feet and took off his shoes and I did not care if he thought I was a much travelled catamite. I hurried to make him naked; I strewed his clothes on the floor. I was between his legs; I put my face against them, nuzzling his lean thighs, kissing till I came up to his crotch and pounced, my lips around his prick, which filled my mouth and tipped into my throat. I was ecstatic, slobbering and panting – O, I covered his cock with kisses and O how badly I did want that in me. I lifted my adoring eyes to him, and he raised me up and kissed me very hard till tears came to my eyes. I flung my arms around his neck. He almost slung me on the bed then, face down, and I lay shaking, enraged that he had grease to hand for juicing me, and almost intending to pull away and sulk, as his fingers separated my arse cheeks, confident aggressive handling by one who had done that before and often. I spread my legs and he eased himself between.

"O," I whispered, "take me, take me…" I was excited as never before, and at his entrance I could not help spurting all my juices hot and wet against my belly. He arched his back, leaning on his wrists, gripping my arms like a predator on his prey; and then he dropped on me and fucked me hard, fisting my hair in a handful till I cried; and then as his passion grew stronger he was doing it to hurt, with no thought of me at all save as an object for his lust or something but of small account. I whimpered into the sheet. He took no notice. He said harshly in my ear: "Take it, take it, bitch," and flooded me. His face was against mine; I felt his eyelash on my cheek. His fingertips touched my tear-stained cheeks.

"I hurt?" he said, making a statement of fact.

"You *know*," I muttered. I could feel his heart thudding against my shoulder blades.

"You deserved it." I sensed the anger in his voice. "Coming to me with a letter like that..."

"What?" I said blankly. "'Twas *me* the letter offended."

"You?" That had never crossed his mind. "You knew what was in the letter – you still came to me – what kind of treatment did you expect?"

Sweat trickled between us. I sniffed.

"I know I deserved it," I said contritely. "But I am not what you think – at least, only partly..."

"And what do you think *I* am?" he demanded. "Anthony Wilton sends me a used catamite and a coy letter – if he wants to play games I'll play them and that's what you had tonight. If you are delicate of nature, you had no business tangling with me on those terms. I hope it's somewhat taught you to be more careful to whom you deliver letters."

"O!" I said indignantly. "You were hardly giving me a tutor's punishment. You enjoyed hurting me – I *felt* you enjoy it."

"That's right," he said. "I did."

We moved apart; but the bed was so narrow we were yet very close. With Nicholas in such closeness I fitted like a key in a lock, but even when I knew Kit better, he had not warm affectionate ways like Nicky, and certain that first evening we did not lie like lovers.

"Anthony did not mean anything bad to you," I said reasonably. "All you were receiving was a present. 'Tis me who should feel insulted."

"Evidently you do not, or you'd have torn the letter up."

"But I do! Monstrous insulted!" I squeaked. "How would you like to be called a box of sweets?"

"I cannot imagine anyone ever doing so," he remarked.

I must say I agreed.

"So," he said, "monstrous insulted as you were, you nonetheless presented yourself to be nibbled. Would you like to explain?"

"It was a way to become close to you," I murmured

unashamedly. I sighed. He was not going to reach out and cuddle me, so it was for me to do all. I planted myself firmly against him, so our bodies touched all the way down. He laid an arm across me loosely. "You see," I said confidentially, "ever since I read your poems and went to see *Tamburlaine* I am most sure I am in love with you, and I was prepared to use the letter to bring myself close to you."

"I must commend you on your taste in plays," he remarked, his hand now firming a grasp upon my bum. "And when may I ask did you read poems of mine?"

"'Love is a naked boy!'" I quivered.

"I don't dispute that," he said, stroking my arseflesh.

"I read those poems which we brought from Canterbury," I explained, "about Corinna. You remember Angel Pollock, who gave them, whom you hit? Well, I am with that company. I sing solos with the lute and play ladies. We are at the Cross Keys."

"*Are* you now? Nicholas Henshaw and that fat blond, and the amazing dragon, and now *you*. How curious quaint! Peculiarly of the last century. You might mention to Nicholas that you have the ingredients for a morality play there. Angel could play Anger, and the simpering blond Sloth, and Nicholas could play Envy." He sniggered. "You could play Lust."

"If you join us and play Pride," I said scowling.

"Whereby the angels fell," he agreed comfortably. "Why not?" He settled himself ready to hear compliments. "So – how did you like my play?"

I had no criticism to offer, I was all adoration. I poured out what I had felt watching it, from delight at the spilt brains to joy at the poetry and glitter, and the shameful confession of my secret arousal, which did interest him immense.

"*Which* parts?" he insisted.

"The naked panting slaves and the cage and the threat of being whipped naked."

"What a provocative boy you are..." he observed.

"Am I?" I beamed.

"Yes, you abominable Gaul," he said, pinching my flesh. "And I assume from your blatant ease in my bed that you think compliments and the use of your sweet arse entitle you to sleep here? Or are you planning to limp off to the Cross Keys through the midnight streets?"

224

"O – please don't send me away," I wheedled. "You haven't tasted all my flavours."

"Behave yourself then, and do as you are told," he said severely. "Abject devotion will please me most."

"Yes, Kit," I said happily.

He put his finger on my lips almost affectionately. "I like the way you say that," he said half sleepily; and I pulled the sheet around us both.

I cannot say that we slept well. I was used to Nicholas' shape, and Kit's bed was so narrow. He turned much in his sleep and I was on the outside and I was half knocked out of bed. But these things are small discomforts when one sleeps with one's hero, and I was bleary eyed and happy. When it was morning I watched the light of day fill up the room, I saw his individual eyelashes and the hairs of his eyebrows and the veins of his eyelids, and his awakening brown eyes – all bloodshot at the corners!

"What did you say your name was?" he asked, squinting.

I moved the hair out of his eyes adoringly. "Marc."

"Tell me you were joking, about the King of France."

"I was joking."

"If you were joking I'll black your eye."

"You told me to be obedient; very well, I was not joking. You have spent the night with a Valois mignon."

"And poxy uncomfortable," he said. "Go home now, Marc; I'm bad company mornings."

I got out of bed and started to dress. He swung his legs off the bed and sat, rubbing his eyes hard. He stood up and went over to the table, all naked. I bit my lips as desire stirred instantly – O how I longed to kneel down and begin to kiss him! But while I was thinking about him and lust and kisses, he was leaning over his books, and flipping pages over, and I might as well have been invisible.

I finished dressing, taking longer than I needed, hoping he would remember me and say something about the future. Or about me. I could hear street sounds below, the yells of traders, the barking of dogs, the clattering of a hammer. My heart sank at the thought of explaining what had happened to Nicholas. But what would I have to explain? I spent a night...it is all over now...and anyway it was nothing.

"And now I leave," I said importantly.

He gestured vaguely with his hand, not turning.

I coughed with meaning; this had no effect.

"Kit, I'm going now. I'm going now, but may I come back?"

He turned round and looked surprised.

"Of course you come back," he said. "I thought it was understood."

II

"His glistening eyes shall be my looking glass,
His lips an altar, where I'll offer up
As many kisses as the sea hath sands;
Instead of music I will hear him speak,
His looks shall be my only library."

I WAS possessed.

As I tripped back to the Cross Keys in the sunny morning, all I wanted from Nicholas was the assurance that we were still friends; whether he still loved me for the moment mattered not. I would have liked advice and support and his continued affection, but all this was for the present not as important as that I could go back to Kit's room and make love to him.

To my shame, Nicky's feelings for me were as deep and strong as they had been from the first.

It was strange. We sat together in our garret space, subdued and calm, discussing my situation as if it were a family calamity, as if, say I had just lost all my ships at sea or had my house burned down, and one must still live one's ordinary life.

"'Tis not that I do not understand," said Nicky calmly. "I was angry about your night with Sir Edward because I knew you did not care about him and it seemed to me that you might sleep with anybody for a favour. But this all seems so logical. I suppose I knew you'd fall for him if ever you met. Godamercy, I don't like him, but I can see he is attractive, much the sort you'd like. He somewhat glows..." he finished glumly.

"Tis not that I think any the less of you, Nicky. Tis something other."

"I know. Like a lodestone that draws all to it."

"Exactly. I am grieved-it was him, Nicky. You not liking him."

"It would probably be worse if it was somebody I liked. If I liked him he would probably be a worthy sort of person who would be good and kind to you, and then I should surely lose you. As it is..."

"What?" I demanded.

"Well...you *know*," Nicky hedged.

"What?" I persisted.

"Don't make me upset you, in your exhilaration. O, I simply mean it cannot last. He's very glittering – like a jewel. Jewels are very bright and very cold. And though I doubt he'll properly value you, you'll offer him something for a time. And so, enjoy it. I truly wish you well."

"I'm not going away," I protested. "I'll still be here."

"O, you're going, I assure you," said Nicky ruefully. "You'll have been all round Trebizond and the Euphrates before you've finished, O yes, and the Terrene Sea as he has to call the Mediterranean in order to scan! You'll be up in the rarified air of classical geography and solemn works from the Walsingham library. No more faery rings now!"

"O Nicky," I quivered. "I'll never really leave you. I do believe in our magic, I mean good magic, the flowers in the forest and the ring, and the petals falling from the bough; nothing changes that."

"I think you may find it harder to reach...He makes his own magic, and I wish I could say it was wholesome. O, whatever I say will sound sour, Marc. So confident am I that he will let you down, that all I can feel is a kind of dread sympathy for you. All I can say is that I'll wait for you to come back to your senses, and I'll patch you up when you're ready."

"O! How sombre you are, Nicky."

"Should I laugh?"

"I'm surprised you yet speak to me. Tis horrible what I am doing to you."

"And to yourself!" Nicky observed drily. "And tell me,

where do you intend to sleep, so I may know what to expect?"

"With you, as usual," I mumbled.

Nicholas laughed, though not entirely mirthfully.

"You have a marvellous talent for eating two kinds of jam at once."

I wriggled; reasonably enough, for I did feel very like a worm.

"Oh, moreover," said Nicholas brightly. "Angel and I went to see *Tamburlaine*. We did not like it over much. It has no honest homely folk, but little story, and a surfeit of words. And as for those spilled brains!"

Twas easier for me to put Nicky's remarks down to rivalry, so I just laughed.

That afternoon we performed *St George* and after, with a swiftly beating heart, I changed my clothes back to apple-green silk and cream, and I bought a new baked loaf and wine and carried that round to Kit's room, hoping to find him in before he went to the Phoenix, and thus avoid his drinking friends and Robert.

I was lucky. He was sprawled on the unmade bed looking somewhat unkempt, writing where he lay, the inkpot on the floor, a pile of quills strewn, and himself attractively dishevelled, his shirt open to the waist, and no shoes on. Without more than looks passing between us, he directed me to plates and goblets and a knife, and I did arrange this little meal, and most pleasing to me, I fed him bread while he wrote; and then finally he lay back and stretched, and the bed did creak. O, I thought, his lovely legs, how grown...they had no puppy fat, were not the kind that gentlemen did pinch, like mine.

My eyes strayed to the black inked words he had just writ:

> For she is dead! Thy words do pierce my soul
> Ah sweet Theridamus say so no more;
> Though she is dead, yet let me think she lives,
> And feed my mind, that dies for want of her.

"It is beautiful," I said.

"Yes," he said munching. "I am tolerable pleased with it."

"But it is a she!" I complained.

"Women often are!" he teased. "You come most opportune, sweetheart, with your bread and wine, for I was set to sink in languid melancholy – it comes to something, does it not, to

228

make oneself upset with what one's writ!"

"What is it? What are you writing?"

"I thought you knew."

"No; it seems to be a play."

"The wonder of his fine intelligence! It seems to be a play!"

"Well, I could read these pages or you could tell me what it is about."

"If *you* were me, what would *you* write next, hey? Tell me what could follow *Tamburlaine*?"

I shook my head, wide-eyed. I could not imagine.

He said with very twinkling eyes and in a secretive stage whisper: "*Tamburlaine – Part Two!*"

"O!" I said.

"Prettily gasped. And speaking of gasping, do you know how to fill a pipe?"

"No."

"Would you like to learn?"

I knelt by the bed, head bent, while he initiated me into the mysteries of folding and packing tobacco leaves into a pipe bowl, and I watched in fascination and concern as the smoke clouds rose and the scent began to permeate the room.

"Kit, I don't think it can be good for you," I said anxiously. "You might be burning your insides...you know how a chimney looks, all black – well, what if your throat went black also, and your teeth and tongue?"

"You sound much like my mother," he said, comfortably puffing. "Here, try it."

Cautiously I sucked in a huge mouthful while he watched amused. Smoke filled me up and choked me and I panicked and could not breathe, my eyes streamed and I gasped and gasped, my throat making horrible noises.

"What did I do wrong?" I gulped.

"Almost everything," he smiled, "as I supposed. But fear not – later I will find you something your throat shall like better."

My gut quivered with a wicked thrill. I turned over the loose pages, the ink barely dry. I mused happily about the way he had written of love. Full of admiration and emotion I expressed my rapture at his words.

"You promise to weep then and start the others off?" he teased; but he was pleased.

"How do you write so perfect about love for a lady?" I burst out.

"I have to assume it's the same," he replied, but so serious and straightforward I knew he was laughing. Then he said: "I thought of Alexander. To me he is one of the world's great lovers. This golden boy who changed the world, who took the map of his own time and then rewrit it to his own design. His lover by his side, Hephaistion. And then Hephaistion to die... all sudden, they still young, with everything yet to be achieved. How must he have felt, Alexander? The spoils of conquest glowing at his feet, his lover dead, so sadly mortal. We are teased, I think. We are almost gods, we see the world spread out... and then we die... and once we've seen the jest of it, all that's left for us is anger, and we stand and fling our stones against the sky like impudent boys at windows... I thought you came to divert me, Marcus; pull your breeches down or something."

"Certainly not," I said, so dignified and poised that it was a challenge. He laid down his pipe carefully and lunged at me, and we rolled over on the floor in a struggle. We lay side by side, his hand inside my hose, the other wiping back his hair.

"She had to go, Marc. It was necessary."

"O?" I sulked, preferring the romp.

"She was in the way."

"Well, you are a plain and simple murderer then, to kill her off so coolly."

"She would have been too much a helpmeet. Truly he did love her and would probably have listened. But I need him free. And a little crazed."

I shifted my arse about to remind him I was still there.

"Alexander," he said, "never recovered from Hephaistion's death. He burnt the city where it happened. He erected colossal statues, built a huge sarcophagus. A madness lay hold of him. It will be the same for Tamburlaine. We shall have much blood..." he said mistily.

I sat up outraged, wriggling clear of his hand.

"You are not natural, Kit! You plan a bloodbath with your hand on my behind."

He reached up and pulled me down on to him, and he kissed me hard. When he finally let me go, my lips were bruised and swollen. I wiped my trickling tears. He stood up.

"Tidy up my papers," he said, gesturing to the floor, and I knelt and gathered up the death of Zenocrate.

"Don't weep on them!" he screeched, horrified.

"Forgive me," I said humbly.

"And then come here."

Kit sat upon the bed, and I went to kneel between his legs. His open shirt hung loose each side of me and my eyes drank in the sight of his lean belly. I took his prick between my throbbing lips; he put his hands on my shoulders and pulled me closer. I devoted all my being to giving him pleasure; it was as if his prick was the axis of the world and I was spinning wide in space, fixed on to it which was my centre.

"Glorious boy," he murmured. "Sweet slut."

He toppled over me like Samson between the pillars of the temple, and I squatted there, my face all wet, the taste of him deep down my throat.

In this pose were we when Robert opened the door and discovered us.

How he did swagger about all gleefully! He said it was like catching Mars and Venus in their net, or in our case, Jupiter and Ganymede. Kit was most amused, as well he might be, having had his satisfaction – I was the more vexed, being not so fortunate, and I knelt and scowled.

Robert whistled. "If ever I did see a used boy! His lips all swollen and purple – his face all glistening with love juice. He is a peach, Kit. I swear he almost makes me want to turn sodomite!"

"Well," Kit agreed languidly, almost as if it were a compliment to him, "*I* do like him."

"So," chatted Robert, poking around at the papers. "Did you kill off the lady?"

"Yes, she is gone – amid a welter of sighs and tears. This sentimental soul," indicating myself, "was pleased with this: 'Wounding the world with wonder and with love.' Myself I think some high flown passages have come out well. Here – 'Batter the shining palace of the sun, and shiver all the starry firmament...'"

"Stars and firmaments, yes, tis very you," laughed Robert.

They bent over the table, Kit absentmindedly adjusting his

clothes to seemliness, Robert carelessly swigging back the last of
our wine. I sat upon the bed. They were discussing the coming
evening and who would and would not be there. Kit suddenly
turned to me.

"Will you come eat with me then, sweetheart?"

I stared astonished. Robert smirked. "Poor lad, he is quite
overcome. What do you say, O sweet and obliging one, will
you share our humble supper?"

"Do you *want* me, Kit?" I said surprised.

"I do want you, yes," said Kit frankly. "And in my bed
tonight."

I went pink with pleasure.

"Do come," said Kit, curiously winningly. "If you don't stay
with me I shall be morbid and lie thinking about death and
mortality."

"Heaven forbid," groaned Robert.

"Heaven does not; Heaven loves us to be morbid," Kit
scowled. "It keeps us in our place. Good and troubled."

"We will have you cheerful," Robert promised.

"Tis true, you know, I did monstrous sadden myself today
writing about the death of lovers. How vile it is we have to die!"

"Ah, Kit," said Robert with praying hands and a holy tone.
"We have eternity!"

"Fuck eternity," said Kit with feeling.

"O," cried Robert. "That! From you!" He turned to me
flamboyantly. "There was never such a villain greedy for
eternity as this!" He slung an arm round Kit's shoulder. "Do
you hear me, sweet boy? When he says 'fuck eternity' just laugh.
He would sell his soul to be eternal and to believe Heaven was
true."

"Anybody would," Kit muttered grudgingly.

"I would," I maintained stoutly.

"What, you?" Robert laughed. "I thought you were but a
fabulous arse! You mean you have thoughts too?"

"Yes," I said reasonably. "I have always wanted to be eternal.
I do believe we have eternity in God but we want it on earth too.
I do. I can think of nothing better than to be famous down the
ages."

"Ah, he is one with us," Kit laughed fondly. "You cannot
fault that, Robert, tis what we all demand. How did you

propose to achieve this fame, my little plum? You are surely not a secret writer?"

"No," I wriggled, pink and petulant. "I have no particular talent. I thought perhaps I might have been a famous courtesan, when poet and lute player seemed unlikely. I live in hopes."

"I tell you what," Kit said merrily. "We'll compromise. Tis I shall become famous down the ages and if you want to become a famous courtesan you can be mine. We'll be up to the elbows in the Castalian Spring together."

"Up to the crotch, more like," grunted Robert.

"We shall fuck in it," Kit agreed.

"You'll fuck and be forgotten," Robert shrugged. "You cannot offer this boy fame on those terms. If your odd little amity is bruited abroad you'll be arrested for sodomy, and all your masterpieces will never be writ."

Kit laughed. He had not been serious. He cared not two pins whether I achieved my fame. There was only his to consider.

"Meanwhile," he said, "shall we starve?"

As we made ready to go out, he said: "Not one word, Robert, not in jest or even drunk, about what you came in on. Even drunk, Robert, not a hint."

"I swear it," said Robert. "And he shall say it was a girl who kissed his lips to bruising."

And so that night I ate at the Phoenix, amongst people who have almost all since become famous. Kit ignored me; he was too busy expounding his opinions and telling everybody what to think. Sometimes I had to shudder at the things he said, for it was very raw and frank and lacking in respect for everything he named, and I dreaded that a member of the Watch, or worse, was present, lurking. But everybody swore vile oaths, and swapped lurid tales of foreign travel and dark deeds and loose women, and much politics was talked, and much sneering at what was old-fashioned and past. And Robert Greene was quite as bad as Kit in what he said, and truly I was glad it was not him I loved, for if his tales were true, he must have had the pox ten times over.

Afterwards I went back home with Kit, and he was somewhat drunk. But even drunk he hurried. I always did think with him he was conscious of time being in short supply. When we were safe in his room he took me in his arms. His kiss tasted of ale and

233

tobacco, and I found it a far more acceptable way of taking the weed than through a pipe.

"Come to bed," he murmured. We took our clothes off as we stumbled across to the bed, dropping them behind us on the floor like footsteps. He groaned as he eased himself down and laughed also. Each time one drinks too much one swears never again to do so. I was tipsy also. We lay there warm and naked in the lust-streaked sheets, the bed seeming to roll like a ship.

"What do you *want* from me?" Kit suddenly said, puzzled.

"Want? Nothing."

"No lies, wag. A prosperous courtesan doesn't attach itself to a poor poet. Why did not you try for the Earl of Oxford? He likes boys."

"I care not for fame," I announced dramatically.

"Liar."

"I renounce fame. I want this, what I have now."

"What? My drunken breath in your pretty pink ear?"

"If you like. I want anything you give me, anything."

"You know what *that* will be!" he sniggered. "But there can be nothing more, you know that, do you not? You would be a fool if you hope that I shall love you. I have not time."

We heard a church bell strike some hour or other, with horrible appropriateness. We laughed uneasily.

"You would think God listened," Kit remarked. "He's the supreme dealer in stage effects. Forked lightning is nothing to Him – burning bushes – parting seas – a very minor angel would have been sent to ring that little bell."

"Why do you say you have not time? What demands do you think I would make?"

"None, because I would prevent you. Do you think you are the first boy I have taken up with – you are not! They all begin by promising no intrusion, perfect sweetness. In truth, they are like women, greedy and grasping – for time, affection, presents, feelings that have been affronted – and you will be the same. I will not be involved. My thoughts are too important, and my head is bursting with them. You stay here on my terms, no more, no less, and I am not easy."

"I love you," I said in holy tones.

"Christ! I half admire your stubbornness. I'm glad you're here tonight. I was not lying when I said I was like to be morbid tonight. I would have brought wine back with me, but you are preferable. Am I to lose myself in the sweet flesh of your ample arse? Will you be especial good to me?"

I held his face in my hands and kissed him, feeling our shared excitement mount.

"Mon cher amour," I said ardently.

"Turn over, angel arse."

We groaned together in the warm sweaty darkness. Without finesse we hurried to our satisfaction.

"Ah," he breathed, "my little love."

Yes! He did say that! Tears trickled from my eyes, I was so happy.

"I love you," I said, and sniffed.

"Constant repetition never convinced me of any truth," he murmured sleepily.

As we drifted into dozy slumber I reflected seriously about life. Against our fears, our pain of being mortal, all we have is – and like a good Catholic I replied Faith. But another voice was louder. It said Faith is all very well, but it is not so effective as something else: two bodies lying close in the dark, pressed together by the sweat of lust, comforted by the other's breathing and his sweet warm smell.

And when the church bell sounded out the next half hour, that might have reminded us of time, we did not hear it.

III

"Come, Ganymede..."

I BELIEVE it was a chance remark of mine that made Kit press for me to stay next morning. If I had not said it I am sure he would have all careless sent me off to the Cross Keys while he began what happened after Zenocrate's death. All I said was: "Well, I'd best be leaving now; I have to go to church."

"You have to go to church!" Kit cried, as disbelieving as if I'd said I'd had to slit babes' throats. "Why do you?"

235

"It is Sunday."

"Indeed it is, and tomorrow may possibly be Monday. Use your fingers to help you count, and you may list all the days in the week, and after, we might try harder matter, like the months of the year."

"Do not laugh. I always go to church."

"I'd have sworn you'd been a Papist."

"Yes I am, but not very devout. Nicholas says as it is the same God I should dispense with scruples, for a quiet life."

"Nicholas has the makings of an archbishop," Kit observed drily. "One that might last through several reigns."

"I do not overmuch enjoy it," I admitted frankly. "Tis a very plain service."

"Mm, yes, I prefer a good Papist show, tis marvellous pretty for ceremonies. Organs blasting away, and the elevation of Mass, and all those singing men and golden-haired choirboys with rosebud mouths all making an O as if they were offering up. They're hypocrites, Protestants. I cannot bear stupidity and they are stupid. I was trained for the church, you know; I have seen it from within."

"O! You were nearly a priest!" I was astonished.

"But the church was spared, fortunately. I'd have been a rat gnawing at its bowels. Excommunicated by now, no doubt, as all the best people are."

"Why did you change your mind?"

"I saw the light."

"What light?"

"That there is no God but Man, who has created God in his own image."

I shivered, half expecting a small thunderbolt.

"See," shrugged Kit. "You can say anything – God doesn't stir an inch. Listen: There is no God; I deny God; I say God is a fool. There. Was I struck down? No. I am yet here with you in this bed, uncomfortable but aroused, and no devil has been sent to prod us with a pitchfork. You try – come, say what I just said."

"O no! I could not!"

"What are you afraid of? *Are* you afraid?" His brilliant eyes close to mine radiated mocking amusement.

"No – yes – in truth, I am."

"I order you not to be. And I will prove your fear is groundless. Say what I just said. Say it now."

"No," I wriggled.

"O yes you will," he stated firmly, and he took hold of me by the ear ring! Imagine! He twisted my head down and up and I do not exaggerate to say it was agony, and pierced ears can go putrid and abscesses form; truly, the pain was immense and I was terrified for my ear, and I said all the things he wanted me to say.

"Well," said Kit, releasing me. "Are you struck down? Are you encircled by crimson demons prodding at your vitals?"

"No, but —"

"He has not even given us boils, not even one little pimple."

"Maybe later?"

"Then it will be inconclusive. It would only have an effect if it were immediate."

"O," I moaned. "How easily I did submit. I was so fearful for my ear. When I think of all those saints and martyrs – roasted on gridirons, sawn in two pieces, disembowelled..."

"Yes, darling, it would seem you are not the stuff of which martyrs are made. So, is all proved? Whatever deity He is up there, He's tolerant to the point of apathy. He also has but small opinion of us His creations. He sends us crafty shifty prophets and a text fraught with inconsistencies and lies."

"As what?" I demanded.

"For instance, this one: If God is everlasting, invisible and immortal, then how can Jesus Christ be God, and be born of Mary, mortal, visible and subject to change?"

Naturally I had no answer.

"And the story of the Creation. Everybody knows, from nothing can nothing be made – Ex nihilo nihil fit. Moreover, there were Indians living in the Americas before the Bible was writ. And if the Garden of Eden was in Africa or by the Mediterranean, how did there come to be people in the Spice Islands? Not from Adam!"

"Kit, will you have a look at my ear and make sure that it is well?"

"Are you listening to anything I'm saying? Pea brain! I am giving you cogent reasons why we should despise the early writings in the Bible."

"Yes, Kit."

"And look at Moses who was a cunning old Egyptian. Anyone who takes a map and looks can see that he could have led the Jews to the Promised Land within the year – so why did he take forty? And the foolish Jews went stumbling after, covering the same ground again and again, passing the same thorn trees they saw twenty years ago, without noticing. And these God *chose*! Was it for their stupidity, so He could pass on his word where it would have most effect? Fishermen, I ask you. Are fishermen intelligent? What do they know except one fish from another? No wonder they believed in miracles – all they had seen before was fish!"

"What do think happens when we die then?"

"Nothing at all," said Kit gloomily.

"Do not you believe in Hell?"

"I think Hell's a fable."

"But the flames and demons...people have always believed . . ."

"No; tis a plot to keep us good. I daresay politics gave birth to it. If there were no Hell, sweetheart, no fear of damnation, what's to stop us committing any crime? Peasants toil and sweat from fear, that if they rise up and revolt, they'll go to Hell. If they but chose to think it out they'd see that they are damned already. Stipendium peccati mors est – right? The reward of sin is death. Si peccasse negamus, fallimur, et nulla est in nobis veritas – if we say that we have no sin, we deceive ourselves, and there's no truth in us. Well then, it follows we must sin and everlastingly die – what kind of doctrine is this? Intelligent people aren't fobbed off with such inconsistencies."

"No Hell then? No Heaven either?"

"Heaven is here," he said to me meltingly, "or can be if you kiss me."

We indulged in a long and lovely kiss.

"You are lovely," he said. "You have no business being at church; you are all temptation. Stay with me. If you have a mind to worship, worship me." His voice cajoled, smouldered, persuaded.

"You would be a cruel god."

"Yes, but would give favours. It shall well please you to become my acolyte."

238

"I fear so."

During the morning while he sat and smoked, he let me rifle through the wondrous treasure house that lay strewn across his table, I mean his books and works. He had history chronicles, and Ovid with illustrations, and the writings of Machiavel alongside the Bible, and an enormous thing called "Munster's Cosmography." He had Ortelius' world map, and Richard Hakluyt's Journeys, and books with maps about the Turks and the nearer cast. Travellers recounted how they had sailed the mighty Euphrates, from Balsara through the Persian Gulf to the city of Ormuz and thence to Chaul and Goa in East India. There were descriptions of Gibraltar, Constantinople, Alexandria, Cairo, Tunis, Goletta, Malta, Algiers and Tripoli, Santa Cruz and Asafi, Morocco, the Isles of Cape Verde, Benin, and the dreadful Cape of Bona Speranza. I make a list of them because I understood with him the magic in the sound of names – he said: "I just like saying them out loud", as if it was a foible. But with him he translated them into poetry, and in the mouths of Sigismund and Orcanes and the rest, the map did come alive and seem magnificent. He said:

"Alexander *knew* those places, saw them for himself... all the gold, the rivers, all the burning deserts and deserted tombs and palaces. Ah – to think they all *exist* – and we not there! If only there were some way – if we could turn magic to our advantage and go where we would – life never could be long enough..."

I said: "O Kit, and you have some French books too – 'Le Tocsin contre les Massacreurs' – this is a Huguenot version, you should read both sides, you know – and here is Jean de Serre's 'Commentaires' on the Civil Wars – Kit!" I accused. "You can read French! Why don't you speak it?"

He laughed lazily. "Because it suits me very well to enjoy your charming accent, which I find endearing and amusing. But I'll go hang before I give you the privilege of thinking that of me!"

I sorted out his Ovid elegies for him, the ones that we brought up from Canterbury. And this I read out loud:

"Lo, I confess, I am thy captive, I,
And hold my conquered hands for thee to tie."

And Kit looked at me speculatively, as a fox might look at a chicken.

239

And I found in verse that belief we all held dear – Nicky and Amyas and me, and all, as we discussed amongst the daisies the best way to achieve immortality on this earth:

> Garments do wear, jewels and gold do waste,
> The fame that verse gives doth for ever last.

"O Kit," I sighed. "You will be famous down the ages."

"Yes," he said thoughtfully, "I will be, if my work is not lost."

"You must publish," I said earnestly. "Do you have a patron?"

"O please to advise me," said Kit with heavy sarcasm. "Your great knowledge of the literary world would prove invaluable."

I did somewhat blush. Kit relented.

"Have you heard the name of Walsingham?" he said.

"The Secretary of State?"

"No, no, not him; his cousin Tom, who lives at Scadbury. Whose beauty..."

Kit smiled dreamily at memories I chose not to enquire about. But my question was answered; he did have a patron. He added: "Edward Blount will publish me, but there is not yet enough. Translations – a couple of plays, tis nothing – I need at least two lifetimes – one to live and one to write..."

"Oo, look," I remarked. "Here is a lewd one!"

"Where?"

> "'And eagerly she kissed me with her tongue
> And under mine her wanton thigh she flung
> Yea, and she soothed me up and called me Sir
> And used all speech that might provoke and stir
> Yet like as if cold hemlock I had drunk
> It mocked me, hung down the head and sunk.
> Nay, more, the wench did not disdain a whit
> To take it in her hand and play with it –
> But when she saw it would by no means stand
> But still drooped down, regarding not her hand...'

Kit, this is well told! Has it ever happened to you like this?"

"No indeed," he said huffily. "It is a translation – as you very well know, impudent. And now tis time you came to church, it

240

being Sunday. The shrine of Saint Christopher, you being a traveller."

How curious well together we blended, I with my need to worship, he to be worshipped. He sprawled languidly back in his chair, and tapping his nail on a knife, he made a metallic sound; he said: "That is the bell that summons you."

I went. O I was wicked! I crossed myself and then knelt down at his carelessly spread legs and put my hands together as if I were at prayer. And him encouraging me and prompting me, I said holy words and he laid his hands on my head and blessed me, and I confessed that I had lain with him and he made me describe it, as if he had not been there!

"But, did he enter you? What, at the arsehole? O peccatum peccatorum! And how was he? Very mighty and strong, say, ten inches? O nomine Domini! So much! And did you yield to him most willingly? Misericordia!"

And then he absolved me and forgave me. "Go away," he said sepulchrally, "and sin no more."

But on the contrary, our wickedness had so excited us, that when I looked up at him and fluttered my eyelashes mischievously, it led immediately to carnal pleasures; and shortly afterwards I limped home.

I did not care to think too much what I had done. I hoped that God would think it was all in foolishness and understand that we were not being serious in mocking holy things. Uneasily, though, I knew we had been serious, both so. I was besotted by Kit; he could have commanded anything of me, and when I had covered his feet with kisses I had been lost in adoration. So my conscience did trouble me somewhat as I returned to my company.

The air was full of the ringing of bells, and the streets of honest sober citizens. Here, I felt, were the dutiful, going to or from church, their thoughts upon spiritual matters, their religious views all conformity. I felt marked by a stain of sin by what I had been doing, and I am not now speaking of the stickiness that was in my hair. I felt the Devil had access to me, and I looked about me warily. I half expected to see grinning fiends in doorways, their pointed tails flicking like a whip's end.

To my alarm, as in an old morality tale, I did see one grinning in a doorway. It was not a fiend, at least not one with pitchfork

and with flame; no, it was that gaudy beggar I had noticed in
Paul's churchyard, all covered with grisly sores and in that same
patched cloak. He saw me, that was clear enough, and recognised me, and leered, as if he knew what I had been at, as if it
was an intimate secret we both shared. I gulped and put my
hand to my throat. What did he want with me? Was there to be
retribution for my unholy day? I do believe I wondered whether
he was sent from on high, because his being there disturbed me,
like the Good or Evil Angel that attends our secret wishes and
intents.

He took a step forward from the doorway in which he stood
and raised his crutch. I gasped. O! Surely he did not mean to
speak to me! What could he have to say?

But even as I stared, a churchgoing family passed between
us, buckled shoes picking their way through the muddy ruts –
father, mother, children, and there were servants too. The father
raised his fist at the beggar.

"Be off with you, you poxy devil," he said in ringing tones;
he was as big as if he were a tanner or a blacksmith on a weekday,
and very fierce. The beggar fawned and whined and slunk away.

"Our laws are not severe enough," said the worthy fellow to
his wife. "Filth like that should be outside the city walls and
booted to some other town, not squatting here where decent
folk must look upon them on their way to church."

And I ran home no easier in my mind that I had been before.

It was comfortable and reassuring to sleep that night with
Nicholas. I think there are two kinds of people, those who put
their arms about you, and those who wait for you to put your
arm about them, and Nicky was the first. When I tentatively
asked if he would look at my ear for me he did. He said it was a
little swollen and told me to take the ring out, and he bathed my
ear with a potion and tweaked my nose hard for the company I
kept. I was an apologetic docile patient.

We did not make love, but lay warm and slept, with heaps of
apples piled about us.

The gossip from the inn, said Nicky, was that Francis had
been paying court to Phoebe and had bought her a cap with
ribbons, and Angel was monstrous discomposed, and had come
to Nicholas asking him to write a sonnet to her charms and

Nicholas had obliged. When Francis heard, he knew the sonnet was not Gabriel's and had demanded one of Nicky for himself but different; and Nicholas decided it was only fair if sonnets were to achieve the lady, so Francis must have one too.

"But why should she want Francis?" I marvelled. "He is so ugly."

"He is not. And he is most reliable of nature. He would make a better husband. He never wastes his money. He would be a provider, in so far as a player can be. Maybe she is being practical."

"Yes; women are mysterious," we decided.

Nicholas was touching up an old play called *The Letter*, in which I was to have a bigger part than usual. It was a comedy of misunderstanding, all hingeing on a love letter written by a lady (Amyas) whose name was Alice, to her lover, without her husband knowing. I was the confidante, Perdita, a sweet and clever girl who manages to burn the letter before the husband's very eyes, swearing it was but a paltry sonnet I had writ that I was burning because it was so bad. So all are laughing at this silly maid's discomfiture, when really she is saving her mistress's honour. The lover Nicholas gives me a kiss in gratitude, for if he had been discovered he would have been disinherited and sent away. It was a jolly play to do, most droll, and the lines easy to learn.

"I would have liked," said Nicholas, "to write a play around you, Marc; you as the heroine. I wondered whom I could create who spoke with a foreign tongue, all the rest being English. There are divers queens, you know. But Margaret of Anjou was such a bitch. I thought perhaps Elinor of Aquitaine. You know, the Court of Love..."

"Oo yes – beautiful!" I beamed.

"'Tis pity Joan of Arc was such a clown and whore – otherwise we could have made a wondrous tragedy..."

"Nicky!" I screeched. "What are you saying? She was a saint!"

In vain did I tell them the truth. I was a lone voice in a wilderness of scorn and disbelief. I became enraged and upset. These people thought the holy Jeanne had slept with the army entire, that she practised witchcraft with Gilles de Rais, and that she was a bumbling, clodhopping imbecile. Otherwise, they all agreed, a wondrous poignant play could have been writ, all soul and fire; if only she had been a virgin martyr – she *was*, she *was*, I cried (they ignored me). How moving then her death scene – how terrible the inquisitors – how appealing I would be, portraying that. I agreed. I begged Nicholas to write that play.

"No," he sighed. "We'd be laughed off the stage."

Our opposing views on Jeanne d'Arc did not constitute a large difficulty. We realised that politics were strange things; and in spite of our differences, everything between me and the company of players was very affable, and we always cherished warm feelings together even when they were misguided and I was touchy. They placated me with hugs and compliments, and feasting soon took precedence.

We had the feast late one night in the kitchen of the inn. We drank cider and beer with our immense meal, and we sang old ballads. There were all the inn folk present, and some of the guests, so there were women too, and all in a merry mind. Amyas read us portions from a novel he had bought in Paul's churchyard. It was the tale of Sir Lucas de Barbarole, a rich Italian cut-throat, who lived entirely upon a diet of peacocks of the Ind, and passed his days robbing and murdering and abducting ladies. Amyas liked to read the ladies' playnts:

"Thus with her aged husband lying in death's extremities in the room above, poor Corisanda had no one to whom she could call for help. The villain pressed her to the floor and tied her arms together *with her own long hair*!" (We gasped.) "And there he took his wicked way with her."

"I would have kneed his balls," said Phoebe.

"But Corisanda was too gentle," Amyas reproved. "Like to have been a nun. Well! This is what she said when he had gone: O stars! O moon! O heavenly arc that lies above and sees all our woes! Shed not your light on one who here lies shamed. For now is death welcome to one who has lived to see her chaste treasure despoiled. O woe, O bitterness, no more the day shall dawn –"

We had to silence him or he would have railed all night. But there were many more delights within the book, for finally Signor Lucas was brought to justice, and what a fate was his!

"He was spread out upon a wheel –" Amyas jumped upon the table to read it out, so all were obliged to hear. "– Upon a wheel," he continued menacingly. "Upon his eyes choice morsels were placed so that crows would fly down to peck at them." (We shivered loudly to show how terrified we were.) "Gnawing worms were put up his nose" ("Ugh!" cried Phoebe. "Up his nose?" "It is disgusting," agreed Angel, with his arm about her, pretending a sensibility he did not have.) "And in his ears!" glowered Amyas. "And a rat was let loose in his throat, his mouth then muzzled..."

"I have heard a tale like this where the fellow was fixed with his nether parts in a barrel," said Francis mildly. "A rat was in the barrel also. The rat then sought the only hole he could find..."

"I have heard of a snake's egg hatching in the stomach of a woman," agreed Jack. "The snake then grew, and also looked for a way out."

"Did it come through the throat or bite its way out through the belly?"

"At the Dagger Inn in Fish Street," said Phoebe, "a rat crept into a pie that was to be baked. They baked the pie, that rat being in it, and there he was discovered, all cooked, with the apples and cloves."

"That rat, at least, should have been able to get out," Nicholas observed.

"How so?"

"Being a pie-rat it could have fought its way out with a cutlass!"

"I have not yet told what happened to his stomach," Amyas interrupted the laughter, stamping his foot, which shook the boards and caused everyone to clutch at their cider. "His stomach was Cut Open and in it was put a nest of ants and then – and then –" (we waited, awed) "– *fireworks were attached to his privities*!"

"More cider, Marc?" said Phoebe.

"Thank you, yes."

The women, I noticed, did not appreciate the proper seriousness of the climax of Signor Lucan's punishment, indeed, some sniggered; but several of the men did wince, I saw it. Satisfied, Amyas returned to his seat.

We passed around a book of jokes; some were amusing, some were foolish. There was: Why should a lady seeking a lover travel westward? Because then she will find the Isle of Man. And there was: A fruit has rind and pith. Where is the pith, within or without? Answer: Neither; the pith is in the pot beneath the bed.

But we did laugh at all, and then we moved the table back and had a dance, and revels lasted well into the night.

Madge put her arm round me and drew me to one side. She was rosy with cider, and merry as one walking out one midsummer morning; and very warm and sweating close to. She said: "Are you happy with us now, Marc? You do seem so. Are you going to stay with us, and make your home here?"

"I am most happy tonight; I feel most comfortable."

"We are glad to have you. Don't go back to France. I hope you'll think of us as your family now. We are a rude and noisy crew, I know, but we mean well, and we will never let you down."

I kissed and hugged her and said I would stay, I would stay for ever.

I am obliged to compare that merry time with an evening at Kit's a few days later, when divers of what Nicholas had once called "his unpleasant cronies" came round all to get drunk together.

I daresay that night the conversation was as brilliant and literary as ever conversation could be in the land, with ideas and wit like tennis balls bandied about so swift you could hardly tell where they went. Because I was pouring drinks and passing them around of course I was called Ganymede, and Kit was congratulated on having found someone so pretty and winsome, who was moreover so compliant and amenable. You know, even intelligent people, I think, believe that if you speak with a foreign accent you are not in fact as intelligent as they, and are considered as something akin to an amusing toy, and this explains their attitude to me. The more tipsy they became, the more lewd in language. There were no women present, and I suppose their mischievousness was logically like to fall on me.

I sat at Kit's feet, he idly toying with my hair, and when they called for drinks and such I jumped up and obliged, and sometimes I did marvel that here was I, scion of a noble house, waiting on the likes of merchants' offspring and (with a dark glance at Kit) cobblers' sons. In a way I did not care, but I was treated very cool and scathing, as servants are.

I know well enough who it was pointed out that Ganymede is

often represented naked – it was Robert – and I believe he said it to challenge Kit, to see what power he truly had over me. And because it was Robert, Kit responded in kind; and when they teased Kit that I would not do it even for him, he ordered me to strip. For him I did oblige, though I resented that the suggestion had come from Robert. They made a circle round me, and encouraged me as if they had been farm labourers visiting a stew. I received their comments with fluttering eyelashes and a sort of modest smirk. I knew that I was beautiful. I was quite happy to be naked and admired; also it pleased Kit mightily to parade me. I carried on just as before, filling cups, going where I was beckoned, and of course I was much pinched about my person. I returned dutifully to Kit's feet and sat upon the floor.

This was when I first heard Kit's daring assertion that God would not be shocked to look upon our little scene, since He permitted love between His son and the blessed saint John. This being so, was not boy love the correct way to behave, and all who went with women, deviant? But Robert said that women were best, and boasted of a drab in Southwark who gave more delight than any boy. And some said that if all boys were as perfect as I was, they would be tempted, and Kit laughed and said no, he would not share. Soon after, he told me to get dressed.

I point out that on the two occasions – the celebration at the Cross Keys with people who were fond of me, and the evening being Ganymede to people who did not value me at all – my pleasure was equal. I do not understand why. Nicholas said that in me the ratio of animal and soul was equally mixed, that the qualities of man and beast in me were entirely parallel. I was mud and air.

I do not know, but it was so. I loved the warmth and joviality of one, the wanton lasciviousness and provocation of the other. Perhaps it was due to being a Gemini.

EIGHT

I

"Ay, this is it: you can sit toying there,
And playing with that female wanton boy..."

How to explain the tyranny of love? I would have let Kit treat me any way he liked – indeed, I somewhat did – and since there were people who misliked him, even hated him, it must be that he was not considered perfect by all. Yet to me he was. I could see that there were disturbing aspects to his character, but they counted for nothing beside his dark attraction. Just to look at him was enough, to watch his long slender fingers, the curve of his neck as he bent over his writing, the falling forward of his long brown hair, the sudden shock of his intense eyes as he looked at me, the curl of his lip. I remember some mornings when he allowed me to stay and watch him work, and with all the holy devotion of an acolyte at an altar I prepared his quills, cutting one end and sucking the tip to the appropriate softness, saying nothing, except when he told me to, needing diversion. I saw him write the lovely words:

Thou shalt not beautify Larissa plains
But keep within the circle of mine arms.

I saw those words first writ; I saw the ink wet.

But Kit's mind was not on love when he continued *Tamburlaine Part Two*. First he was all deep involved with the technical aspect of warfare, and from a book of weaponry and a clear remembrance of Canterbury's great walls, he was all concerned with ditches and counterscarps, bulwarks and ramparts, countermines, artillery and cannon. And his thoughts were fixed on war and blood, of which there was much in the play, and much of piercing bowels and blows and bloody wounds and lancing flesh. I think Kit would have been a gentler companion if he had then been engaged on *Edward the Second*, for that is much to do with love.

He once asked me thoughtfully: "What is the wickedest thing you have ever done, would you say?"

"O . . . well, some would say that I have done in bed," I shrugged.

"O come, let's not be ridiculous. Fucking is naught. You disappoint me, sweetheart."

"Well, there was a time when I took pleasure in killing things," I mumbled.

"What things?"

"Chickens and cats."

"How did you do it?"

"I drowned the cats. I wrung the chickens' necks . . . I know these are customary ways to kill, but it is the intent behind the deed. I did it for pleasure."

"Indeed . . . and . . . *was* there pleasure?"

"I fear there was."

"Why, do you think?"

"I think it was because I was unhappy. I hated to see these stupid creatures pecking and squawking and being alive, not troubled with fancies and fears. I thought: well, you shall suffer."

"We all have it in us," Kit said. "If you had limitless power, would you be tempted to kill again – not necessarily chickens – would there be pleasure then?"

"Do you mean kill *men*?"

"Yes, I do; yes, that is what I mean."

"O no! I don't think so!"

Kit began to lose interest in me as a subject for probing. I could not help it. I think if you are in love there is no room in you for revenge and blood. Kit was nurturing the seeds whence grew *The Jew of Malta*, one of the most sinister plays I have ever seen. But I was the one who had stood in a garden by the river one glittering morning, full of excitement and freedom, waving my arms at the golden barge of the Queen. The sun in all its warmth is stronger than blood, and makes it look no more than rust. And I had long since sold my dagger.

Twas fortunate I was not a chaste and modest boy, for my

sensibilities were not spared when Robert visited Kit and found me in his bed, which happened divers times. There may be lovers who hide their boy away or call out Do not enter; but Kit was not one of these, almost the opposite, parading me with the nonchalant pride of ownership, and I was pleased for him to do it.

"Look at him," marvelled Kit. "Is he not sweet? Look at that arse, Robert, those downy cheeks like fat ripe peaches. And you say you want women!"

"Yes I do," laughed Robert, "and as many as I can have. But I grant you this is tasty, for a boy."

"May I get dressed please, Kit?" I asked politely.

"You leave us, Ganymede?" enquired Robert.

"Marc is a working man," said Kit severely. "He is a marvellous important player in Sir Edward Knollys' company."

"Is that so? I have not heard of them."

"Few have," sniggered Kit.

"We are very good," I said stoutly, pulling on my stockings.

"Are you? What is your repertoire?"

"We do *The Spanish Tragedy*, shortened."

"O? Who plays Ned Alleyn's part?" enquired Kit with interest.

"Jack Unsworth," I said defensively. "Who else?"

"Ah yes, fat Jack," agreed Kit seriously. "Who else indeed!"

"If I were in your company," Robert remarked, "I would be praying that Tom Kyd did not come marching round to see how you have mangled what used to be his play!"

"Tom Kyd? Is he one I have met?" I frowned.

"I believe he was down at the Phoenix the other night," said Kit vaguely.

"Yes – that time when you were spouting somewhat about Moses!"

They grinned, as if Kit's views on Moses were well known.

"So? He laughed as loud as anyone. He is good company and I like him," Kit maintained. "I used to think his plays were better than mine. But now," he added languidly, "I do not."

"He will perhaps write better when he is a full grown Goat," decided Robert smirking. "Even so, he will not like his play dismembered."

I shrugged. "What can he do? A play once writ is anybody's."

250

"You would do best to stick to your ancient clownish tales more fit for country players. What else do you perform?"

"We do *Saint George*, and a pastoral called *Sir Calidore*, and we are rehearsing a new old play about a Letter."

"A letter?" Kit sniggered. "H for homespun?"

"O for old-fashioned?" agreed Robert.

"No, the kind of letter you read," I said, dignified as one can be adjusting hose.

"Not the kind of letter *I* read," chortled Robert.

"We must not tease him," Kit said seriously. "It is great drama with which he is involved. What can be more thrilling, more world-shaking, more inspiring than the loves and hates of shepherds and their nymphs? We are on holy ground here."

"Ah yes," breathed Robert. "Who shall milk the cow today? Let us speak homely philosophy among the rabbit turds – O the simple life – so pure – so innocent! We sit and watch the wriggling sheeps' bums and we possess all wisdom, for we are pure of heart!"

"And we are all called Corydon and Phyllis and Carmela!"

"And those of us not called Corydon and Phyllis and Carmela are called Doron and Cynthia and Corin and Amaryllis!"

"Robert, what was that humorous one you wrote? The one with cucumbers in it, that was so merry?"

"Let me remember, and I will give you a rendition. This is how it goes:

'Ah, Doron! ah my heart! thou art as white
As is thy mother's calf or brinded cow;
Thine eyes are like the slow worms in the light,
Thine hairs resemble thickest of the snow.

Carmela dear, even as the golden ball
That Venus got, such are thy goodly eyes;
When cherries' juice is jumbled there withal,
Thy breath is like the steam of apple pies.

Thy lips resemble two cucumbers fair,
Thy teeth like to the tusks of fattest swine;
Thy speech is like the thunder in the air.
Would God thy toes, thy lips, and all were mine!'"

Kit and Robert between them had worked themselves into a near frenzy with mirth. I carefully buttoned up my doublet.

"Is your pastoral like that?" Robert asked, almost hiccoughing at his own humour.

"Not at all," I said haughtily. "Ours is very beautiful."

"O," groaned Kit, "it cannot be, and a pastoral. They are monstrous, pastorals. They are old, so old and ancient they creak like floorboards or old men's knees. They are quaint as the old church plays. The most exciting thing that happens is two shepherds wanting the same nymph. And when a spot of action is required they have someone carried off by a bear!"

"Or a lion," said Robert. "But the beast's a whoreson fool and never eats the silly swain, who is always restored in time to sing the closing ballad. What part do you play, fat bum, the bear?"

"Don't call me that," I sulked.

"You heard him, don't call him that," said Kit, "even though it's true. He plays a girl."

"Amaryllis, a nymph," I said icily, now dressed.

"I'll wager you sing a song about the joys of country life," said Robert.

"That's right, I do. To a lute. Tis a solo – 'O sweet woods, the delight of solitariness'."

"By Sidney," Kit added pleasantly.

"I know who wrote it," Robert grinned, thumping him. "And tell me, Amaryllis, how do you keep warm in Winter? They never tell you that, do they? The snow six feet deep, the lord of the manor taking all the logs, the sheep frozen on the hillsides. I suppose they drape themselves in fleece – and what's left over they can use for slippers. I see her now! True desirability. Fair Amaryllis in big round slippers, like the hooves of a mythical monster. She clomps through the snow thus, beloved of all who see her. Is it played like that, Marc, your pastoral?"

"No," I muttered. "It takes place in Summer."

"O excellent!" they marvelled. "We did not guess! We are so surprised. What a neat idea, to play it in Summer!"

"If you have now finished," I said huffily, "I have a play to prepare for."

"You know," said Robert evilly, "I have a fine mind to go see this play."

252

"O no," I gasped blushing. "It is everything you say. You would find it amusing..."

"Exactly," said Robert. "A little diversion. And so much more wholesome than that bloodthirsty chronicle of conquest and rapine that's on at the Rose, eh, Kit?"

"O I do not despise a little blood," Kit protested modestly.

"Yes, but in this instance we talk about very much blood!"

"Ah! Very much, eh? Well, that makes a difference. We should certainly go see Corydon and Phyllis."

"Please, Kit," I whinged.

"I thought all players liked to have followers who came to cheer them on. Don't you want admirers to come and stare at you, sweetheart? Off you go, and put your pretty dress on."

I prepared for that afternoon's performance with a sinking heart.

O! It was every morsel as bad as I feared. For as we performed our pastoral to the admiring throng in the innyard, Kit and Robert, who had certainly dined on ale, did cause a merry disturbance in the crowd. They made witty comments on our lines that did cause the crowd to laugh – they made remarks about sheep and cows and udders and turds. Some of the crowd told them to be silent and let the play go on, but then someone recognised Kit, and there was a whisper of "Tis Kit Marlowe!" and then they did gather round him in eagerness, and tell him how much they enjoyed *Tamburlaine,* and ask when he would write another, and one did fetch ink, quill and paper, for Kit to sign his name so that the admiring could take it home and say they had his signature. We had to stop the play, and Jack came forward and urged them to give us their attention. Amyas, all golden and blue as Pastorella, begged most winsomely for their allegiance.

"Do as the maiden says," called Robert, "or she will set the sheep on us, and they from regular fighting with bears are powerful strong and will gore us all to death!"

"Is it true your skin is so white and pink from rubbing it with a paste of rabbit shit and honey?" Kit asked.

"And I would rub it on your tongue, Kit Marlowe," Amyas scowled aggressively.

"That is no way for a maiden shepherdess to speak to an honourable man."

"I see no honourable man, just a bawdy crude poet. Spill out your brains for us and show us how tis done!"

"Do you want a real live wolf to run amongst your sheep?" Kit challenged.

Me, I was astonished and most fascinated at the disruption – Amyas and Kit slanging so vehemently, Jack bellowing and gesturing, the apprentices cheering and booing at whatever pleased or displeased them.

Nicholas strode forward irritably, very manly in his shepherd's thongs.

"Get you gone, Marlowe," he said.

"Hooray!" Kit cheered. "Tis Nicholas Henshaw, the celebrated writer, poet and playwright with a string of successes to his name – everything he turns his hand a success two hundred years ago!"

"Give us a song," yelled Robert. "Give us 'Greensleeves'!"

(This being an old song which everybody knew, even schoolboys; even the variations were well known to boredom.)

"Leave *now*," said Nicholas from the front of the stage. "Or I will tell all here the matter of your next play."

"He does not know it," I gasped, horrified to think Kit would suppose I had told Nicky what I'd seen. Twas a good deceit however, and I knew Kit would go then, but not without a gesture.

"We'll have the song from Amaryllis, then we will go. 'O the sweet delights of December on the hillsides', that one."

"It does not come yet," I protested.

"We want it now."

It was decided to appease them, and much blushing I was escorted forward, where I sat upon a rustic stool and sang my solo. I was much applauded, Kit and Robert clapping loudest and longest, and somewhat more than my song deserved. I grinned and fluttered and looked from under my eyelids.

"A flower for your admirer!" Kit demanded, with a sarcastic bow, ogling the big white daisies that swayed and dangled from my flowery head-dress. I removed a daisy and handed it to him. He stuck it between his teeth and stomped off, Robert with him; and we continued with our pastoral.

Well, it certainly made a diversion. Afterwards we talked of nothing else – how shameless he was, how vicious, how drunk,

254

how boisterous, how vain, how sneering, how arrogant, how handsome...Some even considered me partly responsible. I screeched denial. Jack said if I had any influence over him I was to tell him never to come here again. I laughed ruefully. Influence over Kit – a fine jest!

Unfortunately there was some trouble for me with Kit, when I entered his room that night. He got up from his table quietly, and then he seized me by the hair and punched my nose, which bled.

"What – why?" I screeched, shivering with fright.

He hung over me like a dark avenging angel.

"Have you told Nick Henshaw what is in my play?"

"No!"

"You sleep with him, do you not?"

"Yes, but –"

"I trusted you – I let you see anything you wanted."

"I know – I was very grateful –"

"Why did he say that then? How would he know about it? What have you said?"

"Nothing; he knows you're writing a play, that's all. Everybody knows that. Robert knows it, everybody at the Phoenix knows it; tis no secret. I told nothing. Nicky said it to make you go away."

"If anybody knew what my play was about it would ruin it," he said, marvellous angry.

"It would not," I sulked, seeing the violence was past and he was pacing rather than punching. "There are yet the words."

He paced, thumping his fist into his palm.

I stayed where I was, watching the blood drip on to my doublet. There seemed much of it. A familiar feeling came over me and I slid gracefully to the floor in a swoon.

When I came to I was lying in Kit's bed and he was squeezing a watery cloth over my face.

"God's Teeth, how troublesome you are," he told me, patting my cheeks. "You swoon from a nosebleed – I have never seen the like."

"It was not my fault; it was yours. You had no need to hit me, and I do swoon at blood."

"You should try and be more manly; you are too much the fool."

He said nothing to my comfort. I was made to feel all was my fault. He covered me with a blanket.

"*Did* you tell Nicholas?" he insisted.

"No, I swear it."

"If you do..."

"I never will," I promised.

He tucked the blanket round me and suggested I went to sleep. Then he went off to the Phoenix, leaving me. I felt very shaken. I lay and watched the darkness fall around me, on Kit's books and papers and the table. He came home early; he had not been gone two hours. He lit a candle and came over to me.

"Here," he said fondly. "For one who likes pastorals."

He put into my hands a spray of rose hips filched from a garden. The summer leaves were still on them, and the stem bore prickles, which made it hard to hold. I lay there clutching it, not speaking, looking up at him, the candlelight laying shadows over his face, darkening his brows, picking out his cheekbones and his sensuous lips.

"Que tu es beau," I found myself saying, every bit as sentimental as he believed.

He breathed out, like exasperation or sadness.

"Let me tell you something, my sweet boy," he said. "Pastorals do not exist. Pastorals are a weakness, a poor attempt fools make to pretend the world is other than it is. Perpetual summer, true love, songs under shady trees. Fantasy. Pastorals are so easy to ridicule. Anyone can do it."

I felt upset; my lip quivered. Ironically, I had said the very same to Nicholas. I told him the world was bitter and cynical and not like a pastoral. He had told me then that love was thus all the more necessary. And now Kit was doing to me what I had done, and me, I was the one who wanted pastorals to be true. Foolish tears came to my eyes.

"I want you to go home," Kit said.

"I may come back?" I gasped alarmed.

"Of course. But you need sleep and care and I am not the one to give it."

This was true. Once more I would have to limp off to Nicky, for him to pick up the pieces.

I got up from the bed, my bunch of rose hips in my hand. I reached the door and turned.

"Kit, how did you spend Midsummer?" I enquired.

"I have forgot."

"Did you celebrate?"

"No...I don't remember even where I was."

"So you did not gather roses or watch for elves or anything like that?"

Kit had lit another candle and was preparing to write some more. He had his back to me.

"Certain, I did not spend Midsummer dabbling in the dew, no."

"If you do not believe in pastorals," I said, "and if it is foolish and weak and fanciful, then why did you bring me the fruits of the rose?"

He did not answer but I knew that he had heard.

"The flower of love," I added.

"Because it was to hand," he answered. "Why else?"

Despondently I walked back to the Cross Keys in the darkness, and indeed it was very dark. The little doorway lanthorns shone, small glow worms of light in an immense night, and an autumn wind soughed mournfully around the overhanging eaves. There was nobody about, and underfoot the mulchy leaves were slippery and sodden. The signs above the shuttered shops all heaved and creaked, distorted music, with a tabor-thud as woodwork pounded wall.

When I crawled up the slatted ladder to my crow's nest on high I found Nicholas seeking – and finding – consolation with Amyas. All in all it had not been a good day for me.

Whether Kit felt any contrition whatsoever, I saw none of it, and he did not refer either to his display of temper or to his thoughts about roses. He believed in my good faith, however, for which I felt curiously humble, because he never hid away his manuscripts and I could still read as before anything I wanted. He had been amused by the sight of me costumed for the play, and he dared me to walk to his place from the Cross Keys in my dress, and come play him some lute music. Easily perverted, as my horoscope said, I agreed.

And thus one evening found me walking somewhat tentatively along the dim-lit streets dressed as a girl and carrying a lute. The vivacious daisies I had left behind and I did wear a small neat cap from which my long hair dangled. My bodice, sleeves and kirtle were green – love's colour – my gown of cream silk. I had white stockings and ribboned garters, and sweet pointed shoes with small green bows. Around my hips the bum-roll caused my skirts to sway voluminously about me. I walked daintily and reached Kit's room without mishap.

"Ah – you are lovely!" he cried delightedly, laughing as he surveyed me. "Walk about – turn around – O, beauteous! Come and kiss me, luscious nymph!"

I minced over to him, stood on tiptoe, and pursed up my lips, my hands upon his shoulders.

"Christ," he laughed. "I can't get near you! What have you there about the waist that will not let me feel your loins?"

"A bolster," I murmured. "It is the fashion."

"Show me! This is all amazing!"

I modestly lifted up my skirts and showed my white stockings.

"Higher, you wag. You should not tease an admiring swain!"

I lifted my skirts then all the way, very coy, and when the bolster finally showed, it was not the focus of Kit's attention. My pressed together thigh flesh bulged over the top of my white stockings and ribboned garters, and there was all the evidence that I was not female, and I stood there showing it to Kit. Suddenly he darted down and kissed my prick, which leapt up and out as when someone treads on a rake's end.

"Over the table," he said roughly. "I must have you now."

"O Kit," I demurred, "My dress is property, not my own; I must not have it soiled. Let me take it off."

"I must and will be pleased," he said, "and you shall yield. Now bend."

I did as I was told. I gathered up my skirts and went against the table. I laid my face against the table surface, carefully shifting the volume on warfare and the inkpot, my eyes catching sight of the latest piece of writing. I did smile at what I read:

> I feel my liver pierc'd, and all my veins,
> That there begin and nourish every part,
> Mangled and torn, and all my entrails bath'd
> In blood that straineth from their orifex...

I must have presented an alluring sight as Kit prepared to mount me. Skirts and petticoats all billowing around a plump white arse framed in a crimson bolster, much, I would imagine, like a target in archery. I realised, as all progressed, that Kit was taking pleasure of a mental sort also. He was fucking pastorals, swiving what was out of date, unnecessary, illusion, baggage, things we did not need in order to be men alive now. He was fucking out the weakness in himself, any need he might yet cherish to be soft and foolish and naif. It was exciting him, the intellect mingling with the lechery, the mind's action performed bodily. Pastoral disintegrated into a quivering climax, the two of us merging in a passionate groan, bodies sprawled across the table, hearts pounding, throats gasping, as men needing water.

He returned to the bed and lit a pipe, and told me to play to him. And thus perfumed with lust and bodyscents I did settle on to a low footstool and began to play my lute. I played "The Woods so Wild" and "I saw my lady weep". He said lute songs were an excuse to cover up bad verse, for anything passed disguised about with music. He swore he'd never write anything for the lute and have fools miss the words for listening to the music. I had to disagree, for there were beautiful poems set to music, and I played him "They flee from me that sometime did me seek", which of course he knew and liked, and then my favourite: "O happy dames that may embrace the fruit of your delight", and he said that was beautifully sung and he would love that one for the singer's sake.

"D'you know, my sweet," he said, "how appropriate is the gown that you are wearing for this occasion – those long green leaves embroidered all over it are myrtle."

"I had not much thought of it. I just saw long green leaves."

"Groves of myrtle are planted around the temples of Venus. It is her plant; and it is dedicated to the goddess of love. They also," he added carelessly, "decorate the brows of poets with it."

"You may put your brow in my skirts whenever you choose," I assured him provocatively, and we did smile, as those who shared secrets.

And then a man I had not seen before arrived, mudstreaked with travelling, to talk to Kit, who did order me home.

It was odd the atmosphere which this man brought with him. He was not one of Kit's literary friends, that was clear enough – he did not jest and laugh or seem at ease there in Kit's room. And more strange, Kit did not seem comfortable either. I had never seen him so discomposed, so irritable and shifty. He knew the man certainly, but not as a welcome visitor, and he was displeased to see him here.

"Your journey here was wasted," he began.

"Nevertheless," replied the stranger. "I have that which must be said."

Kit shrugged.

"Send your boy away," said the man, with a contemptuous glance at me — no doubt with some cause, for I was most assuredly a strange hermaphrodite sight at that moment.

Kit flashed a look of anger at thus being ordered.

"He was about to leave. Go home, Marc."

I hesitated.

"I could wait outside," I hinted.

"No, no; go home; I shall not want you tonight."

I do not think it crossed Kit's mind that a young girl walking home at night down Cheapside might risk a bad encounter. How much more perhaps a young boy dressed as a girl! I blanched somewhat at his indifference, and left, clutching my lute.

All went well until I was three-quarters home. A man coming out of a tavern saw me and came alongside and pushed me into an alley, and held me so hard about the arm I could not shake him off.

"What hurry, darling?" he said beerily, and held me facing him, my back against the wall. In comedies at this point one hits him with the lute upon the head, but if you care about your lute I found you hesitate, and cluttered up with petticoats even a well-aimed knee would have no effect. So I just stood stiffly there and waited for him to realise his mistake. He began to paw and kiss me, and when I did begin to struggle at last, it only excited him more. He sniggered gloatingly and scrabbled amongst my clothes. When the truth dawned he screeched like a marsh fiend, and leapt back off me, wiping his lips and choking.

"Jesu, a boy!" he wailed. "Sweet Jesu, I have kissed a boy!"

That was for him to fret on, not for me. I turned and fled. He screamed abuse after me, but someone from the inn said reasonably: "Tis but one of those motley players," as if that made all clear. It proved a jolly tale later at the Cross Keys, but Nicky said I had been provoking trouble, and was lucky all that befell me was a kiss. But Amyas said it was most droll and he wished he could have seen.

As to the stranger who visited Kit, indeed it was not my business to ask, and I did not, though I thought it strange that Kit knew someone who had the power to order him about. Whether Kit would be ordered or no was another matter, but that stranger did think he had that right. Large, blond-haired and passing fair, he bore himself as one who considered himself important. I could not understand who he might be.

II

"A man compact of craft and perjury..."

ONE DAY, however, Kit had a visitor whom I knew very well indeed, whose appearance there, in Kit's room, languid and easy, made me gasp. It was Anthony Wilton! There he sat, lounging on Kit's bed, his shoes off, smoking a pipe, and looking marvellous at home.

"I believe you two know each other," Kit smiled. He was sitting at the table, his shirt open to the waist, untidy and amused.

"I am most happy to have brought you two together," drawled Anthony. "It seems to have been mutually profitable."

"O!" I seethed, pink. "Well may you talk of profit. You robbed me!"

"I left you some," he shrugged. "Ah, you must be charitable. I was in dire straits; I had to have money."

"Why?" I demanded.

"Have you no idea?" he enquired carefully. "Did nothing occur at the inn which might have led you to believe my plans had changed?"

Quick thinking I replied: "No", in a tone of such righteous innocence that he could not but assume I had seen nothing. I believed Nicky when he said I could have been murdered for what I had seen. So I played very innocent; but in my mind I thought: This man had a rendezvous with a Spaniard; they exchanged papers... And in outrage I remembered how he had treated me! But I rapidly composed myself.

"Will you return my money?" I enquired with dignity.

"Well, I have none with me at the moment, not expecting to find you here," he said suavely. "Another time and I will bring it round."

"You had no business writing such a letter!" I seethed. "Boxes of sweets... nibbling... it was monstrous of you."

But he and Kit both laughed at my annoyance, so I knew I would find little sympathy. I sat upon the low stool and sulked.

"We should be friends," oozed Anthony. "Each one of us here has made love to the other."

It was a familiarity I did not relish, the more so when Kit grinned: "I hear that Anthony was so eager to make your acquaintance that he bribed sailors to attempt a rape."

"You – bribed –?" I gasped. I was insulted beyond belief. Had those sailors on the boat not even coveted me then? Had Anthony paid them to molest me, so that he could rescue me? It seemed so. I seethed!

"Forgive me," Anthony said blandly. "I did so want you to feel obligated and to come with me."

"I hate deception," I said coldly. "I would have gone with you simply if you had offered me your cabin for warmth, as one traveller to another. You had no need to be sly."

"Ah, my way was more like the old romances – a rescue, a maiden in difficulties..."

"It is a long time since I was a maiden," I said loftily.

"*He* could take them," Anthony suddenly said to Kit.

"Very well," Kit agreed. "You'll do a small favour for Anthony, will you not, sweetheart?"

I smiled in a way that was like baring my teeth.

"*What* favour?"

They wanted me to go to a village called Paddington and deliver some broadsheets to a house there. I grumbled heartily, but they convinced and persuaded me. They would give me money to hire a horse and I could take a friend with me and have a holiday, and the countryside was pretty – I liked pastorals, did I not? I could have a real pastoral there amongst all those daisies and buttercups.

262

"There are no daisies and buttercups now!" I cried.

"O pardon me!" laughed Kit. "I thought that in the country it was always Summer."

He added that if I would oblige in this matter he would later take me over to Southwark and give me a sight of some interesting places I had not been to. So come now, darling, do not be difficult; do this for us and all shall benefit.

"*What* broadsheets?"

A pile of them lay on the table, the kind of thing they stuck up in Paul's churchyard. I read them. They were mildly satirical religious tracts, somewhat provocative, the kind you had a little smirk over and then forgot. None of them were as angry as Nathaniel Gods-Will's. I fancied they would appeal to Kit in one of his more foolish moods. I knew it would be no use asking him if they would be considered politically seditious, because he would shrug and talk about fools and bigots. But these tracts seemed to me no worse than others I had seen, so I said if Nicholas agreed they were not seditious I would take them.

They teased me for needing a tutor, but those were my terms. I did not stay much longer after that, for bluntly I so misliked Anthony, and I was also somewhat scared of him because he was a man without scruples and had lied so shamelessly and was a spy.

Nicky said there was nothing wrong with the broadsheets. He could not understand why anyone would want them delivered. They were, as I supposed, but comments about the state of the church, indifferent naughty, but not Jesuit nor treasonable. He said I was stupid to run errands for lazy people, but I wanted to please Kit, and Amyas offered to accompany me.

Indeed, a glorious day was ours. We hired a horse, which we sometimes rode together and sometimes led, and the way to Paddington village was idyllic. We rode between high hedgerows which were gleaming with blackberries and scarlet hips and haws, and the pale sunlight glinted upon every spider's web. In the deep grasses and on fallen tree trunks we saw strange mushrooms, and on the little winds came flying past all manner of leaves, red, brown, gold, tawny. We saw squirrels scuttling up and down tree bark, and beneath clumps of beech trees that we passed, the ground was thick with nuts. We stopped to eat; we had bread, cheese and cider, and blackberries from the hedge. We sat on a log and chewed beech nuts and played spitting nuts to see whose would go farthest. Amyas showed me how to make a weapon from a conker and we played at that. Then we continued on our way.

It was a large manor house to which we must deliver the broadsheets. There were twenty, all neatly folded in a leather pouch. The manor was a hidden sort of place, tucked away behind tall trees, with many panes of glinting glass, and upon its walls a brilliant crimson ivy, so covering over, it was like a coat. Smoke curled up from the many tall chimneys, yet once inside I found the place felt chill, as if the stones of its floors brought coldness up from the earth to all the rooms.

I left Amyas outside for he would mind the horse and was happy to divert himself by finding whether fishes in the ornamental pond would come to him by whistling. Indeed I would have rather stayed with him and seen if it was so, than follow that smooth serving man who escorted me within. This man had manners most impeccable, walked with a graceful motion, and engaged me in brief conversation, turning a wide smile to me, as if he would well know me. He enquired my name, I gave it, but he then made me repeat it and he said it to himself again, as if he would remember it. I had to suppose he found it or my speech too foreign-sounding to digest, and this offended me a little for they understood me well back at the inn. He brought me to the lady, and he waited there against the wall and would not be dismissed until she turned and sharply told him go.

The lady of the house was tall and pale, of middle age and wrinkled much about the eyes. Her hair was fair and curled in pretty disarray beneath her jewelled velvet cap. She wore a dress of honey-coloured silk, her sleeves and kirtle tawny. Pearl pendants hung at her ears, and from her waist a long gold slender chain with some dark jewel at its tip. She would have been most fair when young, and even now had beauty still upon her, but for a look of such world-weariness and sadness, that did cloud the fair she yet retained and made her seem thus older. I could see nothing in my arrival to occasion her more anxiety, yet it seemed so, and she bade me follow her, with a palpable urgency which to me seemed marvellous out of place.

She led me along many low dark-pannelled passageways, her

soft skirts rustling on the stone. I caught glimpses of carved oaken chests, and views of trees beyond the leaded latticed windows. In the silence I heard a door bang suddenly, and a swift draught stirred some leaves that had blown in. I turned my head to look but I saw no one; I felt as if someone had hurried away.

I was brought into a small room where a fire was lit, and now by contrast, the windows being shut, the air in here seemed unwholesome and confined. The logs that burned gave off a sweet perfume, reminding me of incense. Upon the wall hung a beautiful clock, its face under an ornate wooden canopy, its body a curious carved, almost conical tail, and in the cloistered space its ticking sounded monstrous loud. Clocks like that made one startlingly aware of life slipping past, I thought. I undid the pouch, eager to get the business done. I took out the papers, and the lady received them with nervous hands.

"Are you of the faith?" she enquired.

"Catholic, do you mean?" I said surprised.

"Assuredly – what else?" she said brittly.

"O yes," I said reassuringly.

"You are not English?"

"I am French."

"But lately arrived?" she frowned.

"I arrived on the first of May." I thought she wanted to converse. She is most surely lonely, I decided. I said pleasantly: "I am a player at the Cross Keys inn. If you come into London you should come and see us. We will make you laugh."

"I doubt it," she smiled, as if the weight of the world were on her shoulders. Then she looked sadly at me. "You seem so young," she said.

"I am sixteen."

"As I supposed, yet young. It seems such a shame. Ah, but then it is most often the young who achieve. You have an innocent face."

"O!" I protested. I did not think so at all.

"Did all go well on your journey?"

"Yes thank you," I said, comfortably remembering how Amyas and I had gulped down blackberries and carolled madrigals. "Perfectly."

"Good. Well, much thanks for your trouble. Have you

been recompensed?"

"O yes," I said hurriedly. "All that is arranged."

She was not at her ease. Her gaze now flitted to the window, now to the door, listening and waiting, yet as one who would deny she did.

"Well. To better times," she murmured, and escorted me once more into the passageway. That servant with the bland enquiring smile was waiting for me, and though the distance was great before we reached the hall and the main door, he accompanied me in a marked silence, as if in some way to assure me that he knew his place and must not speak. And he watched me from the doorway as I walked off in search of Amyas. I know because I turned and looked. I frowned. Did he think that being mere raggle taggle players we might damage something as we left? What monstrous impudence! But no, he seemed to look beyond us, down the track that curved behind the trees. I wondered then whom he expected.

Gladly I rejoined Amyas. The strands of his hair all dripped with water from leaning too low over the fish pond. He swore that he had proved that fishes came to whistling; he would show me if I cared to wait. I did not care to.

"Let's away," I told him. "That house was strange – too quiet, but yet...I did not like it. Something was odd."

"How could that be?"

"They did not seem the kind of people who would want to read those jolly tracts. And why did they need so many? And why did it matter if I was young? Or French? And Amyas, do I seem innocent to you?"

"A puling infant," Amyas assured me firmly, palpably impatient with my mysteries. "And I will tell you why."

"Why?"

"Because," he said importantly, "a person who was wise and worldly would not pass up a chance to see fish come to whistles!"

Happily I abandoned my disquiet and thought no more about it. We rode home through the leafy lanes, the smell of wood fires sweet upon the air. A man on horseback, coming from London at speed, near mowed us down. We stared after him, grumbling at his haste and carelessness. I wondered if he was the one they waited for, and what he brought withal.

266

The evening found me gathering up dried rose petals from the big pot pourri on the staircase at the inn. Amyas watched me quizzically.

I packed them in a pouch. "They are for Kit's bed."

"His bed? That will be monstrous itchy!"

"Bumpkin! It is a beautiful thing to lie in rose petals."

"Ah, Marc, you should give them to Nicky."

I coloured up guiltily. "In a way, yes," I said. "But you see, Nicky knows about roses."

"Kit does not?" said Amyas scornfully.

"No, not in the way that Nicky does. I cannot give roses to Nicky in the same way, because Nicky believes in magic and faery – he has all that richness. Kit for all his fine words and fame does not seem to have access to that simplicity. I want to be the one who puts rose petals in his bed, because if I do not he has no one who will do that. They are all so sophisticated and clever; they are above rose petals."

"But Marc, how much longer can you go on assuming Nicky's love and never feeding it? One day you might turn round and find it is all dried up for lack of nourishing and for your carelessness."

"I do not think so," I said despondently. "I do believe tis love, you see, and love does not dry up. I know this to my cost. I love someone who does not love me and I will always love him, into eternity. It will be the same with Nicky. If he loves me I can depend on it."

Amyas became very sweet then, and without saying another word he began to help me collect up rose petals.

O, but my education of Kit was not a success. That night some of his friends came round, fortunately not Anthony, who had once again disappeared. He was spoken of, though.

"O, yes, Anthony," Kit laughed ironically. "That one is so doubled up in double dealing that he'll end up eating his own tail. Is there not some kind of snake does that?"

"Should you laugh?" enquired Thomas Watson. "Do you not share the same problem?"

"Not at all," retorted Kit. "I am not confused; I merely confuse other people."

"Is Anthony confused then?"

"Anthony has his fingers in many pies."

"Foreign pies?"

"O, do they make pies over the seas?"

"Indeed they do, and bring them over here disguised as homely fare. Then off comes the pastry, and out pops – whatever was put in it."

"I' faith," someone declared, "I can't believe that Anthony is involved with anything worse than passing on snippets that he hears abroad; and everyone does that."

"I hear a tavern in Howlebourne was raided again; the man escaped by hiding in a farm cart."

"O, Calais is in a panic all the time, and what they hear there seems to shoot to London like an arrow. Some den in Blackfriars was stacked full of books and vestments, and it was discovered there was an underground press in one of those villages some way out of town – East Ham, or was it Barking?"

"What can you expect? Rheims sends Jesuits over with every tide. They hide in the seaweed, you know!"

"Don't their cloven hooves give them away?"

"Godsooth, we need not fret ourselves – Tis *next* year that the world will end, not this. Astrology foretells it – the Annus Mirabilis!"

"Annus Mirabilis?" said Kit cheerfully. "But that's what Marc has between his arse cheeks!"

And in having a hearty laugh at my expense, they dropped the subject of Anthony and double dealings, which I was finding peculiarly disquieting. I was relieved that it was only mildly satirical broadsheets I had taken to Paddington.

But they all stayed so late that Kit was drunk and tired and grumpy afterwards, and blew out all the candles very irritable, and in this mood I could have gone or stayed, he would not have cared. He would not relight the candle, and though we slept together it was uncomfortable and sullenly.

In the morning, after an irritable night, I stomped out of bed in a great fit of sulks, and over to the leather pouch. I seized it and returned to the bed. I pulled the blanket off him.

My knees weakened at the sight of his beauty, where he lay on his back, his arm crooked over his face against the light. His prick lay limp in its mass of dark crotch hair; his lean belly glistened lightly with sweat. He shifted a dark hairy thigh. I prodded his shoulder.

"I know you are awake," I scowled. He did not move.

"Wake, wicked sinner!" I cried. "The Devil is come for you!"
He removed his arm and stared at me.

"Please, Marc," he reproved quizzically. "That is not very
kind, first thing in the morning, before a fellow's first pipe of the
day."

"Monster," I accused.

"Ah, leave off; my head throbs."

I undid the bag and shook countless petals down on him.
There he lay, naked, strewn with petals, old dried rose-heads,
shrivelled scented flecks nestling in his hair, dappling his chest,
floating on to his eyelids.

"I brought you rose petals!" I cried. "I thought to strew our
bed. You could have slept in rose petals. You missed the chance.
You were so busy being clever and political and entertaining all
your clever friends. And you will always be like that – a person
will bring you rose petals but you, Kit Marlowe, will be so busy
making pronouncements and being the centre of attention, you
will not notice. You will not have rose petals in your life. You
will have admiring friends and fame, yes, even down the ages –
fame, but never rose petals; you will always put out the candle
upon the chance of rose petals –"

"Yes dear, the point is clear enough," Kit said wrily.

"You should care about Midsummer! You should celebrate
these things. But you, you know about Aristotle, and Turkish
warfare, and ancient gods and goddesses, but the daisies beneath
your feet are too small for you to see."

Kit sat up, letting the rose petals fall and tumble.

"Yes, you say true, you little reprobate," he said, "and if I did
not feel unfit and therefore tolerant, I might beat you for your
presumption. Strew your rose petals if you must, but tell me
once more that my vision of the world is wrong and you will go
out of here head first and my boot under your sweet fat arse."

We stared, I with a thudding heart, he with a glowering brow.

"Daisies are too small for me to see, exactly as you said," he
told me. "I am up where sometimes even the earth itself is too
small for me to see. You know nothing of my horizons – or of
my torment. If what I am means doing without daisies," he
spat, not even contemptuously, "I do take that chance."

I did not even speak. There was nothing I could say. A river, a gulf, an ocean was between us. I dressed and left.

That night I lay thankfully in Nicky's arms. We made love most affectionately, and I wept small tears of happiness – or maybe I cried because it was not Kit. I was overwrought. We put out the candle, and the moon shone in at our tiny window, silvering our bodies and the glistering sweet-smelling apples. Mice rustled companionably nearby, and the apples shifted. The ancient woodwork creaked, reminding me of a ship. The wind muttered outside and a loose board rattled somewhere.

Must it be, I thought, a choice? Must it be aery regions or the earth? Why must there be a difference? Why must we all be so separated and apart? Why must I myself love both, irreconcilables?

III

"For I will fly from these alluring eyes
That do pursue my peace where'er it goes"

AND YOU might think, and reasonably so, that I would sort out for myself the sensible path and break away from that most beloved tyrant – but no, I did not, and within three days or so I tremulously returned, half wondering if he would even want to see me.

"By heaven," he said, "I'm glad tis you" – so pleasantly and friendly, that I half wondered if it had been two different people who had argued about rose petals and the vision of life. "I am most ready to quit these quarrelling kings." He put down his quill. He had ink on his lips, where he had been sucking it. I found it endearing, and he would have been furious to have been thought endearing.

"I gave serious thought to your proposition," he said. "And this is what I decided. You have a need to strew rose petals and I have not. Needs make you weak. I do not need these rituals; rituals are a burden. To dance because it is Midsummer is a burden. I kept your rose petals in the bed, but it made no especial difference. The difference is in the mind. Petals clutter up the process; tis better to abandon the trimmings and let the mind be clear. There is nothing stronger than the human mind and it needs to be free – it needs not to need. It cloys it to douse it in sentiment; it clouds clear vision. The vulgar seem to need these props. Not I. D'you see, you strew the roses for yourself, not for me – for your own need, not for mine...Is there anything you want to say?"

"In my defence?" I laughed – I felt like an accused!

"Defend your viewpoint if you can, or dispute with mine," he invited.

"No; it is enough we are yet friends."

"Friends?" he said amused. "Is that what we are?"

"O very well," I sulked. "I am pleased I am yet someone you fuck."

"You are not exactly a great disputer," he remarked. "You could have maintained your initial premise – your outburst about my conception of the world."

"No, you have Robert for that, and he will add as many Latin proverbs as he needs to back his thesis. I don't ask to be that to you."

"What would you like to be? My what?"

"Your anything."

"What?" he challenged. "Captive? Slave? The choice is very wide – my anything."

"Captive, slave, anything you want," I said, and our eyes ran lightly over each other, arousal sneaking upon us both.

"Footstool?" he dared me.

"If you wish it."

"I do wish it. I order it. Come over here."

That day I learnt many refinements of servitude. I yielded breathlessly to all his requirements, my helplessness exciting us both, for O he did bind my hands and use me with such cool mastery that my bondage began to seem entirely natural, and it amused him mightily to converse with me on ordinary topics while I was in the pose of footstool. He asked me about the Valois court. His questions were most serious and his interest true. I told him all he required – how it was at court, the personal appearance of the King, what he wore, ate, drank. Did I receive presents?

"The very belt I wear today, there, with the amber studs, that was a present, and gloves and ear rings."

He wanted to know more about the Duc de Guise and what his ambitions were and did he hope to be king? Was he capable of murder? – was Henri? Did I know all about the famous massacre – was it true the Catholics wore white crosses on their helmets and white scarves on their arms, to know each other, and all not dressed like that were slain? And a bell rang, and they were to kill for as long as they heard the bell and cease when it stopped? And we thus discussing the state of things in France the time did pass, till suddenly I squeaked in alarm – it must be two o'clock. I should be at the Cross Keys – I was performing!

"You are too late now; best remain."

"Kit! They expect me!" I moaned. "Set me free."

He did not.

"Which of your appalling productions is it today?" he asked.

"*Saint George.*"

"Whom do you play? Some fainting female, I suppose."

"Yes, the lady's maid."

"Tis not important. There are but two characters necessary in that play, and one of them breathes smoke. They will not miss a lady's maid. Let the lady tie her own ribbons today. Tis Amyas, is it not – let the little monster fend for himself."

"Tis principle...loyalty..." I stuttered. "I must be there. We are a company. O! Please untie me!"

"No," he said pleasantly. "I have a mind to keep you here."

He laughed at my protests. When he finally relented, it was far too late for me to be in time, and before he let me go he made me say that he could treat me as he pleased and it was my pleasure to oblige him. And O! It was true!

Jack was as much as anything plain surprised that I had not turned up. He was angry also, but if I had given a proper explanation he would have tolerated it the once. I apologised sincerely, but I did not stoop to making excuses; I just said I was with Kit Marlowe, and let him think what he would.

"But what kind of a reason is that?" he cried with dramatic gestures of his hands. "I am disappointed in you, Marc. Don't you understand we have an obligation to each other? Our loyalty is understood...I have to warn you, Marc, there are a host of ready players who would jump into your shoes like a shot. Be not so careless – the next time it happens I will think nothing of beating the hide off you..."

I hurried from his presence sulkily. Even Nicky berated me. He said, 'fore heaven, what was I thinking of? Did not I care about the company? We had to rely on each other; between players that was everything.

We were busy rehearsing *The Letter*, which was coming on well, and I did like this play, for in it Nicholas kissed me before all, in his role of grateful lover, for my burning the letter. In a way I was almost the heroine of that play, for my cleverness saved Alice's reputation – that is, Amyas – whose part was more of a gentle simpering sort. He played that well, it being his own nature!

But I did something unforgiveable on the first day it was to be performed. I was eating at midday with Kit and Robert and George Peele, in Kit's room. I remember that the talk absorbed me, for that was the first time I heard Kit confess to his growing interest in necromancy. He said the thinking man began with philosophy, and then tried law and physic and eventually divinity, and all were found wanting. There was only magic that could open the secret doors of the mind, and he had heard of certain conjurors and learned doctors that could do what common folk would call miracles – call spirits up, summon people back from the dead and make them speak. I listened with huge eyes, so absorbed that Robert said I was too young and innocent for this conversation, and Kit sent me to the apothecary's for some tobacco. I went reluctantly; I knew he had been going to give examples to back up his claim, and I missed them all. When I came back they were talking about astrology.

"Here he returns," Robert observed, "and in good time, since I have heard arse-trology is his speciality."

I asked Kit what was his birth sign; he said Aquarius, who being a water carrier is sometimes believed to be the personification of Ganymede. I asked what were the characteristics of Aquarius, and Kit said the good aspects were: profound in imagination, reserved in speaking, patient in labour, a grave disputer and arguer.

"Reserved and patient!" hooted Robert. "So true!"

The bad aspects were: envious, mistrustful, sordid, sluggish, stubborn, malicious, never contented. We said the bad aspects suited Kit very well; and he said the list was writ by one jealous of Aquarian brilliance. He said one had to pick one's astrologer.

This led to a discussion on free will, and the conflict between the animal in our natures and reason our heavenly part. Kit believed strongly in free will. He had no time for old fashioned magic – the most magical thing of all, he said, was our human spirit, which was stronger and better than any number of wizards' rings and amulets. The questioning mind could break all bonds and soar to unimaginable heights. It should dispense with conventional religion, and value learning only as a means. Believe nothing, discover all for yourself, challenge all precepts, carve out your own way.

"The most important thing in the world," he said, "is the freedom to think whatever you choose. No man has the right to tell another man what to think."

"No man," agreed George, "But what about God?"

"God? What of Him?"

"I believe He has something to say on the subject of what we should think! Hasn't He transmitted through His word-pieces – the prophets, the apostles – certain indications of the ways of thinking which He prefers?" suggested George wrily.

"Yes," mused Kit. "He has laid down His laws. But laws are made to be questioned, and if found wanting, to be broken. If God were supreme one might expect Him to be more alert. A mere landowner has guards that lurk about the grounds. God has the serried ranks of angels and archangels at His disposal – yet He never sends them out to threaten us or punish us when we transgress. Believe me, I *know*! How much does it take," he wondered, "to rouse God up to action? What does one have to *do*?"

I sensed it must be time for me to go, and yet I did not. Hearing Kit talk was an experience to me, and when he and his friends were in full flow forgetting I was there it was exciting. It was like that time with Sir Edward Knollys when we had talked about the spheres and the sun and the idea that anything was possible, perfect freedom of thought. It was like watching little flames spark up. I just stayed sitting where I was, and knowing that I should be going. It was the first performance of *The Letter*,

274

and I was needed. It was not like *Saint George*, where they could do without me. I was the one who burnt the letter. I was necessary; and I did not go. It was not even lust I stopped for; it was just to hear him speak. Kit in relaxed expansive mood was like a scene from his own writing come alive; he scattered words like monarchs strew largesse. I stayed, like one by magic turned to stone.

O – they did talk about whether one could write about the things one really wanted, as, could one write about love between men? Kit said he would like to; he did think perhaps Richard the First and Blondel; but Robert said because it was not generally known, the people would resist it and he would be on safer ground with Edward the Second and Gaveston. Safer! they sniggered. How would Edward Alleyn take it, making love to a boy upon the stage! And they talked about the ideal of manly beauty. Did such exist? Could one ever find it strolling around London? Perhaps as well not, Kit laughed, or I'd write no more plays but spend my time pursuing him.

"But is not that your intention?" Robert teased. "I thought you *had* found him, and that this paragon walks the earth at Chiselhurst. The beautiful Tom . . ."

"O, your wild fancy . . ." Kit said with an easy laugh.

"Is it not true he has long rippling curls?" Robert drooled.

"Tis true, yes," said Kit offhand.

"Which would you prefer," said Robert, "an ideal man, like that, who took you away to an idyllic country manor and fed you grapes between his fingers and called you Love – or by a hairsbreadth to pass by such a man and never meet, but by missing him, to be famous down the ages? Love or Fame, Kit – which?"

"Fame," said Kit.

Eventually I slunk home. My presence and my absence had been scarce noticed, yet myself I felt richer, and I never regretted staying. I had seen inside a magic box, a lid was lifted and I had breathed in something precious.

I was received with rage and icy disapproval. Without me they could not perform *The Letter*; they had had to do *Saint George*, and they were savage. They gathered round me accusingly, as if all wanted to be the one to grind me into pulp. How could I explain? I was like one who had been to Olympus and returned, wisps of heavenly cloud about my ears, ambrosia streaked across my cheeks, and shepherds now screaming at me for abandoning a herd of scrawny goats.

"You were with Kit Marlowe," Jack accused.

"Yes. I am most shamed to have let you down."

"I do not understand you. Are you possessed?"

"Yes."

"Possession is no excuse. These are not the olden days. I'm going to tan your hide and try to beat some sense into you."

I stood there, traces of Olympus swift receding. I did feel marvellous ashamed. I cared about these people; they were my family. They had taken me in and given me a way of life, security, affection, when I had none. I hated to betray their trust. I hated myself for what I must seem – feckless, wayward, unworthy. Jack glowered at me, waiting for some kind of reaction, explanation, squeals of protest; but none came. I surveyed the floor between us, innyard cobbles, flecked with straw.

"Do you agree that you deserve a beating?"

I shrugged.

"You understand – any man would do the same."

Poor fellow, he was sorry for me, even while being angry. Well, I was no stranger to beatings, and I reckoned Jack's would be a deal gentler than my brothers', if only because he needed me in the play tomorrow. I looked up. All around were the faces of the company, Nicky perplexed and concerned, Amyas with bulging eyes, and Angel somewhat scornful; and Madge beyond, exasperated. Others also, curious and staring.

"Right," snapped Jack. "Will you take it like a man or must you be held?"

"I'll take it."

Jack leathered me with his belt on my bare back against a post. When he had finished he held me against his chest and ruffled my hair hard.

"Don't let me down again," he said, gruff and upset.

"No; I promise," I gulped, and rushed away to weep.

Nicky came and sat with me up in our garret.

"No more, Marc," he said. "Push your luck and Jack'll have to throw you out. Have some sense. Don't keep putting *him* first. You'd be crazy to ditch the company. You fit in so well.

We need you – you need us."

"Kit says tis weak to need."

"I don't want to hear what he says. He lives by another planet's influences. And you do not."

"Part of me does."

"I speak to the other part then. The one who guzzles strawberries and thinks Joan of Arc was holy. The one who sold his dagger and believes in faery rings."

"O, him."

"Tis painful to me to stand by and watch what's happening to you."

"I cannot help it," I replied unhappily. "I feel, like Jack says, possessed. As if I am not responsible for what I do, and yet I know I am. You see, I do not even regret that I was not with you; I was glad to be with him. And at the same time, I'm shocked I could have stayed away from the first performance of *The Letter*, and spoiled it for everybody."

"O, Marc – be careful. Don't put everything at risk."

I heard his concern and advice, and the love in his voice. My passion for Kit was playing havoc with my life. For the hot fervent lust we shared, for the sound of his voice and the adoration of his words, and much careless treatment and for unkindness and indifference, I was upsetting the people who cared about me, betraying them, and much tormenting myself. But worse was yet to follow.

Not simply on that occasion when my sore back might have been the reason, but at other times before and after, it seemed that Nicholas and I could not make love as happily as we were wont. I told him I was tired, and so I was, but he would not take an excuse so simple and believed that matters had befallen so for wider reasons, more disquieting.

"It seems I do not please you as I once did...I had rather you be honest...so tell me if you have grown tired of my lovemaking."

Perversely I said nothing to his comfort. I thought he should have known me better than to suppose I was so fickle. It was true I had deserted him for Kit, but Kit was as some dark magician whose powers could not be fought against – I thought that Nicky understood that, that I was helpless, like the victim of a spell. I felt that he demeaned himself to talk of petty things, as if he would oblige me to pay him compliments and praise him for his skills. If he loved me, could he not be patient? My head so full of Kit could not take bedtime wrangling, dumps, recriminations. And if I said: "I am not tired of you; but simply tired," he seemed not to believe me, saying things like: "Then why make no response? Why do I feel nothing from you when I touch you? Why do you lie half turned away?" – all of which were true, but for no reason that I could convey. And so the air lay heavy with unspoken thoughts and nothing was resolved. Sometimes we kissed before we went to sleep; and sometimes we did not. And I thought: Nicholas will find another lover...I will lose him by my carelessness...But I did nothing that might have put matters to right. I felt like one that in a little boat goes where the water will, no oars, no steering, just the current's flow, that takes it who knows where.

I forced myself henceforth only to visit Kit *after* a performance, so I could not be seduced into staying with him instead of playing my part. On one of these occasions I spoke to him about something that was making me anxious.

We were lying on the bed, all naked after fucking, the late evening twilight upon us like a lovely cloak. How different our bodies were – his so lean and dark, so male, so fully grown; and mine so smooth and softly firm, and my crotch hair the only smudge on my body.

"Kit," I said hesitantly. "Forgive me for – advising you, but I don't like Anthony and I wish you did not see him."

"You know him not, dear. You don't like him because he stole your money."

"Well! I've never had it back, have I? And he knows where I may be found," I said reasonably.

"'Tis true, he is a villain, but so are most of the people I know! And that makes them more interesting – they do not live by vulgar rule."

"Yes...that I know. But Anthony is...sinister."

Kit laughed so much the bed rocked.

"O Kit," I wailed. "I fear he may be concerned with dangerous things which – I don't care if he is caught and discovered, but they might think that you too – because you know him..."

278

"In the Devil's name, what do you mean? What do you know?" Kit was tense and angry now, and I was scared, expecting to be hit.

"Nothing," I mumbled unhappily. I dared not say what I had seen at the inn, for Kit would probably have told it to Anthony as a great joke, and I would be in danger for knowing.

"You're an ignorant brat," Kit told me scathingly. "Curiously simple for one who has lived at the Valois court, everyone dropping dead around you from poisoned grapes and perfumed gloves. You've taken against Anthony because he upset your dignity. Your dignity! A humorous notion, for one who is willing enough to play the footstool when I require it." The thought restored his humour. "Listen darling," he drawled. "'Tis no secret – even you must know this – gentlemen travelling overseas – in France and Italy and such – they keep their eyes and ears open and they notice things. And when they come home, they pass on what they know. They receive a small fee if they are lucky. That is not dangerous. That is all Anthony does. I do not want to hear any more childish burblings from you on this matter. 'Tis not your place to wonder at things beyond you. Your place, insofar as you have one, is at my feet. 'Tis understood?"

"Yes," I muttered. But I knew that I was right. I supposed it would not matter. Whatever Anthony did in connection with some Spaniard he would not tell, and if Kit knew nothing about it, he would be safe. But my conscience was uneasy somehow. I was convinced Kit did not know about Anthony and his Spanish rendezvous. Or if he did he was being monstrous cool.

NINE

I

"What stranger art thou, that dost eye me thus?"

I HAD often wanted to visit Bankside by night, for the most part because Amyas had painted such a picture of its depravity, and because I had in my head Cuthbert Hodgkin's quivering description of the melancholic brooding playwrights who frequented those low dives and alleys. I would not have dared to go alone, but when Kit said I could go with him and the others I was all agog with pleasurable excitement and alarm.

Thomas warned me to leave off my brightly coloured clothes, for at our destination such would attract the eyes of thieves and villains and cause trouble; so I dressed in dark clothes – a rough shirt and a leather jerkin, with grey hose and a wide flat woollen cap. They laughed and called me Kit's apprentice.

We did not set out till very late at night, passing through the dark streets whose doorways were lit only at intervals by glowing lanthorns, all decent folk being fast abed. It monstrous pleased me not to be decent folk! I felt my life was exceptional exciting, excellent rich. More, we did not go over by London Bridge, we went over by boat, and I saw for myself the foul-mouthed watermen so spoken of by voyagers who had suffered their abuse. Ours was delightfully foul-mouthed! I sat next to Thomas Watson, who laughed and told me to close my ears, and Kit and Robert did answer the boatman back oath for oath, as if his conversation had been perfectly polite. Also the boatman did know them by name, and he kept up a string of abusive chat as he poled us over, as: "So, Master Greene, so you are trafficking in pox tonight then, bringing one sort over from the north bank and taking another sort home...you'll not reach thirty-five, mark my words...And I see Master Marlowe has brought his own, that poxy cattlemite boy all made up like a whoreson wench...The wickedness of the world keeps me in work..."

Tom and Kit began to sing an ancient ballad which began: "The ferryman was old and grey, He crooked his quivering hand: O bitter is the price ye pay, Before ye shall touch land."

The river was wide, much wider than it seemed by day, and the bridge by night was beautiful. Pinpoints of light illuminated the houses, reflected lights danced in the black water, and before us and behind glowed the lights of each bank of the Thames. A group of swans close to the boat showed up eerily white; the boatman drove at them with his oar.

We disembarked at a row of drenched and slithery steps beside some tall jumbled houses whose foundations were right in the water. Lanthorns twinkled at many windows and the yells of brawls and revelry floated on the beery breeze. We walked up wet and twisty streets, which stank mightily of fish and filth, and Thomas had amusement treating me as if I was innocent and must be protected, shielding my eyes from the painted ladies in the doorways – and almost smudging my make-up. From what I noticed the women looked tawdry and uninviting, great breasts spilling out of their bodices, and some had bad or no teeth, and they were very old, at least thirty. They called out to us as we passed:

"This way, gentlemen..."

"See anything you like?"

They twisted their bodies about to flaunt the curves of the flesh beneath. One had a dress slit to the waist and showed all her thigh and beyond. Their hair was quite unkempt and they did not smell wholesome. Yet into one of those doorways we did soon lose Robert. He has no finesse, I thought.

We reached a certain tavern which we entered by going down some steps, as into a cave. It was full and noisy, hot and boisterous. Thomas remarked in my ear: "The secret of enjoying this place is to get drunk as quickly as possible." We sat and began to do so. I was fascinated by a metal appliance nailed to the wall and stared at it blinkingly, for it looked something like a bridle, till Matthew said cheerily: "Looking at the chastity belt, dear? Like to try it for size?"

Wafts of conversation teased my ears – Kit reckoning that in prison you could pick up any number of illicit trades and he knew someone who had literally made a fortune counterfeiting; Matthew recounting intimate tales of Women he had Known, and horrible accounts of How to Take a Virgin.

And here Kit told a funny tale. It seems there was a young man living in the country (ah, all tales do so begin!) and he awoke one morning thinking all was not quite well. Indeed it was not, for looking down at his belly he discovered that his tool was gone! Yes! He had no pizzle! He guessed that he had been bewitched, and all in a terror he ran to the village priest to ask what should be done.

"No pizzle? How can that be?" enquired the priest. "Pull down your breeches and let me see."

So the hapless youth unloosed his hose and showed his parts, or rather where his parts had been, and so the priest was forced to believe the truth of what he saw.

"You are indeed bewitched," he said. "And what you must do is go to the old witch's house in the forest and beg her to give you back your tool." And off the young man went.

The old hag took pity on him. "Yes, I have your tool," she told him. "Climb that tall tree and you shall see it with some others in yon bird's nest."

So the young man climbed the tree, and there in a bird's nest he found several privy members of all shapes and sizes, and one exceptionally large. "O," says he, "can I have this one instead?"

"No," said the witch. "That belongs to the village priest."

So he left that one, and took his own, and sped away before he landed in worse trouble.

"You would think that that was just a silly tale," Kit remarked amongst all the laughter that followed his telling. "But no, it was originally offered in all seriousness by judges in past ages as an example of the power of witches. They believed this story to be true."

While some then marvelled at the credulous, someone else asked over my head: "Would Marc like a girl?" There were mutters about the possible prospects and how much they cost, and another more discreet murmur of "...Kit's ingle." And later: "Does he want a *boy*? Do you want a boy?" "No thank you," I replied; and then we all moved on to another tavern, further up the street.

I had a shock as we emerged – I saw again that gaudy beggar. How he seemed to dog my footsteps! He was lurking by a lanthorn, crooked upon his wooden crutch, the bulbous sores upon his face all hideously shadowed by the light. I would know him anywhere – his fearsome aspect, his menacing leer, and that tawdry cloak so brilliantly patched, that hid – O, what? A body scarred and pitted, putrid with decay? A skeleton where rotten flesh hung all in shreds like beggars' weeds? Unnatural dread suffused me and I pressed close against my jovial companions to be hid. But he had seen me.

"Here it is!" said Matthew cheerfully. "You will feel more comfortable here, young Marcus."

Thankfully I went inside the tavern, where we mounted rickety stairs to an upstairs room, low-beamed and full of shadows, fugged with smoke. Here were no women, and several young boys very painted, and as if to acknowledge my realisation Kit caught hold of me and sat me on his lap. I was very proud as well as very tipsy. Here we met Anthony Wilton once again, and a painted boy came soliciting him as we sat. I watched with interest, and I guessed he thought Kit had bought my services. The boy assessed me maliciously and I returned the compliment. Anthony fixed a price for him, and the boy twined himself around Anthony, but ogled Kit. I scowled and put my arm round Kit, implying This is Mine. I was marvellous attentive to Kit, and lit his pipe for him and kissed his cheek, and he in the midst of talking did pause to kiss my mouth or my nose, and to tickle inside my thigh, so I did smirk with pleasure.

I liked it in this place, but Matthew and George wanted women and were impatient and pressed for us to leave; so we went on to another tavern down near the water's edge, and part of it was a wooden balcony on struts jutting out into the river, and under it the water very black and stinking, with smears of reflected lights wriggling in the murky slime.

This tavern had one large low room. Kit disentangled himself from us somehow; I could see him further off in the corner with a man, deep in conversation, backs to the room. I sighed to think that there was so much of Kit that I would never know. Ours was not a true friendship, I reflected. O he did favour me, and sometimes he could be sweet; but I was his ingle, like they said, and he cared nothing for the intricacies of my humours. I downed another swig of beer.

"Where has Roberto gone?" said Thomas.

"O, that lad..." said Matthew, and he turned to me. "Did you know that Robert has a wife at home in Lincolnshire, and a child withal?"

"No; I know but little about Robert."

"Ask him sometime what he did in Italy and Spain! He has tales to tell of vice and spurring that would make your hair stand on end. I daresay there is not a wench – or boy – in all of Italy that has not had some experience of him! And then, having surfeited himself on pleasure, would you believe, he suddenly repented! He was in a church in Norwich, and he swears God spoke to him. Quivering and shivering, Robert heard the masterful tones of the Almighty and promised to forego his wicked ways. Next thing he knew he was a married man and settled down. But his repentance only lasted till he had spent all Dorothea's dowry. Now he lives with that slut Em Ball in Holywell, half the ruffians in London are his neighbours, and he knows the inside of every stew in Bankside. Roberto loves the low life, but he fears Hell fire. He does, yes, whatever he may say to the contrary. Roberto," Matthew told me beerily, "is not a man in whom the humours are equally mixed!"

I stood up and went looking for Kit. Near to him now, I recognised the man he was with – it was the fair-haired one who had come to Kit's room unwelcome when I had been sent away. Their voices were low, but anger suddenly raised them.

"Tis not a question of my loyalty," Kit snapped. "Surely you have someone else you can send."

"I say it is. I say your loyalty is very much in question. And it would be much in your own interests to provide some proof of it."

"Other matters weigh more important with me just at present; I have not the time."

"What other matters can be more important?" demanded the man, grasping Kit's arm urgently.

"If you have to ask me that," replied Kit coldly, "I cannot possibly explain."

There was a pause. This was a conversation I was not supposed to hear, and I hurried to make myself scarce. A man started talking to me and asking would I like to try one of the girls from the stews. He was a sailor and he told me I need not be

284

coy. It was in order to avoid his unwelcome interest that I went out into the street.

How the next part happened I really do not know, but in the dark street puddled with river slime I was surrounded by sailors who would not leave me alone. I say surrounded; there were four. They began mauling me about, and drunk as I was I could not make out why, until the bizarre truth dawned on me that they were picking on me because I was French. My prettiness and my make-up no doubt had something to do with it, but the insults were directed at my not being English – *French* catamite, *foreign* slut, come over here and give us the pox, would you? And all this done with shoving me and pulling at my clothes, and then throwing me down in the dirt, at which I began to scream. That brought figures to the doors and brawling all around us.

Thomas hauled me clear of the fray, just in time to see Kit with his dagger raised against a sailor he had pinned to the wall, their shadows monstrous and immense.

"No!" yelled Thomas, seizing Kit's wrist, the sailor ducking and disappearing.

"Christ! You are a fool!" cried Kit, his hair dishevelled. "I could have turned on you."

"Have some sense," gasped Thomas. "They would have traced him straight back to you by way of that boy. Who else trails a French catamite in his wake?"

"Damn him," scowled Kit darkly. "Someone take him home."

I stood limp and filthy, shivering with reaction.

"I don't want to go home," I sulked.

"Devil take him," muttered Kit. "D'you know –" and he laughed in sudden great amusement. "It had completely slipped my mind the little minx was French!"

"Please don't send me home," I quivered. "I won't speak to anyone."

I was ignored. I was a constraint, an irritation; and Kit never bothered with these. He simply disappeared and shrugged me off, and it was left to Matthew to take me home, a person I had not had much to do with, and who only took me home because he was ready to go himself.

"We never thought," said Matthew chattily. "The country

constantly expecting to be overrun with French and Spanish troops, they're very jumpy down there at the wharves. Sailors especial, since they're the ones who must fight. You should have kept your mouth shut. You cannot blame them. I suppose looking like you do does not help! You somewhat draw attention to yourself, even in tonight's sober garb!"

With talk like this to listen to, and the general indignity of being sent away like a child from a feast, I naturally would not be fobbed off this way. Monstrous affronted at my treatment, I ran away from Matthew down a side alley, and I lost him rapidly as I ran hither and yon amongst poxy little streets more gutter than pathway, and underfoot I swear was gushing shit. Mostly in order to take my shoes clear of the stuff, I turned into a tavern doorway, and in as obscure a seat as I could find I sat and ordered beer.

It was a dark and squalid hole, my refuge, but I had rather be there than ignominiously sent home, and I began to look about me. A bunch of female whores were sitting around a table with two well-dressed customers; a game of dice was in progress in the corner, hunched figures in tall hats; and there were a couple of sailors – Dutch, I thought – with a map between them on a stool. As I stared, I saw that the man who had brought my beer was Lionel Fulbrook, whom I had met at Charles' lodging in the Rue St. Honoré before he set out to become an underground priest. I peered again to make sure I was not wrong – no, it was he, in humble attire, his lank dark hair all greasily hanging down; and I admired his disguise, for no one looking at him would ever think he was a seminary priest. So, this was his bolt-hole, the cookshop in Southwark, and I had stumbled into it by chance. And he had not recognised me, in my muddy apprentice gear – one does not recognise what one does not expect to see.

I wondered whether to make myself known, but I decided not. My brief experience with Sir Philip and his secret mass, the terror I remembered, had taught me to steer clear of clandestine religious matters. The beer was vile, I drank a little and began to leave, but then I paused and stared. Another man had detached himself from the murky shadows and was now speaking to Lionel. He was wearing a long dark cloak, but his fair hair showed beneath his hat. It was Anthony Wilton, talking privily to Lionel, and across that tavern room I felt the same sensation as I had done when I lay feigning sleep in the Blue Boar Inn, on my first night in England, that same dread and knowledge that it was not wholesome for me to be seen.

I stood up and edged my way to the door but was not swift enough. Anthony saw me and our eyes met. I ran out of the tavern, and outside I ran down the dungy street, and he followed. I hoped at first he did not follow me, but was simply leaving because he would; but I knew at heart that he was in pursuit.

Familiar panic seized me and I ran, this way and that, not knowing where I went. The river smells hung on the air, the stench of fish and foul water. The surface of the street was runnelled and slimy; it was distaste that slowed me down, and stupidly I blundered down a narrow alley lit at one end – but where was I, a coal-black cul-de-sac and I was caught there.

Panting, Anthony blocked my way, his bulk filling the alley; and we faced each other, with features white and eerie from the wind-shifting lanthorn just beyond us. Backed against the wall I waited trembling. The wall was wet, chill and repulsive to my palms.

"Are you following me?" said Anthony frowning.

"No!" I squeaked. "You are following me."

"Yes, to ask you that. And what you were doing in the Bent Nail."

"The what? O, that tavern," I shivered.

"Yes sweetheart, that tavern. How much do you know?"

"Nothing at all, I promise you."

"I believed you last time. But now I'm not so sure. You saw me talking to the man who brought the ale. Do you happen to know his true identity?"

"No!"

Anthony loomed nearer. I wondered how I'd ever thought him handsome; he was terrifying. I cowered back and tried to ward him off. He put his hand on my throat.

"What did you see at the inn?" he said.

"You know what I saw," I gulped out. "You were ordering beer, I suppose, the same as me."

"No," he said angrily. "Play not the innocent. I mean at the other inn, the Blue Boar. Where you put your talents to such good use for me." His lip curled. His eyes looked monstrous odd. "What did you see?"

"Nothing," I tried to say, but no sound came and his hand tightened on my throat.

"You saw me with the Spaniard – I half suspected it all along – and now tonight – The risk is too great – you understand, I have no choice – "

I closed my eyes. O! to die in a vile alley far from home and friends, all unprepared – it was too cruel!

And Fortune must have agreed with me, because it did not happen. It was Anthony who sank to the floor, his grasp unclenching from my neck, his body crumpling till he fell heavily in a heap; and I was standing there face to face with the gaudy beggar, whose oozing sores I recognised only too well as he looked at me, the crutch in his hand whereby he had knocked Anthony senseless. Or worse.

"O! Is he dead?" I gasped.

"No," said my deliverer. "Now come and give me thanks."

I squealed. From one disaster to another I was tossed like a tennis ball.

"O no –" I whispered, buckling at the knees.

With a very strong arm the beggar supported me and lifted me over Anthony.

"He was trying to kill you?"

"I believe he was."

"And did I rescue you?"

"Yes, but –"

"Then you shall thank me."

"Will you take money?"

"Yes. But also I will take you."

"O please," I whinged.

"Every time I see you," said the beggar, "you are running away. Always running. And now you hope to run from me."

I gazed into his repulsive face. His eyes were very merry.

"It is my sores that bother you?"

The understatement nearly made me laugh.

"If I must be honest," I began politely.

"O, we must all be honest! Is there any other way to be!" And he took my arm. "Come with me."

As we moved out of the dark alleyway a couple of shadowy

figures hustled past us.

"I said *come*," said my companion more urgently.

"Why?" I turned to look behind, but he hurried me away. From one dark street to another we went, past bulging house walls, the sagging timbers shored up with makeshift buttresses. We stopped. The beggar reached inside his cloak and brought out a great black key. He unlocked a door, an unexpectedly sturdy iron–rimmed thing, and we bent our heads and entered a low room. The beggar locked the door behind us. There was no room to move, only sacks, and the most exquisite smell.

"Lie back," the beggar said.

"It seems to be spices."

"It is spices. Nutmegs, cloves, and there ground cinnamon. Lie down."

"But how are spices here?"

"I put them there. Don't ask questions. Dealing in what I steal is one of my many professions. Tis a wicked world and one makes one's way."

"It seems you have always been following me. So many times my path has crossed yours."

"Chance, that is all."

"But I have noticed you so often."

"I assure you, except for tonight those encounters were chance. Most certain, each time I have seen you I have run my eyes over you and swore I'd use your body if I had the chance."

"O! And would I have had some say in such a plot?" I demanded.

"No. I have always intended to ravish you."

"And is that your intention tonight?" I quivered.

"Tonight it was not mere Fortune. Tonight I did watch you. The man you were with would have not been good for you. So I made sure I was there. This is a place where I bring valuable things."

I settled upon the sack of nutmegs, shamelessly flattered.

"Give me your hand," said the beggar in the darkness. "Now put it on my arm, and feel." I shuddered. My fingers closed on a sore upon his arm.

"Touch it...pull it..."

It was grotesque to lie there in the dark, to hear his voice say that, to touch the bulbous lump, and all the while to feel the air so close and perfumed with warm cinnamon. Between my fingers that sore shifted and its texture seemed like ointment, smooth and oily.

"Tis a great skill to make sores," he told me.

"Make sores?" I gasped. "You mean it is not real?"

"Tis a fine art. It begins with crowfoot, spearwort and salt, and later ratsbane and torn bits of cloth. It is no easy matter. I need not have told you this. But as I intend to have you, I prefer you should enjoy it and not be quivering in revulsion. Beneath my self-made sores I am a whoreson handsome fellow."

His hands loosened all my nether garments. I lay back upon the spices. With no choice then, as he said, I had best enjoy it.

"Lift your legs," he murmured, and his gaudy cloak came down around us both.

In that small dark place I could see nothing, but my other senses did very well. I felt his rough lips kissing mine, his monstrous bulbous self-made sores scraping my cheeks, the bristly hairs of his body brushing my skin, his hard long shaft within me; and all the while the heady scent of spices, cinnamon, nutmeg and cloves all merging together, stronger every time I shifted, filling my throat till I could taste it on my lips. As he intended, I enjoyed it, yes, it was most pleasing.

When he had finished with me he gave me one more kiss and helped me to the door.

"Stay with the people you know," he said as we parted. "Bad things can happen in these murky streets. I am not a bad man, but if I had been, who would know? Who would come looking for you here? Go back to what you know." He pointed. "The river is down there."

I saw the treacly waters of the Thames down in a gap between the dark shapes of two houses, steps descending. A swinging lanthorn showed a boat below.

I never saw that place again; I never knew where I had been. I limped down to the water's edge, smelling of spices.

II

"Sit on my knee and call for thy content,
Control proud Fate, and cut the thread of Time:
Why, are not all the gods at thy command,
And heaven and earth the bounds of thy delight?"

I HEAR that Matthew lost you on the way home?" Kit
enquired amused, the next day, his arm about me on the
bed. "Where did you go?"

"I drank beer at the Bent Nail," I boasted, prepared to make
of it a tale of adventure and bravado. "So you see, I am quite
able to look after myself. I saw many drabs and doxies, I saw
dicers and sailors, and I was most comfortable. You need not
have sent me away."

"So I see," Kit laughed. "I am impressed."

"Um...did Anthony rejoin you?" I said cautiously.

"Anthony? No. Why?"

"He was there also."

"He was? No, I have not seen him since."

"O Kit!" I blurted out. "I must warn you again – Anthony is
not a good man. I know it, believe me; and I'm frightened."

"Why?"

"There is a serving man at the tavern whom I know to be a
seminary priest. I met him in Paris. I recognised him again – and
Anthony was talking to him. And when he saw me he behaved
most guiltily. They must certainly be plotting – the priest once
told us he could deliver messages in pies..."

"A seminary priest in Southwark!" Kit said amazed. "Disguised as a serving man?"

"Yes – but he is not the problem – it is Anthony. We must not
see him again, Kit; believe me, he does not wish me well."

"I have no plans to see Anthony again; calm yourself now;
there is no reason to fear him." He suddenly laughed. "Messages
– in pies!"

I sighed. So much of Kit's life I would have liked to change. I
did not like how at ease he seemed in sordid taverns. Over the
river – O, was that not a secret name for witchcraft? – lay that
jumbled expanse of twisty alleys and disreputable people, and

291

Kit was comfortable there. Who was it that he had met and talked so earnestly with? What had he done there after I had left?

"O Kit! You know such strange people. I wish you would abandon them and only write. Kit, why not leave London altogether and go and live in the country?"

He burst out laughing. "I know nothing about country life!"

"I'm sure tis safer there."

"O come," he sniggered, only too apparently glad to drop the subject we had been discussing. "Everyone knows that country-folk are continually being eaten by bears! What kind of security is that?"

"No, Kit, that is not true," I assured him.

"Is it not? You have marvellous cheered me – I'll go buy a sheep cote somewhere and live an idyllic life beside a stream. King of the pastorals!"

"O Kit – it would be so agreeable!"

"I suppose you'd come and keep house for me and sing pretty songs all day? It would of course be May all the year round."

"We could bathe in the stream. Tis beautiful, that. Buttercups and cowparsley come right down to the water's edge, and cows come to drink and flick their tails about, and the sun shines on the water."

"Cows – what do I know of cows? In all seriousness, what does one do in the country?"

"The peasants work hard, and the rich continue much as they do in the town."

"And since we are neither peasants nor rich, where do we fit in?"

"Only in fancy," I said glumly. "In an idyll or a dream."

"In other words, not at all," he said plainly. "Listen, Marc," he said. "The world is not as I would like it. How can it be, when we have to die? How can we be satisfied with the Almighty plan? If we come of poor stock we are marvellous abused. We use our talents to rise, and at once we encounter a wall. That is forbidden, this is forbidden, thoughts are forbidden, the way one chooses to love is forbidden. Men setting themselves up as little Gods, privy to God's counsel, dictate to the vulgar – everything is wrong. But losing oneself in Pastorals is not the answer. In the Americas there is rumoured to be a city of gold and one day it will be discovered. But it is possible to reach that city *now*, without even moving a limb, do you see what I mean, through the power of what you choose to think, each new thought an exploration, each idea that goes beyond ordinary fear and proscribed limits..." He laughed. "Come, this is idle talk, and opportunely there is someone at the door."

It was Robert and Matthew come to fetch Kit out to supper.

"The magician, with his familiar!" Robert teased us.

"You say true!" said Kit amused. "And you interrupt us about to concoct a spell for questioning the dead."

"Indeed you do not," I protested. "We were doing no such thing."

"I do wish to question the dead," declared Robert, clearly in a merry mood. "What must we do?"

"I the questioner," said Kit, "must drink a wine compounded of poppy heads and powdered hempseed, the infusion strained through cloth woven by the hand of a poxy drab. An incense must be made, of camphor, ambergris and goatsblood and the innards of a mole, mixed up with the body of a bat that drowned in blood, and four nails from the coffin of a disembowelled villain. So tonight we shall go dig up graves!"

"'Tis always vile things," grumbled Matthew, "that the dead require. What manner of man would seek to mix a brew like that, and drown a bat in blood, and slit a mole?"

"The highest in the land," shrugged Robert. "Did not Lord Robert Dudley keep company with witches and employ that necromancer Dr Dee to conjure up the dead? And that same Dr Dee was astrologer to the Queen and privy to her close counsel. He enquired of spirits when she should be crowned and then advised her of the day. Why, Kit himself has friends who dabble in such matters; and *they* are *lords*!" He strutted somewhat. "All we who are learned men concern ourselves with mystic things – the choleric and melancholic influences in our bodies lead us to pursue the unlawful. We have no choice."

"I do confess," said Kit, "a curiosity in the power of circles, symbolised by those dragons that do swallow their own tails, and the magic properties of blood and bone; and holy words writ down in such a way their meaning changes."

"In France," said Robert, turning then to me, "there is much witchcraft and much burning of witches, is not that so? I have heard that in the south there are ten thousand witches and they copulate with demons. They worship boars, and kiss the beasts' backsides."

Kit laughed affectionately. "And is that so, Marc? Up and down the waysides as one travels, does one see much of that?"

"I did once know a witch," I said, but sombrely. "But it was long ago – besides, she is since dead."

"And did she show you all her skills?" Robert pursued. "Indeed, you have the witch's marks, those moles upon your face. Were you her helpmeet?"

"In a way I was."

"What think you, Kit?" Robert asked. "Would he be a useful adjunct to our purpose?"

"Ah yes," said Kit in a low thoughtful voice. "But this is not the time. Get dressed Marc, and be off with you." We both began to hurry into our clothes.

"Witches' marks, they call them," Robert continued. "For secret power lies within a facial mole. Are you a witch's brat, boy? Come, you may confess."

I thought he was but jesting so I did not reply.

"How say you, Kit?" said Robert evilly. "You bragged he would do anything you told him to. I dare you to seek whether he has a hidden source of power."

I gasped. I suddenly realised what he wanted Kit to do. I clapped a hand over my lips. My resistance and alarm sparked a response in Kit.

"Most sure I dare, and he would do it, but I have nothing small enough. A pin is needed, something small and thin."

I watched in trepidation as Robert took off a brooch from his shirt front and handed it to Kit. Kit, to be just, did look annoyed, but his reputation counted to him more than my feelings, as was his custom.

"You'll let me prick your mole for an experiment," he remarked. It was a statement, not a question.

"Must I?" I quivered.

"Yes, you must."

"What if I am marked?"

"How can you be, by a brooch pin?"

"First," said Matthew, business-like and brisk, "you have to hold it in a candle flame."

"Why?"

"I know not. We always did it when I was a child."

"You were a witchfinder, were you, in your nursery?"

"No! I mean whenever we pricked boils or blisters. We always had to hold the pin in the flame."

"Very well; light a candle and we'll do that."

I stood by, sullen and wary. They were like little boys. I could imagine them poking about in the innards of a dead cat; or stretching out a frog's carcase to look for the little key-shaped bone that you can use in love spells. They were serious and merry, absorbed and curious. For all that, when they turned to me, I shivered all over, my unwillingness patently apparent. But they were excited and aroused, as in a rape, and they took hold of me and bent me across the table on my back and held me still and hung over me. I did not struggle, but I was much afeared. How could Kit bear to do this to me? I marvelled, as his face came close to mine, concentrating, and the pin hung near my mouth between his finger and thumb. I felt the pin prick and I screamed, more from panic than pain. The air was curiously close, and at my scream Robert and Matthew recoiled; not Kit, he stayed calm, and removed the pin with steady fingers. His forehead was beaded with sweat.

"Pass me a handkerchief, Robert," he ordered coolly.

My teeth were chattering with fright.

"We let out the Devil, I think," Kit smiled, dabbing my abused mole with the handkerchief. Upon it was a little drop of blood. I started to calm myself. I was after all still alive. I looked up into Kit's face, and I knew that Kit had enjoyed what he just did. Diable! How many people could bring themselves to prick a mole on someone's face coldbloodedly like that? It takes a strange disturbed and special soul to relish it. And I know Kit felt something weird and mystic about it. I remembered what Nicky said, about Kit's magic being unwholesome. Kit kept that handkerchief, I know. It was pure white, and it had this one red spot of blood on it.

"Brave boy," Matthew praised me. "He'd be a fine addition to our ceremony, Kit. Make him come."

And this incident here in Kit's room became the prelude to a stranger, far more dreadful one; and it was the wickedest thing I ever did for Kit.

It was two days later. In the darkness of midnight we went by boat to a majestic house that bordered the river. It was not a Thames boatman that rowed us; it was someone from the house. In the presence of this servant no one spoke of the business that brought us here, but we seemed like conspirators, wary, secretive, uneasily jesting.

The house, fronting on the Strand, was a nobleman's property. It had ceased astonishing me, the vast strata of Kit's acquaintance – to think that he knew disreputable tavern villains and the dissolute literary gang at the Phoenix, and then these elegant wayward lords. I simply went along, obedient, almost trance-like, and yet on this occasion my part was central.

The boat nudged along the wet slimy wall. The house soared up above us, enormous and black like a castle, with battlemented turrets just visible in the faint lustre of a cloudy moon. Here and there lights showed. A shivery wind blew chill across the river from the Lambeth marshes. Leaves above a low wall rustled and shook. The boat scraped a row of steps, and the water plashed about them. An arched wooden doorway opened at the top of the steps, light flowed down on to our faces, and we were beckoned in.

We entered a cold passageway lit by burning brands that flung our shadows monstrous and misshapen on the ancient walls. It led to a small circular room whence a stairway wound upward to the floor above. Here in a room of similar shape, but hung with tapestries and lit by many candles, were gathered a group of men whose clothes and bearing were noble. They were cloaked against the cold but I caught glimpses of pearl-studded doublets, jewelled scabbards, finest leather boots. We were warmly welcomed and wine poured for us.

Two of the men embraced Kit with more passion than in common friendship. One of them was the handsomest man I had ever seen. He was six feet tall, with a swarthy complexion, black curly hair and beard, and beautiful clear grey eyes. I almost thought him a Spaniard, but when he spoke it was with an odd kind of English accent, which now I know for Devonshire. As it dawned on me in whose presence I now was, I felt a frisson of delight – a man so high in favour with the Queen herself, whose expedition to the Americas had made him famous beyond the seas, a man reputed to be daring, bold and witty, yet violent and cruel withal. I much admired his clothes – his white and silver doublet, his white hat, its feather buckled on with a great ruby, the lining of his cloak all set with tiny pearls, the double pearl-drops at his ears. He held Kit hard against him and did kiss him on the mouth.

The other man that embraced Kit was slim and young, with long fair rippling locks, and I knew who he was as Kit cried: "Tom! You came! Ah, I am so content."

My face hardened into a scowl. Beside me, Robert softly laughed:

"I don't like him either."

But this was not the time nor place for Robert and I to delve into why we reacted adversely to young Tom Walsingham. That he was pretty and that Kit was palpably smitten with him was reason enough. I knew that his family estate was at Scadbury in Kent and I knew that there were leafy walkways there, green glades and ancient trees and a lake all fringed with water lilies, all places where two lovers might walk unobserved and talk of love, and I knew that Kit had been there and was like to go again. So I did not overmuch like Tom, but nor did Robert, and he never told me why.

No other names were mentioned directly, though I did hear one man addressed as Hariot – a man with troubled brows and close-cropped hair. Robert told me afterwards that he had a brilliant mind, but of the many things he told me Hariot could do, the one I remember most is that he could explain exactly what makes up a rainbow, and I never look at a rainbow now without thinking of Hariot who was so clever.

And now in the silent room we all drank wine, and they did see that I was heavily imbued with it to prevent too much thinking, and it worked very well, for I had no conscience, no scruples, nothing; I did all they wanted. And next we repaired into a private chapel, and there the ceremony did take place.

Now I must insist that this was never a Black Mass, but simply an experiment, a scientific experiment such as any alchemist or astronomer or any learned man might perform. The purpose was to create a situation where a summoned spirit would feel at his ease – assuming that spirits ever did feel easy, something which we cannot know! We gathered in the little chapel and the gentlemen did kneel or sit, all looking toward the altar, which was covered with a golden cloth that spread in heavy folds, and glinted as the glow of candle-flame picked out its metallic strands. It being night there were many shadows, and a heavy silence, and the deeper darknesses beyond the glimmering light. Around the altar upon the slim stone steps were symbols writ on parchment, within a circle – Jehovah backward and in anagram, Hebrew letters, mystic signs, and names of saints and demons mingled. Then I was led forward wearing but a cloak, and this was taken off me and I was put naked on the altar on my back, spread out, and Kit arranged me and did mark my flesh with ointment, on the chest and belly. I lay limp and let him do all that he would, a wicked sensation of excitement rising in me to be thus displayed.

Then Kit stood behind the altar like a high priest, and he said the summoning words. They were these:

"Sint mihi dei Acherontis propitii! Valeat numen triplex Jehovae! Ignei, aerii, aquatani spiritus, salvete! Orientis princeps Belzebub, inferni ardentis monarcha et Demogorgon, propitiamus vos, ut appareat et surgat Mephistophilis, quid tu moraris? per Jehovam, Gehennam, et consecratam aquam quam nunc spargo, signumquae crucis quod nunc facio, et per vota nostra, ipse nunc surgat nobis dicatus Mephistophilis!"

Floating with the effects of wine I lay and looked up at Kit making the sign of the cross, scattering holy water, as he spoke the words. He did seem like a priest. I wondered how he would have been if he had stayed within the church. He spoke the wicked words so beautifully, more inspiring than the Protestant preachers in church on Sundays, almost as a lover might call up the beloved, sensuously. His arms were raised, his eyes were bright, as if when the spirit came he would embrace it.

In the stillness following the summoning I sensed a mood of true fear. Twas as if all held their breath. Spirits *had* been summoned – astrologers summoned angels, everyone knew it. When God gave Moses the Ten Commandments on a tablet of stone he gave him the Cabala too, and those who understood it could call angels thereby, but by possessing the secret magic given by God they can be sure no bad angel will come. But we were calling Mephistophilis, and though these were discerning intellectual gentlemen who logically expected no spirit to answer, there was a moment then when they must have wondered secretly whether after all there was a chance. We waited.

Of a sudden someone sniggered fearfully and loud; and one sardonic voice observed: "Perhaps another has called him already, and he is elsewhere."

"Come forward now," Kit ordered, breathing quick and hard. "We are by no means finished."

One by one they came up to the altar. Kit poured wine into a chalice. Silver it was, set with emeralds and rubies, one that must have been hid in secret and escaped the ravages of the Protestant purge. Down through the ages since men had worshipped, lips must have kissed that holy cup in reverence. But now the lips of the worshippers were put to other use. After each had sipped the wine, each bent his head and lightly kissed my prick. Whatever the symbol behind the act, the pleasure I received did raise me to erection, and I lay there thus, and I was on the altar! On an altarcloth! And Kit said holy words, as a priest does, when they kissed me. And some but brushed their lips against my prick, but others lingered longer, finding pleasure of their own, winding their tongues about me and touching me with fingertips, their long hair caressing my skin as they bent their heads. I was not so far gone with wine that I did not notice who did what, and to this day I swell with pride to think that one who kissed me passionately was that handsome hero, favoured of the Queen, whom some called cruel and proud as Lucifer, but whose lips were warm as a lover's are.

But for all our profanity and our lechery we did not achieve our aim that night. I lay there till they had finished, immobile as the altar I was upon. Eventually I was lifted up to sitting, and a cloak was placed about me. Matthew supported me and we all made our way out of the chapel, down some steps and out into the darkness, which was startlingly cold after the candle warmth. We gathered in a courtyard, talking in low voices. I found I was shivering.

Someone near to me said: "I did not think it would work. We are too innocent. There should have been more – we were too nice –"

"What, would you have us slit a chicken and drink its blood, like hags under a hedgerow?"

"There must have been things we did not do..."

"Kit spoke the words right. If demons do exist, one would have come."

"I for one am glad we failed."

They were subdued, relieved, belief in rational things sustained.

It had been very shocking what we did. But to me the most shocking part of the night was then, for Kit went marvellous strange and not like I had seen him hitherto. Whereas the others all were thoughtful, analytical, reflecting on the event, Kit was noisy and frenzied.

"Once again, *nothing*!" he shouted. "What do we have to *do*? What is *bad* enough? Christ! We spread a naked boy on His altar – we kiss the prick aroused – we call up Mephistophilis in faithful aping of the sacrament – and nothing!"

The lords I thought were uneasy then, probably because Kit's voice was loud, and anyone could have heard.

"Damn Him, damn Him," Kit screamed, "Again and again I try – He never answers, never. He *shall* exist – He must. I dare Him to exist! Answer, damn you, strike me, here I am, prove it – what do I have to *do*?"

I stared aghast at his control all gone, him standing there shaking his arm at the huge black starless sky, his head thrown back, his voice all strained with rage and pain, howling on God.

Thomas Walsingham hugged him. Kit collapsed in his arms sobbing wildly; Thomas soothed him.

Matthew put his arm around me.

"All well, Marc?"

"Thank you, yes."

"A strange affair, eh?"

"Most strange."

"Do not be troubled, will you? Twas but a prank. It meant nothing."

The group began to disperse. Thomas Walsingham and Kit went inside with their arms around each other. Matthew laughed, like one trying rapidly to return to ordinary things.

"Kit will be well by morning."

"I doubt it not," Robert agreed unpleasantly, passing by.

"O!" Matthew added to me, as an afterthought. "Had you heard that Anthony Wilton was found slain?"

"Slain?" I gasped. "No, I had not."

"It must have been soon after we all met him in that sailors' den. The night you gave me the slip! Yes; he was stabbed in an alley, by villains after his purse."

III

> "Not from my heart, for I can hardly go;
> And yet I may not stay."

I SEE NOW that it was that dark experiment which was the turning point in my relation with Kit. When I did see him there so vulnerable, so tormented, I did think: I shall never leave him, he needs me, someone in his bed whom he can turn to. If Kit had for a moment admitted this to be true, then for him I would have left the players, left Nicholas, left a life I liked, and swapped it for a life that scared me, just to be his helper. But he never did.

Afterwards, when I did see *Tamburlaine Part Two* performed, I realised that it deals much with challenges to God, though it is to Mahomet that Tamburlaine calls, so as not to offend too much:

> Now, Mahomet, if thou have any power,
> Come down thyself and work a miracle:
> Thou art not worthy to be worshipped
> That suffer flames of fire to burn the writ
> Wherein the sum of thy religion rests:
> Why sendst thou not a furious whirlwind down...
> Or vengeance on the head of Tamburlaine
> That shakes his sword against thy majesty,
> And spurns the abstracts of thy foolish laws?
> Well, soldiers, Mahomet remains in Hell;
> He cannot hear the voice of Tamburlaine...

And Tamburlaine does all he can to anger Mahomet, horrid bloody things that cause the audience to gasp with horror and juicy relish, and Kit's most famous scene, the "pampered jades of Asia". But to me it was sad and moving, an anguished cry of one who seeks the Lord and never finds, a strong man looking for a leader good enough for him to follow. O I ached for him; and he did not care a whit. But mighty conflicts in the mind leave no place for an ordinary loving friendship, and although it may not seem so sometimes, I did have some pride, and his constant scorn and sneering did not suit me.

When I did meet him first after the ceremony, he behaved if anything worse to me than previously. He called me "this good Papist boy", with a great sneer, and it did seem to anger him that I had not been struck down and dared to be still breathing.

"Here he is, this good Papist boy, who lay down naked on an altar and was kissed by worshippers, and yet his God has not punished him, not even with a rash of boils. Either God does not care about you very much, my dear, or you are a fool for praying to an empty space."

We were eating at the Phoenix. There was much discussion about Anthony's death.

"He was found by a boatman returning home, they say."

"Stabbed many times; yet it was thought he put up no resistance...no one heard the sounds of fighting."

"No one would admit so, even if they had!"

"His purse was stolen..."

"*Was* he a spy, do you think?"

"I had heard so."

"What do you think then – his masters having no further use for him dispatched him?"

"Or he could have been double-dealing and discovered at it."

"It is a murky mist, the twilight world of the intelligencer!"

"So they say! I know naught of it!"

"Pure as the snow, yes, we know, as are we all!"

Myself I thought that, horrid though it be to feel gladness over a murder, I was glad that Anthony was dead. Whoever had stabbed him in the alley had done me a kindness, for I knew that Anthony would have come after me again. I did not care too much what exactly had happened or who his murderers had been; but I shuddered to think how close I had come to witnessing it.

But it was another conversation that stood out in my mind from that evening. It was some news that Matthew told us. He said:

302

"Just nearby where we were the other night they have discovered one more Papist hide-out! I was passing by the Bent Nail this afternoon – I'd been to the playhouse – and I found the tavern is closed down! They told me there had been a printing press hidden in the cellar, and the whole place crawling with Jesuits... You remember the Bent Nail, do you? A poxy little hole... And do you know the oddest thing of all? It seems a simple pieman was a seminary priest disguised! I thought that somewhat merry – we said one time at Kit's that Anthony had his finger in many pies! Well, if he had been coming away from the Bent Nail on secret business, then so he did, and we were cleverer than we knew!"

Everybody asked eager questions and wondered if Anthony's murder were connected with the discovery of the undercover priest, and how it was that the Jesuits were found out; but Matthew knew no more – the tavern was closed down and boarded up, and all the people who worked there taken away for interrogation. Scant sympathy was shown for them by the drinkers at the Phoenix – admiration for their cunning, merriment over the pies, a shrug of the shoulder for their ill fortune in being so discovered; then on to other matters.

A feeling akin to the queasiness of mal de mer came over me, and I wriggled clear of the company and decided to go back to Kit's room. My thoughts were confused as I trod the dark streets, because I could not help believing that I had been the only one who knew the true identity of Lionel Fulbrook. How could anyone else have known? Had Lionel betrayed himself in some way? Or had Anthony turned informer and passed on the secret before he was murdered? I could believe him capable of anything.

I reached Kit's lodgings, climbed the stairs, and found to my surprise a light within.

Robert was there alone, lying on Kit's bed, and somewhat tipsy from the contents of a leathern bottle, and I recollected that he had not been with us at the Phoenix.

"Ha! Come in, sweet boy. Don't hesitate – join me – I am just in a mind to rail with you upon our mutual friend."

"O," I scowled. "You and I have nothing to say to each other." I shut the door and eyed him dubiously.

"Why have you never offered me the same respect, I

wonder?" Robert mused beerily. "Is it talent you admire? – My books are brilliant, yet I do believe you have never read one. The play that I am working on will be every bit as great success as his and Kyd's, and yet I am much in their shadow. But why? They say he is all air and fire. I say no – all wind and smoke! I speak as one who knows," he told me, nodding sagely.

"I have no wish to join you in carping about Kit," I began with dignity.

"True, for your carp avoids deep waters." Robert sat up and pointed at me blearily. "I warn you, sweet bum, he will be no good for you, as he is no good for me. It is one thing to jest in taverns, and another entirely to fool about in a holy place, and he will find this out. The Lord is biding his time, but retribution will come, mark my words – my words, Marc – We will all be punished for that night when we defiled an altar. Yes, even he whose house it was, who seems to be in such high favour with the Queen. The mighty fall, you know, when Fortune's wheel is tilted. The angels fell, Lucifer fell, and so will he!"

"O Robert," I winced uneasily. "You sound much like a Puritan. What you say is foolish – and also very poor poesy."

"O I don't claim to be a poet; there's room for one poet only in this place," scowled Robert. "But as the ripest fruit contains the worm, the strongest tree the most withered twig, there be some men most fair who have most foul within...I shall distance myself from him a while; I fear contagion." He looked at me then, eye to eye. "Did you not tremble, there on the altar? Did you not fear the wrath of God?"

That idiotic church bell chimed outside. We both jumped, and Robert crossed himself. I refused to be discomfited.

"I did tremble, yes. But I was cold."

"You were frightened," he corrected. "And you were not the only one. I saw them; they were monstrous discomposed. Tom Walsingham, whom I was close by, was white as a shroud."

"His complexion is naturally pale, perchance."

"Tis caused by double dealing – too much hiding in the shadows, listening for plots."

"What do you mean?"

"Surely you know his uncle Spymaster uses him upon missions to catch Papists?"

"No I did not, but I suppose tis reasonable."

304

"And Kit too."

"Kit too? What about Kit?"

"He dabbles in intelligence for Walsingham. Why, that was how he first met the fair Thomas. Upon a staircase, I believe, in Uncle Spymaster's house in Seething Lane; and then much more at Cambridge. Love at first sight, Kit told me," Robert bellowed dramatically, blowing a kiss. "The only kind of love there is, says Kit."

"I do not comprehend you – are you saying that Kit and Tom have worked as spies?"

Robert mimicked my tone. "Worked as spies? Well yes, my dear, I am. You should be proud. The rumour is that Kit helped bring to justice those who plotted to set the Queen of Scotland on the throne. That pretty young man Babington, who ended his days stripped and disembowelled, and his privities cut off."

"But why should Kit work against Catholics? He prefers the Catholic religion. He has no strong feelings for the Queen."

"He does it for the money, dear, what else? Or maybe because it keeps him close to the Walsinghams. He is besotted with Tom."

I turned away from Robert, all my nausea returning.

At this moment we heard Kit coming up the stairs. Robert heaved himself to his feet, and when Kit entered he shook him by the hand and behaved as one in a play who parts from a friend, with wringing of the hands and beating of brows.

"Farewell," he hiccoughed. "We may meet again. The Lord will make his purpose clear. I had intended favouring you with explanations, but this obedient familiar will tell all. I shall not come too close to you – I see a demon on your shoulder."

Kit stared after him as he stomped off down the stairs.

"And what ails Robert?" he enquired. "Or is it simply Robert's ale?"

"He is much troubled about the time we called up Mephistophilis."

"He would be much more troubled if Mephistophilis had answered! *I* am more troubled that no spirit came. It leads me to the grim conclusion we were calling out upon thin air."

"Did you tell Tom Walsingham there was a Catholic priest in Bankside?" I demanded.

"No!" said Kit affronted. Then he added: "Yes. What of it?".

"As I supposed. For Tom to tell his uncle?"

"He would tell his uncle, yes."

"O! Kit! And you heard it from me!" I wailed. "So it becomes my fault. I have been the cause of arrest and interrogation and worse...and he was someone I knew! And I had decided I would keep his secret for him."

"But you did not, did you?" Kit observed drily.

"But I only told *you*! I did not for a moment suppose – but is it true what Robert said, that you work for Walsingham, that you are a spy?"

"On your own admission you are something of a blabber-mouth. I am hardly likely to chat freely with you on such a subject."

"But Catholic priests if betrayed are condemned to that most horrible death – and it must be upon your conscience – and mine too now. How can we bear it?"

"You are too impressionable," said Kit roughly. "Priests know the game; they take the gamble."

"You heard what Matthew said – All were taken away for interrogation. You know what that means, do not you? It means torture. In France we know all about what happens to captured priests – there were pictures painted which made all clear – the dripping blood, the mangled limbs –"

"Calm yourself or you'll be swooning again."

"Do you know why I decided not to betray him?" I said, much overwrought. "It was because of you. You said we must all have freedom to think anything we choose. And Lionel thought the same. Much as I did not like the idea of Lionel Fulbrook being free to pursue his ideas, I know he cherished those ideas dearly and I thought he must be allowed to have that same freedom..."

"So he did, but then he was found out."

"If you believe in thinking freely you should have left him alone. Or is there to be freedom for you to think freely, and different laws for others whom you do not agree with?"

Kit drew his breath in between his teeth.

"The whole sorry business has nothing to do with free-thinking; it has a far more practical origin," Kit lounged upon the table's edge. "'Tis true I did some work for Walsingham, and once they get their claws into you they are loath to let you go. I have been much pestered lately – I believe you saw the man they sent. Your snippet of news was like a plum that dropped into my hand – a golden ball to cast into the path of Atalanta, and stave off pursuit! Give us some proof of your continuing loyalty...Christ!" Kit suddenly yelled, banging the table with his fist. "Nobody seems to understand! All I want to do is to be left alone to finish my play!"

His words hung in the air for a moment as we stared at one another.

"And so you shall!" I cried with much dignity. "For once it will be easy to give you what you want."

Any player would have been proud of the exit I made, the swirl of the cloak, the toss of the head. But in truth I was much distressed and bitterly chastened. It was ended, I knew it; all ended.

It was an odd thing that brought it home to me.

It was to do with Amyas. Those apprentices whom he did call his followers, upon one of their holidays, when all Hell is let loose upon the streets, and decent folk do hide indoors, and football is played up and down Cheapside and heads and limbs are cracked – on such a day, for fun, did these followers kidnap Amyas in his gown and challenge Angel to restore him, Angel being St. George and Sir Calidore, the embodiment of knightly virtue.

They had stolen Amyas away, though in no way secret, for they sent a letter saying where he was – or should I say she, for she was in a dress. She was tied to a post in the yard of the Bull Inn and guarded by apprentices, and there were to be challenges for her release. They had decorated her with ribbons, and O she was a picture! She was loving it. She beamed and smirked, dressed all in white, and calling out: "Nicky! Marc! Angel! Have you come to save me?" while the apprentices fed her comfits and gave her kisses.

We were all there, and to rescue Amyas we took part in contests with the apprentices. Nicky beat his opponent in a race round the innyard and we screamed encouragement as they belted past us. He won, but was overcome at wrestling. I won easily a contest singing to a lute, apprentices not being especial known for the melody of their voices! But I was ignominiously defeated at cudgel play, unwilling to have much to do with pain.

Angel won wrestling and walking on hands for longest – and O! he was beautiful even from that angle, as I know from close observation. Francis won at wrestling but lost at vaulting. I won a bout of swordplay, marvelling that this skill, which had been taught me in France for serious intent, was put to use in the yard of the Bull Inn with boisterous lads to whom I bore no ill will. I mentioned this to Nicholas, but he was unmoved, indeed ungracious – but I put it down to the bruises he had received.

Between us all we had done very well and honours even, and so Angel was permitted to untie the maiden and lead her blushing and flower-bedecked to a trestle table where we all had bread and cider. It was merry and carefree, I thought, as we sat there guzzling and laughing and nursing our wounds, and I could not help but suddenly compare it with my outings in Kit's company. *Here* was my place, eating and drinking in the day-light, with companions who were proud of me for the games I had won. I could not fit with university wits who tolerated and humoured me and treated me with disdain, who took me out and abandoned me, who involved me with dangerous company and torments of the soul.

All through the feast, when I seemed most merry, I thought out these things. I knew I had gone eagerly to be debauched and I must take the blame. But now I saw things clearly. I looked around at my good friends, a merry group all warm in fellowship; I felt that I belonged. A surge of happiness pos-sessed me and I smiled and laughed. I tried at times to convey somewhat of my good humour to Nicky, though lost amid the general merriment it was not easy; yet I thought he would be pleased to see me glad at last and I was looking forward to revealing my changed state of mind. And so, secure in the prospect of pleasures to come, I beamed like any sunbeam and joined in with foolish jests and noisy songs and thumping on the tables, muddy from my battles, much content.

I may be made of earth and air in equal parts, I thought, but I have free will. That is the strong part, the part that overrides both and makes me what I am. And I must choose. There may be the two halves of my character which are equal real – I mean the one that lay naked on the altar, and the one that whistled with its fingers in its mouth so Nicky would be inspired to win his race, mud flying till it streaked our clothes. But neither must rule me – I must rule them. I could not take any more of Kit's mistreatment; and though I loved him I must say goodbye.

Feasting ended, the players began to stroll home. I took Nicholas' arm affectionately and reached up to kiss his cheek. He roughly shook me off; I supposed he did not like such a display of feeling in the street.

"Nicky," I said winsomely. "I have some news for you, some good news that will make you glad."

"I heartily doubt," he said, "that any news of yours will make me glad."

"This will," I assured him. "It is about Kit."

Nicholas turned on me, enraged.

"Listen Marc," he said with narrowed angry eyes. "I never want to hear that name again. I have been tolerant too long. I thought that I could master my true feelings but I cannot – I am not a saint and you have tried me long enough. Nobody would have suffered your carelessness the way I have. I thought I loved you and so it would not matter. Maybe I was wrong – you certainly care naught for me."

"I do care!" I protested shocked.

He ignored my interruption. "Watching you just now," he said, "I saw you as you truly are – selfish, shallow, with no heart. You laugh and play as easily as you rant and weep. You are a child, with a child's eagerness for gratification. I was stupid to take up with you and to hope for something different."

"Nicky, the thing I wanted to say..." I began.

"You can have Kit Marlowe or me," said Nicholas, not hearing my words at all. "But no longer both. And maybe," he added quietly, "maybe neither."

He strode away from me to join Francis and Ralph, and I stared after him aghast.

Everything he said was true, I knew it. I had treated him badly; but had I truly caused his love to falter? Shaken, I thought on it. I knew that first of all I must follow my design without any prompting from Nicholas, and say goodbye to Kit. When this was done I could return to Nicky, my action speaking louder than my intent, and surely then he would not doubt my love for him and my earnest wish to act more soberly in the future.

And so I set off directly to Kit's room, to cast him from my life.

I knew this would be hard, but I was not prepared for the pain of it.

I climbed his stairs, heavy hearted, firm of purpose but desolate. When I opened the door and saw him sitting at the table, my heart turned over with love and sadness. He was hunched and writing, his left hand clenched in his hair, and he half looked up and waved me to one side carelessly with his quill, strewing blots and swearing.

But I would not be shoved aside by that Scythian shepherd any more. I closed the door behind me.

"I have come to say goodbye," I said, in the hollow tones of a messenger announcing total defeat.

"O?" said Kit squinting, finishing his sentence.

"I have not much demanded of you," I began, "and at first it did not trouble me that you do not love me, and I was happy to receive at your hands whatever you were pleased to give. But..."

Kit looked across at me, laying down his quill, so startling handsome that my heart turned over, the lump in my throat greatly hampering the clarity of my speech.

"But I love you too much – or is it too little? – to devote my life to your indifference. I know you find me troublesome..."

"Indifferent? I am not indifferent to you..."

"...and you put up with me as something sweet, a sort of toy, and I did not care because I would have had you on any terms...As soon as I saw you I wanted you, any way you liked...and..." I was by now weeping profusely at the thought of what I was losing; all I could see was his beauty and his writing; his cruelty quite forgotten.

"I do understand," he said quite kindly, yet palpably unmoved by all.

"I am but ordinary," I floundered on. "I like to play with fire, but it does not make me happy, and with you I am always burned."

"Darling, enough! Your explanations are not necessary," he assured me.

"But I love you, you see, and I am leaving you. I have to explain." Tears poured down my face like rain down a window, unstoppable. "I have had to choose, because I was all divided. You may not know that Nicholas loves me and has been very sad about my coming to see you, and I have under-stood it was wrong to make him unhappy. Also there are the players, whom I cannot give myself to as they deserve while I am close to you, and I choose them. Although I choose these things, if you want me, all you have to do is say, and I would stay with you..."

"Ah, Christ," he muttered, ruffling his hair. "This always happens...so messy..."

"And I thought, if I say goodbye now, it will save there coming a time when you tell me to go. Which would be worse."

"Well, that time might have come soon, because I intend to quit these lodgings. However, it would not be because I was tired of you that I would ask you to stay away; simply that I shall not be here. I would never have kicked you out, you know. You'd have left of your own choosing eventually – tired of my unpleasantness. Even as you are doing!" he laughed brittly.

"I do not want to leave you," I wept.

"Listen, sweetheart, you are right, I do not love you. If that troubles you, then be resolute and leave. Go to Nicholas. He's an agreeable cove, though he'll never be a playwright...You need not tell him I said that!"

"Well...I will go," I choked. "But I want to thank you for...for...it was very beautiful – you will never know – I shall never forget – I was, Kit, I was *honoured* – to be – to have –" Sobs overcame me.

Kit leaned on his elbows and looked at me.

"Yes," he said thoughtfully, "in spite of being such a villain I did give you something, didn't I?"

I turned and rushed away. I hardly knew where I went. My eyes were full of tears and the streets were dark. But soon I would be with Nicholas. I would tell him all and relish his delight in the brave stance I had taken. As I thought about the night to come, when we would lie in each other's arms, my heart lifted and I believed that after all, things would be well.

Evening it was now, and I made my way back to the inn. As I drew near, a man approached me. Silent as a cat he moved out of the shadows, and stood in my path.

"Marc Morny, the player?" he asked me.

I admitted that I was.

"I was expecting to find you at the Cross Keys," he said. "I

311

have been waiting for you."

"Usually I am there. I am on my way."

"I think not," he said firmly. "I have a message for you, from a gentleman in Howlebourne. You are to attend him immediately."

"O!" I protested. "I cannot. I have to return urgently to the inn."

"You must," he said gravely. "It is the Queen's business."

I was perplexed and vexed, but stupidly I did not guess what was his purpose with me. Howlebourne was a pleasant place with many gardens; and I wondered whether it was anything to do with Sir Edward Knollys. For this reason I accompanied the man who accosted me, and I answered dully to the trivial conversation he engaged me in. When we reached the place he indicated, two men dressed all in leather drew near to us, and thus it was I found myself arrested, and in Newgate prison.

IV

"And yet I am not free – O, would I were!"

YOU MAY wonder which of my many crimes it was which at last had brought me to the notice of the authorities – *I* certainly did, for I was not told. Since I had first placed my elegant finest leather boots upon English shores I had been regularly involved in sodomy, and I was told this was a felony which carried with it the sentence of death, though none, it seemed, had ever seen such a sentence carried out. I had also mixed with atheists and heard a good deal of seditious talk. I had played without a licence, and defiled an altar. And the manner of my arrest was very strange. Everyone else I know who has been arrested, has been so in a public place and carted off in noise and bustle; mine was so devious and secretive. I was winkled away by this mysterious message, and the men who arrested me were not the Watch at all.

Sharply I shook myself clear of the dazed and preoccupied

state of mind that had possessed me and turned to grapple with this sudden unexpected shift of Fortune.

The tower of Newgate is a frightening thing with its barred windows and the teeth of its portcullis. My thoughts chased each other like frightened mice as the formidable walls closed around me. All very well for Kit to say prison was nothing and you could pick up a useful trade there – well, I was very frightened indeed, and only the hope that there had been a mistake prevented me from frenzy. A couple of years later Kit himself spent thirteen days in here, when he and Thomas Watson were arrested in a street fight on suspicion of murder, but they were released when it proved to be self defence. I know some people were very nonchalant about Newgate, but I was not – I was a quivering heap of panic and dread.

My gaoler, clanking a chain of keys as he went, bent down and lifted up an iron ring. A trap door rose, and a vile stench with it. He straightened up with an oath, rubbing his back.

"Down you go," he said gruffly, and I gawped in wide-eyed disbelief at the uninviting cavity revealed.

"Yes! Down you go," he insisted, and what could I do but obey? Beneath the hatch there was a small black space lit by a candle. By its light I saw a bed of straw and grimy black stone walls. Here I was incarcerated; I was there all night.

O! What a dreadful night that was! Alone in that dark hole I was left to direst imaginings. First of all I was confounded and outraged at having been arrested thus and given no explanation; then I was terrified because I had done much that was against the law. I began to remember pictures I had seen in France of martyred Catholics, their bodies torn limb from limb, their entrails burnt before their eyes in a fiery brazier. What did they do to prisoners in Newgate? I tried to remember any tales I had heard, but all I could conjure up was Kit laughing disdainfully, and saying Newgate was a useful place for making handy contacts and meeting interesting villains; he did not seem to take it seriously. But it was a prison! In the Bastille they used the Boot. They put your foot inside it and added wedges till there was no space and the bones were crushed. The victim was able to hear the crunch of splintered bones and know he would never walk again. I looked down at my feet encased in best leather and vowed that I would tell immediately all I knew. But what did I know? Wherefore was I here? Confusion returned, and I tried to apply philosophy, knowing that "It is fear that I stand most in fear of; in sharpness it exceeds every other feeling." How true that was!

When the candle burned out, such light as there was came through the iron grill in the roof. I had always fancied prisons to be silent places, the silence of many thicknesses of stone and the slither of moat water, with rats maybe, and a distant scream or moan to chill the blood. Newgate was as noisy a place as I had ever been in. I heard the sound of drunken carousal all night, the tread of boots passing overhead; I heard scuffling and fighting; at one point a body fell across the grille and blocked out the light, then it was dragged away. A face peered in and spat and belched. I settled on the straw, huddled in a heap, extreme frightened and alarmed and wary.

And now somewhat late it began to dawn on me that nobody knew where I was. Worse, my friends would assume that I was with Kit, as I had been so often before, and Nicholas would think that, threatened with the withdrawal of his love and his justified anger, I had chosen Kit and decided to be the bedboy of that disturbing playwright instead of Nicholas' true lover. It was unfair. I could well lose Nicholas because of this. Even now he would be thinking I was with Kit, that I could be that callous and unfeeling. He would harden his heart against me, as he had begun already to do. He had said he might not love me any more. He would never know that I had said goodbye to Kit and was on my way back home to him to tell him of my love. O! Fortune was too cruel. How long would I be incarcerated, and all that time Nicky believing me so careless and unkind?

O! What if I was never released! The full weight of deepest dread now descended upon me. I knew very well that when the gates of prison closed upon a victim, he passed from ordinary existence and from men's knowledge. Years could pass. You sank into oblivion. You lay, chained and emaciated, all sense of time forgot. You did not see the light of day, the change of season, you knew nothing of the world's shifts and fortunes. Eventually, with the sensibility of a plant or a stone, you became fit for naught, and upon release you trailed your wretched life uncaring, pitiable, a beggar in body and spirit.

If I could get a message out, so that someone knew where I was! How could I do that? Was it possible? One might reach Sir

314

Edward Knollys, my patron. He would help me. O! But why was I here? What was my crime? Had somebody told the authorities that I liked to lie with men? Who would do such a thing? Or was it for something I had seen or knew? Was it to do with Anthony Wilton? Those two men I had seen slinking along the alley, on their way to murder him...had they recognised me? Was this their work, to stop me telling what I had seen?

Remembering that moment, and the wild and whirling world of Bankside by night, I thought of Lionel Fulbrook, now taken away for interrogation. Was he in here? O! Surely it was not Kit's doing that I was arrested? If he had told Thomas Walsingham about Lionel, there was no limit to what he might do to appease those he worked with in his vile profession. I felt this thought to be unworthy; but then so bemuddled was I that all unspeakable things seemed possible.

For so long now my everyday life had led me into situations that I did not understand, and the sinister, the treasonable, the devilish had been my daily bread. I mixed with spies – I had almost seen murder done. Would I, like Anthony, pay with my life for the things I had done, the people I knew? I had lost my liberty and the love of Nicholas – was the ultimate loss to be mine also?

Prey to such thoughts I sank into a troubled sleep, commending myself to every saint in Heaven.

It may have been morning when the trap door was lifted and a gaoler let down a ladder and ordered me out. He took me to a recess in a passage, where one sat at a table.

"What garnish have you?" I was asked.

"I do not know."

He grunted irritably. "What money have you about your person?"

I showed him.

"With that you can go to the Masters' Ward. There you can have beer and company."

"Choose that one," my gaoler recommended. "The Middle Ward is packed solid. And your only other choice is the Stone Hold."

"And there," cackled he at the table, "you will die!"

"Quickly, by fever, or slowly, by starvation," added the other.

A third gaoler who had been standing in the shadows, now

stepped forward. "No, he is to come with me."

I was taken down to a room, along passages lit by wall brands, and in this room at a table sat a man with two attendants, and on the table in front of him some papers. I was so relieved to be with people in power, in order to make my position clear and protest my innocence, that eagerness for a moment overcame my fear.

The man who interrogated me was serious and firm, square jawed and dressed in black. He had a dark curly beard and scary eyes that seemed to look into me and out the other side.

"You are known as Marc Morny, a player living at the Cross Keys Inn," he established. "But presumably you have another name, a French one?"

I told him what my name was. What would my ancestors think of me, saying our family name in the confines of this sordid place? How had I sunk! "You are French," he said seriously, and I almost giggled, after having said my name out in its entirely.

"Yes," I said.

"You arrived in England on the thirtieth day of April in the merchant ship Bonaventure."

"How do you know that?" I gasped.

He did not say. "In the company of Anthony Wilton."

"No – well, I met him on the ship, that's all."

"You left the ship in his company, in a small boat, landing at a secret beach, and avoiding the customs at the port of Dover. May I ask why?"

I gawped.

"Because I was seasick."

"I repeat, why?"

"Seriously, that is why. Anthony had a boat ready and I went with him to get off the ship because I was seasick and he said I needed a rest and he would take me to an inn."

"Avoiding the customs..."

"Only by chance. He said they would detain me because I was French, and since I was vomiting all over myself I did not want such trouble, so I went with Anthony."

"You arranged to be on the Bonaventure together."

"I did not!"

"Merely a fortunate concurrence," he sneered.

316

"No – a nothing. I had never seen Anthony before that day. I had no idea who he was."

"Of what did your conversation consist?"

"Of seasickness."

"Do not play games, young man."

"But tis true! I was not human. I was reduced to a wreck. I could not talk seriously. I simply groaned and puked. And he put me in his cabin and covered me up and let me sleep. And so the journey passed."

"I want a truthful reply to this. When was the first you met Anthony Wilton, not on the ship, but aforetimes?"

"Monsieur, I assure you...he was a total stranger to me."

"On the basis of so short acquaintance, you put your life in jeopardy for him?"

"When did I?" I demanded amazed.

"Do you deny that you have ever seen one of these?"

He thrust a paper at me. And now I saw it was one of those broadsheets I had taken to Paddington.

I frowned. "No," I said.

"You know what it is?"

"Well, yes...tis a paper with a satire writ upon it."

"I told you, boy, *do not* play games."

I shrugged, marvellous confused.

"What have I done wrong?" I said.

"You are Catholic, are you not? You told the woman of the house you were."

"Yes I am; but so are almost all of my nationality. It is an accident of birth. France is a Catholic country."

"Less of your impertinence. As a Catholic, your sympathies are with the Pope, with France, with Spain, with everything Catholicism represents? You hope for the restoration of the faith to England. You work actively for its return."

"No, indeed," I gasped. "There are degrees of dedication; mine is very slight. Of course I believe in God and the Virgin and the saints and the tenets of the faith, but not to excess; and since I have been in England all my friends are Protestants, and every Sunday I go to church with them. I have not been to Mass since I left France. I have no sympathies with Spain at all. I am entirely loyal to the Queen."

My interrogator sighed.

"Look at the paper properly," he suggested.

I looked. It was then obvious that between the lines of the satirical tract there were other words, writ differently. I peered closely, trying to decipher them.

"Your satirical broadsheet was a cover for one more Popish plot," he observed, "to be distributed amongst the faithful. Invisible ink was used. The writing emerges when immersed in water. We have details of a ring of sedition, hopefuls ready to rise up to receive the invaders. The little plot has failed. You were a rather foolish choice of messenger. Your foreign accent warned a servant. All was revealed."

All I could think of was that lovely day when Amyas and I had ridden along leafy lanes, in the sunshine, eating blackberries. It seemed so unconnected...

"I knew nothing of this," I said flatly.

"Why did you take the message?"

"I was offered a holiday — a hired horse. I went for the pleasure of it."

"Where did you meet Anthony Wilton for him to give you the broadsheets?"

A bell rang in my head. Instinct, warning. Kit must not be involved. With his religious views he would be highly suspect by ignorant authorities, taken away...

"By chance," I shrugged. "In Paul's churchyard, a chance meeting. I can only think he picked me for my ignorance. Only somebody stupid would have done his bidding, and I do begin to feel I was that one." I was angry at my duplicity. I burst out: "I hope you do not think I have regard for Anthony. I hated him. On the voyage he robbed me of money and deserted me, and now I see he has taken advantage of me and has landed me in trouble. We never talked of politics. I had no idea of his views. I certainly do not support them."

"Why did you come to England?"

"A purely domestic reason. To visit my cousin Gervaise Blysshen of Ashford, which I did. You can ask him; everyone saw me there, Gervaise and his friends, and an important merchant called Thomas Hodgkin, and his son, a Puritan, Cuthbert Hodgkin; they all knew why I was there. And after that I joined a troup of players, and ever since I have been hard at work doing plays. I have had no time for politics. Ask anyone.

And our patron is Sir Edward Knollys, the friend of the Earl of Oxford, and he will support me. He knows me very well."

Then I was taken back to the cell and left, and for two days and nights, except for a guard who brought black bread and but a thimbleful of ale, I saw no one. Then again I was taken back to the interrogator and questioned again on the same themes, more closely, with much about Anthony and my beliefs, and all that happened on the day I took the papers. There was a sudden breakthrough when the word Felipe cropped up as I described the night at the inn (without the lust and without the letter). Suddenly they were all alert, and of a certain this was news to them. I had to explain how I had lain seemingly asleep, and what I saw and heard; and as far as I could understand anything at all, it seemed to me that Anthony had been a secret agent for the government who had decided to work for Spain as well, that this had been suspected, and now was all proved. I sensed a more lenient attitude to myself for being the means whereby their suspicions were confirmed. They became less hostile and aggressive, a little more exasperated, as if indeed I was foolish beyond belief and as naive and stupid as I seemed. Then I was taken back to the cell.

It was most wearisome to wait there, and I wished I could be sent for again, and my innocence finally proved. I know the mention of Sir Edward Knollys had helped. I felt sure I would be saved. But all was not yet over.

Guards then came and ordered me downstairs. They took me to a different place, a low chamber supported by pillars. In the gloom there were hideous shadows. I knew what they were and trembled. I saw the shape of a rack, with its pulleys and ropes and the iron wrist clips, and on the floor the straw was foul and stinking and I shrank back, but they shoved me forward, and made me climb some wooden steps.

My wrists were fixed in iron gauntlets and lifted above my head and fixed to iron staples in the ceiling. I was streaming sweat. It ran down me in rivulets. It was a dreadful moment, like a nightmare frozen halfway through. The guards were gruff and grim. They did not talk to me; fixing me in place they muttered about wrist sizes and adjustments. I felt so lonely, arched and stretched and shaking and unspoken to.

Two did lurk in the shadows, idly touching the hideous

instruments as if they were any ordinary object, patting them, like friends, all careless – I even heard the rack creak. The third did stand before me and look up at me.

He showed a disregard and detachment which seemed to me curiously shocking. Then with a snigger he asked me if I was comfortable.

He said: "Let me tell you what happens, there, where you are fixed. The steps you stand on now are taken away. You hang from your wrists. Are you thinking about what it would be like? You feel a gripping pain... You feel it in the chest... belly... hands and arms." And he traced his dirty fingers over all those parts of me as he spoke. My tongue had gone so dry it was like a piece of old boot in my mouth. He surveyed me placidly. "The blood will seem to rush up into your arms and hands. You will think that it is oozing from the ends of your fingers and the pores of your skin... but it is only the sensation of the flesh swelling above the irons... The pain will be most cruel."

"O please don't hurt me," I whispered, terrified out of my wits, "please..."

Gratified, he grunted darkly.

"It does the same job as the rack," he said, "*eventually*. Your own weight will dislocate your limbs."

"Please... have pity on me," I moaned, half swooning. I could not feel my arms at all. My head swam.

He turned away from me, leaving me stretched and whimpering, and did mutter to the others over in the corner, and they did tap the metal and feel the wood and stroll about. After a while they turned back to me. All the time they were taking me down and unfixing the gauntlets, he kept up this conversation: "Yes, I've seen strong men break under this... not just little codlings like you... your paltry bones'd not hold up a baby. Your frame'd crack like a gnat's."

My legs gave out, my knees buckling, and I sagged, and they half dragged me over the filthy straw. The feeling returning to my arms brought aches from neck to wrists. I was hustled along passages and I ended back in the interrogation room, where a low stool was slung forward, and me on to it. I sat cowering.

I see now what it was. They had decided I was innocent and rather gullible and they were pleased that my testimony had convinced them finally of Anthony's double dealing. But they were angry with me, and they thought my carelessness deserved a punishment – perhaps another time I would think twice before accepting strange commissions. "*Frighten* him a little," I am sure they said. And this is what they did, and well succeeded. I was terrified.

"I want," said the man at the table, "the names of everybody who was in the room whenever you were in the company of Anthony Wilton – in other words, everyone whom you knew to be acquainted with him."

I went blank. It seemed like another life. He helped me with a list.

"Thomas Kyd? Matthew Royden? Thomas Watson? Robert Greene?" He had all their names, and others that I did not know. I mumbled assent; they would have to look after themselves. "Christopher Marlowe?" At this point, his assistant murmured: "I believe in that instance he is to be left alone."

"God's Blood," replied the inquisitor, "he will answer like the rest of them."

I said yes about Kit the same as I had for the others. He marked his list. Then he leaned forward to me.

"I am going to release you," he said. "I believe you have been foolish rather than treacherous. I cannot believe that a cunning spy would choose such a plainly suspect accomplice, except as a dupe. Your bearing and your answers have convinced me of your ignorance, unless you are an exceptionally skilful counterfeiter, which I doubt. I release you with a word of warning. Confine yourself to pastorals. Stay clear of spies! Go to church on Sundays. Do that you are good at, and do not meddle with that you do not understand. You have been lucky this time; but you may well be *observed* in the future. Life," he told me earnestly and very sententiously, "is a path. Follow it; it offers much. But do not turn off and plunge into the undergrowth. In the undergrowth there are roots and stones. And under the stones...loathsome evil things. The *unexpected*."

"Yes sir. Thank you sir."

And then can you but fancy what next he said! He said, in all seriousness: "I hope the rest of your time in England will be happier. Now go home and act prudently in the future."

"Yes sir, thank you sir," I repeated, grovelling fervently.

It was night. I made my way shakily along the cold dark

streets and finally up the rickety stairs to wake up sleeping Nicholas. I hammered on the door. He opened it and pulled me in. He fell on me like a starving beast, seizing me to him, eating me with kisses.

"Marc – I've been out of my mind – all this *time* –"

"O Nicky! I was arrested. I was in prison. It was to do with spying! Anthony Wilton was a traitor – maybe one will believe me now. I said always he was dangerous. No one believed me. I was right..."

I spilled out the facts to Nicky. He swore. He kept holding me and touching me; then he mumbled, "Christ! You'd better have a bath. You stink."

"Nicholas," I wept. "I was not with Kit. I have told him goodbye. I shall not see him again. O Nicky! *Do you still love me?*"

He stared at me stupidly. It suddenly dawned on me then that he had forgotten our last dreadful conversation. He had spoken in anger, to hurt. Anxiety had overlaid all else since.

"Of course I love you," he replied soberly. "And I knew you were not with Kit. I asked him where you were, and he said he did not know."

At once I realised how distorted one's thoughts become in prison, rudely uprooted from family and friends. It had never occurred to me that Nicky would speak to Kit, so obvious an outcome.

Dressed now, Nicky opened the garret door, and we set off down to the kitchen. Nicky roused people up, and he ensured some water heated for me and put into a tub, and he woke Jack and told him why I'd gone missing. And Jack came in his nightshirt to speak to me, and there in the inn kitchen I was reunited with everyone, with many kisses. And I was given scented herbs for the bath and I sat in it and also washed my hair; and Master Meeres the innkeeper poured best wine for me, knowing I liked wine more than ale, and I drank it in the bath, my knees poking up out of the yellow foamy scum.

When the excitement had died down, and Nicholas and I were alone in the kitchen and I was feeling safe and much recovered, I spoke to him of something that was troubling me.

"I know," I said, "that they will question all who knew Anthony, to see whether any were in league with him. And they

322

will question Kit, when his turn comes."

"He has nothing to fear; he will be but a name on a list," Nicky shrugged, sitting on the table.

"That would be so, but I know Kit has some copies of that broadsheet in his room. He kept them for the satire. If they are found it will be known that Anthony was in his room, and it may be assumed that Kit knew the secret between the lines."

"Perhaps he did."

"No. Kit is not political. He does not care who is on the throne as long as they leave him alone. And he would not have let me take them if he'd known."

"You think he'd care about protecting you?" Nicky asked dubiously.

"No," I winced. "He'd think I'd be discovered and the plot would fail...The fact remains, those papers are in his room, carelessly strewn among *Tamburlaine Part Two*, and I must go and get them."

"You? Never!" he said. "You're going straight to bed."

"It is a problem. They said they might have me watched. I might be the means of leading them straight to him. But he must be warned. They would arrest him, and he has not finished *Tamburlaine*."

"A plague upon it," Nicky snapped. "I will go myself."

"But will it be safe?"

"I will take care; I'll see I am not followed."

"But you hate him. You would not care if he was arrested."

"You little swine. Of course I do not want him arrested."

"O Nicky," I cried from the bath, "I do love you so."

"You're a shameless minx and I am a fool."

Yes, I had wanted Nicky to go. Who else could I trust on that delicate and important mission? Visions of Kit arrested, disbelieved, unable to finish his great work, tormented me. He had to be saved.

When Nicholas had gone I emerged from the tub and dried myself before the fire, and pottered about the quiet kitchen grateful to be returned. I sipped wine, I ate a small hard apple (my mouth tasted like ditchwater) I stroked the vast striped cat who blinked and purred, I watched the firelight and the candlelight shadows, and I listened to the shifting of embers. Then I sat wrapped in a big blanket toasting my toes by the

323

fire, one candle burning low, and waited for Nicky's return.

Phoebe came in, in her night gown, with her long fair hair loose about her shoulders, to ask me if I was well and to make me a posset. We stoked up the fire a little and drank the brew she made.

"Tell me, Marc," she said. "What would you advise? Both Gabriel and Francis wish to marry me. If you were me who would you choose?"

"Neither, but a man from hereabouts who will not have to travel, as players must."

"That is no kind of answer to my question."

"Are you sure it is *marriage* that Gabriel proposed?" I wondered dubiously.

"Yes! And your advice is not very helpful."

"Well," I pondered. "Francis plays a very good clown and can turn good somersaults."

"That is not what I would be requiring him for," said Phoebe reasonably.

"Nicholas says he is steadfast and true."

"I would guess as much," she agreed. "And Gabriel?"

"Well," I remarked. "Marry him, for since he does seem drawn to married women he will be drawn to you!"

She did not look best pleased with my reply, and shortly after betook herself off to her bed. I remained, reflecting that my envy of her situation did not make me the most suitable person to give advice.

I was truly surprised that Angel had asked her to marry him. She was not as beautiful as many of the conquests he had made along the way. Love is strange, I thought – not the first or last person to make that observation. Half dozing, I let time pass, and the next I knew Nicky was touching my bare shoulder.

"Is it done?" I gasped.

"Yes, and all successful. We burnt the papers."

"Was he there?" I enquired tremulously.

"O yes," said Nicky grimly.

"O Nicky! You spoke to him then!"

"I certainly did," he said with feeling.

"Nicky! You weren't – critical?" I said awed.

"Just a little."

"What did you say to him?"

"It doesn't matter what I said. It didn't have much effect on him, I daresay. But he had some things to say about Anthony. His majesty is somewhat sore about being duped."

"Yes...he thought Anthony was just an ordinary spy."

Nicky laughed wrily. "Spies...prisons...arrests. Your life has become somewhat too eventful lately. I think I shall keep you on a leash henceforth – like a dancing bear. At least I'll know where you are."

"O Nicky! Yes please," I smirked, nuzzling him. "Nicky, did I ever tell you how very much I love you?"

"Once," he observed, a little cuttingly. "Just now."

I leapt into his arms, the blanket tumbling away; I hugged him with all my might.

"Nicky, I love you! I see it clearly now. I am humble and ashamed for taking so long to love you. I had scales before my eyes and now they have dropped away. I was bewitched but now I am free, and I do love you. I will love you always, I will never leave you, I will be your faithful swain, your own true love. And will you be mine?"

"Yes, of course I will, you evil little frog."

"Kit called me an abominable Gaul."

"Then I never shall. I suppose there will come a time when you stop mentioning him in every other breath."

"Nicky," I said in holy tones. "You have saved him for posterity."

"I hope posterity is duly grateful."

We stood pressed close together, embracing, I quite naked and scented and warm from the bath, my wet hair dribbling, Nicky licking the drops. I rubbed myself against him, arousing myself.

"I am full of love, Nicky, and full of happiness. I am the happiest boy in the world. Come to bed, Nicky..." I was dotting him with kisses in between words." Come to bed and let me love you as you deserve to be loved and as I long to...I will kiss you everywhere...I will love you with all my heart and with all my body..."

It is not surprising that Nicholas gave no resistance. As we climbed up to our garret, I daresay we believed that our troubles were over and happiness entire was just beginning for us.

TEN

I

"How long shall I with grief consume my days...?"

As if to make up for lost time, I devoured Nicky feverishly, which I almost believe was a way of casting out my memories as much as indulgence of true passion. Seemingly I recovered rapidly from my horrible experience in prison, but deep down it had shaken me immensely; not just the most plain – the loneliness, fear and threat – but the remembrance of myself so weak and whimpering, half melted from the sweat of terror, pleading in tones of childish desperation not to be hurt. Kit had once teased me I was not the stuff of which martyrs were made. It was fortunate I did possess no important information; I would have told it all. But Nicky said I wronged myself, for I had the wit to keep Kit out of it, when questioned. But he had not known how scared I was. If they had known what questions to ask I daresay in the end I would have implicated everybody.

An odd and topsy-turvy time followed. It was not easy to be parted from Kit for I marvellous missed him. My friends were kind to me and sympathetic, though they must have been entirely glad to see me breaking free. But even Amyas did not jibe, and no one said I told you so. I did my work with tears sometimes dropping on to my hemming, and they had to change my lute solo to a sad one, as I usually broke down during it.

One day inexplicably I hungered to speak my native tongue, and went and sat in a lace maker's shop and talked. There we sat, this elderly man and I – the subjects we covered, and all in French! – his wife bringing in a small glass of wine, and samples of lace around us. But the strangest thing of all was that the man was a Huguenot! He had fled to England during the troubles, to escape from Catholics. I think I had reached true free thinking at last! The man was marvellous agreeable, and not at all a monster. Neither of us poisoned the other. He said that I was charming. I felt soothed as I came away.

Memories of Newgate prison assailed me in my sleep and in my waking hours. I shuddered as I struggled to forget. And eagerly I shut out bad remembrances with lust, and O indeed our nights were wonderful, deep in our blankets beneath the sloping roof, with the creak of wood, the twitch of straw, the pallid moonlight that did pick out our body shapes and shadows. I loved to kiss the little curls on Nicky's neck and trace his body with my lips. I loved to kiss him erect, slowly moving down from his chest and his belly, and all round his hips and loins, licking the taste of him, and so to his curly brown crotch hair and his quivering prick. I took it deep down my throat and licked it wet all over; I held it between my fingers and softly kissed it, and it bubbled at the tip and Nicky groaned and writhed and pleaded for me to finish. And sometimes I would greedily suck it down, and sometimes all passionately I would plead: "*In* me, Nicky, deep in me..." and he would do as I longed for, and slide on to me in the combined sweat of our heated bodies, till we both gasped and moaned and came together, breathless, floating, enraptured. And in the daytime I would look at him with love and wonder, for as we went about our ordinary work it did amaze me, to have such passion at night, to feel such tenderness by day. Reading through a script together, holding a nail for him to hammer, sewing up a rip in the dragon's tail, fetching cakes and cider, hearing Angel say his lines, tuning my lute as I sat on a barrel, correcting my English to Amyas' self-important dictation, most afternoons a play to perform; these sort of things were the fields in which my newly planted love did grow and bloom. Of Nicholas I did sing that song of Sir Philip Sidney's, the words being true: "My true love hath my heart and I have his," a song which I could never believe, as some said, was writ as if he were a woman. Why should he want to do that?

The details of ordinary life do not speed on my tale, and of the many days that passed in pleasant pleasures and work and eating, I will not say much, except that Nicholas and I found each other most congenial for company, and in the small things of this life we grew to value each other as friends. I mean the talk of childhood and of thoughts, things which are endearing between lovers as they twine closer together but which have not much import to observers. People were happy for us. Jack's wife Madge did one day give me a great hug as we sewed up skirts together.

"I am so pleased, for Nicky's sake," she said, most mother-like. "Nicky does not tell his thoughts; he seems so balanced in his humours, all busy with his writing – but I feared what would become of him. I doubted he would find true love – he would not go with girls and I did shake my head – his chance of happiness with a boy – well, the odds are much against it. He's not like Amyas, who's a shameless little fruit! No, he feels...I cannot tell you how pleased I am – everyone can see you are in love."

In love! Indeed, we were. And it was not light love, superficial love, skin-deep, born of a swift desire, a passing fancy – no, for we had much endured and been apart in bodies and in thoughts, that now were close together. Warm in our blankets we lay close, only too aware of how near we may have been to losing love.

"Love is not easy," Nicky said. "No wonder poets never can describe its ways...I thought that I was strong and tolerant and could stand by and wait and be your firm support...I learnt that I was weak and vulnerable, as jealous as the next, ready to rail on Fortune with all the turbulence and passion of any of the characters I create in plays. I thought I was as Jupiter mani-pulating mortals, and found I was instead as humankind."

"I have been so unkind...but not again, never again. I am all yours and so will be. Nothing will part us."

"Stay close, Marc," Nicky said with kisses. "I am so deep in love with you I could not bear to lose you. Stay with me always. These last weeks...they have not been easy...I think I could not bear it if something else should happen, something come between us...to know such great unhappiness again..."

"What could, Nicky? What could part us? All the sadnesses are finished." I hugged him tightly to me, smiling at his fears.

328

The days grew chillier, the evenings early dark. Upon the trestle stage we sang of the delights of Spring and Summer, shivering in our shepherd's fur, blowing on our fingers before we could play upon the flute and lute. But yet our hearts were warm, our friendships firm.

The players worked to make me laugh – and sometimes it was by mistake. One time we were performing and Francis as Horatio must enter with Bellimperia to declare words of love before they are surprised in the arbour and he is slain. But Francis blundered and came up on the wrong side of the stage. Amyas was all ready, simpering sweetly, and he saw Francis across the stage and gasped. And Francis to put matters right got down on all fours and came crab-like across the back of the stage, behind the two stacked benches covered with a cloth of grass. He arrived beside Amyas dishevelled but triumphant and could not understand why there was laughter – for all had seen his raised backside traversing the stage behind the benches!

I have mentioned that our plays were sometimes disrupted by Puritans, who did try and preach sermons to us as we played. Well – to my astonishment one day I did recognise the Puritan who spoke. It was Cuthbert Hodgkin – as pallid and uninspiring as ever, his long nose and straw-coloured hair protruding from under his tall black buckled hat. When the performance was over, he came especial to seek me out and talk to me.

What an amusing sight we made – he in his black and white and buckles, all severe, and I like a painted doll, in my cherry red dress and white stockings, daisies in my hair, and lip salve and powder feminizing my face! I was frivolous in attitude too, and he was solemn. We stood in the innyard and he tried to convert me.

"I did warn you Marc, before, as we sat at your cousin's table. O, had you listened to me then! Now how much farther are you on the downward path – how much more desperate your need for salvation! If my prayers were enough – but I doubt that, while you are constantly in the company of sinful players. I blame myself. I should have worked on you before."

"Trouble not, Cuthbert. Tis very merry being sinful. I have never been so happy!"

"O Marc, do not jest. We are talking of your soul."

"No – of my friends, and my livelihood!"

"You must be rooted out of this morass of iniquity. Your innocence has been played upon. You were a wandering lamb – wolves found you. Look at you. *You have painted your face!*"

"Yes! Like the whore of Babylon!" I giggled.

"Licentious tongue – sinful heart – the Lord will put his finger on you!"

"Ooooh!" I minced and quivered.

"Dissolute – disreputable –" he wailed as one tormented. "I *will* save you. You shall be my purpose!"

I should have been forewarned, but I was not. I merely laughed. I thought he was repulsive and hilarious, no longer sinister, as I had thought at first. A couple more times he did come and speak some more of the same. Hell fire was mentioned. None of us players took these ravings seriously; we knew we were not wicked. So I gave no thought to Cuthbert, teasing him, and acting lightly, answering his warnings with giggles and silly wit. Amyas sometimes abetted me. It became our great delight to play the fool with Cuthbert.

"Cuthbert is back again! He could not keep away – he must have his daily dose of sin..."

"He comes to learn about all those things he would know more of...singing, poesy, lechery..."

"Listen to me!" Cuthbert cried. "I have your welfare at heart. You would do well to pay heed to what I say..."

"Or he will set Nathaniel Pig-Swill upon us!"

"And to push us toward the flaming pit he will prod us with a naughty little fork."

"Ooooh!" we wriggled.

In the midst of my giggling I suddenly stopped. Beyond Cuthbert, up there in the gallery of the inn, I could see the gentlemen who came to watch the play. One moved in the shadows, and I recognised his tall impressive build, his dark fur robes – Cuthbert's father, who had propositioned me, who had told me that he always achieved what he set his heart on. Of a sudden I felt cold. What was he doing here? Had he merely accompanied Cuthbert, or was his presence anything to do with me? So uncomfortable did he make me feel that I had no pleasure in further teasing, and to Amyas' surprise withdrew.

So, Thomas Hodgkin knew where I was. I put him from my mind, but he lurked there, a recurring shadow. I guessed he

330

would not have been there solely to watch the play. I could see him again walking in that procession with the city fathers, the regalia of their offices born upon velvet cushions. These were the same people who passed laws against players, whose minions buzzed about the inn yard to make sure we were breaking no rules, nor sounding trumpets when we should not, anything that could give them an excuse to close us down. I knew that if Thomas Hodgkin had any plans for me I would soon be hearing about them.

And I was right. Next day, after a performance of *The Letter* Francis told me that someone wished to speak to me upstairs. With a sinking heart I climbed the steps to the balcony, and indeed it was Thomas Hodgkin who was waiting for me there.

As I stood there in my cherry coloured dress before him, I had a feeling that I was in for another nasty little tilt from Fortune's wheel for my pride. I had spoken scornfully to him that he had risen through commerce and I had called him a relation of a pig. So now although my face was bold, my stomach was churning. And with good reason, as I was to find.

First of all he praised me on my performance, but in a cool and cutting manner.

"Your departure from Ashford was somewhat sudden," he remarked. "Surprising, and if I may say so, a little impolite."

I did not feel that a discussion on manners was relevant. I pursed my lips.

"Perhaps," said Thomas Hodgkin carefully, "you remember the details of our conversation at your cousin Gervaise Blysshen's house."

"Yes," I laughed uneasily. "We talked of iron smelters." And lute players, I remembered uncomfortably then, one who had been abducted and forced to serve in the galleys at the whim of some nobleman.

"We talked of my wish to have you as my page," he corrected me sternly. "Now let me advise you, Marc. You waste yourself here. You are acting in a way not proper to your station. You are nobility, Marc. Have you forgotten? Why do you consort with these garish wanton folk?"

"Because it pleases me to do so," I shrugged. I noticed briefly that this appeal to the dignity of my ancestry, which some months ago would have struck an answering chord, now

331

weighed with me nothing at all.

"I am older than you, Marc," he said. "And age brings wisdom. I know better than you the ways of the world. You tarnish yourself living here, living this kind of life. I am offering you a return to respectability. I have a house in Bishops Gate. Important men meet there. In future years these men could be useful to you, contacts, advancement. This is a wise way of looking at the world – not what you are doing, living from day to day, careless of the morrow. Believe me, I am right!"

I said nothing. I looked at his silver-ringed hands and the rich dark fur of his robes and I sensed the inevitability of his power.

"I came here today on purpose," he told me. "Cuthbert explained to me that you were here. I am not one to be thwarted, Marc. I am determined to bring you into my household to our mutual advantage."

"Do my wishes count for nothing?" I demanded.

He made a snort of contempt. "You do not know what you want! How can you? You ran off with these folk on impulse, to be clear of Gervaise. But you are too high born for this company. You should be amongst a different class."

"What do you know of class or high company, being a merchant?" I spat.

"Do you intend to come willingly?" he asked with a monstrous cold politeness.

"You are crazed!" I seethed.

He curled his lip – the sign of any villain. Kit did it all the time.

"I am not a vicious man," he said steadily. "But I will have you for my page and you shall come with me this very day."

"I will not," I said with gathering dread.

"You have a choice. You will accompany me, or I will have your friend young Henshaw arrested for sodomy. I am a magistrate."

I said that I would go with him.

As I looked through blurred eyes down at the innyard, where my company was working to dismantle the stage, I knew the trap I was in. It was Gilles all over again. When they had used Gilles against me I had vowed never to love again. I had tried the cold loveless life, the brittle carelessness. But Kit had unleashed my passion and Nicky had nurtured my love. And now I was

332

love's victim once again; one could not escape love.

I felt almost proud. People might use love against me, but only if I denied love and impoverished myself would they have a true victory. Very well, I would have to go with Thomas Hodgkin, but I would never deny love again, and it would all be for Nicholas' sake.

The matter that troubled me most was that the company would be once again affected by my disappearance. What an impediment I was to them! Well. They had plays they used to do before I joined them. They would manage.

Thomas Hodgkin went down to speak to Jack. I never knew exactly what was said; I think he gave Jack money and I believe he indicated that I went of my own free will. I ran to find Nicholas and to blurt out the sorry tale to him.

We stood in the dark cold passageway that led from the yard into the inn. Warm wafts of smoke and kitchen smells blew from the open doors, and I felt envious of those who ate and slept and toiled, phlegmatic folk that were not the prey of passions or events. O! to sit and turn a spit for hours on end, dull-witted and unnoticed – bliss indeed.

Nicholas laughed bitterly. "I perceive that some malign fate does not wish me well. If I had fallen in love with Amyas it would be his foolishness of nature alone which might distress me. But I chose you. I set about to make you happy and lose you your fear. All for the delight of Christopher Marlowe as it then turned out. You finally break free from that fair tyrant and it seems we share true love. How foolish of me to suppose a pleasant future!"

"It may not be for long," I said eagerly. "If I am not a satisfactory page he will soon tire...he will regret his choice..."

"Why should he? A nobleman would find you lovely, let alone a merchant. He will not give you up."

"O Nicky, do not look so despairing," I wailed.

"But I *am* despairing! Why should I not look so?"

"There must be something we can do."

"How may there be? Jack dare not offend a city magistrate. What would you have him do?"

Nicky sighed and looked away. I felt then desperate. O, what a trouble I had been to him! Was I to lose him now? With a sudden chill I remembered how he had said he could not bear it if anything more should come between us. What did he mean exactly – surely not to cease loving me? I clutched his arm.

"Nicky! It will not make a difference to our love! We may have to part – but all it means is that we must be strong."

"I am not strong," he said soberly. "And," he added, "nor are you."

I gulped. My mind worked frantically. And then of a sudden an idea came to me. I clapped my hands. I had the answer!

"Nicky, do you think that Sir Edward Knollys could help us?"

"Your fancy nobleman friend!"

"Our patron!"

"Well, yes, I suppose he might," said Nicky. "But it seems like clutching at straws."

Yet as we slipped away, leaving Thomas still talking with Jack, it gradually began to seem as if Sir Edward would be able to save us. He was our patron. He was a lover of boys himself – he knew the Earl of Oxford, and Kit said he too was of that fellowship. Surely the nobility were more powerful than the merchant class. It must be so! Our hopes were rising, with every step we took towards the Strand.

It was already dark, and lightly raining. We did not speak, but hurried on apace. I knew Sir Edward would be our salvation. I remembered our sweet night together, and how we talked of life and thought – why, I still had his ring, and as in so many tales of love and messages I would present my ring and he would say: "Yes my boy! I said to you if ever you were in trouble, present this ring and I will answer..."My heart leapt. I saw us taken inside his sumptuous rooms, and me presenting him to Nicholas. They would find each other pleasing, and he would invite us both to supper. There would be candlelight and firelight – maybe with his Yuletide preparations it would be a special meal with many delicacies. He might ask us both to stay the night! Why, I would even bear it if he found Nicholas attractive, I could be that magnanimous for the favour he would do us. And in the morning we would all go back to Gracechurch Street or maybe he would see Master Hodgkin privily and send him about his business! Back to his nutmegs! I chuckled.

Nicholas gave me a wry look as if to warn me not to expect too much; but he too was excited, I could tell, and he squeezed my hand.

It was exceeding dark now, and the lanthorns lit, and at first I could not remember which of those tall houses had contained Sir Edward's lodgings. I flitted from one to another, Nicholas tense and exasperated behind my back. The main doors were open, and I recognised it now, leading the way into the forecourt. We were crossing towards the far door, when a porter accosted us in the uncouth rustic manner of porters:

"Oy! Where do you think you are going?"

"We are friends of Sir Edward Knollys!" I gasped, elated to be at our destination, vexed at having to explain myself to a menial.

"Then you will know he is not at home," replied the porter, as if he did not believe us.

"Not –? When will he return?"

"Why? Are you thinking of waiting?" enquired the fellow, with a studied insolence I found most offensive. We glared across the dim-lit courtyard.

"Yes indeed," I said haughtily. "Since we are his friends he will not object if we sit in his rooms and wait for him."

"I hope you have brought food and drink and blankets then, young sir; for your wait will be somewhat lengthy."

"How so?" said Nicholas, like one who has already seen the golden bubble drifting away.

"How so? Any friend of Sir Edward would know that the gentleman has gone into the country to celebrate the festive season and that he will not be back until well into the Spring."

We could feel the pleasure which this repulsive servant took in imparting this information to us. We stared, unwilling to believe, and yet knowing in our hearts it must be true.

"When did he leave?" I asked faintly.

"Last week."

"And where has he gone?"

"To the county of Warwickshire."

"Where is that?" I demanded tremulously.

"It might as well be the moon," said Nicholas glumly, "for *our* purpose."

"Are you sure it is true?" I wailed pathetically to the porter. "You could not be mistaken? It is exceeding important to us. We

335

need his help."

The porter relented a little.

"Look up there. If you know his rooms you will see there is no light at any window. If I could show you for myself I would, but the entire tower is locked and will be till the Spring. Why he wants to leave a merry town like London is a mystery to me but there, he does. What is there in the country, I say, but trees and fields? But then, tis different for the nobility, who can kill stags for pleasure to pass the time, and eat and drink themselves to bursting, in each other's country houses! No disrespect to your friend," he added as an afterthought. "I am sure Sir Edward is a monstrous dainty eater."

"It hardly matters, does it!" Nicholas observed, "since he is eating daintily in Warwickshire. Come Marc, there is nothing for us here."

I hesitated, unwilling to abandon all my so tangible imaginings. Like spirits vanishing before my eyes, the candle-light and the firelight and the eager welcome faded almost visibly, I could almost clutch them as they sped. And we were there in a cold courtyard, the rain falling hard now, and our hopes all gone.

"Nicky," I said. "Let's run away."

He shrugged impatiently. "In December? Where would we go?"

Taurus, I discovered, has its feet on the ground.

We trailed despondently back to the Cross Keys, much wetted by the rain, chilled in heart and body.

"Fortune is too cruel!" I burst out. "To permit us to become true lovers and then to part us!"

Nicholas said nothing.

"O Nicky!" I said, holding tightly to his arm. "Promise me that even though we may be separated, you will always think of me and be faithful to me and never love another for all your life!"

"I cannot promise that," said Nicholas soberly.

"Why?" I screeched. "I am prepared to promise all those things."

"That's because you find it easier to deceive yourself, and others."

"Nicky, how can you be so cruel? We may be parted for years!"

"Exactly," he remarked. "And so how can I promise all those things?"

"Then will you send me away with such meagre comfort?" I demanded.

"I simply do not want to say the extravagant things you wish me to."

"I thought we were true lovers!"

"'Tis time alone will prove that."

I lost patience with him, with his dull reasonableness.

"Perhaps you will be glad to lose me?" I shouted, standing still in the street.

"How you are at the moment," he agreed, goaded.

"We have Master Hodgkin to thank then," I said icily, "for giving us what we both want. You can be free of me to pursue whoever you like. And I can live amongst important people who will value my worth."

"Your worse?" Nicholas suddenly sniggered, noticing my pronunciation. "I doubt you could become any worse than you are now!"

Another time I would have laughed with him. I knew we were both bitterly disappointed with the outcome of the evening, and our bickering was due to that. Instead I sulked, and we continued on our way, mostly silent. Although we spoke again, it was a grudging neutral kind of communication; and because Thomas Hodgkin had chosen to wait for me at the inn, there was no time to patch up our differences. We parted like that, diffident, unhappy.

II

"Let's see what tempests can annoy me now..."

THOMAS HODGKIN lived in a tall half-timbered house in Bishops Gate, a neighbourhood much favoured by the rising wealthy. There were divers fair inns nearby, and also Crosby Place, an old majestic mansion where the last of the Plantagenet kings had his home. (Kit said that Plantagenet had been true king and a good man in his time. He said the Tudors stole the crown like a band of thieves who break a window for a jewel. He said they won the throne with foreign rabble, and Walter Raleigh had more claim to wear the crown than Queen Elizabeth.) The street itself was as dirty as any though, and even here the piles of rubbish stood at the street corners, where dogs sniffed at it and the gusty wind carried its stench in all directions. But a newly built conduit brought fresh water, and it was surely one of the better parts of the town, and the Hodgkin house was new.

It had a most splendid staircase with carved balustrades, atop of which ran a gallery with many windows of glass. The large bedrooms were panelled with oak and had wall hangings with bright patterns. Thomas slept in a bed almost as fine as Sir Edward Knollys'. I mention this only in amazement, to think that merchants may live like lords; it had no conncection with me – my bedroom was a small one at the back, with a trundle bed.

Downstairs there was a dining parlour, all panelled, with fine pewter displayed on a sideboard; and a living parlour with a fireplace like the gatehouse of a mansion, with columns and carved figures of females carrying bunches of grapes. We ate breakfast in the stone-flagged kitchen, where the housekeeper, manservant and maidservant worked. There was much talk about a tapestry from Antwerp, which had not arrived. It was the main subject over breakfast day in, day out – it was delayed at Dover, it was delayed at Dartford, it was lost, it was misdirected, it was at Lincoln – each day when I came down I waited eagerly for the next instalment of its whereabouts. I blessed that tapestry, for Cuthbert had been sent in search of it, so he was not here.

"Make your Christmas preparations as usual," Master Hodgkin told the servants. "We'll have the pastries and the marchpane and all the trimmings, yes and holly boughs and bay leaves too, in spite of Cuthbert's new found austerity."

I hoped the tapestry was by now at York. But I should not laugh. One had to be most rich to own a tapestry from Antwerp, even a lost one, and I could not but he impressed with his wealth, and he had earned it all himself. He had begun his life with next to nothing. He had risen through his own efforts.

338

Even our chamber pots were pewter! My experiences of life had certainly changed me, because previously I had only sneered at merchants. Now I could not help but admire. He was very much wealthier than I had been, except in terms of land, because his wealth was actual. The elegant house and fine furniture were all new, and it was Venetian glass with every meal and extreme good food. Though we did not daily dine off peacocks of the Ind, I had not eaten so well since I dined with Sir Edward.

Although I was his page – a situation which could sometimes be ambiguous – my position was most respectable, which thoroughly surprised me. I went sullenly, expecting to be degraded for my previous unmannerliness, and maybe I would have been had I been arrogant; but because I was doing this for Nicholas I was determined to behave impeccably, and give Master Hodgkin no cause for complaint.

I had a room to myself, with wainscotted walls painted red, blue and gold, and through the latticed window a view over the garden at the back of the house. He gave me a suit of new clothes – cream-coloured stockings, cream shoes in soft leather, a buff-coloured brocaded doublet, small flowers embroidered all over it, tawny trunk hose slit to show yellow, and a cream shirt, and a stiff white ruff and wrist rufflets.

When I first arrived, I had to sign a paper. This paper said that I, Marc-Alphonse du Plessis Mornay, did of my own free will agree to become the page of Thomas Hodgkin for as long as he desired it, and did promise to devote myself to his service and do all duties as required. I signed it.

"I suppose I am to call you sir?" I sneered.

"Indeed you are, and may I say it will not ill become you to show natural respect for your elders."

Of course, I had been a page before, in France. There I had been quietly debauched, flattered and teased, and at night my services had been somewhat divers. In my cynicism I half expected similar treatment here. But Thomas Hodgkin did not take advantage of me. If he was indeed a sodomite, he was the kind that wanted to but refrained. My duties were domestic. I had to wait on him in the morning, in the evening, in his room, passing him clothes, and water to wash in, and tidying up; and when he ate and drank to pass him food and pour him wine. I waited on him at table. I did all this with good grace. I felt it was

339

a penance for having taken Nicholas for granted, and for all my other little sins which I was not quite easy about. I do not mean I was happy; I was not. I was miserable and I missed Nicholas.

Of course he wished to parade me, and many evenings we dined out, I waiting behind his chair, when at his beck and call I would step forward and pour his wine or hold his cloak. Similarly when we entertained at home, I was polite and deferential and a fine example of what everyone desired, a French page with good manners. He had no rowdy friends or thigh-pinching cronies. If they had faults they were pomposity and tediousness and dull conversation. They envied him my services. We had the Lord Mayor to dine one evening, and I felt not a little proud of Thomas, to be so important.

The merchants did not gossip nor joke much – what do you expect of grocers? And Thomas was a grocer and had risen by spices. He used to have a shop in Swan Alley and now had warehouses in Bucklersbury. Their talk was all of aldermen and elections and standards of workmanship and how to prevent foreigners buying and selling in London and the cost of endowing almshouses. But then one evening it became more interesting when they spoke of maritime ventures – and suddenly I stared, because for a moment it reminded me of being with Kit.

"...The East Indies, the Americas, the coast of Africa, and Tartary, Muscovy, Persia, India: all of these are now within our grasp."

"El Dorado, if it exists..."

"El Dorado? I was never sure whether that was a place or a man."

"The story as I heard it was this. There was a Spanish expedition to Guiana. One of the sailors became separated from his fellows and he was captured by the natives. They blindfolded him and made him walk for miles through perilous country. He lost all sense of direction. Eventually, when he could see, he was in a city. Everything was made of gold. It near blinded him – the sun being exceptional bright in those far off parts. There came forward a king – El Dorado, the Golden One. His body was naked and golden. He seemed a man of gold."

"How could that be? Tis impossible."

"No, tis done by anointing the body with oil and then rolling over and over in gold dust. The effect must be spectacular!" (I agreed, wide-eyed. Naked and golden! I wished I had seen him!)

"There were, moreover, in that same place rivers that ran with liquid pearl and mountains of emeralds. So the man said."

"Who can trust what a Spaniard says?" one dismissed the tale.

"Indeed. And if he returned to tell his story why did he not then take an expedition and capture the place? And then kill the so-called Golden One. That is the Spaniards' way," they chuckled cynically.

"He could not remember the way. And so the fabled city lies, somewhere beyond the sunset, untouched, unspoiled, and waiting."

'Tis a fine idea; one might make a philosophy from it! The El Dorado of the mind. The goal which one strives for and never attains."

"Does that make money?" one sneered. "An El Dorado of the mind? Give me some sturdy ships and money for an expedition and I'll show you what you can do with the mind!"

I asked Thomas about it afterwards, when I made him ready for bed, his gold chains stored in his coffer, his sheets turned back beneath his warm embroidered coverlet.

"An El Dorado of the mind? No, I have no time for that."

"But do you not think the mind must be free to go where it would? That the freedom to think whatever we like is the most important freedom of all?"

"No I do not, and nor should you, young man. It is not true. Thinking, as you put it, whatever you like leads to doing whatever you like, and doing whatever you like will land you in the Clink."

I twitched. Had he heard about my trip to Newgate?

"We must have free thought," I said doggedly.

"It is not necessary," said Thomas. "Knowledge of the word of God is all that is necessary for a good life. Directions for thought are all in there. Reading Holy Writ is a worthier thing to do than wandering in the dangerous regions of free thinking. That leads to atheism, and that leads to treason, punishment and death."

"You must not let your religion make you blind to other ways of thinking," I insisted. "Montaigne says that he knows what he thinks, but he knows other men are different and he would not

341

impose his way of life upon them. We should all keep a small back room of our true selves, a private place where our true selves lie..."

"A small back room?" laughed Thomas. "It has a huswifely ring to it, with hams hanging."

Even in his night robe Thomas was majestic. He put his thumbs where a huge fur collar would be if he had clothes on, found no fur collar, and gripped instead the nightgown.

"I incline to a famous speech by Sir Nicholas Bacon," he told me, "Lord Keeper of the Great Seal, and Privy Council member. He said that nothing should be advised or done that might in any way breed or nourish any kind of idolatry or superstition, and so heed must be taken, lest by licentious or loose handling any occasion were given whereby contempt or irreverent behaviour towards God and godly things might creep in. You would do well to think on that, Marc. You have a nature that inclines itself towards what is wayward and untoward."

"I know that," I admitted.

"When Cuthbert returns," said Thomas thoughtfully, "he shall instruct you more. He is a devout boy. It would be good for both of you. It cannot be easy for you, coming from France, of Papist origin, trying to fit in. Religious discussion with Cuthbert will make the way clearer."

"I think I can do without Cuthbert," I maintained, alarmed. "I am a loyal subject of Her Majesty and have not found that such religion as I possess has been too much of a hindrance to thinking freely."

"Nonetheless..." he told me severely, "Cuthbert shall instruct you. Daily recourse to Cuthbert's preaching will be a very suitable antidote to an excess of El Dorado of the mind."

He liked me to be interested in his work, and he obliged me to accompany him to his warehouse down by the wharves.

Huge vessels floated at anchor here, taller than houses, ships that had travelled to the places on Ortelius' map. Thomas had a copy of that map in his study – the very same map as Kit possessed! The spices that made Thomas rich came from the places Tamburlaine had conquered – there was relation. It was eye-opening to me.

The choppy grey Thames water crackled against the quay's

edge, the wind rattled the doorways of the store sheds, and rain pinpointed the puddles on the cobblestones. We climbed over hard wet tangles of rope and heard the mighty creaking of the timbers and the mew of sea birds. This wide stretch of water so neatly bordered by the two opposing shores was that same water that led to the wild oceans of the world; these same painted prows had maybe rested in blue bays by trees of palm, while natives wearing necklaces of shells brought cinnamon and cloves.

We entered the warehouse which was dark and dry out of the rain. On all sides were stacked spices, in sacks and baskets and barrels. A heady scent hung in the air. Upon a small raised dais in one corner sat a clerk at work upon a ledger, candles burning on his table giving light in the murky gloom. Master Hodgkin and he bent over the accounts.

"And how," I heard him ask, "have my night watchmen fared? I trust there have been no more missing sacks."

"So far this month all is accounted for."

"I would give much to know who our thief is – if he has a network of accomplices – a hiding place. I would very much like to see the villain brought to justice."

"So far he has proved elusive..."

Thomas grunted in dissatisfaction. I ran my hands through an open sack of nutmegs.

"That is the fruit of a tree that grows in the Tropics," said Thomas, pleased. "And the clove is an unopened flower bud, dried. Cinnamon is tree bark. A very precious commodity, spices. We've had a spate of stealing – someone must be doing well out of it – I daresay they have their dens hidden about the more disreputable parts of London...They'll have no trouble finding a market – spices will always be in demand as long as we have to preserve our food by pickling and salting. Yet even I," he added, with a softening of his sententious manner, "allow myself the pleasure of considering their romance. Can you not feel it, Marc, that spices do provoke emotion – a sensuous feeling, to do with smell and touch...?"

"Like lechery," I agreed, my hands in a sack of ground cinnamon, my thoughts with the gaudy beggar who had made love to me on a carpet of spices.

"Lechery? No!" snapped Thomas brusquely. "Nothing like

that. No! I was speaking of commerce."

Of course he was. I smiled, and curiously I warmed to him, for I knew it was like lechery, for all he did deny and frown. Rapidly he told me how much each cost by the pound.

"They praise Sir Francis Drake as a hero," said he, "and rightly so, of course. But I can never hear his name mentioned without remembering one act of his which was unforgiveable. You will have heard that he sailed around the globe to the great glory of our nation. Upon that historic voyage he concluded a treaty with the Sultan of the Spice Islands, giving England the trading rights – unlimited possession of spices. He took six tons of cloves aboard. But then his ship foundered on a reef. In order to free the vessel he had to drop three tons of cloves over the side to lighten the load. I shudder every time I think of it, and for all he burned the ships in Cadiz harbour I can never forgive him the abandoned spices!"

I laughed at myself when he obliged me to study some recipes to see why spices were desired. Milk and almonds, boiling rice and flour, adding wine, cloves, cinnamon, raisins, saffron and salt – why, I would be making gingerbread next!

Not far from the warehouse on our return I noticed in the street my gaudy beggar, lurking by the gutter, covered in sores. He winked at me and I pinkened. I clutched at Master Hodgkin's arm.

"That pitiful fellow...O! May we give him a penny?"

"What? O, if we must," and my generous master dropped a shilling in the proffered bowl. The beggar blessed him noisily.

I accompanied Master Hodgkin to the Royal Exchange on Cornhill, where the London merchants met. It had a central courtyard and arcades. Upstairs was a gallery of shops – milliners, booksellers, goldsmiths and armourers. In the milliners you could buy mousetraps and birdcages, and from the same metal, ruff supports which went under the fine starched lawn. I had never been obliged to take much interest in shops before, but I did now see them as the means of a livelihood, and admired the ingenuity and invention involved, stopping to watch all those at work within.

I saw something too of his view of life. He believed in the

importance of education. It was too easy to sit back and say that such and such was God's will and do nothing about improving your lot. The olden days could be forgiven for this fatalistic attitude, but in this modern age there was no excuse for not making the most of all opportunities offered. That was why merchants liked to endow colleges and schools, using wealth to improve everybody's wider knowledge.

Incredibly, this was the same view as Kit's and as Sir Edward's. Not spoken the same of course, but in essence. It made me see that life is not compartments, but a river flowing everywhere, into all, making one whole of human thought.

We did speak together often. Master Hodgkin talked to me about his long dead wife, and all his past, and how he made his wealth, and of his problems, even of his health, his purgings and his physick.

"You should marry again," I advised him sagely.

He sat upon his high-backed settle by the fireside, and I sat on a cushioned stool.

"I had thought about it," he admitted.

"You are a good looking man," I told him frankly. "But a little too serious, and your clothes are too sober."

"I must dress so. Clothes are for warmth, not for ostentation."

"Even so, they can be elegant. Wear black if you must, but edge it with gold. I'll help you choose; I know about clothes."

That made him laugh outright.

"When I saw you at the Cross Keys you were wearing cherry red and a headful of daisies, white stockings and cork-heeled slippers!"

I laughed too. "Tell me, did you come to see the play or, as Cuthbert, to convert us from our wicked ways?"

"I came to see you. But I did enjoy the play. I was surprised at how agreeable it was."

"Not seditious at all?"

"I found it inoffensive. Though I do not approve of boys in female attire and painted faces."

"Have you ever been to a play at the playhouses?"

"I have not."

"You should. We might go together! O! Please! And it would be so good for you!"

I was delighted that he allowed me to persuade him. We went to see *Tamburlaine*, and to my joy it was a performance of *Part Two*. How quickly brilliant Ned Alleyn had learnt his part, and how splendid were the spoken words! We sat in the wealthy seats – and I must say it was a vast improvement upon being a groundling, particularly as it rained a little and was exceeding chilly. How I pitied those below that shivered in the cold, for it was not so warm even here on the cushioned seats. I watched enrapt, hands clasped, my mouth dropping open at the spilled blood, little cheers and boos coming quietly and circumspectly from my lips, sighs when it was beautiful, and squeals at the cannon shot, when they shoot the proud Governor of Babylon as he dangles from the turret! And when I recognised a line that I had seen still wet upon the page, a terrible tug at my heart made me recognise that my love was still as deep, and always would be.

"You loved it!" Thomas said, like a tolerant uncle, sitting back and drawing his fur about him.

"I did, yes. And I know the author," I added modestly.

"Well, tis not my style. Skilful, I grant you, but bloodthirsty and boisterous. You know, I think I prefer *your* company's. I like the kind of plays they act indoors, after supper. More courtly..."

"But *Tamburlaine* will be famous down the ages!"

"And so?" said Master Hodgkin. "We shall not be there to see it!"

He liked me to play some lute music before he went to bed, to soothe him, and I did. That was no hardship. I sang mostly of love. "Si Fortune" he liked, and "If Love now reigned", two melancholy songs. It fascinated me how all of us seem to have that strain, however seemingly well proportioned our humours appear, however firm our feet are on the ground, the easiness with which we slip into sad and thoughtful ways when hearing music.

In my spare time he let me use his library, mostly books of travel, and I would take a volume into my room and sit there dreaming. From my window I could see the garden. At this time of year there were no flowers to see, and all seemed dead down there beneath the grey and lowering skies, the afternoon

346

darkness. You could see the cleverly worked out shape of the intricate patterns in which it was laid, garden plots arranged in curves and triangles about a central walk, with little paths leading off and round.

"It was created on the same lines as a Persian carpet," Thomas said. "We owe the happy notion to the Crusaders. They also brought back leprosy!"

Looking down on that December garden, I sat and thought about my love for Nicholas. I realised that at last I had learnt true love and knew its beauty. O! But was it all too late? We had parted so unpleasantly. Was Nicholas unhappy too? Or had he already eased his need with Amyas, or with anybody else? O! He had all London to choose from! At least (I controlled my wild fancying) all of London who were sodomites – and that was plenty. Did he still care about me? Would he still be waiting on my return? O! When would that be? I could not ask him to wait months, years! Just as he said, he could not promise eternal fidelity, and I could not expect it. I did miss him horribly and longed for him, but I dared not sneak off and meet him, and I was too proud to ask favours, as that he might visit. Perversely, I blamed him somewhat for not trying secretly to see *me*! Many a night I peered down at the garden hoping he might have leapt over the wall (love giving him wings) as lovers do in stories, and we could have conversed over the sill of my window and called each other's names by moonlight and promised our undying love – or at least agreed that we did still love each other.

Comfortable upon my tapestried cushion, my book idly open in my hand, I would gaze down at the bare branches of a little tree, its twigs all beautified with pendant rain drops, and I would sigh. It was comfortable indeed here at the Hodgkin home, within this little room, but how I missed my apple garret and Nicholas. I wondered how long Master Hodgkin intended to keep me. I had signed a paper to say I would stay there for as long as he wanted – but what if it were years! O, but then, I thought, I am sixteen already – one cannot have a page of twenty-five – one has to let them go. But was I working against my interests, being so affable and obliging? Was he growing fond of me, dependent?

I pitied him a little. All he had was Cuthbert.

347

"See what strange arts necessity finds out!"

CUTHBERT had finally located that missing tapestry in Lincoln, and now he and it arrived to take up residence. The tapestry was an embellishment – a forest scene with huntsmen, deer, intricate patterns of foliage, and many, many rabbits – but Cuthbert was not. He was if anything even more severely dressed, and yet more pallid and ill-favoured than when I saw him last. And he did screech like a mandrake when he heard his father had been to see a play.

"In the den of the ungodly!" he wailed. "Where whores do make their assignations, where men hustle to sit next to women and to touch them privily, where filthy words of love are whispered in dark corners . . ."

"I suppose the oranges we bought were lascivious also, being round and plump and two together," I said amused.

"I thought this player boy was brought here as your page," snapped Cuthbert, "and if so why does he interrupt, and why is he allowed to sit with us at table?"

"'Tis true he is my page," said Thomas, "but I do allow him more liberty than is usual. In your short absence, Cuthbert, I have found his company congenial, and have somewhat relished the levity of his conversation."

"'Tis as well I am returned," said Cuthbert with pursed lips. "This is a boy who needs our guidance, and I am glad to have the opportunity to work on him. Remember, father, he has worn female garb before the populace. Petticoats, and kirtles . . ."

As I noticed Cuthbert's quickened breathing I added delightedly: "White silk stockings. and a soft embroidered shift, which rustled . . ."

"Marc has turned his back upon those days," said Thomas severely. "At least for the moment. Since he has been here his behaviour has been almost impeccable. Many of my acquaintance have congratulated me. He has also, Cuthbert, shown more willingness to please me than others have this many a year."

And Cuthbert scowled and made a great business of shuffling his spoon and trencher.

Almost at once he set about trying to convert me. Our conversations at the table became extreme sober. When he told me what he believed I wondered what would be left in the rituals of church after he had finished with them. He and his sect would do away with priests, of course, and bishops, and with surplices and vestments, and with the wedding ring and the sign of the cross and with kneeling down to take the sacrament. Ministers and elders would tell us what to do. What to do? It was far more a religion of what not to do. There would be no playhouses if he had his way, no maypoles and no Yuletide festivities, nothing abandoned and joyous, and none of the old country things that folk had always done without being entirely sure why. I suspected that included celebrating Midsummer; for certain, faeries and elves had no place in the serious virtuous world that Cuthbert envisaged.

One afternoon some cronies of his, with the same ideas, came round to the house to eat, and I waited at table, listening to their discourse.

"The better to present our case to the populace we must be seen and heard more than we are now."

"Another sermon in Paul's Square?"

"That is too mild. They are as sheep, the populace. Anyone may manipulate them. Whoever speaks last, he it is they follow. A sermon therefore has but slight effect."

"So what do you suggest?"

"I would like to see more action on the streets. Civil unrest...I thought perhaps beginning with a disturbance on London Bridge, with banners, so that none might pass. And some might sit down in the street...The city north of the bridge, the roads of Southwark, all would be impassable, for as long as we chose to keep them so."

"Or till the Watch moved in."

"The Watch! Who pays any heed to them?"

"*We* should. For they represent the law, and the law is all important. And whatever we do must be within the law. There must be no unruly action."

They all agreed, vociferously so. The one who had suggested action allowed himself to be persuaded. I felt some regret. I poured him extra wine in sympathy. Disturbances on London Bridge had seemed to me an excellent notion.

It is always thus with Puritans, I thought in scorn. Watery and drab, they will always keep within the law. Themselves sheep-like, they pose no threat to anyone. I found their conversation tedious, and when I had done all that was needed I came away.

I found Thomas standing by the door that opened into the garden. Outside, there was mist. We stood there in the doorway. The voices of Cuthbert and his friends sounded beyond the inner door, low and earnest as they planned their world.

"Tell me," Thomas said, looking out at the silent shrouded garden, "does Cuthbert frighten you at all?"

"Diable, no!" I laughed. "He is ridiculous."

"Yes; I had supposed you would think that."

"When I first saw him I admit I thought him sinister. But that was because of the troubles in France – I thought he was like the Huguenots. There has been so much war with us, so much blood spilt, for so long...Tis not like that in England. Cuthbert is not the same...all this preoccupation with Sin..."

"Had you realised that his sect have become vociferous in Parliament?"

"No I had not. I thought they were mere stupid people who spoilt our plays. You mean there are more of them? That people take them seriously?"

"They should do. There is a curious cunning about Cuthbert's philosophy which has somewhat about it of the stamp of success." Thomas frowned. "Have you seen those pamphlets in Paul's churchyard, purporting to be the work of Nathaniel Gods-Will?"

"Yes! Do you mean that he is Cuthbert?" I cried delightedly.

"Worse, in fact – he is nobody at all. O, Cuthbert has somewhat to do with it, as do several of those within...I was brought up to revere our nation's heroes, Marc, and God knows we are fortunate in possessing an abundance. Bold men, some of whose ideas I may not agree with, yet could admire for their courage. A hero sets himself up, and, being human, he can be brought down. There is an honesty there. Now one might even admire Nathaniel Gods-Will, for his leaflets are read and he seems a dedicated man, if misguided. But Cuthbert's brethren want no heroes. Nathaniel Gods-Will can never be apprehended or accused – he exists wherever a Puritan pins a broadsheet – anywhere and everywhere, growing like a weed in the cracks of the paving stones, infinitely renewable. And weeds thrive. I speak," he added mournfully, "as one with a garden."

"O," I said disparagingly. "I cannot believe that Cuthbert is dangerous, even so. He is too droll."

"Marc, do you fear the Queen? I mean, respect, and accept her divine authority to rule?"

"O yes; assuredly."

"And so do I. I never question it. But Cuthbert does. They are not afraid. I dread to think what would happen if he ever found himself in the presence. I listen to Cuthbert and his friends. They think their beliefs entitle them to say anything."

"Well, it is so, you know, sir," I said with my new tolerance. "They have the right to believe what they like. I must allow them that."

"Marc, what do you think is the most frightening thing in this temporal world?"

"O! Prison – the rack – the chains – pain..."

"Certain, yes," said Thomas abstractedly. "But there are more subtle terrors. You know, the city fathers fear your plays – the threat of seditious ideas, a gathering of crowds, the kind of bold bombast your author friend lets his hero spout, the pursuit of lechery... These are not the real dangers, Marc. They are mere butterflies compared with... Look outside – what do you see?"

"A very grey garden. Grey sky and no flowers." I looked at him perplexed. "What is it that you fear, then, more than chains?"

Thomas replied: "If ever power was to be given to those whose only philosophy is Thou shalt not, thou shalt not, without having formulated a philosophy to replace it." He laughed tersely. "Let us hope that Cuthbert continues to seem ridiculous. And come back within. These vapours breed disease."

Thomas Hodgkin had obviously disquieted himself with his gloomy fancies. It was as if he had convinced himself that for the moment, at any rate, one had the power to choose the delights that were available here and now. I was delighted when next day he left off his habitual black and wore dark green, and when he asked my opinion as to whether a box of ginger would please a lady as a gift I was happy to assure him that it would. Within the week he had invited the lady to dine and I was happy to wait on them.

I could barely control my glee. When Thomas let me know he had a lady in mind to court and marry, I imagined a starchy widow of mature years whom he would prize for her house-keeping and marchpane making. But Tabitha Featherstone could have been no more than twenty-one, a lovely fresh-faced girl with a skin like peaches, and large grey eyes. She came with her father, a merchant like Thomas, and as far as I could tell, she really did find Thomas attractive – and why not, for he was so. Her clothes were indeed sober, and her mien at first demure, but she was one I could favour myself, had I been inclined to women.

I chortled to myself as I passed the trenchers. Ho, Thomas, I thought, admiringly, you are no fool! I foresaw a row of pretty children, and Thomas mellowing in her tender love, and best of all, Cuthbert much offended.

That Cuthbert was already monstrous out of joint was clear to all. They spoke of it in the kitchen, sniggering as they made the Christmas pastries. And as I bore the wine into the dining parlour I could hear what passed between the Hodgkins as they glowered across the snowy tablecloth.

"It is our wealth she seeks!" cried Cuthbert. "She has learnt from her father that the spice trade is a lucrative proposition. 'Fore God, and I would even say that he had said as much to her, and hinted that she should come try her luck, as at a country fair!"

"You credit me with more diversity than I possess," smiled Thomas. "But in your supposition you are at fault – her father is as rich as I – they have no need to line their purses so."

Cuthbert scowled. "Very well. So she is not in need of money. But let her father provide for her – why should you? We have enough commitments of our own and every penny precious."

"I do not grudge a penny spent on her. Indeed if it would please her I shall spend much more. I begin to think that I am sudden grown aware of pleasant things that one may buy with money." He caught my eye and twinkled. "The playhouses, for

instance...I think my Tabitha might be glad to see a play...
perhaps not *Tamburlaine* – but there are theatres nearer home,
and other plays..."

Cuthbert squealed in mortification. "Are you entering your
dotage, father? A man such as yourself, known in the city for his
business sense, and now you talk of squandering your money
upon plays and women! All the world will poke fun at us. And
what will my friends say?"

"Maybe they will compose a special pamphlet?"

"Ah, father, think again!" Cuthbert leaned forward earnestly,
his face an unbecoming yellow in the candlelight. "You are not
young. You have heard what they say about the union of May
and December – they laugh at it, the pitiful old man, the maiden
who in time, unsatisfied, takes lovers – serving men, minstrels,
passers-by..."

"Zounds, you are indelicate!" Thomas interrupted, beginning
to be angry and then pausing and reflecting. "Cuthbert?" he said
quizzically with a raising of the brows. "What can have been
your reading matter lately?"

I was amused but Cuthbert was not. He took a breath.

"My friends and I," said Cuthbert, "value chastity. We
understand that the flesh is weak and subject to temptation. But
forewarned is forearmed. I *pride* myself on my virginity. No
woman, with her fleshly lusts, shall subdue my chastity and
make me vulnerable. And father! I would wish the same for
you." He wrung his hands. "This woman is but young. She is
more my age than yours. She is young enough to be your
daughter. *What will people say*?"

"That I am fortunate?" suggested Thomas wrily.

"They will say it is unseemly!" Cuthbert hissed. "At your age
your thoughts should be on spiritual matters. You should be
settling your account with God, looking back on your past life,
contemplating your sins and seeking forgiveness. Indeed, some
pious gentlemen of your years do sit and gaze at a skull which
they acquire for that especial purpose, the better to fix their eyes
on man's mortality. And I," he said, with folded arms, "would
be best pleased if you did that, and so would all my friends."

"Then let them all find skulls and stare them in the hollow
eye, and leave me to gaze in the eyes of the living." I recognised
in Thomas that content which comes of love's security, that

353

does not rise to anger because it sees the world a rosy place. "And I am not December, Cuthbert," he added drily. "More late September, when the berries are luxuriant."

The presence of Tabitha as a visitor to our house affected not only Cuthbert but myself also. She often came to dine and I would wait at table. I had ample opportunity to observe her – her large grey eyes, her full wide lips and milkmaid complexion. Her hair was chestnut and her dress was russet and tawny, her ruff of finest lawn fresh-starched, her perfume rosewater.

"O! Does Marc play the lute?" she cried. "I love lute music. Would he play for us? Would you, Marc, for me?"

Assuredly I would. I was happy to delight her. She knew the names of songs, she knew which she preferred and longed to know of others, and so many an evening we spent happy times with music. And when she said that she had once played on the virginals and hoped to learn its skills, lo and behold a virginals appeared, which Thomas bought all suddenly for his beloved (and which Cuthbert saw as the realisation of his direst fears and told us so in quivering tones as one would tell of Hell fire and the Second Coming). So then we played and sang together, and to add to her perfections that delightful maiden possessed a voice as sweet as any lark.

So, partly I was happy, partly I was sad. I saw that she and Thomas were in love. Upon the high-backed settle in the parlour they would sit beside the fire, the curtains drawn against the rain and wind, and I upon the little cushioned stool, and Cuthbert unaccountably from home.

I sang sad songs of love most feelingly, and while I envied their good fortune I could not but compare their lot with mine. I longed for Nicholas and I remembered Kit, and neither brought me joy. I had lost Kit for ever – to posterity, to Walsingham, to some other light o' love, or to his work, which love came first with him. Yet O how sweet our time had been together – our hot embraces, our shared words, and his dark beauty which I never would forget. Remembering made me sad, and so I thought of Nicholas. But what help was that to me? – He was not here. And if he were, did he still love me? Why should he so, after all the trials I had put him through? O! If I could but once again lie close to him and reassure him all was well, that I would be his love for ever...

Meanwhile, Cuthbert never faltered in his determination to convert me. But he did it in a marvellous strange way, leaving me alone by day to minister to his father, and yet taking to entering my room at night!

The first time I was astonished. The door creaked and I awoke from sleep to sense a figure moving about in a muffled kind of way as if he wished not to be heard. And as the candle flickered into life, I saw then who my visitor might be. I sat up in my bed, warm and naked, ruffling my hair.

"Cuthbert! What do you here?"

All unconcerned he sat down on my bed as if this were most usual.

"I have some tracts to read you. In sleep one is most innocent and closer to the angels. Be still and listen."

Some dead leaves flew in through my little open window and fluttered round the candle flame while Cuthbert read me of damnation. And then he made me pray with him, I yet in bed, and then he blew out the flame and left, leaving me surprised.

But this set the pattern for every night. At first he only read me tracts and we prayed, the papers shifting on my bed cover. But then one night he told me to get out of bed and kneel while he read, upon the hard floor for better penance.

"I have no nightshirt on," I mumbled modestly.

"It matters not. Sinners are usually portrayed naked. Do as I say."

I emerged hesitantly from my white scented sheets, and kneeled upon the floorboards. Cuthbert watched me critically. He made me adopt a praying posture, and I had to shut my eyes too; and while I knelt there thus, he read the nightly tract about sin and repentance, and I did wriggle and twitch, my knees all crimson and sore. And then I was allowed back into bed, and now this was the pattern for the next few times.

Next, to make my penitence more personal he did write some special tracts for me to read out loud as I knelt there on the floor. I read whatever he brought. It was simpler, and it meant he would leave the sooner. I asked the Lord's forgiveness for my wicked life, my play acting, my bad companions, my way-wardness of spirit, and I promised to be wholesome and righteous henceforth. That I was shivering with cold seemed to give him great satisfaction. Perchance he supposed it was my fear of divine wrath.

Then one night, Cuthbert said: "You are voluptuous, Marc."

"I am not!" I said, looking at my chest.

"Your – your behind," he whispered awfully, as if he was swearing in church.

I glanced around at the object in question. I had often wondered whether Cuthbert had noticed. Seemingly he had. I patted it comfortably.

"Tis just a little plump," I shrugged.

"Tis a temptation!" he accused.

"Well, usually I keep it covered up."

"It is like Eve. It is like the apple."

I sniggered into my hands. He ordered me back into bed. I could not help twinkling and smirking. He was so serious.

The next night he had written me a special tract about temptation and voluptuousness. I could hardly read it for laughing. I had to apologise for being a temptation! And Cuthbert could not take his eyes off me. He was pink and white and flustered. I began to giggle as I fumbled through my speech.

"You are shameless!" he gasped. "You do not understand... it is for the good of your soul."

I snorted and stopped reading.

"Stay there," he ordered seething. "Wait till I come back."

He was gone just a short while. He returned with a little bendy stick.

"I must chastise you," he said, and closed the door.

My face fell.

"Must you?" I grimaced.

"Yes, and you must permit me, or I shall tell my father you were disobedient."

I swallowed. "How many?"

"Six."

"O, very well. But not too hard or people will hear."

"Bend forward." His voice quivered with excitement. And since I recognised that excitement it was with much apprehension that I obeyed him, dropping forward so my elbows leaned on the hard floorboards.

Cuthbert contemplated me, and I felt sure that an excess of righteous zeal in no wise blinded him to the pleasure of the sight in prospect.

"This is for your own good," he told me. "To make sure

you understand that, you must say so. Say it!"

"This is for my own good," I groaned.

Down came the thin stick. I twitched. Again and again; I made a little gasp. Three more times. I caught my breath in through my teeth.

"Thank me," he panted.

The curious tone of his voice made me sneak a glance at him. His habitually pallid face was flushed and he was breathing hard. I swear the hand that held the stick was trembling.

"Thank you, Cuthbert."

"Get up now and – think of your sins –" He sounded overcome. To look at him you would think it was he who had been the victim. Even as I twisted painfully around and stood, I saw his hand stray to his crotch and he gulped. Suddenly without explanation he gave an odd little gasp and pushed out of the room. I believed I understood clearly enough.

Gingerly touching my stinging arse I thought carefully about what had occurred. I blew out the candle and climbed back into bed where I lay most uncomfortably on my stomach. Everything was different now. I had tolerated the tracts and the praying, but (by the twenty-four balls of the apostles!) I would not put up with any more of what I had received this night. I would speak to his father, but cautiously. O! How little I relished the prospect.

It was late afternoon next day when Thomas and I were alone in his study. I stood at the window, looking out on to the garden. Beyond the diamond-leaded panes thin flakes of sleety snow were falling, like grey rain from a grey sky. Upon the green leaves of a holly bush it turned to water, clear droplets hanging from the twigs amongst the glistening leaves. I turned back to the room.

Thomas sat beside the fire, a book upon his lap – a travel book, his favourite kind – and indeed I would have much preferred to talk with him about the wonders beyond the seas. The room was dark and warm, the firelight picking out the painted roses carved amongst the wainscotting, and the smooth surface of the great globe that, tilted to an angle, showed seas and dolphins and Neptune blowing monstrous waves.

"You may read also," Thomas observed good humouredly.

"Idly wasting time does good to no one."

"When is it that I shall go home?" I blurted out.

Thomas put his book upon the table and closed it carefully.

"I fondly assumed that your time here was not proving too unpleasant?"

"It is most pleasant," I assured him. "But I ask again: when do I leave?"

"When I am ready. Remember, you have signed a paper..."

"I remember. Now that we know each other better and I have given you good service, do you yet stand by your original threat, about Nicholas? Or are we almost friends, and may forget such barbarism?"

There must have been something about my manner. I daresay I looked a little shifty.

"Why do you ask?" said Thomas frowning.

"Only that...if we are to accuse Nicholas it might be that we will have to accuse Cuthbert too. I would not want to think that it was different for him. For he is worse than Nicholas and does not even know he lusts."

"Cuthbert? What do you mean? What has this to do with my son?"

A burst of indignation overcame me.

"He has been coming into my room at night and he made me kneel and pray, without my clothes. I did not mind the praying – well, not too much – but now there has been more..."

"It is perfectly permissible for Cuthbert to instruct you in prayer; and if his manner of praying is not what you are used to, you must blame it on his religious fervour, which as we know is excessive."

"But there was more!"

"What more?"

"This!" I did something very undignified; I pulled down my trunk hose and gave him a good view of all my welts, alarmed for the moment in case they had worn off during the morning, for they were certainly less smarting now. Relieved I saw there were yet marks. Justifiably piqued now I added: "And this did monstrous excite him, and I have had enough. For I do know hot lust when I see it!"

"Cover yourself," said Thomas, palpably offended at my lapse of taste.

I pulled up my hose, embarrassed.

"We need not despise Cuthbert for his outburst," I began, intending to show wisdom beyond my years. "It was too much for him to see you so content. How must he have suffered, a virgin unloved, and you and Tabitha so deep in love, and songs of love sung every evening, and then he to go alone to bed all cold and full of longings..."

"Marc, you outstep what is seemly," said Thomas with a very serious mien. "'Tis not your place to speak to me of Cuthbert so. To talk as you are doing does not become you and it well reminds me of the company you used to keep."

"O Diable!" I cried. "I should have known you would take Cuthbert's part. I thought now that we understood each other better I could speak to you on any matter – but I see that I was wrong and all we are is what we seemed – a city merchant and a bawdy player."

"You have always had the stain of voluptuousness about you..." he began.

"And you would be more pleasing if you had more so!"

"God's Bread, you go too far!"

"I know I do, but I am monstrous vexed!"

Thomas stood up. O but he was impressive standing! One day, I thought admiringly, he will surely be Lord Mayor!

"I have no wish to talk further with you Marc, while you are tedious and peevish. Tonight I sup out, as you know, and I shall not require you."

"Why will you not?" I demanded aggrieved. He was going to Tabitha's and I had been looking forward to seeing where she lived.

"Because you mightily displease me," he replied severely, "and if you were to spend the time reflecting on –"

"My sins?" I screeched. "As Cuthbert said?"

He turned his back, his fur-lined robe falling in heavy folds about him.

His silence filled me with alarm.

"I have done all you want since I have been here," I reminded him anxiously. "And I have not seen Nicholas, and Nicholas has not come secretly to see me; we have been most circumspect, and it has not been easy. I do ask pardon if I have spoilt it all..."

I waited, but he had no more to say, and so I left the room.

359

O! What an evening drear and dire I spent! I sat within my room, a prey to bitterest fancies. Had I truly angered Thomas – would he punish me? Or, worse, had I put Nicholas in danger? What was Thomas after all but Cuthbert's father, and in extremity one sided with one's own. He would ask Cuthbert if I spoke the truth and Cuthbert would say no, and it would be believed I had told lies to achieve my release from the bond that I had signed. It was not so! I would not have stooped to deception to gain my ends – he should know that. But I felt guilty also, because I knew as like as not that Cuthbert would not bother me again, now that he had felt and I had seen his palpable arousal. He was cognizant enough of shame to recognise it in himself, and it could well be that he would see his nightly attempts to convert me from my wicked ways for what they were. But, I told myself hotly, I could not know this, and I had no desire to receive any more of his visitations, for whatever purpose. Indeed I was still sore when I sat down!

I tried to divert myself with reading, but when I picked up a book it was no other than a book writ by one Robert Greene, which Tabitha had lent us, assuring us it was a lively tale. When I read that it concerned those who "guided their course by the compass of Cupid, and either dash their ship against most dangerous rocks, or else attain the haven with pain and peril", I decided it might suit me well. But when Robert in his preface compared himself to "Pan blowing upon an oaten pipe a little homely music", I did laugh aloud, knowing well his thoughts concerning pastorals. And when I perused the subject matter, I could not read it, for what good to me were characters in the "misty clouds of despair", "plunged in perplexity", "oppressed with care", "cumbered with choleric cogitations" and "sipping the sour dregs of sorrow"? It was all too much like my life! And only that it was Tabitha's book and mine to borrow prevented me from flinging it across the room.

I was on my best behaviour in the morning, exceptional polite and obliging, and giving Thomas every chance to tell me of his thoughts. But he maintained the dignity I had associated with him from the first, showing no portion of that agreeable softening of nature that had been his since we had known each other better. He told me that he would be from home during the day, and that if I had nothing to do I should make myself useful in the kitchen. There was a time in my life when I would have found such a suggestion monstrous offensive, but now I did not, and I was glad to have pleasant employment.

Outside light snowflakes fell, but in the stone-flagged kitchen beside the hearthfire all was warm, and much to do. Mistress Rowe the housekeeper was good company and over the course of the day we boiled beef in ale, which process saw me sitting at the table surrounded by vinegar and treacle, thyme, sage and rosemary, and mace and cloves and many onions, shedding more tears in the chopping then even I had shed as Isabella. When we poured the ale on to the simmering brew in the pot above the fire, the scent was delicious and filled the kitchen with its odour. To be busy, it seemed, was diversion, for I was in part distracted from my "choleric cogitations" and all the unease and foreboding which I felt about my future. But not entirely. Just as the warm kitchen with its tubs of apples and parsnips, its bunches of dried herbs, its basket of logs and its bread fresh from the oven all spoke of things secure and plenteous, yet there hung beside the hearth two blackbirds dead and stiff and shifting slightly in the fire-draught, and I would see them from the corner of my eye. And thus, I thought, however self-composed the mind may seem to be, there oft times lurk dark spots which trouble and dismay.

When Thomas came home, late in the afternoon, there was an air about him which much mystified me. I lifted his snow-flecked cloak from him and saw upon his face an expression both merry and severe, and I hoped some explanation; but all he said to me was that I should take my supper in the kitchen, and surely that was not the smell of onion upon my fastidious fingers?

I asked Mistress Rowe if she knew aught; she said all that she knew was that we were to have company tonight after supper, and she had cakes to bake.

After supper Thomas came into the kitchen and told me to go up to my room.

"You will find a change of clothes there," he told me. "I have a mind to see you in the outfit, so you will oblige me by coming downstairs in such garments as have been laid out for you."

I knew by now that something was afoot, and that Thomas would tell me in his own good time. So I did as I was told and went up to my room.

As I opened the door and set the candle down my heart did skip a beat. For there upon the bed was spread my cherry red dress, the one I wore when as Perdita I play in *The Letter*. All my accoutrements were there – my high heeled shoes and stockings, garters and petticoats, the famous bum-roll and my jewelled cap. I slipped off my page's clothes and dressed, shivering as the chilly silk brushed my bare skin. By the candle's light I made myself beautiful. I could not help but think of the many times that I had clad myself thus in more happy circumstances. How beautiful had been the summer, when I first grew to know the players, whom I now thought of as my family! I found myself recalling incidents that I had half forgot – conversations in village taverns, idling in the meadow daisies, setting up the stage and decking it with flowers and green boughs, and country fairs and dusty waysides, and feasting in the twilight before sleeping in the wagons. How far away all that now seemed, elusive as a dream.

Indeed, as I emerged from my bedroom I marvelled at the power of dreams – as sleepers do on waking – for the voices I had summoned by my thoughts seemed to be in the air around me. In the gallery I paused and listened, my hand upon the great carved balustrade. It was no dream. I could hear Jack – one always could, even three or four rooms away – and the boys' high voices, and a giggle that I knew to be Amyas' when he was excited. Crimson as my dress I went downstairs and Thomas Hodgkin met me at the bottom of the staircase.

"We are having a little play tonight," he said. "Nothing extravagant. A seemly and old-fashioned kind – no blood, no spilled brains, no battles. I want you to take part."

There in the parlour was all my company assembled, to play *The Letter*, and only needing me. All the Hodgkin servants were the audience, and some of Thomas' sober friends, and Tabitha and her father, but not Cuthbert. Tabitha particularly was so smiling and dimpled and merry that I felt sure she had had somewhat to do with this.

I was too moved to speak. I looked across the room at Nicholas, my heart all full, and he at me, a look most full of love. Yet we behaved most circumspect, before this gathering. I did not run to him, but made as if I had come with the company, to perform at a merchant's house one dark December evening. But all knew otherwise – Jack was beaming even when his part would show him sad, and spoke his lines too loud; Amyas cavorted like a country bride, simpering and bountiful, lovely as a lily, in white. Angel was dignified and handsome, his hair more yellow than the buttercups – O! how excellent fair he was! O fortunate women that might know his sweet embraces!

Both Nicholas and I forgot our lines, and in low whispers asked if all was well. How did you fare without me? – I was desolate – How much did you miss me? – I thought of you constantly – so did I of you – But did you not take other lovers? – No! How could you think that of me? Do you trust me so little? – I do trust you but I know how it can be – Tell me that you love me – You know I love you – But say it –

Amyas pinched me hard and prompted very loud. It was fortunate our audience was easily pleased and tolerant and had no eggs or oranges to hand, for that performance must have been the worst we ever did, and I have no recall of how I spoke my lines. But in the final scene where I do burn the letter, as I approached the candle flame Thomas Hodgkin stood up from his chair, and took the letter from my hand and silently exchanged it for the deed I had signed, that bound me to his service.

"Am I to burn it?" I whispered tremulously, and he nodded.

I certainly did burn it, and my fingers too, for holding it too close. Then came the part where Nicholas the grateful lover approached to kiss me. A small and delicate peck it should be – O! – but Nicholas did kiss me with fine hunger and possession and I did respond. For a moment there we spun in aery regions, dizzy and enraptured. Then Jack did hustle us apart, half laughing, half severe. Somewhat sickly Nicholas spoke his final lines. Amyas and Angel turned to each other for the final loving scene, and Nicholas and I held hands as tight as a lock, and suddenly we were all bowing to applause.

I felt dazed and tired. All I know is, Thomas gave us food and drink for our performance and I never let go of Nicholas' hand; we drank our wine with arms and glasses intertwined, and many healths were drunk – to Health and Love and the goddess Hymen and the Queen and prosperity to ships at sea – and we laughed and fooled and nestled. And Tabitha asked me how I

363

had liked Robert Greene's book and if it was true that I knew him, and I said the book was excellent and Robert a sweet kind person who gave much to the poor; and that night when it was all over, I went home with the players.

EPILOGUE

> "O sacred love!
> If there be any heaven on earth, 'tis love..."

O NE DAY very near to Christmas, about midday, when I was fixing holly boughs to the framework of the stage, a boy came looking for me.

I noticed him immediately, because he was yellow-haired and pretty. A little pasty, perhaps, but winsome, a pert tilt to the chin, a dainty button nose, sweet lips too worldly to be virginal.

"I'm looking for the French boy," he said loudly, and those about the inn yard directed him to me, where I stood ankle deep in holly leaves.

"Yes?" I enquired languidly. "Yes, dear?"

"I've a message for you from Kit Marlowe," said that youth somewhat aggressively. "You are to go to him at once."

I lost all my composure instantly. I went a deep becoming pink and dropped an armful of holly. It quivered about my feet, a gleaming, rustling, red-berried heap.

"Kit wants me? Why?"

"I do not know. He did not say. He just said come."

"What, now?"

"Well, certain, if you want to know what he wants."

He turned mincingly.

"Wait..." I began. "Is he... well?"

"Most sure he's well."

"Are you – with him?"

"In a way."

I smiled ruefully, with a painful little tug of the heartstring. How well I knew that "in a way".

"Listen," I said. "I cannot come. We are to rehearse a play and I am needed. I could not get to Kit's lodgings and back in time, so say I cannot come. Truly, I regret – but –"

365

"Very well," shrugged the youth, and strolled away.

"O Marc," said Nicky, who had come to stand unnoticed by me. "Was that wise? What if it was important?"

"It will not be," I said wrily.

"But are you not curious?"

"O yes. But what I said was true. I have to be here."

Nicky squeezed me fondly, and adjusted the necklace of ivy leaves about my throat. We were rehearsing Christmas fare, jovial masques and dances, merriment for evening banquets. We were marvellous busy, and in the New Year we were to perform for Thomas Hodgkin's wedding. Our days were monstrous full and very merry.

Upon a stage bedecked with holly, ivy, mistletoe, rosemary and bay, we rehearsed our play, and when we finished I came down off the boards wearing my cap of flowers and my green kirtle and rubbing my hands against the cold. We had a brazier burning in the inn yard and I made for it, the flames throwing up a mist of billowing smoke, which for a moment hid the one who stood the other side. It was Kit. O! *He* had come to *me*!

I had not seen him since we parted. O! He was so beautiful! My knees weakened, my mouth dropped open, my eyes adoring.

"O," I said inadequately. How dark his hair was, lightly wet with rain, how smouldering his eyes – how sensuous his mouth! Beneath his cloak his white shirt was open at the throat; he wore a black doublet. His cheek was faintly smudged with ink.

"Well, darling," he said. "We meet again."

" O – Kit –"

"I'm only passing by. Calm your fluttering heart. I've brought you a present. Tis this."

He handed me a piece of paper and I took it.

"It is for you," he said. "I want to see you read it; read it now."

This is what I read:

> Come live with me and be my love,
> And we will all the pleasures prove
> That valleys, groves, hills and fields,
> Woods or steepy mountain yields.

And we will sit upon the rocks,
Seeing the shepherds feed their flocks
By shallow rivers to whose falls
Melodious birds sing madrigals.

And I will make thee beds of roses,
And a thousand fragrant posies,
A cap of flowers and a kirtle,
Embroidered all with leaves of myrtle.

A gown made from the finest wool
Which from our pretty lambs we pull,
Fair lined slippers for the cold,
With buckles of the purest gold.

A belt of straw and ivy buds,
With coral clasps and amber studs,
And if these pleasures may thee move,
Come live with me and be my love.

The shepherds' swains shall dance and sing
For thy delight each May morning;
If these delights thy mind may move,
Then live with me and be my love.

"Of course," Kit said airily, "the idea comes from Virgil."

"Kit," I whispered. "It is a pastoral."

"That's right. The silly sort of thing you like. And damn me if I ever write another!"

"'Tis beautiful," I trembled.

"I know," he admitted. "Do you see – all the relevant pieces? All our past conversations? That time with Robert when we talked about the slippers and the sheep? Your amber studded belt, a present for services rendered!"

"The bed of roses...my cap of flowers...and the dress that I wear even now."

"Take it, Amaryllis," he laughed "Get some fool to set it to music. You wanted to be famous down the ages, did you not? By next year all London will be singing that. As long as they do, you'll have eternity."

And without caring who saw, he took me in his arms and kissed me.

I was left with the poem in my hands, the kiss on my lips. All gathered round to see what it was, and I passed around the poem, more precious than gold, and never to leave my possession. We stood around the curling flames, players in an inn yard poring over a new song to sing. Kit was right. He circulated many copies of his pastoral – the best that was ever writ – and everyone who heard it loved it.

We passed the winter months in London. Phoebe chose Angel, which makes me think that women, for all they are considered wise, are every bit as foolish as men, for she rejected one that would have been true and steadfast in favour of one she knew would please her in bed. In Spring we were once again on the road. We saw the beacons lit that showed the invasion force was near, but it did not land. *Tamburlaine Part Two* was a roaring success, and other great successes followed.

The portion of eternity I have on this earth I give to Nicky.

But my secret heart will stay with Kit; who has made me famous down the ages.

POSTSCRIPT

All the chapter headings come from *Dido Queen of Carthage* by Christopher Marlowe.

"Out of this welter of experience no one knows when or how, but by the crystalline precipitation of genius, there came Marlowe's one most famous and popular lyric 'The Passionate Shepherd to his Love'. This is the poem by which Marlowe still lives today to millions of English readers who do not know his plays or the thousands of other lines of verse he wrote in his brief life...a haunting poem, full of nostalgia and longing for what can never be..."

A. L. Rowse, *Christopher Marlowe: A Biography*

History has always told us that in 1593 Kit Marlowe was killed in a tavern brawl in Deptford at the age of twenty-nine. The circumstances of the murder were mysterious – was it political, sexual, or a horrible accident? But Kit had powerful friends. It is not inconceivable that they contrived his escape abroad to save him from the consequences of his recent arrest by the Privy Council, and that in plague-stricken London an unknown body was buried in the unmarked grave purporting to be his. Some believe that he lived in Italy for several years and later returned to England where he eventually died of natural causes, in the arms of his lover. We can but hope.

also by Chris Hunt:

STREET LAVENDER

In the busy West End streets of 1880s London, young Willie Smith quickly learns to use his youth and beauty as a means of escaping the grinding poverty of his East End background.

"Among its many unlikely pleasures, *Street Lavender* brings us an old-fashioned paladin, struggling from ignorance and penury to true love with honour untarnished. The rhythm of salvation and perdition – from reformatory to male brothel to good works among the teeming poor, via a superb episode in Bohemian Kensington – is fearlessly sustained. The effect of this harlot's progress with a silver lining is irresistible" – Jonathan Keates, *Observer*.

"I read all three hundred and forty-three pages in two compulsive sittings. Chris Hunt has produced an accomplished amalgam of Victorian literary styles . . . Both a funny study of a young gay's mounting consciousness and a voyeur's guide to the seamy side of Victoriana" – Patrick Gale, *Gay Times*.

"For all its playful mocking, and cherishing, of the gothic adventures and romantic sexual manipulation of pulp Victorian fiction, *Street Lavender* takes its political and sexual cues from Dickens, Edward Carpenter and nineteenth-century political novels based on urban working-class experience. Sexy, romantic and adventuresome reading, a fine merging of history and pride, politics, and cheerful Cockney bravado. Thank you, Chris Hunt!" – Michael Smith, *Epicene*.

ISBN 0 85449 035 3 (paperback only)
UK £4.95/US $9.95